TO KILL AGAIN

PART THREE

DARREN HOWELL

ISBN: 9798361715046

darrenhowell.com
facebook

For Mum and Dad.
X

CHAPTER ONE

Since the inauguration of Harry S. Truman in 1945, the White House Communications Agency has assigned a unique codename to all presidents and members of their first families for use by their Secret Service protection. Generated from a list of 'good words,' as they are known, the monikers chosen are purposefully unambiguous, simple to understand, and easily pronounceable in communication regardless of tongue. Traditionally, all family members' codenames also start with the same letter wherever possible. For instance, Ronald and Nancy Reagan were Rawhide and Rainbow; their children: Rosebud, Riddler, Ribbon and Reliant.

Robert Garrett's codename was Trumpet...and he hated it.

Not because it reminded him of *that* man—that would've been an easy, and reasonable, assumption to make. But that was not the case. Garrett despised his call sign because it brought back unwanted memories of the musical instrument he had been forced to learn as a child. The complexity of its mastery had baffled him at such a young age; his tiny fingers clumsy on the pistons and the hideous musty smell of its valve oil had turned his stomach then, and the memory of it still made him want to puke. But, above all else, it had been the god-awful racket it would make, or rather, *he* would cause it to make.

When approved for presidential candidate Secret Service protection and assigned his codename, Garrett had considered asking to swap it for some other brass section-inspired nickname—his wife was Trombone, his son Tuba—but it had seemed such a petty matter in comparison to winning the election and getting the country back on track that he'd just let it slide.

Trumpet! Trumpet! Trumpet! As if they were purposefully mocking him with its continued use, it was all he had heard while drifting in and out of consciousness since the security breach at the hotel.

Garrett had no recollection of the events that had led to his current situation, relying solely on information fed to him by his personal physician, Malcolm Jakobi. A man claiming to be a London police detective, the doctor told, had gained access to the first floor to wander unimpeded into the Eisenhower Suite. The stunt had nearly cost the man his life, only a random phone call saving him from a hail of Secret Service bullets.

The ball had been dropped, and heads would roll as a result, Section Chief Callahan had informed Jakobi in between screaming the codename into his phone or handheld radio over and over. Callahan had referenced the last Secret Service screw up—not on his watch, he hastened to add—when a married Virginian couple had managed to attend a state dinner at the White House without invitation in 2009. Intentions motivated by the wanton desire for fame rather than to do harm to the then president, Barack Obama, the fallout had been embarrassing, to say the least. If there was ever an investigation into this incident—and given the covert nature of its occurrence that was unlikely—it would be thorough and catastrophic to the career of the guilty parties, Callahan had ensured the doctor adamantly.

Garrett sat slumped on the tan leather in the back of the black Chevrolet Suburban, with Jakobi attentive and ready at his side. His head rolling from side to side, the president found himself vaguely aware of the sensation of movement. They were travelling. Travelling fast.

The Suburban was sandwiched in the middle of four equally dark, brand-new Range Rover P800s, the convoy the vehicles created cutting a swathe through the afternoon traffic like a mechanised black snake.

A presidential motorcade could consist of anything between twenty to forty vehicles depending on a location's specifics. There were route cars, pilot cars, big SUVs called Halfbacks, Roadrunners and Watchtowers—all tasked with performing a specialised duty. A Hazard Materials Mitigation Unit, in the shape of a big black truck, would scan the area for nuclear, biological, or chemical threats to the convoy, and there was always an accompanying ambulance for emergencies. The Secret Service's Counter Assault Team travelled in CAT trucks, heavily armed and packing enough firepower to start a war, with the whole thing finished off by a 'rear guard' of local law enforcement cars and motorcycle outriders. The president's safety was paramount, and nothing was left to chance, with every possible scenario accounted for. Even the Beast, the presidential Cadillac, given the handle of Stagecoach while the president was aboard, had multiple identical copies that would run in the motorcade and switch running order with the real Stagecoach to confuse any potential attacker. With the president sometimes visiting up to three cities in a day, organising such processions was a logistical symphony that took months of careful planning and cooperation between numerous agencies and departments.

But there was no such scrupulous preparation here—the playbook on presidential safety shredded and thrown to the wind. There was no additional assistance from the host government or police because, to the world, Garrett was already back in the US. Corners had not only been cut to facilitate the ruse; they had been slashed and torn: the life of the world's most powerful man put in jeopardy for the sole purpose of saving that very life. It was a ridiculous paradox. And all the bidding of the mysterious—

"Brad Ratski," the president mumbled.

"What's that, Robert?" Jakobi asked.

Garrett shook away the doctor's enquiry and pulled at his tie, yanking it down until it hung like a loose scarf. He tried to gain some focus on his surroundings, squinting through the bulletproof privacy glass, desperate for lucidity to flow. Everything was a blur. Nondescript greys and browns interspliced with flashes of light. Garrett was no stranger to London—he and his wife had honeymooned there in 1995—but the UK's capital was a big city, and nothing registered as familiar beyond the windows of the Suburban.

Finally, strobing flashes of clarity blasted away at the confusing fog. He remembered being unceremoniously bundled into a wheelchair and hurried out of the Eisenhower Suite, surrounded by a protective ring of armed-to-the-teeth agents moving as one. Wheeled into a service elevator that stank of flowers and grease, they had plunged into the underground loading bay of the hotel. The Beast had already returned to the US along with the president's decoy, so he was manhandled aboard the remaining Suburban that had stayed behind in London. But even for a machine as powerful as the United States Government, the move had taken time to arrange.

Eighty-seven minutes to be precise, Jakobi had informed him.

The delay was caused because Ratski couldn't be reached. Underground, his phone left with an injured Secret Service agent, the news of the security breach wasn't relayed until he returned to the rented office in Whitechapel. A ferocious argument had erupted between Ratski and Callahan regarding how best to handle the situation: the latter demanding the charade end and that the president be allowed to return to Washington. In the end, Ratski won, the president groggily agreeing that he remain in London and for the subterfuge to continue.

Four Range Rovers were leased from a car hire company in Belgravia that specialised in luxury vehicles, acquired under false identities, while the black helicopter that clattered high overhead was sourced from the United States Air Force base at RAF Lakenheath; the Ministry of Defence's air traffic control centre advised it was providing aerial support for the transfer of a classified VIP, which wasn't exactly an untruth. Next, a destination was chosen to accommodate the president from a long list of US Government-owned properties throughout the UK: an ex-CIA safe house located in Wimbledon selected due to its relatively short travel time from Mayfair.

"Punch on through," an authoritative voice from the lead car ordered from the speakers of several handheld radios.

Functioning as one sentient being, the convoy slipped onto the wrong side of the road as the traffic lights ahead turned red and the vehicles in front all stopped. The president gasped at the terrified face of a cyclist who appeared inches from his window, the Suburban screeching through as instructed. The risky manoeuvre resulted in a minor pile-up of oncoming vehicles. Horns blared and expletives were screamed, the convoy accelerating away from the collision it had caused.

"Jesus..." Garrett shuddered, just catching sight of a road

sign through the window that read FULHAM HIGH STREET as the Suburban's rubber squealed, and he slid on the leather.

"Intersection clear," the radio chatter declared. "Arrow Tip proceeding…and through."

"Trumpet case clear," the agent in front of the president replied.

Trumpet case. Garrett gave Jakobi a look that was one-part grin, two-parts eye roll.

"Fletching clear," the rear car checked in on a crackle of static.

"Fletching!" the president harrumphed noisily. "Who comes up with this shit?"

He peered up at the black helicopter high above. Providing 'overwatch' as it was known, the bird had no doubt been saddled with some archery related pseudonym. There would be two scout snipers up there, one on either side. He had flown similar missions back in Iraq, with burly camouflaged marksmen hanging from his rear doors, affording protection to some high-ranking top brass with more medals than courage.

"Arrow Tip to Arizona One, Trumpet case entering onto Putney Bridge Road. ETA nine minutes out. Say again, nine minutes."

The caravan swooped into the central reservation, cleaving the door mirrors off a long line of waiting cars going the other way as it tore along, ducking back in before it ploughed through the pedestrian island that rushed up to greet it. Nifty, breakneck speed driving got the convoy onto the bridge, the river below as grey as the sky above. The traffic was heavier there, the vehicles slipping into the bus lane on the left and racing through the jam; the camera installed to catch bus lane violators working overtime as they roared past.

"Arizona One to Arrow Tip. All received." The serious voice lightened in tone slightly, breaking from the strict radio protocols such an operation demanded. "We're about ready to roll out the red carpet here."

The airwaves hissed, and then a calm voice spoke from the rear car. "This is Fletching. Advise you hold off on celebrations. We have a local PD unit on our tail, closing fast."

It had been a busy shift for the pursuit car of Wandsworth police station. Under the capable hands of seasoned advanced driver, PC Jason Lincoln, Whiskey One (the call sign for the vehicle) had attended two robberies, three assaults, nicked a violent, thoroughly unpleasant Krok dealer, and stumbled across half a dozen examples of bad driving, that ranged from piss-poor to downright dangerous.

So far, the hectic bustle of their day had denied them a meal break, so they had parked up for a couple of minutes in front of what was reputedly Putney's best snack bar. It was a quick pitstop: the crime that infested London's streets would have to hold fire for a couple of minutes.

A sausage roll in one hand, coffee in the other, PC Dean Harris sagged in the passenger seat of the big Vauxhall Centro, alternating trips to his mouth. Heat be damned, he shovelled the pastry into his asbestos mouth, his waistline seemingly expanding with every hearty bite.

"So," Harris munched, smacking his lips together, "she's like, '*I ain't done nuffink, pig!*' And I'm like..." He stopped chewing, his eyes narrowing to fix on something through the rain-streaked windows.

"You're like what?" Lincoln prompted, not looking up from his phone or sandwich, or sounding particularly bothered whether he found out what Harris was like or not.

His stare intensifying, Harris' mouth slipped open to reveal a mashed-up lump of meat and pastry. He shot forwards in his seat as a convoy of black SUVs weaved its way through the traffic towards them. "What the bloody hell's this?" he chomped, powering down his window for a rain-free view.

Curiosity sparked, Lincoln finally glanced up, just in time to see a long streak of black slip past the windscreen, leaving a trail of spray in its near-silent wake. The iMessage back and forth he was having with his wife put on hold, he tossed down the phone and his half-eaten sandwich and fired up the Vauxhall's powerful dual electric motors. "I dunno, but they're not hanging about, are they?" He flipped through a line of switches and shouted over the siren that instantly flooded the car's interior. "Call it in and show us as responding," he yelled over the din, jutting his chin at the car's main-set radio.

Harris grabbed the handset from its mount as the car screeched out of Gonville Street and headed for the bridge. "MP, MP from Whiskey One, active message, over."

Under normal circumstances, a reply would be near-instant. On this occasion, however, there was nothing. The radio silence continued as the car's lightning-fast acceleration pushed Harris back in his seat.

"MP, MP from Whiskey One, active message," he repeated. "We're in pursuit of a high-speed convoy—possibly Range Rovers—

"The one in the middle wasn't!" Lincoln interrupted.

Harris swatted away his input. "—heading south on Putney Bridge Approach. Requesting additional units to assist, over."

When still no response came back, he unclipped his personal radio and tried that instead. Nothing. He shook the radio and shrugged at the driver, glancing out of the window in time to catch several pedestrians doing likewise with their phones.

Harris snatched Lincoln's phone from the centre console and eyed up the screen quickly to find there was no signal. "What the...?"

The Secret Service agent in the passenger seat of the president's Suburban ducked and weaved his head to try and get a better view of the police car between Garrett and the angry face of Doctor Jakobi, waving his phone inches from his face.

"I was trying to call my wife!" the doctor cried. "You cut me off."

"We cut everybody off," the agent said routinely, pointing at the string of people on the sidewalk staring dumbly at their phones.

The Suburban, a Watchtower surveillance vehicle retitled Stagecoach due to the president's on-board status, was equipped with a host of aerials and domes fixed to its roof for jamming communications and detecting incoming projectiles. Consequently, it played major havoc with cellular phone technology when activated.

The agent behind the wheel, his dashboard of high-tech screens and monitoring equipment extending well into passenger territory, flickered his steely gaze to the door mirror to see the police car, lights flashing, dipping in and out of the line of cars that separated them, getting closer and closer. "Law enforcement communications contained, but threat remains active," he summarised robotically. "Suggest non-lethal countermeasures."

The passenger nodded and tapped a black earpiece he wore. "Trumpet case to Fletching, you are authorised to deploy NLCs."

"Deploy NLCs, roger that," came the reply.

In the Range Rover codenamed Fletching, the Secret Service agents got to work. Aside from the driver, upright and rigid at the wheel, there sat another three men with matching suits and military buzzcuts. One was perched awkwardly on the back seat, permanently staring at the cop car as if his burning glower would be enough to dissuade their continued pursuit. His companion on the bench opened a laptop, swiping through various menus on the holographic screen until something that looked suspiciously like an aircraft's flight controls popped up. Once satisfied, he nodded at his companion ahead in the passenger seat.

That agent returned the gesture and reached into an attaché case he pulled from the footwell. He withdrew a cake of black plastic the size of a hockey puck from a foam-lined tray full of the strange objects. The agent peeled away a red safety seal circumnavigating the peculiar device and pressed a button on top.

"TEDD is paired," the laptop agent called out with a confirming thumbs up.

"Roger that," the passenger replied as he cracked his window several inches. Ignoring the cold rain that slapped his face, he pushed the puck through the gap and dropped it out of the window. "Package is deployed."

The puck bounced on the wet tarmac, the shock of the impact causing four tiny propellers to spring out from opposing sides. Instantly the blades spun up, the drone—because that's what it was—righting itself into an ungainly, drunken hover. Its systems diagnosed and location mapped in a single second, it shot gracefully to the side to avoid the car bearing down on it. With a whine of its fans, it shot off towards the police car, weaving in and out of oncoming traffic at breakneck speed, the flying skills of the laptop agent precision perfect. When confronted with a stationary Transit van, the drone dropped, scooting inches off the ground to fly underneath. It emerged, altitude climbing, to whizz around a motorbike and curl around the legs of a brave pedestrian attempting to cross the road.

The police car locked in the laptop agent's sights, its occupants blissfully unaware of its approach, the puck slammed into the front grill of the Vauxhall. The Raytheon Transient Electromagnetic Disturbance Drone, or TEDD as it was better known to those who used the device, delivered a short-range but highly devastatingly electromagnetic pulse, blasting a translucent shockwave over the entire car and instantly frying its electronic components.

Inside the police car, the main-set radio vomited angry sparks as the siren drained away and the Vauxhall died in Lincoln's arms.

"What the fuck?" he mumbled, the steering becoming heavy and unresponsive as the ABS suddenly ceased to function. Left with no other option than to use the electronic handbrake—which promptly failed to work—Lincoln repeated his stupefied question as a scream. "What the fuck!"

"*Shitshitshit!*" Harris joined in, gripping the seat, his eyes on stalks at the double-decker bus heading straight for them as they drifted across Putney High Street.

Twelve and a half tonnes of angry red bus slammed on its anchors, screeching to an awkward halt on the wet road, sending its passengers flying and sideswiping several cars in the opposite lane. Collision narrowly avoided, the police car slammed into the kerb, scattering gobsmacked onlookers like bowling pins and crashing through the window of an artisan butcher's shop.

The crash was neither high-speed nor particularly spectacular. Yet, it would forever immortalise the two PCs in the ether of cyberspace, courtesy of the dozen or so phone-filming pedestrians who suddenly swamped the crash site. The final insult came from the pig's carcass that dropped onto the car's bonnet with a thud, causing the unharmed policemen to release a torrent of vulgarities from within.

Back in Stagecoach, the agent in the passenger seat ignored Jakobi's continued grumbling and smiled at the news received from Fletching. He tapped his earpiece and spoke: "Trumpet case to Arizona One, threat is neutralised. You may ready your carpet." He glanced over at the driver and expanded his grin. "And get some fresh coffee on the go."

CHAPTER TWO

The bedroom was devastated—a creation of his own ferocious hand. The two sailors he had found fucking his sister, Mischa, lay dead on the floor, along with Madam Yelena, the brothel owner, her throat torn open, the alabaster makeup she wore in excess, splattered with glossy red.

Jack the Ripper mewed with pain. The bullet had slammed into his gut just below the ribs, the familiar sticky wetness he had felt many times before warming the skin beneath his uniform. The Ripper turned on his assailant, the loving gaze he had given Mischa replaced by rage.

A Tsaritsyn police constable stalked into the room, the barrel of the Nagant revolver he clenched in his hand still smouldering. Old and crooked, his heavy black boots thudded on the floorboards as he stomped towards his prey.

"Don't move, you—" the constable cried, his sentence abruptly ended as the Ripper hurled his bayonet skilfully like a throwing knife before he could open fire again. Despite the agony the motion caused—an agony that would've taken a lesser man —the blade was expertly delivered, with enough force to pene-

trate the policeman's thick overcoat and other garments, driving on to pierce his heart and add another corpse to the body count.

The Ripper regarded the constable's death with a trivial snort and returned to his primary goal: Mischa's salvation. He clawed at the bed on which she lay, muttering softly to herself in her drug-induced state. With trembling, blood-soaked hands, he scooped her up and pulled her to him, cradling her as he had done when first born.

"Mischa, Mischa..." he muttered through the growing wave of hurt, and shaking her awake. His vision blurred as his life oozed from the multiple wounds. "You must...you must rise, sister. We have to leave—" He turned away and coughed, spraying a mouthful of blood over the bed.

Mischa's eyes fluttered, the sedation she had required to service the dead sailors clearing enough for the butchery to register. She stared at him, at the bodies, at the blood, and let out a shriek. She broke their embrace, clawing herself free from the Ripper and slamming against the filthy wall.

"What have you done?" she gasped.

"Mischa, my little Mischa." The Ripper's head bobbed drunkenly as he tried to stave off the pain to replicate the joyous smile he had given his sister as a child. "I promised our mother I would rescue you from this place. You will come with me—both of you. To St Petersburg. You will be safe there."

"No," she said with a terrified shake of her head. "I am sorry. But I am...I am not Mischa."

The statement didn't register at first. How could it? That wretched, scrawny creature downstairs had said this was her room—the room Mischa offered service from. The Ripper stumbled onwards, explaining how her life of desperation was at an end. They were reunited. Brother and sister. She would be safe in St Petersburg, with him and Katerina, his wife. Their mother would tend the small garden and grow herbs and flowers if that was her desire, and Mischa, she would find proper employment and—

"I am not Mischa," *the prostitute stressed. "Mischa passed but a month ago."*

"What are you…? But…but…" The Ripper stared at her, his mouth hanging open and unable to move. When it finally did, the words were delivered with explosive venom. "You lie!"

"I speak the truth! I am Anna—Anna Nikolaevna Pushkina. Mischa was my friend! As much a sister to me as she was you." She motioned to the nearest dead sailor. "She succumbed to an infection caught from beasts like these men." *That final word burned on her tongue.*

The Ripper stared around the room, his body crumpling as police whistles began to shrill close by. Had it all been for nothing? His injuries forgotten, an unearthly groan slipped from his mouth to become a tortured wail. His face contorted into an unimaginable visage, his huge moustache quivering as tears erupted and scorched his flesh. The small child he remembered was gone, forever to remain only a memory.

"You must go," Anna said. "More constables will come. Live. Live for Mischa. Go now. Find a safe place, dress your wounds, and leave this land." She scooted forwards on the bed and pushed the Ripper away while he stared at her, his pain, both physical and emotional, lagging the meaning of her words. "Go!"

The Ripper clambered to his feet, stumbling to the door as a drunkard. He stopped at the constable to retrieve his blade, overbalancing and collapsing against the wall.

"She spoke of you," the prostitute called out as he clawed himself up the door frame, leaving behind glistening red handprints. "She spoke of you often, with nothing but love and pride for a brother." Anna baulked, her face creasing with sadness. "She missed you every day."

He didn't reply. There were no words the Ripper could

assemble to voice his heartache. Little Mischa was gone. And now he would have to go too.

But where?

His eyes snapped open with an accompanying gasp, the haunting dreams of his traumatic past instantly erased by the grinning face staring at him with a mouthful of oversized yellow teeth.

The first thing the Ripper noticed about the shrivelled old man was that he was holding his gun—his *revol'ver*—taken from those men in that strange carriage that moved without horses. It wasn't held in a threatening manner or one that denoted aggression, but more that suggested he had been caught examining it.

The old man peeked up at him and lowered the pistol, his smile blooming even further as if he was greeting a friend or a loved one; the heavy lines on his gnarled face intensified by the layers of dirt and grime to resemble furrowed trenches. Robed in threadbare garments, the man was clearly a vagrant —a *brodyaga*—the reek he emitted pungent and musty and indicating a life lived on the streets. His thick grey hair and beard were irretrievably knotted, his eyes clouded by age and wept dry by some sorrowful pain.

The Ripper responded by pulling himself into the corner as the prostitute in Mischa's room had done. He winced with pain, looking down at the source of the discomfort. His lower body naked but for his filthy bloomers, the black trousers with the red piping he had worn lay discarded in a bundle, the floor of the strange little room awash with drying blood. The tight muscular thigh of his right leg was washed clean and wrapped in a freshly applied bandage.

And then he remembered.

During his subterranean escape from the grim-faced

man, something protruding from the train had sliced open his leg and sent him flying. Almost half a cubit in length, the wound had been devastatingly deep. As the metal beast had screeched to a deafening halt, the Ripper had clambered to his feet and lurched along the tracks into grey daylight and never-ending rain until he found himself in a train station. Bemused passengers gawked at him as he tumbled and swayed, one hand clutching the pistol, the other clamped over the laceration. The rain scouring away the blood he left, they had held up their strange devices to point at him as he staggered through the station and out into the downpour. Like his blood, most witnesses had been washed from the street, allowing him to shuffle along unhindered and duck into a thin slit of an alleyway between two grubby shops. Stinking of piss and littered with detritus, it opened up to the elements and led him into a road he loosely remembered from his daily commute to the foundry in 1888. From there, he'd darted into another street lined with carriages, head down, collars up. He came across a pair of tall, rusted gates. Free from prying eyes, the Ripper had pushed against the slack chain that bound the gates together, widening them enough for him to squeeze through. The area they protected was dotted with yet more carriages, but these were all burnt and rusted, their windows cracked and stained by smoke. The reason for the damage meaningless to him, the Ripper headed for a small squat building on wheels at the back of the yard. There, he found the door unlocked, or rather already smashed open, and so he'd stumbled inside. There was nothing but a table, a broken chair, and graffiti, but it was dry at least. Letting out a laboured gasp, the Ripper had slipped down the wall, and his eyelids had danced shut, returning him to the Motherland once again.

"How do you feel?" the *brodyaga* asked with a heavy Slavic accent. He gestured with the pistol's barrel to the dressing. "I stitch wound and dress while you sleep. Nasty. Many blood. I give to you painkiller. Crunch in mouth as you sleep. It is good job, no? I am like angel."

While he continued to prattle on, the alien words spewed excitedly hurting the Ripper's ears, the killer felt surreptitiously for the outline of the knife concealed within his jacket, gladdened when his fingers pushed against it through the material.

"Your blade is still there, my friend." The old man cackled madly, waving the gun in front of the Ripper's face. "I take nothing but this. You point and scream and shout in sleep. Dangerous and very much noise!" He pointed down at the bloomers discovered when removing his patient's trousers. "Nice pantaloons you wear, by the way. Very fashion!" As his laugher grew, the Ripper watched him with curious contempt. "Where are you from, brother? Slav? *Polskie?*"

The Ripper spat on the floor with disgust. "*Rossiyskaya imperiya!*"

"Russian Empire!" The old man hooted, exposing his big yellow tombstones. "You mad fucking Russians and your delusions of grandeur. I am Aleksander. Aleksander Kowalski. Oh, forgive me… *Menya…menya zovut Aleksandr.*"

"*Ty govorish' po-russki?*" the Ripper cried with an excited gasp. It was the first time he'd heard his native tongue in this twisted version of Whitechapel.

Kowalski made an inch with his dirty fingers to indicate his rudimentary understanding of the language. "*Nebol'shoy.*" He stumbled through an explanation of how his *babushka* on his father's side had come from Volgograd and taught him some words as a boy.

Unaware that Volgograd had been the same city he had visited in his torturous dreams, the Ripper said nothing. An uncomfortable air descended, both men listening to the rain that hammered on the roof of the room on wheels until Kowalski cleared his throat and shook the gun in his hand.

"What do you have this for?" He made an exaggerated roll of his eyes at his stupidity and repeated the question the best he could in Russian. "*Dlya chego tebe...eto?*"

The Ripper seethed at Kowalski's question, his jaw hardening to stone. It was no business of this filthy Polack why he had the gun.

Kowalski detected his annoyance and quickly changed the subject. "You should not stay here, my friend. Very bad people use this place. It was car lot, but someone burn the whole thing. Now, very nasty people use it to sell their drugs and..." He stopped, offered another repentant look, and repeated the statement in slow pigeon Russian.

The Ripper regarded him with a curious eye as he delivered his advice. The mad little vagrant who had attended his wound and probably saved him from bleeding to death was the first person in 2030 to show him any degree of kindness. He was certainly the first person not to brandish a weapon at him or paint him in the glaring light of one of the strange little boxes that everyone carried.

"*Prinyat*," Kowalski said with a toothy smile, holding out the gun for him to reclaim, repeating the same word in Polish and English for good measure. "*Brać, brać*. Take."

A filthy hand caked in dry blood reached out and snatched the gun while Kowalski thought with a contemplative expression.

"I know a place, brother Russian," he finally said eagerly. "You will be safe there. You live with me. As friends. *Brothers!* But it is best we wait until night. I know you are wanted by authorities."

The Ripper volleyed his gaze between the weapon and Kowalski. He could just shoot him in the face and be free of his babbling.

"I have seen your photograph!" Kowalski continued, screeching with amusement and wagging a disapproving finger at the Ripper. "*You are famous man!*" He palm-slapped his forehead and cursed his idiocy and recapped what he'd just said in Russian while thrusting out a withered hand and gesturing for the Ripper to accept it.

The Ripper stared at Kowalski's hand as if plague-ridden and then, with little other option, reached out and clenched it with a wary nod.

CHAPTER THREE

On the pay-per-view hospital media centre suspended above the bed on a hydraulic arm, a stout Indian with fearsome eyebrows and a shock of runaway hair stood beneath an umbrella, Whitechapel District police station in the background. The light of the camera he squinted into made the rain gleam like diamonds as he spoke, a banner at the bottom of the screen announcing the channel as BBC NEWS 24 and the man as COUNCILLOR VIKRAM PATEL.

"Francis Khan is an honest businessman," Patel announced with enthusiastic nodding. "And I truly believe that the barbaric actions of this so-called police officer could further set back the already tenuous relations between the police and the local Asian community."

"Well, whoopy fucking doo!" Secret Service agent Cliff Martin groaned in syrupy Texan, swiping the touchscreen TV to the next channel.

Propped up in a hospital bed in a small private room, Martin flinched and struggled to get himself comfortable as the Sky News studio cut to an outside broadcast live from Whitechapel.

The reporter, thoroughly saturated by the downpour, his mood darker than the street behind, nodded into the camera. "—thanks, Steve. This isn't the first time this particular detective has found himself on the wrong side of the law he swore to uphold after he broke the nose of convicted paedophile Derek Anderson during interview in 2026. Dyson was only saved on that occasion when Anderson himself dropped the charges against the detective, stating that Dyson had only done what any normal person would have done."

A photograph of a handsome young policeman in uniform flashed up on the screen, a title card stating that it was John Dyson and giving courtesy to Facebook from where Sky had lifted the image.

"Dyson himself is currently refusing to make a statement," the reporter continued glumly on his return, "although police sources have informed me that he was charged with assault late last night at Forrest Gate police station and has been released on bail pending further investigation by the Metropolitan Police Department's Directorate of Professional—"

Martin killed the TV with a sardonic chuckle. "Jesus, that guy is so fucked."

He glanced over the room for the thousandth time, thoroughly irked by the bland, vanilla view. The room was small and sterile, with everything fashioned from plastic…including, it seemed, the food. Martin had exhausted the TV and radio and several dogeared magazines one of the nurses had brought him, always returning, a curious spectator at a freak show, to the video he'd discovered on that piece of shit Ratski's phone.

He had watched it over and over until the phone's battery had died, his mind unsettled by the disturbing content.

Before that happened, Martin had searched the device for any indication as to the video's origins. The GPS coordinates of the metadata confirmed the footage was shot where it had claimed to be...but that made no sense, and neither did the date of when the video was supposedly filmed. Both were unfathomable to Martin and hurt his head the more he thought about it. In the end, the agent had settled on the cause being nothing more sinister than a glitch in the phone's software or a freaky chipset that had resulted in false information. That was the only logical conclusion he could draw, although it still didn't explain the horrific content he'd witnessed. Apart from the photographs of the woman and the footage he'd found—and one solitary Petula Clarke song he discovered in the music library—the device was free of any further clues.

Martin blew out a long, deliberate huff and forced his uncooperative eyes to shut. He would be the first to admit he wasn't the fittest agent in Garrett's security stable, but he certainly wasn't used to being cooped up like a chicken in a cage. He liked to jog, leisurely, along the banks of the Potomac when the weather and time permitted, but now he couldn't even walk.

Fifty-five minutes he had languished in that sewer tunnel, shivering and gagging on the stench of other peoples' shit until his friend and fellow agent, Sam Dickinson, finally came to his rescue. After initially finding the humour in his buddy's situation, Dickinson had ripped a length of electrical flex from the derelict cottage's wall and tossed it down to him, Martin rising from the hole, soaked and frozen, his face stricken with pain. They erred on the side of caution and decided not to call the paramedics, struggling instead to the emergency department of the big hospital near their rented office.

That was yesterday. The hospital staff had been fantastic: cleaning, stitching, and dressing his wound and assigning him a private room in a new wing of the hospital. A doctor who looked younger than his own kids had quizzed him as to how he'd received his injury, but preoccupancy in the ball-breaker's video had prevented him from offering any suitable explanation. The doctor shrugged off his reticence, putting it down to shock, and suggesting they keep him in for a few days to ensure he didn't develop an infection.

Martin heard the door of his room click open. "Is that my favourite nurse coming to give me a bed bath?" he oozed with an excited smirk, not bothering to open his eyes.

"Think again," an emotionless American voice replied.

Martin looked up to find Ratski's gaunt, ill-looking face staring down at him from the end of the bed. *Jeez, Ratshit needs the bed more than I do*, he thought while gingerly pulling himself into a sit.

His bedside manner as cold as ice, Ratski took Martin's charts from the end of the bed and scanned through the information. "I need you back as soon as possible," he said without an ounce of compassion or care.

"The doctors wanna keep me in for a few days. For observation, you know? But they don't think I'll be back running for a while."

"But you can *run* a desk, from a wheelchair if necessary."

The agent nodded at his stone-cold stare. "I'll take the couple of days and then head on back."

"Very well." Ratski looked over the room. "Where's my cell?"

Martin reached over and opened the drawer of the white plastic cabinet next to his bed. "Probably gonna need a charge," he said, retrieving Ratski's battered phone and handing it over.

Ratski clenched it, his lips curling into the thinnest of

smiles at being reunited with the device. He turned and made for the door without another word.

"I saw the photographs!" Martin blurted out. Ratski stopped and rewound to the bed, the agent's voice weakening. "And the video. What in…what in God's name was that?"

Ratski came to a stop next to the bed and stared down at him. Impossible to read, he pulled a well-worn Gideon's Bible from the open drawer of the cabinet and examined it for a moment. "God's name…" he whispered, weighing it up and turning it over in his hand.

Martin wondered if he was about to recite some passage relevant to his unauthorised examination of the phone. For a native of a deeply religious Bible Belt state, his understanding of the Lord's work was rusty, to say the least, but he seemed to remember there being something in Exodus about 'laying hands on another person's property,' and he wondered if that was where Ratski was heading.

It soon became painfully apparent, that wasn't his intention.

Without warning, the ball-breaker smashed the spine of the good book down on the agent's injured leg. Martin shot up and howled in agony while Ratski tossed the bible onto the bed and turned to leave again.

"Make it a week," he said coldly, the door snapping shut behind him.

"*Motherfucker!*" Martin hissed weakly through gritted teeth, his face warped by anguish. He looked around for something to suffer a reprisal. Finding only the bible, he snatched it up and hurled it against the wall with all his might.

———

His swollen head swathed in neatly applied bandages, Frankie Khan looked over at the loud thump that came from the wall.

"Keep the fuckin' noise down!" he mumbled, his voice restricted by his bruising and the dressing running underneath his chin. He blinked the eye that wasn't inflated shut and coloured like a drag queen's at the interruption and got back to the news channel on the small flatscreen hanging over his bed.

The news story that followed the recounting of his vicious assault was also from Whitechapel and told of a police probationer called Christopher Haddon who had gone missing on his first solo day on the job. A brief interview was conducted with his tearful girlfriend while several images of Haddon were displayed on screen in the hope of jogging the memories of any potential witnesses.

Innocent of any involvement, Khan laughed along, no less. "Oh, dear. What a shame." He popped a grape as purple as his bruises into his engorged mouth and poked Haddon's girlfriend in the tit. "I'll come round and keep you company if you fancy, Melanie?"

Khan blew her a kiss and killed the TV, pushing the media centre away on its arm.

He had been lucky, the doctors had told him. Dyson's attack had left him with a fractured skull and a nasty three-inch laceration that required stitching, but everything else was superficial. What concerned the medical team who had treated him, however, was the results of the MRI scan they had conducted. It showed an acceleration in his condition; his *glioblastoma multiforme* almost doubling in size. Khan shrugged off the news and offered one of his favourite Shakespeare quotes in response. 'Cowards die many times before their deaths; the valiant never taste of death but once,' he had recited with the flair of a theatrical performer. The puzzled look the doctor had given him had provoked a not so eloquent explanation from Khan: 'Pussies die every day 'cause they're weak and pathetic; brave men like me only die once.' He was brave—braver than any man. He didn't fear death. He had stared the doctor right in the eye at that point and told him that death should fear Frankie Khan.

"'The valiant never taste of death but once,'" he growled to himself, chomping on his grape with a series of exaggerated slurps and only stopping when his phone started to ring.

Buzzing on the cabinet next to his bed, it seemed to vibrate the whole room. Khan cringed at the sound and reached over slowly for his phone so as not to waken the pain.

"*Niiicky*," he cried far too warmly, wincing at the agony his joviality brought. "Yeah, I'm alright, bruv. They're keepin' me in for observation, what with the tumour and shit. Yeah, we'll do dinner before I call it a day. Definitely. You can fuckin' pay!"

The criminal listened as his South London equivalent spoke, giggling like a naughty schoolboy while Nicky Minter countered his proposal. "You get the *whooole* of London when I'm brown bread, you tight bastard. You remember that."

The men had fought once, as gangsters did, for power and territory. But as the body count had risen and the pigs got nosy, the men had called a face-to-face meeting to negotiate a peace deal. Khan had warmed instantly to Minter, and the men had formed a friendship borne of blood—a far better outcome for Minter than Khan's original plan of shooting his competition to death. London was a big enough city for both of them to inhabit, it was thankfully decided.

Khan nodded along, pulling another juicy orb from its vine and hovering it in front of his lips until his features clouded with spite. "My boys are spineless wankers, Nick.

Nothin' but vermin, suckin' the life and the money out of me. But you mark my words… They'll go in the ground before Frankie fuckin' Khan does, I can guarantee you that."

Khan huffed and rolled his eye at Minter's muffled outburst.

"Will you fuckin' calm down, Nichol*arse!* This phone ain't bugged. Bug a dying man? The newspapers would shit all over 'em. I tell you, I've got bacon just where I want 'em. I'm too clever for them. And that's what hurts them more than my face hurts me." Minter placated, Khan smiled and munched his grape. "Now listen… Remember that one boy Paki army you sent me? '*I wanna fight the pigs, innit, Mr Khan.*' Yeah, the one who shit his pants all over me office. Is he alright, is he? D'you trust him?"

A brief appraisal of the boy's abilities and trustworthiness followed, Khan responding to what he was hearing with a growing nod.

"Don't you worry about him bein' a retard. I just need someone who'll do what he's told. Send him back to me, will you? Tell him to come and see me at the hospital. I might've been a bit 'asty before."

Khan rolled his eye again and tutted.

"I told you to relax, you jumpy cunt." He laughed aloud at the question Minter asked, instantly flinching at the pain the humour brought with it. *Fuck!* "What do you think bacon have got on me?"

"Bugger all!" Detective Chief Inspector Colin Sinclair raged at his Directorate of Professional Standards team assembled in Incident Room Two. "That's what we've got on him!"

The usually amiable little man appeared not so cordial as he stalked across the room to send a high stack of paperwork raining down like a ticker-tape parade. Instantly embarrassed by his behaviour, the death of Tom O'Keefe still painful on his mind, he wondered if the influx of anger and violence that had infected Whitechapel was contagious, and he had caught a dose himself. But that was a ridiculous notion; it was the sheer weight of his workload that was choking and pushing down on him. Sinclair had come to Whitechapel to investigate a detective who had blown up his police station's surveillance room: an extreme enough case in itself for the DPS. But due to the woeful state of the Metropolitan Police Department, his team had since been saddled with a killer with access to military-grade weapons slaughtering coppers and another Whitechapel detective who had attacked the man who claimed to have murdered his father...the same man whose dogs had killed O'Keefe.

Frankie Khan.

Whitechapel's local scumbag was fast becoming the primary factor in this whole sorry mess, it seemed. Jerry Mathews had been in crippling debt to the criminal's business partner, and Khan himself had claimed ownership of the murders in Wyllen Close—before retracting his statement prior to his assault. But without much in the way of evidence, it seemed the only crimes they had enough proof to convict him of was being in possession of an unlicensed shotgun and animal cruelty by way of the RSPCA due to the neglect of his dogs. The gun would earn him five years inside —out in half that time with good behaviour—and the charge of wasting police time, and the more serious one of perverting the course of justice, if pursued, would add nothing to his sentence as they would run concurrently. And those parameters depended on *if* they could meet the Crown Prosecution Service's guidelines on what constituted sufficient evidence and *if* Khan himself lived long enough to face justice. He had a brain tumour, his victim statement revealed. *Glioblastoma multiforme.* The most devastating kind. Inoperable and terminal. He was against the clock with no chance of reprieve. If Khan was going down, it was only into a six-foot-deep hole in the ground.

"It's like a bad fucking movie," Sinclair grumbled to himself as he stomped over to a whiteboard of information to thump the mugshot of Khan taped to it. "This bastard is running rings round us. He has alibis for anything we throw at him and claims he made up what he told Dyson about his old man just to wind him up. He's got every Guardian-reading, flip-flop wearing human rights brief queuing up to offer their services, just to jump up and down on us! And it's enough to scare the shit out of the Director of Public Prosecutions and CPS, because if we don't have anything concrete on Frankie Khan, we don't go within a hundred miles of him!"

Sinclair dragged a hand through his wayward hair and pointed at one of his detectives sat at the nearest desk.

"Where are you with the CCTV, Jeff?"

Jeff cleared his throat and delivered the news Sinclair had dreaded. "We have footage of Khan arriving and departing his golf club as specified during interview with Dyson and the following victim statement taken by myself."

He opened a folder and laid some black and white photos across the desk for Sinclair to see. They showed a black Mercedes X55 enter a sparsely populated car park, Khan exiting the vehicle and dashing through the rain. The images were stamped at the bottom with a time and date that corresponded with the massacre in Wyllen Close.

"I've forwarded the footage onto the digital boys, just as a precaution in case someone's fiddled with the timestamp, but it seems kosher to me."

"Who plays golf in the bloody rain?" Sinclair asked with a measure of despair.

"My cousin in Canada," one of his detectives answered, the burning glower Sinclair shot at him making him immediately regret his answer. "Um…he, um, plays…plays in the snow too, with illuminous orange golf balls." He made a weak cough and added "Guv" as an afterthought.

"Piss off, Neil! Carry on, Jeff."

Jeff carried on, laying down another series of images. Blurred and grainy, the washed-out colour photos showed Khan's Mercedes travelling on a wet dual carriageway edged on both sides by faded green fields. One was a pixelated enhancement of the rear number plate, still so indistinct it caused Sinclair to pull a face as he studied it.

CCTV was a concern to many an investigation. Sometimes it was just too poor in quality to be of any discernible use, displaying a wanted suspect as a dark, smudge-like blur that even their own loved ones would struggle to identify. Whole cases had collapsed or been shelved due to a video file's low resolution, lousy compression rate, or a camera's dirty lens, and sheer bad luck would often mean that a camera providing excellent quality was misaligned; missing the vital action so desperately needed to be seen by mere inches. It still astounded many a frustrated police officer that there were mechanical rovers on the surface of Mars capable of sending high-definition footage back to Earth from thirty-four million miles away; while a street camera in London couldn't differentiate a man from a woman or allow for the identification of a passing car.

"These were emailed over from the Highways Agency," the detective explained. "They show Khan's Merc on the A13, timestamped at 10:53 on the morning of the 16th. Which means Khan couldn't have been in Whitechapel."

"Or someone else was driving his motor," someone proposed.

Nodding in agreement, Sinclair plunged his hands deep

into his pockets. "Can we get these images cleaned up anymore?" he said to Jeff. "It'd be nice to confirm it's Khan actually driving the car and not Mickey Mouse."

"Sorry, sir. It was all they could do to get the index."

A female detective sat at the back of the room made a discreet cough. "I hate to be the Bad News Bear, guv, but Khan's debit card made two purchases in the golf club bar on the date concerned, at 13:55 and 14:34. I assume post-game."

"Brilliant," Sinclair groaned, jabbing a finger at yet another detective. "Duncan, where are we with McGruder?"

The young detective he looked to for salvation referred to his notebook. "I spoke to a Captain Saengsingkaew of the Royal Thai Police. He confirmed that Richard McGruder is alive and well and currently a resident in Bangkok."

Sinclair scoffed heatedly at that. He looked around the room and was surprised that no one else shared his suspicions. "In a country where you can buy a hooker or a ladyboy cheaper than the condom you'll wear while screwing it? I'll take that with a very large pinch of salt, thank you very much. Call him back, Duncan. Have him get McGruder on Skype or Zoom, something like that. Until I see him for myself, I don't buy Khan hasn't fed him to the pigs as well and is using his name as a front for his own shit."

He returned to the whiteboard and drew his hand along a dozen ugly looking mugshots pinned along its length. The Metropolitan Police Department's CRIMINT computer database had disclosed them as Khan's employees and known associates.

"*Find Khan's boys*," Sinclair stressed. "Where are they, and why, as the jungle drums are apparently claiming, did they run? It's like a house of cards. One tumbles, the rest will follow. But we need to find them first. And find the lawyer too—and this arms dealer, Barry the Bullet or whatever his name is."

He looked back at his detectives to find them all rooted lethargically to their seats.

"Well, don't just bloody sit there!"

CHAPTER FOUR

Inside Incident Room One, Detective Chief Superintendent Bill Raymond swung an arm over at the television secured to the wall and pressed play on the remote.

CCTV footage started to run, shot from a security camera at Whitechapel Underground station. Digital quality colour film showed the eastbound District Line platform, half a dozen waiting passengers trying their best to shelter under a corrugated canopy from the driving rain that pelted them. There was a sudden flurry of activity as the travellers began to turn in the same direction as if drawn to something occurring off-screen. A couple of them drew their phones as a weighty male figure entered the frame and staggered past, leaving a series of dark dots and splashes in his wake that the rain soon erased.

It was their suspect—the Jack the Ripper copycat.

Raymond's assembled team stiffened in their seats at his on-screen presence, a low mumble circulating the incident room as the footage changed to another camera, following their suspect along the platform.

"What's that he's leaving behind on the floor, claret?"

Detective Constable Marcus Docherty asked in heavy Northern Irish.

The Welshman rewarded him with a condescending snort. "He was hit by a train, Docherty. Unfortunately, it didn't tear him to pieces like he did that poor woman."

The man stumbled onto the stairs, a visibly irate station cleaner following behind with a mop and bucket to wash away his blood.

"How did we get this?" That came from Detective Sergeant Jenny Brent, recovered enough from her ordeal at Khan's farmhouse to return to work.

Raymond swigged his cold tea and made an irritated face. "We've only got it because someone was awake enough at BTP to see the likeness to our suspect. Otherwise…"

He threw his arms wide in despair and then went on to explain how British Transport Police were called to the station the previous afternoon following a collision between an unknown person and a 197-tonne District Line train. It was routine procedure for BTP to attend all such incidents, known colloquially as a 'one under,' the Underground's less than official term for what were generally suicide attempts or the result of drunken tomfoolery. The officer who attended had reviewed the station's CCTV footage and noticed a startling similarity between the fleeing man and the suspect dubbed the Jack the Ripper copycat.

The Welshman pointed back at the television as the footage cut to a bright concourse milling with people, the Ripper moving as fast as his injury would allow to escape the station, the silently shouting cleaner in hot pursuit, erasing any evidence of his presence. The image froze. Raymond tossed down the remote and looked harshly at the detectives.

"And that's where we lose him courtesy of Jerry Matthews," he announced. "But he's out there…and he's injured. I managed to get Horbury to put some uniform out, questioning the locals: stallholders outside the station, shop-keepers, etcetera. Someone must have seen him. But I want…" Raymond unfolded a sheet of paper he took from his pocket. "…Saunders, Henderson, Mohammad and Shaw on the phones. Every hospital, doctor's surgery and walk-in clinic in a five-mile radius. Call them. Have they seen him? And if not, put them on alert to expect a possible visit."

"What about vets, guv?" Detective Constable Barry Henderson asked innocently, his hand raised.

Raymond responded with a hefty sigh, turning to Detective Sergeant Jim Mitchell and clicking his fingers to get his attention. "Mitchell, I want you to backtrack off this footage. Take Knapper with you."

Seated next to each other, Mitchell and Detective Constable Gary Knapper performed a theatrical fist bump, instantly incurring the Welshman's wrath.

"You're here to work, not fanny about!" he cried, sucking on his lip to calm himself. "Find out where he came from and what he was doing. The train driver says he came flying out of an opening for the disused St Mary's station. Start there, work backwards. Questions?"

"Yeah, what are we doing about John, guv?" Detective Inspector Ben Saunders asked.

"John?" Raymond replied with a puzzled scowl.

"*Dyson.*"

"That's out of our hands, isn't it? He was found assaulting a terminally ill man by a DPS detective—"

"*Terminally ill?*" Detective Constable Debbie Shaw spluttered, her high-pitched Liverpudlian shrill and jarring.

Raymond shushed away the stunned faces and shocked expletives of the detectives, the fact that he knew something they didn't amusing him in some infantile way. "Oh, didn't you lot know? This Khan scumbag of yours is dying, so the

Royal London reckons. An inoperable brain tumour. He only has months to live, apparently."

"That's the best news I've heard all year," someone muttered from the back of the room.

Raymond scanned the crowd for the heckler, although he had no reason to disagree with the outburst. "The press are loving it, that's for sure. Can't beat a good police brutality story. If Dyson escapes prison, he'll probably be lucky to be working supermarket security this time next year." He hid the smirk he let slip behind the mug he picked up and drained of tea before continuing. "One more thing... You've probably already heard, but uniform have lost one of their new coppers. PC Chris Haddon. They're handling this themselves for now, but keep an eye out for him, will you?"

Raymond looked over the incident room at the sea of slow bobbing heads, many of the looks mirroring his own perplexity on hearing of Haddon's disappearance.

"Okay, bugger off then." The detectives getting back to work, Raymond headed for the door, beckoning to Jenny with a curling finger. "Brent, you're with me today."

Debbie cocked her head to one side and offered her commiserations by way of a sarcastic grin. "Aren't you the lucky one?"

Raymond crashed through the door into Dyson's glass-walled office.

Ex-office, he corrected himself. There was more chance of Elvis coming back from the dead riding a unicorn than there was of Dyson ever stepping foot in there again. It had been the DPS themselves who had dragged him from his victim, and with high-definition video evidence of the assault, Raymond doubted whether even God himself could save

Dyson now. He was, as the old police adage went, 'bang to rights.'

Raymond grabbed his forgotten phone from the desk. Awoken by the movement, it came alive in his hand, the screen illuminating over a dozen calls and as many messages. All from Pat Carrick, the one-eyed detective chief superintendent he had secretly tasked to follow Dyson.

He thought for a moment and snapped the door shut, glancing back at the woman detective waiting for him in the main CID office and mouthing "*Two minutes*" at her. Rather than trawl through the messages, he opted to call Carrick straight off. The call was answered after the second ring.

"I've been busy, Pat. What is it?" Raymond listened, leaning over the desk and doodling on a notepad while Carrick spoke. "Of course, I still want you to follow him. This Khan thing is completely separate and doesn't change a thing. Where is he now?"

The tails of his Gestapo trench coat flapping on the wind that drove the rain, Carrick stomped his way through the herd of equally saturated shoppers trudging past the swanky, high-end stores of Bond Street. Most gave the unscrupulous detective a wide berth upon seeing his black eyepatch and dour frown, his appearance intimidating and unsettling, looming out of the deluge like some grim angel of death.

With his little Chinese whiz kid still searching for Khan's boys, Carrick had decided to devote his time to Raymond's task; not through any bullshit obligation to the Welshman, but purely out of voyeuristic interest as to where the journey might lead. Carrick had risen early to stake out the soon to be ex-detective's apartment, waiting in the cold, wet darkness with curiosity and two packs of *Gauloises* his partners in crime.

He had shadowed Dyson and the gorgeous bit of stuff with him on leaving the apartment at nine-thirty, hanging back out of sight as they dashed through the rain to the nearby Bethnal Green Underground station. By the skin of his nicotine-stained teeth, Carrick caught the same train as them, hiding himself behind the pages of a discarded copy of the *Metro* while they giggled and canoodled in the next carriage. They had all alighted at Oxford Circus to find that the rain had eased to a fine drizzle, the sun trying its damnedest to push through the dreary clouds for the shoppers and tourists milling about with their branded shopping bags. A couple of hours of lazy, unhurried shopping had followed, Carrick moaning and smoking as he monitored their every move.

Maintaining the leisurely pace set by his mark, Carrick held his phone against his ear while he puffed on one of his French cigarettes, his single eye locked on the woman's arse in her tight jeans who shared an umbrella with the suspended detective.

"Uptown, the posh bit," Carrick said into the phone. "He's enjoyin' a day out with the missus by the looks of it. Crackin' little stunner she is. I'd smash the granny right out of it, know what I mean?" On the other end of the call, Raymond yelled something that caused him to flinch. "Sorry. Yeah, focus. Wait, they've stopped."

Up ahead, beyond the bright illuminated signs for Gucci, Rolex, and Prada, Dyson and the woman stopped outside of an expensive-looking jewellery shop. Big gold letters fixed along the front of the store announced it as GOLDMAN-N'S, 'LONDON'S FINEST JEWELLERS SINCE 1948,' a flowing font beneath the name boasted. Carrick doubted whether that was true but admitted it was certainly a fine name for a jewellery shop if ever there was one. He had never heard of it, although his association with precious metals and things that sparkled had been mostly limited to what he could pilfer from a crime scene whenever the chance presented itself.

Carrick grinned at the woman's reaction to the wares displayed in the window. It was strangely bizarre, as if she had never seen such luxurious wonders in her life before. Dyson motioned to the glass door and pushed it open for her to enter, the sexy little thing nearly leaping for joy at the invitation.

———

While Dyson shook the brolly of rain and stowed it in a golden elephant's foot stand at the door, Mary lightened on her feet as if gravity was less effective within the shop. Almost on tiptoes, she turned back and gasped with wonder at Dyson, their entwined fingers breaking as she skipped ahead, taking in everything.

The interior of Goldmann's was bathed in ultra-bright lighting: an unashamed sales ploy to emphasise the twinkling of its wares. And twinkle they did: from the deep glass display cabinets that lined the glittering stucco walls, the goods they contained tastefully arranged amongst jagged rock and lush flora, to the long polycarbonate-laminated counters —bulletproof to the layman—attired with all manner of beautiful handcrafted pieces, the effect was purely dazzling. The *pièce de résistance* was the massive aquarium that took up one whole wall of the shop. Ten thousand gallons of saltwater brimmed with schools of kaleidoscopic marine fish, while tethered Perspex orbs of varying sizes, each one displaying an expensive piece of jewellery, bobbed and drifted on the rippling current.

On the occasions when Dyson had visited the shop in the past, he had always found the décor a little too pretentious; the ocean-size display of yellow tangs, angelfish, and the little orange and white ones that looked like Finding Nemo giving him some serious aquarium envy and making his own set-up at home seem no bigger than a goldfish bowl.

"It's like nothing I've ever seen before," Mary mumbled wide-eyed to Dyson.

"The tank or the tom?"

"Tom?"

"Tomfoolery…jewellery? *Come on*, you come from the East End!" he pleaded with a hearty chuckle, pulling her into a loving embrace.

Considering he stood to lose the job he loved and was facing the prospect of jail time, Dyson had never looked better. An air of frivolity surrounded him, the stench of work-induced desperation replaced by a favourite cologne. Clean-shaven, his hair neatly combed, he stood relaxed in jeans with a crisp pastel shirt beneath his leather jacket. The twinkle returned to his eyes once more, a weight had been lifted from him, albeit unwillingly: suspension the unorthodox tonic he so drastically needed.

Mary nudged Dyson in the ribs and proceeded to prance jauntily alongside one cabinet, her hand trailing the glass while she examined the contents like a child perusing a sweet counter. She glanced back, mouthing with concern, "*There are no prices.*"

Dyson caught up to her, his answer hidden behind a discreet cough. "If you have to ask the price, you probably can't afford it."

Mary feigned a hurt expression. "You mean you didn't bring me here to shop for an engagement ring, Mr Dyson?"

Dyson looked shocked but not averse to what she proposed. Before he could offer any kind of reply, a glitzy sales assistant glided over, her commission dependant smile firmly fixed in place.

"Good morning, sir, madam, and welcome to Goldmann's," she said warmly. "Is there anything I can help you with today?"

Dyson looked up and returned an equally broad smile. "I think we'd like to see the *special selection*."

The shopkeeper, or 'sales assistant' her lover corrected as they descended a steep set of wooden stairs, led them along a darkened corridor of brick and rusted pipework. Mary trailed behind, concerned by the brutal shift from exclusivity to something resembling a dungeon. The woman led them around a corner, and the passageway opened up on a large workshop. Her smile bloomed as she motioned for them to enter, taking her leave to return upstairs.

Large enough to echo the traditional Yiddish music that played, the room was gloomy and poorly illuminated by a strip of buzzing white light. Festooned with cobwebs and smelling of damp, it was as hot as hell down there. The heat came from a line of bubbling crucibles, their precious contents under the constant roar of orange flame. In the shadows, a handful of wizened old artisans sat hunched over workbenches. They toiled in the unbearable heat, stripped to greasy skin and vests, fashioning their latest creations through jeweller's eyeglasses affixed to their scrunched-up faces.

Dyson took Mary's hand and led her through the workshop. He nodded his greetings at several of the elderly men who turned as he passed, a couple of them waving in return. He had obviously been there before, Mary surmised while he drew to a stop at the end of the workshop, facing a bare brick wall.

Mary watched Dyson quizzically while he ran his free

hand over the rough brickwork until he found what he was looking for. With an enigmatic smile, he pushed on one particular brick. There was a deep hiss of something mechanical, and the wall slid back silently to reveal another workshop. A tsunami of light flooded out, brightening the darkened room as she shielded her eyes.

"John?" she asked, tightening her grip on his hand as they entered the concealed room.

Much smaller than the workshop, Mary noticed it was as cold as the inside of Dyson's fridge. The door slid shut, prompting her to turn on the spot and examine the hidden space. Benches and shelves held all manner of contraptions—things that Mary had never seen the likes of and had no idea as to their purpose. There were bottles of coloured liquids—dyes and inks, she presumed—and a hand-operated press that looked like one she had seen in 1888 once. Dyson marched onwards, pulling her along after him, past computing machines and a camera set up on a tripod pointing at one bright white wall. She knew it to be a camera because she'd found something similar during one of her many explorations of Dyson's home. On a table they passed, Mary desperate for a closer look, stood an inch-thick ream of printed paper, the first sheet topped with an elaborate royal crest and the words CERTIFICATE OF BIRTH printed in red ink.

"What is this place?" Mary said, far too quietly for Dyson to hear her above the old-time piano music playing in the background.

"*Oi!*" Dyson called out theatrically, "*You're nicked, sunshine!*"

The room's only occupant sat doubled over a bench against the far wall. He glanced up casually from what he was doing, not in the least bit concerned by the threat of arrest. Old and withered like the other workers, a Jewish skullcap sat on his head, and the sleeves of the off-white shirt he wore were held up with silver garters. He turned and slid from the stool on which he sat, a smile erupting over his face as he hurried over to Dyson and grabbed him by the shoulders. Despite his years, he was a man in clear possession of his facilities, his mind as sharp as a blade, his eyes unclouded by age and as bright as the lights above. With his white moustache and small paintbrush beard, he reminded Mary of the man printed on the box of fried chicken Dyson had come home with late one night.

"You really need to change that nasty cologne if you want to surprise me, John Dyson," he declared with a laugh that rocked his whole body. "I could smell you from the tube station."

The men hugged, Mary allowing them their intimacy to pick a little blue book from a deep pile of identical little blue books.

"United Kingdom of Great Britain and Northern Ireland passport," she read slowly from the embossed gold lettering on the cover. Inside, she found multiple blank pages printed with nothing but delicate swirling patterns.

The old man broke the embrace and turned to Mary. There was the hint of a foreign accent to his voice, and she thought it sounded German. "And what is this vision of loveliness you have brought with you today?"

Dyson regarded Mary with pride as he introduced her. "Solly, this is Mary Kelly. Mary, this is Solomon Goldmann. The best counterfeiter in the whole of England."

"Stop it, you are too kind." Goldmann made a happy little laugh and swatted away the compliment. He approached Mary and took her hand, planting a delicate kiss on it.

"It's a pleasure to meet you, sir," she said, putting down

the passport like she'd been caught stealing. She began to curtsy until she remembered it wasn't 1888 anymore.

"The pleasure is all mine, my dear." Goldmann watched her for a moment, those shrewd eyes weighing her up. Finally, his mouth curled into a grin and he released her hand, returning to Dyson to adopt a more serious posture. "I see you have gone and gotten yourself into trouble again, you stupid boy."

"Yeah," Dyson winced, pulling himself up to sit on one of the benches to swing his legs in the air. "Probably not my greatest moment. You still owe me that favour, right?"

"You mean apart from the fingerprint gloves?" Goldmann cackled, his withered frame shaking so violently Mary wondered if he might fall over.

She volleyed between the men while they talked, confused as to why a custodian of the law should have such a close relationship with a man who was obviously an illegal forger.

"What is it, John?" Goldmann asked as he hobbled away to a kettle set up on one of the benches.

Dyson made an awkward face and then smiled at Mary. "Well…it's a couple of things, actually."

"This is bollocks!" Carrick spat into the phone, his head bobbing this way and that as he peered through the window of the jewellers.

Dyson and the unknown woman had simply vanished from within. Only a couple of rich-looking Arabs stood inside, inspecting the goods while a cute shop assistant worthy of a good shagging buzzed around them like a wasp.

"I don't know, Bill! They walked in, and now they're gone, know what I mean?" He listened to Raymond and seethed with frustration, jabbing a *Gauloises* between his lips. "Course he didn't make me—I'm not a fuckin' amateur! Look, I'll call you back later if I find 'em. Yeah, yeah, bye."

Carrick growled with annoyance and killed the call with a stab of his thumb. Not a single second passed before the phone started to ring again.

"Fucksake! Yes!" He smoked while he listened to the caller. "What, all of them?" His mood instantly lifted as he laughed out a thick plume of smoke. "Zhang, you're a fuckin' genius, me old China! Alright, let me finish up with this bullshit, and I'll swing by later."

The news was good. Chang Keqiang, the nerdy Triad computer genius he'd hired to find Khan's men, had done just that—found Khan's men. They were spread out far and wide across the whole of the UK, apparently, but he had addresses for all of them.

A sudden thought struck Carrick while he savoured his smoke. "Oi! Ask Ringo if he fancies a bit of work on the side—and his brothers too! If they wanna earn a few quid?"

Ringo, Keqiang's ever-present shadow, had three brothers; named after the Fab Four. If they were all as formidable-looking as him, they would be an unstoppable force against Khan's thugs. He waited while heated Cantonese was exchanged. Chinese could be a very passionate language, he considered. Even a loving exchange could sound like a violent slanging match. Carrick eyed up a pretty little thing that sidled by. He would've winked at her, but the gesture had lost its meaning now he only had one eye.

"Why? Why the fuck d'you think. I'm takin' The Beatles on a UK tour. Know what I mean?"

CHAPTER FIVE

While Dyson made the tea, Goldmann moved Mary into position in front of the white wall where the camera stood, shuffling her an inch to the left...then back half-inch the other way. Humming while he worked, he smoothed out the collars of the shirt she wore and straightened the lapels of her winter coat, taking a moment to brush away any stubborn raindrops that remained. Once happy, Goldmann nodded his approval and returned to the camera, squinting at the small LCD screen affixed to it.

"Now, do not smile, my dear," the counterfeiter instructed.

Of course, Mary instantly smiled. "Why should I not smile?"

Goldmann said something about it being easier for biometric facial recognition systems to work with neutral expressions, Mary's own expression indicating that she didn't understand what any of that meant. Nevertheless, she quashed the smile and straightened up, a series of clicks and flashes bursting forth from the camera.

Dyson came back with three steaming teas. He handed

one to Mary in exchange for a kiss and then gave Goldmann his in a mug with a cartoon rabbi in some mid-air martial arts pose, the words JEW JITSU printed below.

They clinked their cups together as if they were pints, and then Dyson stiffened as he gazed hard at Goldmann. "I need to know, Solly," he said with an awkward grimace.

Goldmann mumbled something unheard and wandered off to a computer terminal. He woke the mouse with a shake, the screen coming alive to show Mary's pale, emotionless face.

"Dear Lord…" Mary wrinkled her nose at the uncomplimentary image.

Dyson told her not to worry; it was customary for everyone's passport picture to make them look like a police mugshot. She accepted his explanation with a cautious nod while Dyson returned to Goldmann, his face hardening into an unpalatable grimace. "Say something, Sol."

The counterfeiter took a deep breath. "John, your father was a good friend. He was like a brother to me. We went back many years. If I am honest, were it not for Alan Dyson, this…" he swept a spindly arm over the room, "…this *understanding* I have with you and some of your colleagues would have never existed."

Dyson knew the story well enough, but he allowed Goldmann his moment of reminiscence as he lifted his cup into both hands as if cradling a memory.

Soloman Goldmann had been one of the first children born after the liberation of Auschwitz in 1945. Against horrendous odds, his parents had found love amongst the hopeless desperation of Hitler's Final Solution, escaping the gas chambers more through luck than any purposeful determination to avoid death. As the Russians marched into the camp, Isaak Goldmann and Rutka Flekstein fled the ruins of Europe for London, where they were married at what would become their local synagogue. Everyone they knew, friend or family, dead at the hands of the Nazis, their only guests were fellow worshippers that the rabbi had managed to bribe with the promise of as many holishkes as they could eat. Isaak Goldmann returned to his pre-war profession as a jeweller, opening a small shop on the prestigious New Bond Street, where rents were cheap with most of the city in ruins courtesy of the Luftwaffe's bombs. Learning all that his father taught him, Soloman quickly became an expert jeweller in his own right, creating the most exquisite pieces that attracted buyers from across the globe. But when Isaak passed in 1974 and the business was handed down to him as their only heir, his interested withered, and he sought new, imaginative ways to express his creative flair. Counterfeiting had never seemed a natural progression for one so gifted with their hands and with such a keen eye for detail, but something so simple as a hotly contested parking ticket, handwritten and so easily altered to exonerate guilt, had changed his mind and set the course for his future path. Goldmann built a select and exclusive clientele—he would never sell his masterpieces to just anybody. He only wanted to help those desperate for escape; the very thing his parents had once needed. Money was never a motivator to Goldmann. He had little need for it: the shop and his legitimate work provided a very generous return. Nor did the counterfeiter ever produce currency itself, considering it disrespectful to the country that gave his parents sanctuary after the war. He did it because he was an artist, because it excited him, and he enjoyed the challenge: a challenge that only grew as anti-counterfeit technology advanced to include elaborate watermarks and hologram protection.

Goldmann had first met Alan Dyson in 1998. Then a Detective Inspector with the Drug Squad, Dyson Senior had been investigating Micky Roth, an ultraviolent drug dealer considered by many to be the East End equivalent of Pablo Escobar. For the best part of six months, he had been trying desperately to convince Roth's partner, a woman called Gillian Mayer, to spill the beans on his operation and give evidence against him. But Gillian knew very little of Roth's nefarious business dealings: the criminal keeping the two sides of his life distinctly separate. Gilly, as Dyson came to know her, was such a sad character, beautiful but damaged and eternally terrified of Roth from the years of mental and physical torture she'd suffered. She was desperate to help put him away but had nothing to offer, which disqualified her from the safety a new identity awarded by the Criminal Justice Protection Unit would offer. Dyson couldn't help but pity her, allowing his personal feelings to cloud his professional judgement. He had urged her to report Roth to her local Domestic Violence Unit, but she was petrified of the repercussions; a rabbit trapped in Roth's headlights of revenge. It was at that point the detective was informed of Goldmann's underground work—a white knight to those in dire straits. Although illegal and a highly unconventional move, Gillian was provided with a new identity, allowing her to disappear and never resurface, but not before she had plundered her lover's bank account of over three-quarters of a million pounds. It was a nice touch, the men agreed, a lasting friendship growing from her escape.

The counterfeiter's features clouded as he took a nervous sip of his tea. "Towards the end, there was a darkness behind his eyes, a blackness to his soul even, and I would wonder if it was the same man I had known for all those years. On occasions, he would pull these thick piles of money from his overcoat—you know he was always easy with his cash? And he left your mother very well provided for, yes?"

Dyson gave him a hesitant nod. "Yeah, but…but that was from the properties he invested in, surely?"

"And from where did that money come, John?" Goldmann argued. "He was a detective. I would ask him sometimes where he had gotten it; I knew your police do not pay too well. He would tell me that it was better that I did not know. I am not saying he did what this Khan fellow claims, but—"

"But this is the man who saved Gilly Mayer, Sol?" Dyson defended. "And the others he helped. And then, what? He goes from saviour to extortionist? *To a rapist?*"

"I do not know, John," Goldmann shrugged with regret. "My father would tell me of men he knew. Good men. Proud, honest men within the Jewish community, becoming the camp stooges of the Nazis. *Sonderkommandos* they were called. They would feed the bodies of their own people—friends and relatives—into the incinerators for cigarettes and a few extra scraps at mealtimes. My father never looked upon humanity with the same eyes after that. How would I tell you over the years that the man you idolised, as any son should their father, had a darker side? Would you have even listened?"

There was an uncomfortable moment, the silence only broken by the counterfeiter's fingers typing away at his keyboard far too deftly for someone of his age. While Dyson stared into his mug, despondent and desperate for the tale not to be true, the image of Mary appeared within a passport page on-screen.

"My dear?" Goldmann called back softly. "Do you wish to remain Mary or would you like to use another name?"

"Um…" She looked at Dyson for guidance.

"It's your call," he croaked with a broken smile, his mind on far more important issues.

"Then Mary Jane Kelly is fine, thank you."

Goldmann shrugged, his gaze finding Dyson's sadness while his hands whisked over the keys. "Date of birth?"

"June the 2nd, 1863," Mary replied without thinking.

Dyson fired her a look and corrected her mistake. "She means 2005. Obviously."

"Obviously," Mary added with a pantomimed look of horror on realising her error.

"Obviously," Goldmann said, those alert eyes volleying a suspicious look between the two. Nevertheless, he wandered over to the blank passports Mary had examined and slid one into a large, hi-tech printer. He returned to the computer and hit a flashing green button, and the printer began to hum and whirl.

Mary skipped off to watch the device do its thing while Goldmann sidled up beside Dyson. "What is she running from?" he asked.

"Who says she's running from anything?"

"Come on, John," Goldmann said. "This deal has been in place for many years now. I tip you or your colleagues off to anyone I consider too treacherous to warrant a new identity, and in exchange you allow me to continue with what I do. I have seen lesser criminals, bankrupt businessmen, battered and abused wives—and husbands—come through those doors, seeking a new beginning. *Everyone* is running from something."

Dyson made a simple nod, contemplating Goldmann's question while Mary squealed with delight and held up the passport the printer spat out. "She's running from what we all do at some point," he said softly. "The past."

"The past…" The counterfeiter stared at him oddly, the word gripping him in a moment of deep consternation, his mind troubled by something other than Mary's plight.

"You alright, Sol? Sol?"

As if snapping out of a trance, Goldmann jolted, his look betraying a hidden knowledge. "There is something you should know, John. It is not my place to tell, but I cannot let you continue believing…that…" Goldmann nodded, his mind made up. "Yes, there is something you should be told." While Mary fooled around, brandishing her passport like a police warrant card, he motioned for Dyson to follow him. "Alone."

Raymond's silver BMW 9 Series crept along Victoria Embankment. Autumnal trees bare and spindly, the pavements were wet with rain and empty of all but the most resilient of tourists and pedestrians. Beyond the stone balustrade that separated river from land, the water of the Thames appeared darker even than the mood inside the car.

The Welshman sat awkwardly behind the steering wheel, his gut holding the car on course while he fiddled with his phone, peeking up every so often at the slow-moving traffic. Jenny rode shotgun, arms folded, desperate to avoid eye contact while flickering disapproving glances at his careless driving. The air between them was frigid and tense, infused with the indelible stink of cheap Lynx deodorant. Jenny tried to instigate a conversation on leaving Whitechapel, nothing too demanding, just where they were heading, but had received nothing but a derisory grunt in reply. Unlike the old river beside them, the conversation had failed to flow, making Jenny question why Raymond had asked her to accompany him in the first place. She had little desire to engage in conversation with someone so blatantly a sexist pig, the likes of which she believed had been purged from the Met years ago, but after what she'd been through recently, silence was the last thing Jenny needed. What she needed was the comfort of mutual conversation…even if the other party was someone as cantankerous and unlikable as Defective Superpretendent Fucky McFuckface. Raymond's nickname had amused Tom O'Keefe, she recalled morosely, a wave of emotion washing over her.

As the Welshman slipped his phone into his lap and slowed at Embankment Underground station, waiting at the lights to turn into Northumberland Avenue, Jenny banished her upset and tried her luck again. She made a delicate cough and glanced over at him. "Can I ask you something, sir?"

"If you must," he replied, not even bothering to look at her.

"Do you have a problem with women in the police?"

Now, he looked at her. Wearing a face that had the potential to go either way, Jenny braced herself, assuming she was about to fall victim to his unstable rage. She had seen how he had the tendency to explode at the slightest thing. Only the previous evening, with the police station still reeling from Dyson's arrest, he had blown up at Debbie for committing the cardinal sin of sugaring his tea.

Incoming…

But instead of bursting with fury, the Welshman softened to the point of embarrassment. He looked clumsily at Jenny, revealing a side rarely seen by the detectives under his command.

"My, um…my…" Raymond stumbled. He fed the wheel through his hands and tried again as the BMW flew past the embassies and hotels that lined Northumberland Avenue. "My wife is sick. Alzheimer's. She's dying."

Jenny opened her mouth to offer her condolences, but Raymond halted her with a raised hand he pulled from the wheel.

"Please…please don't interrupt my flow. As a consequence of her illness—of watching her waste away in my arms, not even knowing who the hell I am most of the time —I…I've begun to hate other women. I know, I know, it's completely irrational, you don't have to tell me. But I find myself looking at women and wondering…why not you? Why can't you get sick instead of my wife? Why my Maggie? What did she do to deserve this? That day I first arrived in Whitechapel, I looked across at the old hospital entrance, and there was this young girl, no older than my daughter, sat on the steps injecting some horrible muck into her veins."

He paused to navigate his way around the Trafalgar Square roundabout, a daunting prospect at the best of times. There were a few cursory blasts of the horn and under the breath mutterings, but Raymond managed to negotiate his way onto Cockspur Street without incident.

"The *old* Bill Raymond," he continued, "would've probably darted across the road and…I don't know, given her the talk about life choices and how there was light at the end of the tunnel if she could only see beyond the gloom. But now…" He took his hands from the wheel and throttled an invisible throat. "I looked at that girl—that child—and I wanted her to die. I wanted her to take Maggie's pain away. Why should some lowlife piece of trash like that, with no respect or regard for life, live while my wife…?"

Raymond dried up and retook the wheel in time to turn onto Pall Mall. The road unusually clear of traffic, the Welshman floored the car angrily to expunge his solemnity. Jenny tensed in the passenger seat, her foot reaching instinctively for the Jesus peddle. The Georgian-fronted properties and exclusive shopfronts blurred into a streak of uniform affluence until he began to slow for a pedestrian crossing, grumbling at the inconvenience. She watched him in profile, staring dead ahead, his bottom lip jutting out as Alfred Hitchcock's had done, his fat fingers drumming on the wheel impatiently at the mother dragging her screaming toddler over the crossing. Jenny found the previous dislike she'd felt for him ebbing away to be replaced by a glimmer of sympathy. He had lost a daughter to cancer, so the Met grapevine told, and now he was destined to lose a wife too. Everyone had a reason for being an arsehole, Jenny had always believed, and everyone deserved a second chance.

"It's not irrational, sir. My dad died when I was eleven. Heart attack. Out of the blue. One minute he was making my breakfast before school, the next... It tore me to pieces. I used to look at all the other kids with their dads. So happy, playing and laughing...and I'd wonder the same thing. Why did it have to be my dad? Why not the dad that was never there for their children or the violent drunk who would abuse their kid? Why *my* dad?"

"'The good die first, and they whose hearts are dry as summer dust, burn to the socket.' William Wordsworth."

Jenny made a thoughtful nod. It was an apt quote and one she would certainly remember. The tension in the car softened slightly.

But only for a moment.

"Okay, my turn," Raymond said. "Cards on the table time." He spread a handful of imaginary playing cards across the top of the leather dashboard and glanced over at her, watching her like he would a suspect. "This Khan business aside, I believe Dyson knows more about our mysterious case than he's letting on. In fact, I'd go as far as to say, he is purposefully withholding information from me. And if anyone's likely to know what his involvement is, it's going to be you, isn't it? His closest friend, ally, and ex-lover."

"That's why you brought me along?"

"That's why I brought you along. I need to know what's going on, Brent."

Jenny shifted in the seat and turned to look from the window as the car turned sharp left onto Piccadilly, immediately wishing she hadn't done so. It was a visible sign of guilt even to those not trained in the tell-tale signs of deceit. To Raymond, it would be as good as a signed confession. She let her eyes slip shut for a moment—another mistake he probably saw the reflection. But how could she answer? How could she betray Dyson with revelations of events and happenings she didn't even understand herself? With The Ritz appearing on the left, Jenny composed herself and turned back to face the Welshman. "I'm sorry, sir. I don't know anything."

Raymond's lips curled into a deliberate smile, the kind a detective made for a suspect when listening to their fanciful tales of innocence. "'Nature never did betray the heart that loved her.' That was Wordsworth too."

Jenny broke eye contact again, watching as the grey and wet buildings slipped past. Without looking back, her voice barely a whisper, she asked: "I'm sorry, where are we going?"

Raymond turned on the spot in the Eisenhower Suite of The Dorchester Hotel, his mood darkening with every revolution.

The double doors of the bedroom that he'd come so desperately close to opening only the previous day had been thrown open to uncover nothing more intimidating than a couple of hotel cleaners: one smoothing out the creases of a snow-white sheet on the impressive four-poster bed while the other raced a vacuum cleaner around and around.

Watched by Jenny, standing at the entrance arms folded, he marched back and dropped to his knees. Where there had been blood and a discarded phone, there was now only spotlessly clean carpet. The bronze bust had been repositioned on its righted plinth, showing no sign of any damage. Raymond struggled to his feet and pulled a cheap wire coathanger from within his trench coat. Jenny gave him a curious look as he tossed it down on the sofa.

"I should've known…" he mumbled.

“Sir?” Jenny probed gently, her question ignored by Raymond, that precarious look returning to his face as he stood on the precipice between rage and regret.

He should’ve known the moment he was able to select the first floor on the lift panel that the restrictions he’d encountered during his off-the-books exploration had been removed—as had any evidence of the US Government’s presence. Raymond glanced back into the bedroom and watched the tiny oriental woman charge around the bedroom with her hoover, a perfect metaphor for the rapid clean-up that had occurred.

“Come on, Brent,” he barked at Jenny, turning on his heels and hurrying from the Eisenhower Suite.

CHAPTER SIX

The president sat propped up in the hospital bed brought from The Dorchester Hotel after his evacuation. His shirt undone to show a visible yellowing of his weathered skin, probes and sensors connected him to the bank of machinery registering his vitals and creating an irritating rhythm of electronic sound. Behind the oxygen mask affixed to his face, his breath laboured, each lungful an effort to inhale. As it had been in the Eisenhower Suite, the second bed stood close by. Empty and awaiting its donor.

With Doctor Jakobi hovering like an annoying bug, the room where the president found himself was vast, its square footage putting the hotel suite to shame. Despite being tastefully appointed and decorated with the most lavish of fittings, it felt desolate and absent of any character. Garrett assumed it had once been a bedroom before being stripped and replaced by every conceivable piece of medical equipment that might ever be needed. He had little recollection of his arrival or location, but Jakobi had filled him in on the details.

Arizona One the house was called, or at least that was the

designation the CIA had assigned the property. Eight bedrooms, three reception rooms, a kitchen the size of Rhode Island, an indoor swimming pool, and a basement converted into a games room, gym, home cinema, and a panic room that could withstand an invading army. Located just off Wimbledon Village, where they held the prestigious tennis tournament once a year, it had been a CIA listening station, a remnant left over from the dark days of the Cold War. But when relations between the West and the crumbling USSR had warmed under Gorbachev's *Perestroika*, and the property became redundant of its intended purpose, it remained part of the government's vast global portfolio due to London's rising property prices. Mounting tensions with the Russian Federation over the recent years had seen it return to a scaled-down version of its old self, refitted and remodelled at the cost of millions of taxpayer dollars. In addition, Arizona One was used to house high-level agents working in the capital...and occasionally for black site interrogations and the holding of wanted terrorists, if the rumours the doctor had heard were to be believed.

A television had been wheeled in and connected at Garrett's request, the news channel he had settled on continuing its coverage of Dyson's assault on one of Whitechapel's villains. The story had gripped the capital, judging by the amount of airtime it was getting. A bland commentary recounted the events for the umpteenth time over footage of the detective pushing his way through a heavy throng of reporters, camera flashes bursting all around.

"Goddamn fool," the president muttered to himself.

Jakobi turned from the machine he was examining to roll up the president's sleeve and attach the inflatable cuff of a blood pressure monitor. "What's that, sir?"

Garrett said nothing. He stewed for a moment, wondering if the pressure the Ripper's escape had put Dyson under had sparked the attack that would cost him his job. The UK police were under intense strain; the president knew that much, the prime minister having told him of their woes at last year's G20 summit in Buenos Aires. For the president to have exacerbated that workload made him culpable to a degree. He felt a shiver of biting responsibility swell through his weakened body, voicing it with a sigh of frustration that filled the mask with a thin layer of condensation. Garret looked away from the TV to find the doctor staring down at him with a curious eye, clearly in two minds whether to broach the subject he wanted to address.

In the end, it was the president who spoke, agitated by Jakobi's dithering. "What…what is it, Malcolm?" he puffed. "Get it off your chest."

"When you collapsed yesterday, you made a very puzzling statement."

"I did?"

"You did, yes. You said that you wouldn't die yet." Jakobi waited for the president to respond. When he didn't, the doctor probed him further. "In fact, you said you wouldn't die until we all…and then you lost consciousness. Until we all what? What on earth did you mean by that?"

"I don't know…don't know what I was saying, my old… old friend," Garrett struggled, the cuff tightening on his bicep. As the doctor glanced down to activate the machine, the president swallowed his deceit and banished it with a wistful shake of his head. "You…you'd pumped me so full… full of drugs, God only knows what the effects were."

The doctor smiled dutifully. "But Evastin has been proven in studies to have no psychotropic effects. In short, Mr President, whatever you were saying, it wasn't because of the drugs."

"Then…I honestly have…no earthly explanation why… why I would make such an outlandish claim."

Jakobi held the grin as the monitor beeped, and he examined the results. "You know, Bob, I have this neighbour. Mrs Florez. The indomitable Edna Florez we call her. She's a crabby old witch, so she is. *Waaay* into her nineties, but bright as a bulb. Been in DC since before gas or electric. Anyhow, when you were running for president, we got to talking, you know, just a neighbourly chat in the yard. I asked her who she was going to give her support to in the election. She didn't know at the time that we were friends and had no reason to tell me anything other than what she was thinking. She looked up at me with this big, proud grin and said she was voting for you. She told me she was a very astute judge of character and that she'd seen the honesty in your eyes. 'That's a guy who tells the truth,' she said. 'That's a guy who tells the truth.'"

Jakobi let the statement linger for a moment while he removed the cuff with the tear of Velcro and packed away the monitor.

"Try and get some rest, Mr President, and I'll check in with you again in a couple of hours," the doctor concluded, heading for the door.

That's a guy who tells the truth, the president thought shamefully as the doctor left the room. He hated to lie, especially to an old friend such as Jakobi, but how could he divulge the terrifying truth that only himself and Ratski knew? It would scare the poor bastard half to death. After the blatant dishonesty of previous administrations, treachery wasn't a quality that Garrett wanted his administration to associate with. Yet there he was: spending billions in black budget dollars and sheltering in a country he had supposedly left while an imposter played president, all under the direction and guidance of man he barely knew. His conduct would undoubtedly destroy the faith Edna Florez had put in him if the truth was ever made public, that was for sure.

But that would be the least of his problems.

The president returned to the TV, but he found little comfort there. The story continuing to play, an image of a younger Dyson in his police uniform staring out from the screen, mocking him. Garrett killed the TV and reached into the pocket of his slacks to retrieve his phone. The screen flashed and came alive, the president squinting to scroll through his contacts. He found who he wanted, the call he initiated answered almost immediately.

"Brad, you…you need to get…Dyson back somehow," Garratt grimaced. "He's…he's too valuable to lose like this."

"And how do I do that, sir?" Ratski replied, quashing the sigh but not the eye roll that followed the question. He pursed his lips at Garrett's response and closed the door of the small office that had become his permanent home, picking up the sleeping bag and blanket from the floor and hanging them off the chair he dropped into. "Mr President…he beat an unrelated suspect half to death. We have no jurisdiction over the Metropolitan Police Department or their internal investigation procedures."

Ratski listened while the president spoke, massaging the banging tension from his forehead that had arrived with Garrett's call. Jamming the phone into the crook of his neck, he fished his pill bottle from the jacket pocket of his suit to pop the lid, shaking a tablet out onto the desktop and gulping it down without water.

"If Dyson's that important to you, sir, I'll talk to him and see if I can persuade him to work for us directly." His face twisted at the pill's bitter aftertaste. "Whatever it takes? I understand, sir. Goodbye, sir."

Ratski placed his phone gently on the desk, the sigh he'd

held finally released as he dry washed his face to scrub away the tiredness. Despite the sleeping bag, he hadn't slept for days, his mind constantly tortured by the terrifying thoughts that the Ripper's continued freedom brought. And now their Ripper expert was gone too: arrested after assaulting his criminal nemesis, so the police radio chatter had disclosed.

"It's beginning to fall apart," Ratski muttered.

If there was a flicker of hope to the nightmare, it was that the Ripper had survived his altercation with the subway train. Ratski had gotten the Secret Service agents to retune their surveillance equipment to the London Underground's radio frequencies, scanning through incident channel after incident channel until the right one was located. For over an hour, he paced the office like a defendant awaiting the jury's return until the radio announced that no body had been found.

That precious Bishop's blood still flowed. The killer was alive…somewhere.

The ball-breaker felt his stomach protest. He needed to eat something, unable to remember the last decent meal he'd consumed or even what it had consisted of. With its streets of swanky restaurants and the endless engagements the White House always seemed to host, he'd eaten like a king in DC once his sickness had subsided enough for him to taste and keep down what he ate. Eating became a pleasure rather than the necessity for survival it had once been. But now, having become a near-permanent resident of Whitechapel since the Ripper's escape, the fine eateries of DC and grills and restaurants of The Dorchester Hotel had been exchanged for the tasteless junk food and cheap curries the local area offered in abundance.

A nod grew, cementing his intentions. He would eat first and then speak to Dyson. Ratski stood and grabbed his phone, reaching instinctively to feel for his wallet in the back trouser pocket it always occupied. A look of confusion swept across his haggard face as he found it missing. He continued his exploration, deep-diving each pocket in turn and then doing the same to his jacket.

"Where the hell is my wallet?"

Ratski manoeuvred around the desk to the unstable hatstand, his coat strategically positioned to counteract the lean. He worked through the pockets until suddenly freezing...but it wasn't his wallet he pulled free. It was the warrant card belonging to the policeman he'd shot in the abandoned subway station. Ratski opened it and stared hard at Christopher Haddon as if he would spring to life and offer the location of his wallet. When he didn't, Ratski tossed the identification down on top of the desk and rushed from the office.

With their time in the bowels of the jewellery shop at an end, a quiet unhappiness had infected Dyson since Goldmann had divulged his mysterious revelation. The news had been unexpected, to say the least, causing Dyson to gasp before desperately trying to laugh it off as a mistake that Goldmann had made. Except...Goldmann didn't make mistakes, not in all the years Dyson had known him. His businesses, both legal and illegal, required an impeccable level of detail that prevented such an occurrence. Dyson had struggled to process the information, his head swimming as if drunk until it had struck him that the news was irrelevant in the grand scheme of things. To a thirty-six-year-old policeman facing a disciplinary and a possible spell *inside*, and with a time-travelling serial killer still on the loose, it was meaningless. But that didn't stop it niggling him like the first bite of a toothache.

He watched Goldmann hand Mary a faded birth certificate as they navigated the workshop of the counterfeiter's underground lair.

"Best you can get, Mary, my dear," Goldmann smiled, turning to look back at Dyson and handing him a slip of paper containing handwritten letters and digits. "National Insurance number." He made a deliberate wink at Mary. "So you can send her out to work!" The counterfeiter cackled with laughter, neither Dyson nor Mary sharing the joke for different reasons. "Anyway, I have taken the liberty of planting a seed in the database."

"Sorry," Dyson said, trying to focus on the matter at hand. "Seed?"

"There is a loophole, a backdoor if you will, that leads directly into the government database. Very few people are aware of it. The seed I have planted is a data packet on a maintenance release schedule. It will bloom all of Mary's details to the relevant government departments." Goldmann held out his withered hand, his fingers springing open to indicate the birth of life. "*Just like that.*"

"Bloody hell, Sol. That's insane."

Goldmann waggled his fingers dexterously and started to gabble about SQL injection, China Choppers, and something called HTran. It seemed inconceivable for someone so ancient to be so computer savvy while Dyson was ignorant of such things, his eyes glazing over as he acknowledged why he'd never pursued a career within the Met's Cyber Crimes Unit. Goldmann went on to explain how he'd given Mary a decent set of GCSE results—she had declined the offer of a university degree—and clean medical history based on a questionnaire he got her to complete, together with a unique NHS medical number.

"You know you're a genius, right?" Dyson flattered, Mary nodding away the bewildered expression she wore at his side.

"Well, of course I am. I am the best. You said so yourself." Goldmann laughed and tapped a bony finger on Mary's passport. "If they were ever to check this, they would find that *they* issued it, her application is on their own database, and that it was printed in Poland as they are now. By the end of this week, Mary Jane Kelly will exist in the electronic ether as much as she does in the flesh, a slave to government bureaucracy just like the rest of us. It is all completely untraceable, of course...providing that you do not arrest me."

"I think a traffic warden's got more clout than me at the moment," Dyson said grimly.

"Because you are very stupid," Goldmann reprimanded, his face wrinkling into a scowl.

"He is," Mary agreed.

As did Dyson. "I am."

"I am sorry, John," the counterfeiter added miserably, "but there is no magic I can perform, no document I can produce that will help you with your situation."

"What situation are we talking about?" Dyson asked with a melancholic scoff.

A silent moment passed between the two men until Goldmann pulled Dyson in for an impressive bearhug —"Come here!"—while Mary studied her passport with a widening grin.

A wealthy Arab haggling brashly with the sales assistant over an exquisite golden necklace, Dyson and Mary exited from behind the counter. Through the window, the rain hammered down on New Bond Street with such ferocity that everything was a slick tide of bleeding colour.

Mary wrapped herself around Dyson's strong arm and

squeezed as they headed for the door. "What did you talk about?"

"Oh, nothing much." Dyson shrugged guiltily, forcing his lips into an awkward smile.

"You're a terrible liar, Mr Dyson," she chided, the pressure of her grip increasing. "You've been as quiet as a church mouse ever since."

Dyson ignored the question, staring at the rain and the people rushing through it like fractured silhouettes. "We need a holiday," he announced, retrieving the umbrella and readying it for the onslaught.

"That would be lovely. Where do you have in mind?"

"Anywhere where it's not raining. How about Japan?"

"The Far East?"

"I want you to meet my sister."

"The teacher?"

"In Tokyo, yeah. I'd love you to meet her." Dyson leaned in and pecked Mary on the lips, the motive in his eyes hidden from her view. "Because I love you."

"And I—"

Ding-ding. Dyson's phone stole Mary's declaration with the arrival of a text message. He grumbled and pulled it out, a message from Ratski opening on screen. I NEED TO SEE YOU URGENTLY.

"Forget him," Dyson said, stuffing the phone away. "I promised you a day out, so we're having a day out."

And what a fantastic day it proved to be. They had started at the London Eye, Mary's face alive with child-like wonderment as their capsule crawled high above the gloomy grey city…until she felt sickened at the height and had to sit, head in hands. The London Aquarium followed; the visit finished with the silhouetted couple kissing passionately against a backdrop of circling sharks. Lunch was taken at an expensive steak house within the Edwardian Baroque façade of County Hall. Wine and cocktails had flowed, the food consumed with gusto until Mary dragged Dyson off with a suggestive grin across her painted lips. The cubicle door of the men's toilets had crashed open—the couple literally tearing each other's clothes off to fuck like animals. After another round of post-coitus cocktails, they had stumbled onto a filthy East End street billowing with dry ice. Victorian sound effects came courtesy of a concealed speaker system, the clip-clop of unseen horses competing with a recorded paperboy crying out the terrible news of another murder. Mary had jumped out of her skin as a top-hatted Ripper stepped out of the fake fog brandishing a rubber knife while Dyson just shrugged, decidedly unimpressed. Laughing and falling about, they exited The London Dungeons entangled in each other's arms. Drunken by alcohol and intoxicated by love.

Free of the building's signal blocking properties, Dyson's phone began to chime repeatedly, a chorus of bells and whistles announcing one missed call or unread message after another. All from Ratski.

His nostrils bulging at the heady aroma of overworked microwaves and cleaning fluid, Khan shuffled away from the cashier in the restaurant of the Royal London Hospital and looked around for a table. He winced with pain; not from the injuries received during his assault but at the cost of the coffee he'd just bought.

'Restaurant' was an overgenerous description, Khan felt. Situated on the fifth floor of the main building, the establishment offered far better views over London than it did any form of culinary experience. With its rock-hard, uncomfortable furniture and unbearable muzak renditions of popular tunes, it was a shining example of a tactic employed by many fast-food outlets: to make the seating so arse-numbingly uncomfortable and the music so bloody awful that punters would eat up and bugger off, vacating their seat for the next victim.

Get 'em in, get 'em fed, get 'em out, Khan thought, the entrepreneur in him appreciating the strategy while staring over a vanilla expanse populated with overworked staff and visiting relatives.

Much to his nurses' objections, the criminal had left his private room, intent on taking a wander to alleviate the boredom. He wasn't well enough yet to venture from his room, they pleaded with him. He had responded by telling them to 'Fuck off and die' as he'd swaggered away, compression stockings pulled up, his buttocks exposed from the slit at the back of the ridiculous gown they'd made him wear.

Khan made his way over to a table situated by the floor to ceiling windows, occupied by an elderly woman, sat alone, sobbing her heart out into a handkerchief.

"What's the matter with you?" he growled.

The woman glanced up, eyes awash with stinging tears. "My…my husband just died."

"You don't need to be takin' up a table then, do you?" Khan snapped coldly, motioning for her to move. "Go on, fuck off."

The woman's face collapsed as she stood and hurried away, Khan's deliberate laughter pursuing her escape as he lowered himself into her chair and gazed out of the window like a lord surveying his kingdom. The rain cascaded down the glass, distorting his already hideous visage as he blew away the steam and risked a tentative sip of his Americano.

He eased a look of disgust across his swollen face and opened the Jack the Ripper book he carried. The five canonical murders all covered in gory detail, the author had moved on to suspects—and there were many. From royals to quacks, barbers to butchers, it seemed most of late Victorian society had been under suspicion at one time or another.

Only halfway through his first paragraph, Khan became aware of someone making a beeline for his table. Whoever it was, they stopped and gave a discrete cough. The criminal scowled at the interruption and looked up to see the wannabe gangster he'd slammed down on his conference table hovering above. Decked out in a loud high street tracksuit, the kid swallowed hard, toying nervously with the rim of his baseball cap. No doubt removed as a mark of respect, Khan told himself.

"Mr Minter told me I should come back and see you, innit?"

Khan smiled and closed the book. "What's your name?"

"Aziz Karim."

"Sit down then, Aziz Karim." Khan sized him up as he slipped into the chair opposite.

Despite the street talk and trackie bottoms at half-mast around his arse, there was a youthful vulnerability behind his wide eyes and uneven stubble. A kid desperate to impress, malleable and easy to manipulate if fed the right incentive, Khan considered. He looked like the boy from that *Who Wants To Be A Millionaire* film he'd seen years ago, where the little Paki kid had fallen in the shit and climbed his way out a winner. But there would be no winning here for Karim.

"You still wanna fight the bacon?" Khan asked.

Karim nodded his head eagerly, his Jafaican accent thickening as he found his feet. "The Feds killed my brother, innit? He was a good kid, shanked up a teacher and sold a bit of weed, but he was mint, man, solid—didn't run with any crew. Fuckers covered it up and said he hang himself in the cell, but I know that's them just chattin' shit."

The kid paused, Khan wondering if he was expected to offer some words of sympathy. Instead, he drank some coffee and scowled. "Six quid they charged me for this, it's fuckin' criminal. It tastes like it's been strained from the lumps out of some old codger's bedpan." Before Karim could reply, Khan surged ahead. "I've got a little job for you, if you're interested?"

The kid bopped his head enthusiastically, reminding Khan of one of those tacky nodding dogs that had been all the rage years ago. "Just say the word, Mr Khan, innit," Karim gushed.

Khan leant over the table and pushed out the words secretively. "In a lock-up garage a couple of streets from 'ere, there's a large quantity of illegal weapons. Guns and shit like that. Amongst 'em are three explosive devices I had specially built. They're bagged up and ready to go. I want you to take 'em for a little stroll round Whitechapel and find yourself three nice shiny pig motors to stick 'em under."

Karim gasped and gulped all at once. "Wait—what?"

"Look, you up to this or not, son?" Khan slammed down his mug for effect, an exhausted nurse glancing over at the disturbance. "Fuck off, nose ache," he snarled, turning back to Karim. "If you're not committed, or you ain't got the minerals, you'd best fuck off too…and I'll find meself another prodigy."

The kid's ears prickled at that. "Prodigy?"

"Prodigy, yeah. I'm lookin' around for a successor for me empire. It's a shame 'cause Nicky Minter only had good things to say about you." He turned away and reached for his book.

"Nah, go on. I can do anything, innit." He gave Khan his

best cocky wink and relaxed in his seat. "Just 'cause I don't eat the pig, don't mean I can't cook it."

Khan thought about that. It was an excellent analogy and one worthy of an appreciative nod. "I like that, very good. Anyway, these devices, they're magnetic, on a mercury switch. You know what that is?" Karim nodded to confirm he did. "Good. Find yourself three baconmobiles—you choose, I don't care. You just stick them under the cars and flip the switch. And when they drive off...*boooom.* D'you think you can handle that?"

"Yeah, of course, Mr Khan."

"Key and address," Khan said as he took a slip of folded paper from within the book and slid it across the table. As Karim reached out, the criminal grabbed his hand and squeezed until he felt the kid tremble. "Don't fuck this up, and don't get caught. It's important this happens today while I'm recoverin' in the competent hands of the National 'ealth Service."

"You...you can...can trust me."

"Let's hope so, *innit?* Give me your mobile number, and we'll meet up later to get the key back. You do a good job, then maybe we can talk about you becomin' a permanent member of the Khan organisation. You'd like that, wouldn't you?"

"I would, Mr Khan, yeah. I'd like that a lot."

"I bet you fuckin' would, son," Khan said, the Machiavellian grin he cast completely lost on Karim.

CHAPTER SEVEN

Forced into scurrying hunches by the driving rain, Knapper and Mitchell followed the station supervisor along the tracks from Whitechapel Underground station towards the tunnel mouth for the District Line. Like the miserable old bastard leading them to their destination, they wore high-visibility vests over their coats and suits: a condition of their admittance the supervisor had told them gruffly, not in the least bit happy at having his day interrupted by the two detectives.

The trip down to the tracks had begun with them presenting their warrant cards for inspection and signing in with the supervisor as visitors. 'Mr Happy' as Mitchell christened him under his breath, proceeded to inform them that although the juice would be off, there would be a variety of potential trip hazards they might encounter along the track and how they should only walk on the ballast and never the sleepers—they would be slippery, the supervisor stressed. It was about that time that Mitchell lost the will to live; Knapper making up for his apathy by nodding away enthusiastically to everything they were told.

The detectives straightened up and shook themselves off

as cold, wet daylight receded to become the dry darkness of the tunnel. The supervisor switched on the 40,000-candle-power flashlight he carried, vaporising the growing gloom with a nauseous white glare brighter than a nuclear explosion. Knapper congratulated the supervisor on his torch, looking down at his inadequate penlight in comparison as they rounded a curvature in the tunnel. There was a stationary train ahead on the eastbound track, its compressors whining away. In the cab, the driver lounged in his seat, reading a newspaper, waiting to return Mr Happy to Whitechapel once the detectives were safely delivered. The supervisor waved, the driver offering only a yawn in reply.

"Controller will be havin' bloody kittens over this," Mr Happy moaned. "You shuttin' his service down like this."

"I'm sure he'll get over it," Mitchell answered, pulling a mocking face at Knapper.

"Once he realises you're assisting with an important investigation," the black detective added to placate the supervisor.

"Is this about that Jack the Ripper copycat business?" the supervisor asked, stopping at a set of steps oxidised with rust that led up to an opening in the filthy brickwork.

"We're not at liberty to discuss that, I'm afraid, sir," Knapper answered, giving the official reply that nosy people generally got.

"Righto," Mr Happy grumbled, adding something neither of them heard while he motioned to the breach in the wall. "Here you go then. There's a door that leads out onto the high street by the mosque. You'll have to go out that way unless you wanna get squashed by a train. And make sure you shut the bloody door properly!"

"Right you are, Captain!" Mitchell saluted, shooing him away to the waiting train as they ascended the steps into St Mary's.

They dropped down into a darkened corridor on the other side of the tracks, a single lightbulb struggling to cast its weak glow.

"Alone at last," Knapper said, firing up his penlight and swinging the weak beam this way and that.

"*Make sure you shut the bloody door—*" Mitchell impersonated Mr Happy, stopping only when his flashlight settled on something on the floor halfway along the passageway. "Is that…?"

He stalked over to a dark red patch on the concrete floor and sank to a crouch, the soles of his shoes crunching on the thick layer of dust. There were other footsteps too, he noticed, choreographed in a way that suggested some form of struggle had occurred.

"Blood?" Knapper said, rushing over to join him.

"No flies on you, are there?" Mitchell joked, highlighting the footprints with his beam. "Plus, we've got multiple persons present; looks to be at least three."

"We're gonna need SOCO down here," Knapper said. "We'll have a mooch around and call them when we're done." He motioned at the doorway at the end of the passageway and illuminated it with his torch. "Come on, Jimmy."

Apart from Ratski and a dishevelled vagrant sitting out the perpetual downpour at a table in the corner, the café used to meet with the detective was empty of customers. The owner stood behind the counter, staring off into space and captivated by some maudlin tune that was playing on the radio. He had been drying the same mug for over three minutes now, Ratski noticed from the table he sat at, appreciating the effect the song had on the man.

He thought of *their* song and hummed the opening bars

of the Petula Clark hit softly to himself. There was little joy or energy to its recital. *Downtown* was a conduit to the past —Ratski scoffed at that—a simple pop song from an era he couldn't even imagine, a melody that brought both relief and heartache. It allowed her face to push through the fog of his unsettled mind, her ever-present smile bringing light in the darkest of times...only for the coldness of reality to snatch her away from him.

Ratski's hollow face twisted, his eyes screwing tightly shut while she invaded his thoughts again. His breath trembled, rattling against his ribs, the ball-breaker desperate for her to be there when he opened them. But she wasn't. Only blurred shadows moved before him, hurrying past the steamed-up windows on Brick Lane.

He snorted away the absurdity of his yearning and stirred his coffee, returning to the early edition of the *Evening Standard* laid out on the table. The glaring headline that warned of the UK's continuing financial woes was of little consequence to him. Nor was the offering of a free eight-page colour Jack the Ripper commemorative pull-out inside. Newspapers were never ones to miss cashing in on a tragedy, Garrett had informed him once after an airliner had slammed into the Rocky Mountains killing everyone on board; the glossy hatchet job one of the less salubrious national publications did on the victims driven into the Oval Office trash can with unpresidential anger. But none of that mattered to Ratski now. It was the date that stimulated his rare display of emotion.

23rd October...

He felt the bulge that blocked his throat grow, choking him, his fingers reaching up to loosen his tie and top button until his breath flowed out as an agonising wheeze. His lips moved silently as if recanting a prayer until the words he wanted to say were released with quiet solemnity.

"Happy Birthday, Myra."

A violently shaking hand plunged into his pocket to retrieve his pill bottle. Ratski fumbled with the container, his annoyance building until one rolled onto the table. He snatched it off the grubby Formica and stuck it in his mouth, sending it on its way on a tide of hot coffee.

"Who's Myra?" Dyson asked as he loomed above Ratski, swaying on the heavy stench of booze.

Ratski cursed his stupidity, the detective's silent approach catching him off guard and sullying his private moment. "You're drunk, Detective," he scolded as he thrust the bottle back from where it came.

"*Ex*-detective." Dyson crashed clumsily into the chair opposite and gave Ratski his best '*Fuck you*' smile.

"Why don't you stop wallowing in self-pity," Ratski said with his obligatory arctic aloofness, "and help me catch this bastard?"

Dyson shrugged, carefree and unashamed by his inebriated state. "Or why don't I just pull you over this table and cave your face in?"

Ratski brushed something from his trousers, unshaken by the threat. "That isn't your…what do you call it, MO?" He made a show of looking around the café, the deliberate smirk that followed aimed directly at Dyson. "And this establishment certainly isn't a precinct interview room." Their glares simmered, bubbling with intensity until Ratski suddenly deescalated the situation with a question straight out of left-field. "What do you make a year, Dyson?"

"What the hell has that got to do with—?"

"I'll tell you then, shall I? £74,786 per annum." Ratski knew that to be true; he had checked the Metropolitan Police Department's website for a detective's pay scale before Dyson had arrived. 'Forewarned is forearmed,' as the saying went. "The president has authorised me to pay you that, per week.

Per week, Dyson. Tax-free. With none of the police procedures you have so much trouble adhering to. You'd be working directly for us. Free to attack whoever you desire—so long as you find the Ripper first."

"I don't want your fucking money, Ratski!" Insulted by the offer, Dyson drove his balled-up fist into the table.

The proprietor jumped out of his trance and peeked over warily at the potential altercation. "Everything alright, John?" he called out.

"Everything's fine, Kostas," Dyson snapped, returning to Ratski. "You can clear up your own shit because I'm out, Ratski. I'm done! And d'you know what? It feels *good*."

"You're lying."

"Am I?" Dyson straightened up out of his slouch to make a lopsided drunken smirk. "Me and my *whore*, we're leaving for Japan tomorrow. Three-week holiday—sorry, *vay-cay-shun*."

A slither of panic rippling his body, Ratski held his composure to eye up his adversary. "I'm no expert, but I'm pretty sure that international travel would be a breach of your bail conditions. Maybe I should check with your superiors?"

He had no idea whether the threat was a viable one, but the president wanted the detective back, so he had to try everything to accomplish that wish. Judging by the drunken chuckling sound Dyson made in response, his ultimatum carried little weight.

"And explain who you are? A fake FBI agent who fucked up and let the *real* Jack the Ripper escape? Sure, knock yourself out."

Touché, Ratski thought grudgingly. He took a long sip of his coffee and decided a change of approach was called for. If he couldn't entice Dyson with monetary reward, he would appeal to his sense of morality. "But these are your people,

Dyson. This is *your* town. You can't walk away from them now. You brought this…this abomination back here."

"And you let him escape."

"Whitechapel needs you!"

"There are other cops. Better than me."

"That is undoubtedly true, but you're the one Garrett wants." Ratski peered beyond Dyson to the steamed window, something out on Brick Lane holding his gaze for a moment. "Not only does the president feel a sense of responsibility for what happened to you, he believes that you're the best man to find this bastard."

"Wow, this must really hurt, huh? Grovelling on your knees, begging me—"

"I'm not begging you."

"You'll be offering me a blowjob next."

"I am not *begging* you. Personally, I don't share the president's belief in your abilities. I think you're a liability." He leant back in his seat and stared past Dyson to the window again. "I mean, a better cop—one not so blind drunk—would have probably noticed that he was being followed."

Dyson didn't even flinch at the revelation. "Oh, you mean the guy with the eyepatch reading the newspaper in the rain? He's been following me all morning, but guess what? *I don't care*. My job's gone. I'll…I'll just have to accept that. Maybe you should too." He climbed to his feet and reached right over the table to slur the standard American farewell into Ratski's ear. "*Have a nice day*."

Dyson headed straight for the counter and plucked a prepacked sandwich from a refrigerator unit. He tossed a crumpled ten pound note down for the proprietor and nodded back at the ball-breaker. "Buy laughing boy there another coffee to cheer him up, Kostas," he said, marching for the door and back out into the rain.

Loitering at the window, the man with the eye patch and the leather trench coat turned away sharply, trying his damnedest to appear inconspicuous. He bumped into a woman coming the other way, a clumsy sidestepping routine between the two costing him valuable seconds.

The woman finally scuttling away, Dyson sauntered over to look the man up and down, undecided whether to laugh at his ridiculous appearance or not. His lips tightly clamped together, the man stewed, raging in silence at being discovered. Whoever he was, he was a copper. While Dyson's warrant card and gun had been seized after his arrest, the well-honed ability of all policemen to sniff out their comrades in a crowd remained. Dyson had spotted him when leaving his apartment, thinking nothing of it until the man had boarded the same tube train as him and Mary and then alighted with them at Oxford Circus. While his lover had salivated over the glass cabinets of Goldmann's sparkly wares, Dyson had glanced up into a fancy mirror on one wall and caught sight of the same person plastered to the shop window. It could mean only one thing: someone had put him under surveillance.

Whoever that was remained to be seen. The operation didn't have the *feel* of officialdom to it; the man's outlandish appearance making him anything but discreet and impossible to miss. There was little need for the DPS to pursue Dyson for additional evidence—they already had enough to sink his career and put him on the wrong side of a prison door. That left Raymond, Dyson speculated, probably calling in an off the record favour from someone in The Job.

"Here," Dyson snarled, dropping the sandwich into the man's crumpled newspaper, "you must be starving." He turned away to stride off along Brick Lane, whipping back around to point at the man. "And get yourself on a surveillance refresher, mate. You look like a Nazi fucked a pirate."

———

It was a minor traffic collision, so the radio message from the police station's CAD room had claimed. But even the most innocuous of events had the potential to develop into something altogether different, especially in London, 2030. Only the previous week, a routine fender-bender in Finchley had escalated from argument to fight to murder, claiming the life of one poor motorist when a knife was driven into his neck multiple times. Even the police were not immune to such violence. The last fortnight in Whitechapel had proven as much: the deaths of five police officers and the disappearance of a probationer still painfully fresh on everyone's mind.

Police Constable Liam Calderwood thanked his lucky stars that this time it was just indeed a minor prang and something not worthy of police attendance. Details were taken, and the issue had been resolved with repeated apologies and zero violence. Nevertheless, the policeman was a seasoned pro, never letting his guard down and always keeping his hand within easy reach of his automatic.

He said his farewells to the motorists and raced back to the Toyota Prius patrol car he had arrived in. Parking had been such a premium on Cambridge Heath Road that the policeman had been forced to double park and leave the blue lights flashing. Climbing in behind the wheel, he scrubbed the rain from his weary face while he fiddled with the seatbelt until it clicked into place. Calderwood sat there for a moment, watching the traffic crawl with the speed of a sun cast shadow. He remembered the missing newbie with a disparaging scoff, sickened by the puppy-dog enthusiasm

Haddon displayed in the canteen prior to his vanishing. Calderwood had been like that once. Jaded and worn down by his years of policing, he conducted a mental reckoning of his time left until retirement.

"Seven years," the PC groaned, his thumb plunging down on the start button and filling the interior with the soft hum of electricity. "Seven bloody years."

Calderwood put the car into gear, checked the mirrors, and pulled away.

The Prius didn't get far.

A devastating explosion tore the car to pieces, opening it up like some perverse flower of twisted metal and sending the shattered interior skywards on a jet of ferocious flame. The blast wave uprooted the nearest cars, sending them spiralling into the air in a perfectly orchestrated ballet of destruction. Doors and windows punched in by an unseen fist, people stumbled and scuttled for cover, flying cars crashing down all around them. Over the unnoticed wailing of multiple alarms, a fragile, ethereal stillness descended on the area until it was smashed by the thud of Calderwood's burning upper torso slamming onto the bonnet of a nearby car. His intestines poured from the terminal wound, unravelling to slide down the dented metal as a chorus of terrified voices began to cry out.

Half a mile from the explosion, two female police officers came running out of a convenience store to their own car, a Vauxhall Centro emblazoned with its fluorescent blue and yellow Battenberg markings.

Even hidden in a doorway over 100 metres away, Karim,

Khan's eager little helper, could hear the frantic exchanges spitting from their radios. A car bomb had exploded in Whitechapel the garbled voices cried.

He had come across the second police car entirely by accident. After hot-footing it away from planting the first bomb to put as much distance between himself and the scene of the crime as possible, Karim had found himself in a narrow side street called Cleveland Way. Clutching a tatty Sainsbury's carrier bag containing the explosive devices, the kid made his way along the road, pounded by the rain and surrounded by shitty, graffiti-daubed low-rises. And there it was, like a jewel in the dirt. A big, fat police car sat outside a grimy supermarket that had seen better days and cheaper prices. Of course, it was parked on double yellow lines. He had ranted internally at how the Feds parked wherever the fuck they felt like when he'd heard the distant *whoomph* of the first explosion. Filled with nervous euphoria, Karim dedicated the blast to his dead brother and got to work. The two bitch women pigs inside, chatting with the shopkeeper and buying food to stuff their pig faces with, the kid had bent down to tie the laces of his already fastened Nikes. As casual as a guilty man, he had reached inside the bag and pulled out a block of plastic explosive the size of a house brick wrapped in greaseproof paper. There were several neodymium magnets on one side, held in place with insulating tape, and a neat arrangement of wires that ran to the flip switch Khan had described on the other. With no pedestrians to witness the act, he had swooped under the car and affixed the bomb with a clunk of attracting metal, flipping the switch that illuminated a red light to show the bomb was armed. Furtive eyes dancing all around, Karim had jumped up and continued his bad man strut until he found a place to shelter and witness the fruits of his work.

The kid held his breath as the two Feds dived inside the

car, his heart racing as the petrol engine fired up and revved. Seconds passed, seconds that felt like hours while he watched the silhouette of the passenger talking into her radio.

And then, the car moved and was no more.

The explosion brightened his face a deep orange, vaporising the car right there on the spot. What was once sleek with smooth rounded lines was instantly jagged and alive with flame. The force of the detonation smashed in the front of the shop on a boiling tsunami of fire, the two cars parked either side thrown along the street as if discarded by a child's angry hand.

"That's for Mahmood too!" Karim growled, spitting on the floor for good measure. He glanced down at the Sainsburys bag containing the final bomb. He had big plans for that, something that would impress Khan and get him deeper within his organisation. It would be the cherry on the cake, the *pasta resistance* or whatever the French called it. He intended to blow up a pigmobile right outside the farm.

That would show real balls.

"Alright, quieten down," Sinclair cried to his team, fanning their chatter with his arms.

The incident room fell silent as Raymond's team began to file inside silently, looking around wearily as they crossed the threshold into DPS territory.

Sinclair cleared his throat, not quite believing what he was saying. "Okay… Situation is this. Within the last ten minutes, two police vehicles have exploded in Cambridge Heath Road and Cleveland Way causing, as yet, an unknown number of casualties." He let the wave of gasps and expletives wash around the room before continuing. "I've been on the blower with the Yard, and they're assembling a Counter

Terrorist Command taskforce as we speak. Until they get here—"

"We're going to run the Golden Hour response..." one of his DPS detectives finished his sentence with a knowing sigh.

The Golden Hour was the period of initial response in any major criminal investigation or critical incident in which time was of the essence, where early intervention and action by police officers was needed to secure and preserve evidence that could otherwise be lost. It was one of the areas that often received the closest scrutiny during post-incident reviews, when people with the luxury of hindsight could nit-pick the actions and decisions their less fortunate colleagues had chosen under nerve-shredding pressure.

Sinclair nodded unenthusiastically. Yes, on top of everything else, that's exactly what they were going to do. "It's all hands on deck until a proper investigation is launched, hence why I asked our CID colleagues to join us."

"This is MIT's bag, guv, not ours," one of his detectives grumbled.

"What MIT, Geoff? Huh?" Sinclair countered, resting his hands on his hips. "They're not exactly crawling out of the woodwork, are they? They had to drag Raymond out of his office for Operation Milton Keynes. There are maimed or possibly dead coppers out there, so we all pull together. We can all argue over semantics later. Now, I'm going to hand you over to DI Fitzpatrick from CTC as this is his area of expertise."

Glad of the breather, Sinclair motioned to the huge slab of muscle standing next to him. Detective Inspector Paul Fitzpatrick, seconded to the DPS due to the explosion at the police station, nodded and took the floor, speaking with the deepest of Yorkshire drawls.

"As this is in its infancy, details are sketchy, but this were clearly a targeted attack against the police," the big man said with a sour expression. "As such, it's highly possible that there are more of these devices out there. Currently, we believe the attacks—if that's what they are—are limited to Whitechapel. Now, until such time as my gaffer and the cavalry arrive, Milton Keynes and the Mathews enquiry are on pause; I want this room used as an interim situations room."

He bounded over and pulled a clean whiteboard in front of the one concerning the Jerry Mathews' explosion and scribbled WHITECHAPEL EXPLOSIONS along the top. He divided the board into two vertically and headed each section A and B. Once done, he turned back and continued.

"Our immediate response is to ensure every single Whitechapel officer is made aware of the potential danger and to get down to the crime scene and collate all witnesses and start taking statements. The Bomb Squad are on route as we speak to conduct a thorough examination of all station vehicles, but until that's done, nobody even looks at a police car. Is that clear?"

As his steely eyes surveyed the nodding heads of the assembled detectives, Raymond and Jenny rushed into the incident room, nearly colliding with Sinclair, pulling himself into his coat and heading for the exit.

"What the bloody hell's going on?" the Welshman squawked. "I heard something on the main-set about—"

"Later!" Sinclair snapped, Raymond's higher rank an irrelevance. He grabbed Jenny by the arm. "You've got your coat on, come with me."

"Me? Where are we going, sir?"

"Khan!" Sinclair hissed.

CHAPTER EIGHT

The television mounted on the living room wall room played shaking smartphone footage of a burning police car. Sirens wailing like some ghostly lament for the fallen, horrified bystanders stood solemn and unmoving, obscured by the thick black smoke that twisted and curled from the wreckage.

Dyson stood rigid at the window; the dour, eternal greyness of Whitechapel reflected in his grim expression. His elevated vantage point allowed a sickening view of the two plumes of smoke that drifted into the grey skies until the wind smeared them away. Sobriety had hit like a hammer when he'd returned home after meeting Ratski, Mary's horrified expression directing him to the images on the TV as a flurry of messages began to chime on his phone.

"I should be out there," he croaked.

Silent and lithesome, Mary slid behind him. She peeled him away from the window and pulled him into a tight hug. He felt so fragile and worthless in her arms.

"Bloody hell!" Knapper cried as a tube train thundered through the abandoned station.

The building shook on its foundations as if the Devil himself had rolled over in his sleep, showering him and Mitchell with a fine dust that twinkled like tiny spots of starlight on their combined beams. He plugged a finger into one ear and pulled an exasperated face, desperate to hear his personal radio pressed against the other.

He thumbed the talk button and gave a little shake of his head as the roar of the train subsided. "Say again? Hotel Tango from DC Knapper..." He lowered the radio and stared over at Mitchell. 'Somebody said bomb, right?"

Someone had said bomb, several times in fact, just before the radio went silent and became unresponsive. After discovering the patch of blood, the two detectives had continued to investigate the subterranean station, backtracking on three distinct pairs of footprints they found in the heavy coating of dust that layered the floor. Knapper had posited that one pair appeared similar to the tread of the boots issued to police officers; Mitchell shrugging off the idea with his typical indifference. The tracks had continued along the eastbound platform and into the passageway where they now stood, wincing at the deafening racket the trains brought when they passed.

"Sounded like it," Mitchell replied, nonchalant to Knapper's concerns. He washed his flashlight over the narrow tunnel, marvelling at the kaleidoscopic patterns of dust caught in the beam. "We're underground. You remember what happened on 7/7?"

Knapper remembered well enough. He had been a probationer at the time, as flummoxed then as he was now as to why his radio had stopped working. The police radio system then had proved to be woefully deficient for operating below ground, severely hampering rescue efforts after the devastating terrorist attack on London. In fact, it had been labelled 'inadequate' two years before, during a training exercise to simulate a chemical attack on the Underground, but nothing was done to remedy the short fallings. Only after 7/7 were the police awarded the updated Motorola Airwave system, which was—

"Supposed to work underground." Knapper shook the radio, more out of frustration than any hope that his action would make it function again.

"*I don't knooow*," Mitchell sang, bored of the conversation. "If someone's blowing shit up, the system's probably gone mental or died or something. There's bugger all we can do stuck down here anyway."

"Where's your radio?"

"I didn't bring it," Mitchell scoffed at the question. "I gotta phone for talking to people."

Knapper huffed at his friend and immediate superior's lackadaisical approach to police work, giving him a disapproving shake of his head before turning off his radio. That was Mitchell: he was a good copper but a lazy one. If there was a job to do, he'd offer up someone else for the task before accepting it himself. But despite his professional shortcomings, Knapper and Mitchell were the best of friends. They had come up through the ranks together, from uniform to suit. Their families socialised and got plastered together, grabbing a week somewhere hot in the Mediterranean when their annual leave allocations allowed or could be juggled into alignment.

Another train tore past the station, the detectives grimacing until the sound faded away. When it did, a door creaked shut somewhere. Knapper jumped, Mitchell laughing and revelling in his discomfort.

"Chill your beans, Gazza. It's only the air pressure, or wind…something like that. You're getting panicky, mate."

"Anxiety comes with age," the black detective mused. "Every birthday you get to, you wonder if it'll be your last."

"Fucking hell, that's a bit deep, ain't it? You been reading Lou's women's magazines on the bog again? Well, don't worry, Granddad. I'll look after you."

Knapper chuckled at the slap Mitchell planted on his back as they trudged onwards. It took only a couple of steps for the grin to crack. "Thing is, Jimmy, you joke about being a granddad, but it turns out Abbie's pregnant."

"What the fuck! What is she, fifteen?"

"Sixteen. Just!"

"Well, at least he waited."

"Yeah. Needless to say, me and Lou are not best pleased."

"I bet, mate. Well, just make sure you don't go and do a Dyson on the little shit who tubbed her up."

"A Dyson?" Knapper smarted. "Is that what we're calling it now?"

Before Mitchell could reply, they rounded a corner in the tunnel to be confronted by a jagged tear in the wall. Blackness seeped through from the other side, together with the gentle sound of running water. The detectives swapped looks and combined the light from their torches into the hole, illuminating what was clearly a sewer tunnel. But there was something else…and it took a moment for the image to register with the two detectives.

On top of a pile of broken bricks, presented like a precious piece of jewellery upon a velvet pillow, sat a black leather wallet.

Laid out on his hospital bed, Khan was in a state of sensory overload. The butchery described within the pages of the Jack the Ripper book, coupled with the carnage displayed on the TV inches from his face, was making him harder than diamond. He slavered at the sights, his eyes glowing with a reflected orange flame from the shaking footage of the burning police car.

The footage froze, and the news report cut back to the studio, the criminal shrugging off the death and destruction and getting back into his book. Read from cover to cover, he was revisiting his favourite bits: the gruesome bits, described in great, gory detail. Currently, he was revelling in the catalogue of injuries suffered by the Ripper's last victim, Mary Jane Kelly.

It was delicious!

As Khan reached down to the swelling in his crotch and considered rubbing one out there and then, the door of his private hospital room crashed open and slammed against the wall. The girlie-looking DPS detective, Sinclair, stormed in, the sexy Jenny Brent acting as his shadow.

"Do come in," Khan said casually, turning the page of his book.

Sinclair was visibly stewing, his features strained and a deep red.

"You alright there, Mr Sinclair? You look like you're tryin' to crimp one off. Hello, by the way, Detective Sergeant Brent. Lookin' ravishin' as always. *Good enough to eat.*"

Jenny tutted with disgust while Sinclair pawed at the linoleum with his cheap shoes.

Khan sighed and placed his book carefully on the cabinet with an exaggerated wince of pain. "What can I do for you? I've already given you a victim statement for the vicious assault I suffered at the hands of your colleague. Have you charged him yet?"

"Investigations are ongoing, Mr Khan." Sinclair fired an irritated look at Jenny. "Been here all day, have we?"

"Of course I 'ave. Where else am I gonna go? I was

brutally assaulted. I'm a nervous wreck. I'm psychologically damaged!"

"You can say that again," Jenny muttered under her breath, Sinclair wagging an angry finger at the criminal.

"We will check," he warned.

"Be my guest." Khan eased a smile across his beaten features. "I've left this room once. Dressed up like a tart with them thrombo stockings they make you wear, to enjoy an over-priced coffee that tasted like…I don't even know what it tasted like, but it weren't coffee, I can tell you that much. What's this about?"

Neither of the detectives answered. He could tell Sinclair was sizing him up, looking for any glimmer of deceit. He was bathed in the stuff, positively swimming in wrongdoing, but it would be impossible to see with his head so swollen and swathed in bandages.

Cheers, Johnny boy, he thought as the DPS detective continued to shake his finger.

"We'll check!" Sinclair reiterated, turning on his heels, Jenny following close behind.

Khan would've puckered up and blown her a kiss if only he were able. Instead, as the door slammed shut, he picked up his book and found his place. "I guess they're gonna check then."

Snaaap!

Mitchell pulled on the second nitryl glove and grinned devilishly at Knapper. "The doctor will see you now," he whispered seductively.

His companion rolled his eyes. "Don't fuck about, Jimmy. Get on with it."

Reaching into the hole, Mitchell retrieved the wallet and

lifted it into the torch beam projected by Knapper. He opened it up to be greeted by a hefty wad of twenty-pound notes, the image of King William smiling majestically. There were a couple of credit cards, a white plastic card of the same dimensions, and two folded sheets of paper.

Mitchell pulled out the plastic card first. It was blank on one side apart from a magnetic strip, but when he turned it over, they were shocked to discover it was a security pass for—

"*The White House!*" Knapper choked. "This is a windup, right? What's a White House security pass doing in Whitechapel?"

Mitchell thought of some witty comeback that would utilise the word that linked 'chapel' and 'house' but failed miserably. Instead, something sparked deep within, his finger bouncing on the image of a grim-faced man at one end of the card. He stared at the photograph intently before speaking. "Isn't…isn't this the twat in the suit who came and saw Dyson the other week?"

"The FBI agent? Ackerman? Oh shit, yeah." Knapper nodded along. "But this says Ratski? Brad Ratski. What the hell?"

Curiosity stoked, Mitchell took one of the pieces of paper from the wallet and unfolded it, the fact he wasn't wearing gloves forgotten by the intrigue created. It was the top half of a front page of *The Washington Post*. Yellow with age, the low portion was torn off and burnt in places. They moved closer together and read the big, bold headline splashed across paper.

The first couple of words ignored, Mitchell summarised what remained. "'…in defence of…' In defence of what? Who?"

"It's burnt off, Jimmy."

"I can see it's burnt off, you bellend," Mitchell retorted,

his words lacking their usual joviality. "Fucking hell, look at the date!"

Knapper did. "Well, that can't be right."

Struck by a sense of urgency, Mitchell pulled out the second sheet and shook it open. It was nothing more than a crumpled piece of paper, slightly smaller than the dimensions of a sheet of A4, scrawled with several handwritten lists. Mitchell read, his mouth moving silently, the resident joker in him absconded.

"What the fuck is this?" he whispered.

Knapper's eyes fixed on the worrying title that topped the sheet, he jutted his chin at the words. "New York, Boston, LA… Paris, Berlin… What the…?"

"Yeah, London too." Mitchell pointed with his penlight.

"What does it mean?"

"Individually, it means bugger all. But when you put it together and look at them as a whole…" Mitchell moved the headline and the lists together and the frightening connection was made.

"It means we're fucked," Knapper's voice rattled. He fished for the right words, but all that came to mind were his family and how much he wanted to hug them right now. He suddenly felt very sick and had to lean forward on his legs for support. "Oh, fucking hell, mate. We…we need to get this to someone."

"Who?" Mitchell yelped, his anguished cry echoing around the station. "Who, Gary? Who the hell do we show this to?"

"I don't know who."

"It's got bugger all to do with our case."

"*Case?* Are you fucking serious? The case means nothing compared to…" Knapper snatched the handwritten sheet from Mitchell and shook it. "This is bigger than any fucking case!"

In the end, the detectives of Whitechapel CID and Sinclair's DPS team devoted only twenty-two minutes of their time to the double explosion's precious Golden Hour. Their budget ringfenced by a continued rise in religious fundamentalism and far-right terror groups, an army of Counter Terrorism Command detectives arrived in a convoy of unmarked vehicles to take charge of the investigation, Fitzpatrick bringing his colleagues up to speed and handing over control aboard an empty bus he had commandeered.

Saturated detectives, worn down by the carless trek back from the crime scenes, trudged along the corridor to their respective incident rooms as Raymond and Sinclair rested against opposite walls. It was an inappropriate moment to catch up, but Whitechapel never seemed to want to give them a break.

They had met over six years ago: Raymond, a DCI leading his own Murder Squad and Sinclair, an overworked DI in the badlands of Romford, Essex. It was the horrific rape and murder of a child that had brought them together. Upon their initial meeting, the Welshman had thought Sinclair too dainty and fragile-looking, lacking the physical presence needed to be an effective policeman. As it turned out, it would be his brain, rather than his brawn, that would find the vital piece of evidence—missed by his own team—that would elevate a minor person of interest to main suspect and onwards to convicted killer.

"What the hell is it with this place, sir?" Sinclair asked, glugging from a can of Diet Coke and looking like he'd aged ten years in as many days.

The Welshman answered with an empty laugh. "I asked the exact same thing. I've never seen anything like it. I've always considered this world to be a brutal and despicable place, but Whitechapel certainly seems to take the biscuit, doesn't it?"

"She's a cruel mistress, indeed," Sinclair replied, his words delivered without humour. "What was the body count in the end, did you hear?"

"Four confirmed," Raymond said, grim-faced. "Three Whitechapel officers and some poor bastard who happened to be in the wrong place at the wrong time. Twenty-six additional casualties, flying glass and shrapnel mostly. Your man, the one from CTC…Fitzpatrick?" He waited for Sinclair to confirm the detective's name before continuing. "He thinks it's a C4 compound triggered by a motion sensor, but it's early days yet."

"Jesus…"

"And what did this Khan character have to say for himself?" Raymond asked.

"He never left the hospital. He's still there. I got security to check the CCTV pronto. It was just like he said. He wanders down to the restaurant—where there were no cameras—and goes back to his room half hour later." He blew out a deep, despondent breath. "Looks like Frankie Khan's off the hook on this one."

"You're not pursuing it?"

"Gently. We're pursuing it gently, skating around the edges while trying not to piss off the human rights mob and the police haters amassing out there. But what do we have at the end of the day, sir? Realistically? Zero bloody evidence and a local businessman—a charitable pillar of the local community, no less—dying of a brain tumour with an alibi for everything we—"

"Boss!" Debbie skidded up in the doorway and nodded at Raymond. "Sorry to interrupt, but you've got a call. You're gonna wanna take this."

She vanished as quickly as she appeared, the Welshman

groaning at the intrusion and saying his goodbyes to Sinclair. He trudged back into the incident room to find Detective Inspector Tecoup holding the handset for one of the desk phones at arm's length as if it were infected.

Raymond snatched the receiver from him and spoke. "Hello? Who is—" He paused, his face clouding as he stared at Debbie and Tecoup in turn. "Speaker? Hang…hang on." He fumbled clumsily with the buttons of the phone and handset the receiver. "Okay, you're on speaker."

"And this is the head of police?" a male voice asked, oozing sinister intent.

"I'm the Senior Investigating Officer in the—"

"Is this the *head of the police*?" the caller repeated impatiently, the way he emphasised Raymond's inflated title causing the Welshman to turn slowly to the Efit of their suspect pinned to the top of one of the multiple whiteboards that edged the incident room. It was him. Their killer.

Their Jack the Ripper copycat.

"I'm Detective Chief Superintendent Raymond of Homicide and—"

"*Ahhh*… I saw you on the television. Your press conference was very…*entertaining*."

Raymond seethed at the dig and washed his tongue over his bottom lip. "Who is this?"

"Come on now. I'm sure they don't promote idiots to the head of police, Mr Head of Police. You know who this is." The cold, robotic inflexion of the voice began to attract detectives like moths to a lightbulb, slowly drawn from what they were doing to gather around their superior.

Jenny pulled out her phone and opened the voice memo app. With a confirming nod from Raymond, she hit record.

As if struck by a bolt of electricity, Detective Constable Mo Mohammad had an idea of his own. He tore his own phone from his pocket and swiped through the apps for one called FONEFINDA. He darted over to the desk phone and typed in the number displayed on its screen.

"*Isn't that illegal?*" Debbie mouthed, nodding at his phone as a Google map of London opened and a set of red crosshairs slowly zoomed in, heading east with the speed of seasonal change.

"So is chopping up women, Debs," Mohammad whispered in reply, placing the phone on the desk for all to see.

"How's your investigation coming along, Detective Chief Superintendent Raymond?" the caller asked with a cold nonchalance. "Only I wanted to ask before I do another one. Before I gut another worthless whore."

"We're making progress," Raymond answered, glancing down at Mohammad's phone and willing it to hurry the fuck up.

"I think you're lying. Did you read my letter?"

"I think most of the world has read your letter." The caller laughed proudly. "No one else has to die," Raymond said, fixated by the crosshairs notching in closer and closer until they settled above Whitechapel.

"The bastard's local," Henderson murmured, trying to giddy-up the phone by twirling a finger over and over.

"Of course they do!" the caller said with a sudden crazed giggle. "I'm Jack the Ripper. They're all whores, they all have to die. They're all *insignificunt!* And I am so enjoying my work."

"And what work is that exactly?" Raymond grimaced.

"Cleansing the world of filth, of course. Do you not look at these whores and sluts with their short skirts and exposed breasts, parading like meat in a market, and feel that they deserve to perish?"

Raymond caught Jenny with a knowing gaze. She responded with a supportive smile through pursed lips. He gulped and thought of Maggie, innocently stalling the conversation.

"I assume your silence indicates that you're trying to trace my call?" the voice asked.

"No, that's not what… Trisha Noble wasn't a whore."

The caller cackled wildly. "You *are* trying to trace my call, aren't you?"

"Don't believe what you see in the movies," the Welshman answered with a forced laugh.

The media portrayal of detectives tapping a few keys on a computer keyboard and homing in on a caller's location was nothing but the stuff of fiction. The reality was sadly very different. Unless the Met's Telephone Investigation Unit were already alerted to a potential incoming call and the expected number was already under surveillance, there was little chance of them assisting with a live call. Their work was also far from instant, especially now they were overworked and understaffed like Raymond's department. A request submitted to them could take days, if not weeks, to address, and with the use of expensive secure cellular networks becoming more prevalent, impenetrable to the TIU's probing, there was an ever-increasing chance of failure. The Welshman could've sent one of his detectives into the incident room next door, asking the CTC detective, Fitzpatrick, to call the TIU—they had a special hotline for immediate phone traces—but he doubted whether he had time.

Mohammad's app, while illegal—it had been central in a recent high-profile stalking case—was a gift from the gods. It would give him the caller's location to within feet…if he could just keep him talking long enough.

"We can only trace a call if it's from a landline, or our telephone people are—"

"I was too clever to use a landline," the voice interrupted with child-like pride.

"You were. You were very clever."

"I won't run—if you *are* tracing it." The caller sang his next sentence, causing Debbie to gasp at the insanity of his words. "*I'm Jack the Ripper, I'll wait right here. I cut them up, I have nothing to feeeear.* Or maybe I will. Run. It'd be such a shame to meet you before I've finished my work, Mr Head of Police."

Mohammad wheeled around and gave Raymond an emphatic thumbs up. Got him!

In silence, the detectives gathered up their coats and jackets and headed for the doors, Raymond transferring the call to a cordless phone and replacing the handset of the speakerphone. "Why...why are you doing it? Hello? Hello!"

There was a click, and the dial tone hummed at his ear. *Fuck!* Raymond tossed away the phone and snatched up his trench coat. He stared at Mohammad for confirmation.

"Railway arches in Pedley Street, guv."

Bursting out into the corridor as one mass of detectives, Raymond stabbed a pudgy finger at Debbie as they hurried along. "Get onto CAD and get me air support and a dog unit."

"Boss!" Debbie pulled her personal radio and initiated a call while Raymond barked at Jenny.

"Brent, go rustle us up some cars."

"Sir!" Jenny said, racing ahead with an impressive turn of speed, considering she was still limping from her numerous ordeals.

As she slammed through the double doors at the end of the corridor, Raymond picked up his pace, hissing under his breath with a determined growl. "I'm going to get you, *you bastard!*"

CHAPTER NINE

It had taken an eternity for Mitchell and Knapper to escape the derelict station. At least it had seemed an age, with adrenalin and fear driving their bid for freedom. Everything seemed to be against them, mocking them and increasing the tension that had followed their shocking find.

The stairs that had once taken customers down to the platforms were long gone, removed at some point after the station's closure—a fact Mr Happy had omitted to tell them. Only a narrow scaffold staircase to street level remained, hidden away in another room behind a door as desperate to prevent their access as they were to leave. The metal steps had clanged underfoot, creating a dreadful toll of doom as if taunting them on their discovery. The exit finally located, they struggled to open the door, pushing on the horizontal bar that the faded sign promised would lead to freedom. The hinges were rusted solid, and it took multiple attempts for the door to budge even an inch. Mitchell had vehemently chastised the Underground's lack of maintenance while throwing his weight into the door again and again. Knapper had said nothing, his throat as dry as the dust that covered them, clutching at the wallet, desperate to share its repackaged contents with Raymond or *anyone* who could validate their findings.

Finally, the door shifted enough for them to slip through into a small triangular courtyard strewn with rubbish; its reluctance to open caused by a thick application of illegal posters advertising everything from concerts to condoms. The rain had stopped—*the rain had stopped*—but neither of them noticed as they struggled to get their bearings. Emerging between the Ibis Hotel and the Muslim Aid Centre on the high street, the police station was across the road to the right. They discounted trying the radio again; it was quicker just to run back. It would only take a minute.

As was the usual procedure, Jenny had attempted to sign out the required pool cars from the civilian keyholder. Sat in her sliver of an office at the back of the car park, she told the detective in the nasal drone of a professional jobsworth how the allocation of vehicles was currently the responsibility of the Bomb Squad. Arriving from their base in Vauxhall, they were in the process of examining the vehicles in the car park, shunting them to one side once declared safe. When they were finished, they would move on to the line of cars out on Vallance Road; those unfortunate enough not to find a space in the undersized garage and currently under the watch of a lone Bomb Squad officer. Those vehicles *were not to be driven until checked*, the keyholder had stressed, glaring down her glasses at Jenny until she nodded her understanding. A Bomb Squad sergeant wearing a dark blue jumpsuit and a hefty ballistics vest assigned her two electric Vauxhall Centros and a battered Ford Focus that looked more 'stolen and recovered' than police car.

Jenny dished out the keys, and the detectives piled aboard. Raymond and Tecoup joined her in one of the Centros, the rest splitting themselves between the other two vehicles.

Her finger hovered over the start button. She turned cautiously to Raymond in the passenger seat, wearing a mask of anxiety as she motioned to a couple of Bomb Squad officers poking circular mirrors on poles under a couple of squad cars. "Let's hope they've checked this one properly."

"Just get on with it, Brent," Raymond ordered, clearly more trusting of the Bomb Squad's abilities than her.

Jenny flinched as she pressed down on the button. The car came alive without incident, the face she made holding while she gingerly massaged the accelerator pedal.

"Chop-chop," the Welshman groaned.

After nearly being blown up by a landmine and eaten by dogs, it was only natural for her to fear the worse, but this wasn't her time to die. The car picked up speed, accelerating up the ramp out onto Vallance Road without incident. She focused on the driver's mirror as she straightened out of her left turn, holding her breath until she saw her colleagues exiting safely.

"Yes, sir," Jenny answered on the rush of air blasted from her lungs.

She relaxed in her seat and stamped down harder on the accelerator, too preoccupied with being alive to notice Mitchell and Knapper waving madly at her from the pavement.

"Fuck sake!" Mitchell panted, staggering to a stop outside the police station to lean on his knees. "Where they off to in such a hurry?"

Knapper watched the three cars disappear along Vallance Road. "I'll…I'll go get us a car," he puffed, the mysterious black wallet still wrapped within his big hand.

Mitchell shook his head. "No need." Face red and tortured by the information contained within the wallet and the brutal sprint they had just completed, he straightened up and tugged a set of car keys from the pocket of his trousers. "I forgot to sign this in." He waggled the bunch and motioned over to the Ford Serreo parked up on the opposite side of the road. "Come on."

The two detectives darted across the street—Knapper just avoiding being clouted by a white van that flew around the corner. The black detective gave the driver the finger as Mitchell unlocked the car with the remote and wrenched open the door, diving in behind the wheel. He pulled the MPD inscribed logbook off the dashboard, left there as a preventative measure to alert traffic wardens that it was a police vehicle, and tossed it on the back seat. Mitchell turned the key and gunned the engine and then…just sat there, staring straight ahead.

"What the fuck do we say?" he asked breathlessly, staring at his friend for guidance. Knapper could barely manage a shrug in reply. "We're gonna look a right pair of cunts if this is some other cunt's idea of a joke."

While alarming, the information contained within the wallet bore no relation to their hunt for the Ripper copycat. Its discovery, however, did relate to the investigation itself, putting a supposed FBI agent and their suspect in potential close proximity. That had to count for something. Mitchell's brain was in overdrive at the possible implications. Was this Ackerman/Ratski character conspiring with their suspect in some way, and if so, what was Dyson's involvement? And how did it all tie in with the chilling information they had found?

Whether Raymond would know what to do with the material they now possessed remained to be seen, but they had to tell him. It was evidence—discovered during their investigation. Plus, they wanted someone else to share the burden of their find.

Mitchell drummed his fingers on the wheel until his mind was made up. "Right, let's do it," he announced to Knapper, shifting the gearstick into first and flooring the car.

The heatwave that washed over them was instant.

It felt cold, rather than hot, like diving into a frozen sea. But that was just the unfathomable shock at what was happening. Then there were the other sensations: of flying, and of being upside down. He snapped his head to Knapper to see his body burning—*inexplicably burning*—the wallet clenched in his hand on fire. And then, he was torn to pieces, violently disassembled, his blood hissing as it was vaporised. Mitchell started to scream, but there was no sound. He looked down and realised that he was on fire too and that half of his body was gone, one glistening pink lung protruding from the massive open wound in his chest, shuddering and struggling to function.

How…lung…looking…at…? he tried to think, his mind as devastated as his body. He glanced back as the wallet turned white-hot, briefly considering how no one would ever get to learn of their discovery before it was scoured from his vision by the wave of fire that cooked his eyeballs right there inside his head. They popped, and the world went black, the sound of his sizzling vitreous jelly the last thing he ever heard. Almost. That accolade was reserved for the crashing sound the car made as it thundered back down to earth, the stench of petrol invading his nostrils. After that, there was nothing but the smothering embrace of death.

Twice the size of the Oval Office, the main living room of Arizona One was an irritating juxtaposition of old versus new. The president had smarted upon his initial entry, joking how it appeared a visual representation of his country's previous foreign policy endeavours: seizing something established and recognised and turning it to crap. Lurid images that were considered modern art hung at wood-panelled walls gnarled with age while several leather couches in colours he thought it impossible to dye cowhide were positioned with random abandonment on a traditional Persian rug; sufficient in size to roll up the interior designer's body and anyone involved in the decoration of the room. There was a grandfather clock against one wall, wrapped in gold leaf and purposefully distressed, its ornate face replaced by the glowing red numbers of a digital clock.

Oblivious now to the décor and its ridiculous cost, Garrett stood at a set of leaded French doors, staring out into the rain that still fell in Wimbledon. What his countrymen would refer to as a yard and the British liked to call a garden, he considered neither. More akin to the grounds of a stately home, the vast green expanse beyond the doors reminded him of a golf course: perfectly manicured with those fastidiously rolled stripes he'd never had the time or patience to create himself. Giant trees and worn statues of women in robes were dotted here and there, and in the very distance, where the weather's inclemency began to blur his view, stood an ornate pagoda wrapped in vines and creepers. Two Secret Service agents patrolled beneath its roof, their machine pistols held ready. As rigid as the decorative figurines, another duo of agents was positioned either side of the doors, windcheaters glossy from the downpour.

Under normal circumstances, Garrett would insist that their shifts were reduced and rotated to allow them to get dry. He had once taken a coffee out to an agent on the West

Wing lawn, frozen and drenched by a sudden deluge the DC skies had tipped down on him. But today, the agents' plight was irrelevant. There were far more pressing matters at stake.

One of the agents turned on spying Garrett in his peripheral. "Mr President, step away please, sir," he instructed with a forceful tone. Unlike the windows of the White House, these were just glass; the only thing they offered protection from was the weather's ingress.

The president scrubbed at the reflected frustration on his face. The phone in his hand trembled against his ear as he nodded and complied with the agent's instruction.

"And he said no?" he mumbled into the phone, listening while Ratski explained the outcome of his meeting with Dyson and cutting him off when he felt it necessary. "I'll think of something." His face soured as he caught sight of the humongous flatscreen television bolted above the fireplace. "I said I'll think of something, Brad. I'm well aware of the gravity of the situation, I'm President of the United States!"

On the TV, Sky News relayed images of a small convoy of rain-streaked vehicles sweeping up to the unmistakable Georgian façade of 10 Downing Street.

"I'm…I'm sorry…Brad," the president apologised, his voice struggling through an increasing bout of breathlessness. "I can't even…even begin to comprehend what…what you went through."

Garrett shuffled away to one of the leather sofas where his oxygen tank stood. He lowered himself down and plucked up the mask, squeezing his heavy eyelids shut to ease the pain that wracked his fragile body.

"Rest assured…I will do…I will do whatever is necessary to stop…stop this. You…you have my word."

His eyes reopened, the discomfort unabated, and settled on the TV.

Under a barrage of camera flashes that bloomed against

the slick vehicles, a tall, impeccably suited black man stepped out of the gleaming graphite grey Jaguar sandwiched between two Range Rovers. The prime minister gave a quick wave at the assembled reporters and hurried through the downpour, disappearing within the world-famous door of Number 10.

"David..." Garrett thought aloud with the thinnest of smiles.

There was a lift in Arizona One. It seemed a wasteful and unnecessary extravagance for what was essentially a three-storey house, but the president was glad it was there. When he'd arrived, sagging and incoherent in the wheelchair after evacuating The Dorchester Hotel, it had saved him the humiliation of being manhandled upstairs by his security detail.

Garrett exited the lift onto the first floor and hobbled along a panelled hallway adorned with more traditional oil paintings of landscapes and portraits of unknown noble faces until he reached the required door. He tightened his posture, put on his healthiest smile, and pushed hard. Made of heavy oak, the door fought back, but he didn't let the exertion it took break his grin.

Jakobi sat behind the desk in what was a large, tastefully decorated office, pouring over a scattering of complex medical documents. The doctor looked up and pulled off his reading glasses, offering a warm grin to his friend.

"Malcolm," the president began with a cheery wave. "I want you to give me a shot of Evastin and...and grab your coat. We're going out."

"Excuse me, sir?" Jakobi replied, his brow knotting with confusion. "What do you mean?"

Garrett strode across the room and slipped into the seat opposite: the patient before his physician. "I need...I need to get out of this place…and I need to see…to see someone. Therefore, you and I—we'll take a couple of guys with us—we are going—"

"A couple of guys! Mr President… *Bob.*" Jakobi held up his hands to block the idea. "Have you lost your mind? I can't allow that. One: you're the President of the United States and therefore cannot just decide to go on a…a goddamn *day trip* in a foreign city. Two: you're not well enough to *go out.* Three: you're not supposed to be in the UK. Remember? Oh, and four: *you're President of the United States!* No, Bob. I forbid it."

"You forbid it?" Garrett cocked his head and chuckled.

"Well…I certainly will not administer Evastin like it's candy. Admittedly, it worked well before, but I am not prepared to give an unregulated drug to the world's most powerful man unless I absolutely have to."

"Don't make me pull rank, Malcolm."

Jakobi smarted like he'd just stepped in something. "Jesus Christ, Bob! Callahan's going shit out a lung over this."

"Let him. I'm POTUS, not Section Chief Karl frickin' Callahan."

"You know," the doctor sighed, "as one of your closest friends I have to tell you, you can be a complete asshole sometimes."

"And that's…that's why you love me."

"Love is a strong word, Robert." Jakobi rolled his eyes at Garrett's adamant gaze, his sigh returning until it faded to nothing. The discussion was over.

A line of squalid railway arches stood on one side of Pedley Street, adorned with multiple layers of spray-painted gang tags, abandoned cars, and dumped detritus that included a mattress stained in its centre with something unpleasant looking. Residents of the long block of beige brick apartments opposite hung from their balconies and windows, filming the unfolding action with their phones. Police dogs barked silently, their incessant yapping lost to the sound of the police helicopter, thumping overhead.

Jenny marched over to Raymond, waiting at the Vauxhall Centro they arrived in. She threw her thumb back at the grubby vagrant being led out of one of the vaulted units by Mohammad and Detective Constable Julius Atangba, an ex-car repair business, so the faded sign on the smashed roller shutter claimed.

She winced at the deafening clatter of rotor blades and had to shout at Raymond to make herself heard. “He said, when he’s convicted for whatever we’re going to charge him with, they’ll put him away in a nice, warm prison. He reckons a spell inside will help sort his pneumonia out.”

Hoax calls, as this had turned out to be, were rare but nothing new. They were something that had to be expected, their claims painstakingly investigated, diverting precious time from the core enquiry. During the reign of the Yorkshire Ripper, West Yorkshire Police received a cassette tape purportedly sent by the killer himself. Taunting the assistant chief constable for his force’s inability to capture him, the arrival of the tape threw the case into disarray, wasting months of investigatory hours. It was only in 2006, twenty-seven years after the event, that ‘Wearside Jack’ as he had become known, was caught and sentenced to eight years in prison.

“Bloody timewasters!” Raymond began his assault, glaring at the grinning down and out as he shuffled past, his hands shackled behind his back. But before he could unleash a barrage of furious expletives at the man and launch into a heated tirade about him wasting valuable police resources,

Debbie rushed over from the Ford Focus where she'd returned to answer an urgent call that came over the radio.

"Boss?" she hollered above the racket, her face grim and frightful.

"What is it, Shaw?"

"There's been another explosion."

The black London taxi pulled through the tall wooden gates of Arizona One and crunched over the gravel driveway to a stop. Instantly, it was swamped by Secret Service agents, pawing over every inch of the vehicle to ensure it was roadworthy and provided at least some degree of safety. Compared to the presidential Cadillac, it offered close to zero protection: a worrying fact reflected in the cold, stern faces of the agents. The driver, the obligatory Cockney cabbie complete with cloth cap, was questioned until the agents were happy—or as happy as they could be given the ludicrousness of the situation—one confirming their findings into the handheld radio he carried.

No sooner than his transmission ended, the double doors of the house flew open, and a swarm of agents exited with the fluidity of running water, Garrett concealed at their heart. The back door of the cab was opened, and the wall of agents parted to allow the president to board. Jakobi climbed in next, and the duo was joined by three blocks of Secret Service muscle Garrett had specially selected. One squeezed onto the bench with the president and his doctor; the other two sitting on the fold-down seats opposite.

Had Garrett gone mad, Jakobi wondered. The doctor watched him closely as he sat peering ahead, his tired eyes aglow with anticipation below the brim of the Chicago Red Sox cap that offered some limited level of privacy. He was sick and dying, but the leader of the free world certainly didn't appear absent of his faculties.

"For the record," Jakobi said discreetly out of the corner of his mouth, "this is the craziest fucking stunt you've ever pulled, you old fool."

"Malcolm, sometimes the severity of a situation demands action that would otherwise be considered...considered outlandish," the president replied with equal prudence. "But I shall take your comment as...as a compliment."

A wily old fox, Garrett had ordered the agents not to take the Suburban shipped over from the US as part of his motorcade. It would be tracked if his ruse was discovered, their location pinpointed long before their destination was ever reached. The same went for the hired Range Rovers lined up on the drive. Likewise, he had requested that all present within the cab leave their cell phones within Arizona One.

Everyone settled, the cabbie flickered his gaze in the mirror. "Where to, gents?" he asked in gruff Cockney, his eyes holding on Garrett with a struggling spark of recognition.

"Horse Guards Parade," one of the agents on the fold-down seats boomed in a voice deeper than the Marianas Trench. A huge African American, he sat scrunched up, his neck bent awkwardly to keep his head off the roof lining.

The cab took off with a whine of electricity, pulling through the gates and out onto the road beyond. Treelined, multimillion-pound homes flowing past the windows, the cabbie continued to volley secretive looks to the man sat next to Jakobi, trying to peer beneath his baseball cap.

"Oi, mate," he cried. "What was all that palaver about then? You look familiar. You on the telly or somethin'?"

The president laughed off a cough. "I get...I get that a lot. I must have one of those faces, I suppose."

"Obviously he's not one for current affairs," Jakobi

whispered.

Garrett made a shushing sound and leaned forwards a little. "Say, do you…do you have a cell I might borrow?"

"A cell? Talk bleedin' English, mate."

"My apologies. A mobile phone? I left in a hurry and kind of forgot mine."

Jakobi shifted on the seat uncomfortably at the lie and volleyed a nervous gaze between the stone-faced agents ahead.

"Right you are." The cabbie poked a smartphone through the slot in the Perspex screen that separated him from his passengers, the big agent taking it and handing it to Garrett.

"Appreciate it." The president pulled a sliver of paper from his pocket and keyed in the number Jakobi had seen him jot down from his phone before leaving. As the call was answered, he dropped his voice a couple of octaves.

"Hi, it's Robert." Garrett paused and made an uncomfortable smile. "It's a long story—which I will explain fully when I see you. Yes, I'm in London. Again, that's right. I'm on my way now. No bells and whistles please, this is strictly off the radar. We'll be coming in through the backyard, so if you could clear a path from any prying eyes, I'd be grateful."

Another pause followed, Jakobi just about able to hear the shocked reply on the other end of the line.

"I'll see you soon," Garrett concluded, ending the call and handing the phone back to the agent, who promptly deleted the number he'd dialled.

Continuing to spend more time studying his mysterious passenger in his mirror than he did watching the road, the cabbie reached out for his phone. The agent returned it, keeping a tight grip on it while bellowed a warning at the cabbie's curiosity, his threatening granite face inches from the Perspex.

"Eyes front!"

CHAPTER TEN

For a man with a reputation of being a ferocious political beast, Prime Minister David Vaughn was deathly silent, a rarely seen vulnerability battling the usually dogged determination in his gaze. A youthful-looking fifty-four, he'd felt his years double as Garrett recounted his story. His jaw was tighter than it had ever felt in the House under the mocking scrutiny and jeers of the opposition, and if the old man had reached out and sucker-punched him in the face, it would've come as less of a surprise than the tale Garrett had relayed over the last five minutes.

Time travel was real.

Science fiction had become science fact. Developed and utilised by the US Government to save their dying leader and accidently releasing the world's most notorious serial killer in the process.

Vaughn had never been one to suffer fools or willingly swallow the bullshit that was rife in the political world. Life had never allowed him such a luxury. As the United Kingdom's first black leader, his rise to the political summit had been far from smooth or meteoric. 'Council estate trash,' he had been called when first running for local election. With an absent, unknown father and chain-smoking bus driver for a mother, Vaughn was never destined to be anything other than an inner London crime statistic. But he had fought hard to prevent the inevitable—fought like a bastard as he'd put it once—to correct the course of his predicted path. Vaughn had risen from the backbenches of Jeremy Corbyn's opposition to offer hope in the hardest of times. Brexit, the devastation left by Covid-19 and the dog flu pandemic of 2026, a stratospheric unemployment rate—the UK had been hammered hard and, like Garrett had in the US, Vaughn offered light at the end of a long and desperate tunnel, scraping a narrow win during the publicly demanded elections of 2028. His election victory brought with it a string of hideous pseudonyms, such as 'Monkey King,' spouted by far-right loons from behind the relative anonymity of their keyboards. Vaughn had already survived one assassination attempt in his two years as leader when a would-be killer attacked him during a hospital visit to Bradford and plunged a kitchen knife into his gut. But his resolve had been stronger than the attacker's blade, and Vaughn had returned to office in less than two weeks.

He watched Garrett from one of the two floral sofas that faced each other. Around and around he went, pacing the faded Indian rug that stretched across the parquet flooring of the Terracotta Room. The sound his loafers made as they scuffed on the weave created an irritating discord with the carriage clock on the carved mantlepiece and the rain that drummed against the windows.

The president was no fool, Vaughn considered. Nor was he the habitual liar that many of his predecessors had been exposed to be. Garratt had despised the woeful state of US politics, he had confided in Vaughn during their initial meeting at a United Nations summit on climate change; an apt venue for two men so desperate to bring about their own change in the political environment. A close bond formed between the two leaders: two men with likewise goals. Yet there he was, the most powerful man in the world, sneaking into Downing Street, frail and near to the end of his life, while a police manhunt sought to find the only man who could save it.

"I had to get out of there," the president said as he completed another lap, his face tortured by the relived events. "It was like I was being…*suffocated*."

The prime minister said nothing. Truth be told, Vaughn was struggling to find something suitable to say that would be considered statesmanlike.

"Say something, David, for heaven's sake." Garrett returned to the sofas and slipped down opposite his counterpart.

Vaughn cleared his throat but failed to deliver a diplomatic reply. "Robert, you have entered this house like some grubby philanderer desperate for an afternoon beneath the sheets with his mistress, only to tell me that your great nation has uncovered the secret of time itself and that you have unleashed a serial killer onto my streets—and not just any serial killer, I might add. *Jack the Ripper*. Quite frankly, I am *fucking furious* that you have acted in this manner without my authority or inclusion. And I would wager the population of this country would feel similarly displeased." Despite the heated content, he spoke the words very well for a kid from Vauxhall.

"I can only apologise."

"Apologies are empty and meaningless when delivered post-event, Robert. We are both fully aware of that. What kind of fool was I to believe that our countries were more than just allies, more than the shoulder-to-shoulder *buddies* that one of your predecessors once described us as. What a fool I was to think you different to those you replaced?"

He paused to drink from a large mug labelled I'M THE BOSS HERE, making damn sure that Garrett saw the message.

"Yet, not content with your nation's perceived John Wayne approach to international diplomacy, here you are adapting it, for what I believed until your arrival, was the stuff of fantasy." He let Garrett squirm for a moment, the president's weary eyes lingering on the message on his mug. "What exactly is it you want from me, Robert?"

"We need Dyson back, David. He's leaving the country tomorrow for Japan. I can't have that happen."

Vaughn shrugged. "But this detective has brought nothing to the table other than shame and dishonour to the Metropolitan Police Department."

"But Dyson knows the Ripper. He was there, in 1888. I believe he's our best shot at getting him back."

Vaughn waved away his defence with a lazy swipe of the hand. "There are undoubtedly more qualified and experienced detectives in London. Detectives who do not assault unrelated suspects during interview. I will speak with Scotland Yard."

"But I feel…a measure of…of responsibility, David," Garrett replied with a pained expression. "He was under pressure."

"He's a policeman. Pressure comes with the territory."

"But…but I don't believe…he would've attacked this… this guy had it not been for me and this foolish…this foolish attempt to extend my mortality. But I need him back."

Vaughn placed his mug gently on the coffee table between them and smiled. He stood and pulled the creases out of his suit trousers, throwing a hand down for the president to take. "Walk with me a moment, Robert."

. . .

The warming yellow walls of the grand staircase that climbed through the centre of Number 10 were adorned with portraits of the fifty-seven men and women who had served as Prime Minister of the United Kingdom. It was tradition to lavish the walls with engraved or photographed renditions of previous incumbents once they left office. They were the ghosts of Downing Street. Pompous looking ex-public schoolboys and aristocrats mostly, born of a life of wealth and privilege Vaughn found impossible to comprehend.

The prime minister led the way, the president trailing a few steps behind, wheezing like the heaviest of smokers. Once past several black and white promotional shots of himself and his current cabinet, Vaughn stopped on the first step of the staircase and pointed at the initial image.

"May I introduce Sir Robert Walpole," he began, sweeping his hand over to the monochrome lithograph of a stout fellow splendidly regaled in powdered wig and gowns. "The country's first-ever Prime Minister, serving from 1721 to 1742. He ended his twenty-one-year tenure with a six-month spell in the Tower of London for taking an illegal payment."

Before the president could question the reason for the impromptu tour, Vaughn raced up a couple of steps and pointed at—

"The Earl of Bute, 1762 to 1763. He had an affair with the then Prince of Wales' widow." Vaughn swung his arm over to the very next image. "George Grenville, 1763 to 1765. One of the very few prime ministers to be sacked by the monarchy because of his complete incompetency. The gentleman next to him is the Duke of Grafton. Augustus FitzRoy to his friends. His government was scandalised by the string of mistresses he openly kept."

The prime minister bounded up several more steps. The next likeness he pointed at was one that Garrett recognised. "William Gladstone?"

Vaughn awarded him a congratulatory click of his fingers. "Ten points, Robert. Prime minister *four times.* Before we introduced the two-term rule, of course. Famed for bringing prostitutes into this very house." He took another step and gestured to an overweight man with an impressively large beard. "Robert Arthur Talbot Gascoyne-Cecil, 3rd Marquess of Salisbury. This mouthful of British aristocracy perpetrated a lie against the people that remains in place to this day."

The president gave him a questioning look, but Vaughn ignored it and tapped on the glass of the next portrait.

"Archibald Primrose, the Earl of Rosebury. 1894 to 1895. He was horsewhipped by the Marquis of Queensbury for having an affair with his son."

Garrett raised his hands in surrender, the reason for the show blatantly obvious. "David, David, I understand. I…I get. They were all involved in scandal. I get it."

"Oh, but it does not end there, my friend. From Walpole to Johnson and beyond, this position has been abused and manipulated by those who have held it. I will not tolerate such actions—I *do not* tolerate such actions. You see, this is not just a history in pictures of former occupants of this house and leaders of the country, it's a rogue's gallery of deceit and dereliction, and I will not see myself added to it for any reason other than the integrity that I hopefully bring to the role." Vaughn paused and let that sink in for a moment. "I am sorry that you are ill, I truly am, Robert, but no man is eternal. The attack on this criminal, this…this *Frankie Khan* has attracted such a following that there is simply nothing within the law that I can do to save this Dyson fellow. Contrary to what you may believe, I do not possess a magic wand that I can wave to make this unpleasantness disappear."

"Then do something above the law."

Vaughn dismissed the notion with a smile and a gentle shake of his head. "You know, Robert, when I was ten years old, I broke this ornament of my mothers. Hideous little trinket it was. A cheap figurine of a girl carrying a pail of water. It was the only thing her mother had ever given her, and she cherished it dearly. I sometimes think she cared more for it than she did either myself or my brother. Anyway, being a rambunctious little bugger with more energy than sense and some serious aspersions to play for Chelsea, I scored a direct hit with this tattered old football I would play with and shattered it into pieces."

The prime minister took a moment, the next part hard to tell.

"I blamed my brother. Younger and smaller and more innocent than I. She beat him like a drum as a result. In a drunken fury, with a belt. He was sobbing and begging her to stop, and in the end, he admitted breaking the damn thing just to make her stop. But she didn't. She wouldn't. She just kept on swinging while I just stood there watching. Now, luckily for Joshua, my mother was so drunk that she completely missed with one strike, and he was able to make good his escape. Unluckily for Joshua, he ran straight out the front door into the path of a speeding car. He died on the spot…innocent and afraid. I never lied again after that."

"I'm sorry, David," Garrett said softly. "That must have been terrible."

Vaughn nodded to confirm that it was. "You see, Robert, every action creates a reaction. A consequence. So, no, I won't operate outside of the law, and therefore I respectfully decline your suggestion to do otherwise. I'm afraid John Dyson must face his own consequences for his actions."

Garrett tugged on his bottom lip and contemplated his next move. The last thing he wanted to do was divulge his most closely guarded secret, but his options were non-existent. He looked up at Vaughn, elevated several steps above him, the most powerful man in the world below what many pundits considered his poodle, and said with the seriousness his declaration deserved: "There's something else you need to know."

There was a tense and sorrowful silence between Dyson and Mary as they packed the two open suitcases laid out on the bed. Music drifted in from the living room, bringing with it the pleasant aroma of a meal cooking, but neither managed to lighten the mood.

Usually so bright and airy, the bedroom felt encroaching and inhospitable, tainted by the harrowing desperation that seemed to seep through the walls. Dyson couldn't wait to escape it—to escape Whitechapel itself—if only for the limited time their holiday would allow. Of course, that had been before the avalanche of messages arrived, informing him of Michell and Knapper's deaths. Now, to run from the carnage just felt plain wrong; seeking shelter in another country while there was so much suffering back home. The ever-present guilt and remorse had continued to feast, its insatiable hunger increasing to sicken him to the pit of his stomach and destroy any desire he had to speak.

Mary finished folding a pile of clothes and placed and them inside one of the cases. She offered him a sympathetic smile and went to him, pulling him into her arms. "Come to me," she soothed, rocking him as one would a distraught child. "This is not your fault."

"Of course it is," Dyson blew with an arctic coldness that

caused Mary to tighten her grip. "Trisha Noble is my fault. George Harford is my fault. Bernstein and Simmons, my fault. This is all my fault, Mary. I thought of nothing but myself and my own self-interest. To be the man who got Jack the Ripper—to solve the unsolvable. And look where it's got me. Look at what's happened, Mary."

She withdrew to place an outstretched finger over his lips. "No! You can't think like that. I won't allow it. Ratski caused this. You warned him, John. But he didn't listen. *He didn't listen.* You told him not to use—"

The sudden buzzing of the doorbell tore them apart. Dyson listened as the electronic warbling cried over and over, the hurried intensity of the sound causing him to pull himself away from Mary, their intertwined fingers the last to break.

"I'll go," he muttered lifelessly, trudging from the bedroom and heading along the hallway towards the racket. He threw open the door to find Jenny standing there, her eyes red and streaked with tears. Her face collapsing, torn apart by grief, she stumbled forwards straight into his arms and began to sob. Two people united by a shared anguish, there was no need for words, Dyson holding her as tightly as Mary had him.

"Who was—?" Mary stumbled to a stop, watching the ex-lovers with an anxious curiosity. Dyson turned and looked back at her with the weakest of smiles.

Mary and Jenny sat at opposite ends of Dyson's dining table, the air chilled by that moment any relationship fears: the meeting of current and ex-lover. Uncomfortable smiles were exchanged while each toyed with their fingers, Mary constantly turning a cheap ring she still wore from 1888 while Jenny picked at the table's wooden grain. Dyson eased the tension with two large glasses of white wine, returning to the kitchen to grab another for himself.

"I'd say cheers if there was anything to celebrate," he said, sinking into the chair between them. Nevertheless, he raised his glass in a half-hearted salutation. "To Jim and Gary."

"Jim and Gary," Jenny echoed, offering a likewise tip of her glass.

They drank in silence, the wine a welcoming relief from the heartache. It was Jenny who eventually spoke first. She snorted away her upset and took a deep breath to look across the table at Mary, the words she said aimed at Dyson. "Are you going to introduce us, John?"

"Sorry. This is…" Dyson paused, looking between the two women. *No more lies*, he told himself, before telling Jenny, "This is *Mary Jane Kelly*."

Jenny looked at him oddly, picking up on the deliberate way he'd spoken her name. "You say that like I should know…" She turned to Mary and apologised. "Oh, I'm sorry. Hi, Mary. I'm Jenny, Jenny Brent. I'm a DS at the station. I work with this idiot."

Mary smiled at Jenny's description. A clumsy handshake was swapped between the two; Mary clearly unaccustomed to women shaking hands as only men had done in her time. "Hello, Jenny. It's a pleasure to meet you."

"Same." The room warming a couple of degrees, Jenny turned back to Dyson with a quizzical look. "You said that like I should know Mary?"

He swallowed hard and sank half his glass in one for what he was about to say. "That's right. You should."

Chugging on a cigarette, Karim waited on the corner of the street as instructed by Khan. The rain had stopped hours ago, leaving only a dull sheen on the pavement, but it was colder than a fridge in his flimsy wet tracksuit now the daylight had gone. He took another shaky draw of his fag and looked around with envious eyes.

There were swanky new apartment blocks all around: big steel and glass monstrosities and high-rise penthouses that reached high into the sky as though frantic to escape Whitechapel. He could easily see himself living in any one of them. Khan would be well-chuffed with his work, the kid felt confident and would surely offer him a full-time position within his empire now. The future was looking good for Karim.

It took balls to kill a man; he had killed five. Five pigs, just like the ones who had murdered his brother. The last bomb had gone under an unmarked car with some official-looking MPD paperwork on the dashboard. There was a copper standing guard, probably due to the other bombs, the jacket he wore emblazoned with the words EXPLOSIVES OFFICER. The idiot had wandered off, fiddling with his phone, Karim hitting the deck and slapping the bomb underneath the chosen target. Still in the carrier bag, he'd found the switch and armed the bomb, clambering back up to brush himself off and continue his swagger, leaving the bag dangling like a piece of rubbish blown there by the wind. He had scored a couple of detectives with that one, so the news had said.

As a result of his work, Whitechapel was in fearful silence tonight. As he savoured the thought of that, and let the smoky warmth of his cigarette wash over him, a big black Mercedes pulled up to the kerb. The passenger window glided down.

"Get in," Khan growled from inside, his bloated face warped into something unsettling by the glow of the car's digital dashboard.

Karim flicked his dogend away and climbed in, sinking into a snowdrift of plush leather. Khan grinned at him and ruffled his hair like his grandmother had done when he was little.

"Right outside of the farm!" the criminal congratulated. "You've got some fuckin' balls, I'll give you that."

The response exactly what Karim was hoping for, he beamed at the praise. He had never really received much in the way of adulation from his parents. His dad had been a professional drunk and his mother…well, the less said about her, the better.

"Yeah, you did well, son. Five burnin' piggies. Not bad for your first day, was it?"

The kid fluttered under the adulation and felt uplifted enough to engage in small talk. "Did they let you go?" he asked, nodding in the direction of the hospital.

"Nah, I discharged meself," Khan said, accelerating away. "I don't need no quacks to tell me I'm a sick man." He laughed aloud at his joke and turned to eye him up as though considering him for another job.

"I'll do it!" Karim blurted out.

"You dunno what it is yet."

"I don't care, man. You can count on me, innit."

"Good boy, Aziz," Khan said with a sickly grin. "Good boy."

Two bottles of Sainsbury's *Pinot Grigio* later, Jenny stared into the dregs of her glass for a long while as if she would find some clarity within its shallow remains.

Time travel is actually possible, she told herself with a derisory snort, wondering how many people had ever had to process that particular thought. Dyson would have, no doubt. Gobsmacked and probably hyperventilating when recruited for his top-secret mission. And President Garrett, upon being told of the outlandish procedure that would save his life. Jack the Ripper even, on arriving in the skewed version of the Whitechapel he remembered.

Jenny had never given much thought to the fanciful notion of travelling through time. On the rare occasions when the subject was raised, usually amongst friends with alcohol in attendance, she had stated that she thought it would be possible one day, but never in her lifetime, and not for hundreds or thousands of years. Technologically, anything was possible, she believed. Mankind had taken some giant steps over the past few years. There was now a permanent mining colony living and working on the moon, courtesy of NASA and a conglomerate of private corporations, stripping it of its natural resources as man had done with the Earth. Closer to home, scientists were successfully experimenting with subatomic teleportation. Jenny had read about it, thumbing through a copy of *New Scientist* while waiting for a recent dental check-up. Oblivious to what much of the endless technobabble had meant, it appeared that the stuff of *Star Trek* was fast becoming a reality, with whole atoms being beamed from one lab to another at a secret research facility somewhere in Europe. On a more mundane front—in comparison to space mining and teleportation—Boeing's new supersonic 800 airliner was capable of carrying 800 passengers (hence the name) from Heathrow to Sydney in a little over nine hours, all while producing zero carbon emissions. And with the Bristol to New York maglev rail tunnel due for completion within the next thirty years, hurtling passengers under the Atlantic Ocean at 2,300 miles per hour, it seemed that the ambitions of mankind were both achievable and limitless. So, if London to New York was possible in thirty minutes, then why not London of the now to London of the distant past?

But for Jenny, her acceptance of the technological possibilities of time travel created a philosophical problem, a logical conundrum that she freely admitted she had insufficient brainpower to answer. If time travel was possible, where were they all? Where were all the filthy rich tourists from the future, coming back through the aeons to gawp and witness significant historical events? Stephen Hawkin, the late theoretical physicist and cosmologist, had often posited the same question, even throwing a party exclusively for time travellers, deliberately not posting out invites or making it public knowledge until after the event. When no one had attended, Hawkin concluded that it was unequivocal proof that time travel was impossible.

The endless supply of questions that crashed and jostled within her fuzzy wine head were only stalled by the deaths of Mitchell and Knapper, her interest turning to the job-related side of Dyson's revelation. At the same time, she watched the interplay between the lovers, their hands entwined tenderly as they waited for her to respond.

"*Soooo…*" she finally slurred, blasting out a huge breath and looking at Dyson and Mary in turn, "this is the *real* Jack the Ripper we're after?"

Dyson said nothing, shaking his head at the situation rather than her question while Mary answered for him. "It certainly is," she mumbled, sounding as intoxicated as Jenny.

"Then who is he?"

"We don't know," Dyson said solemnly, swallowing down a mouthful of wine. "He's Russian, that's all we know. Well, we *think* he's Russian. It's none of the usual suspects anyway."

"Jesus, John," Jenny said, her mouth hanging open for a moment before she continued. "If this gets out, it's gonna cause one hell of a shitstorm. They'll crucify you."

"You don't think I know that?" Dyson barked, slamming his glass down. "Don't you think I know that if I hadn't gone back, Trisha Noble and George—*everyone*—would still be alive? I pushed this snowball down the hill, and it just keeps getting bigger and faster. Do you have any idea how hard it is to sit there and listen to Raymond's bullshit while he's out there?"

"No, I'm sorry," Jenny muttered with a ripple of embarrassment. "He's onto you, by the way. Raymond. He gave me the third degree; he thinks you know more than you're letting on. I've been meaning to phone you all day, but what with everything that's..." Her face crumpled again as she thought of their dead colleagues.

"I think he's had me followed." Dyson reached over and topped up her glass. "I guess I can't blame him."

There was a moment of tense sombreness until Mary looked up from her drunken hunch and threw the conversation on a completely different path. "Jenny, would you like to join us for dinner?"

"*Noooo*...I don't want to intrude." Jenny smiled at the generous offer.

"Stay," Dyson insisted with an eager nod.

"I don't know..." Eating dinner with her ex-lover and his new partner was the last thing Jenny wanted to do, but the wine had given her a ravenous appetite that needed immediate appeasing.

"Please?" Mary pleaded. "It's my first proper creation beyond beans and toast."

"Beans on toast," Dyson corrected her. "Beans *on* toast."

"On toast?"

"On toast, yes." He took back his hand and wiggled one above the other to demonstrate. "They're on top of the toast."

Jenny smiled at their playful exchange. As much as it hurt her to admit, they seemed such a good fit together, and she couldn't help but find a genuine fondness for Mary.

"Very well, I shall try and remember that," Mary said, making a mental note and returning to Jenny. "I've made a pie. I think as many people as possible should suffer the consequences."

"Well, in that case..." Jenny announced, making a drum roll on the table for effect. "I'd love to!"

"It's settled then." Mary gave a little clap as she climbed from her seat and went over to the kitchen area, the effects of the wine causing her to sway.

Jenny sipped from her wine and gestured to her, beavering away in the kitchen to the sound of crashing pots and pans. "I like her," she whispered, not that Mary would've heard over the din. "I probably shouldn't, but...you know." Dyson placed his hand on hers and squeezed his appreciation. "Mind you," Jenny added, struggling to perform the mental arithmetic, "at 167, she's a bit old for you, isn't she?"

Dyson hooted with intoxicated laughter, Jenny joining him until they both dried up and sat in awkward silence.

"You remember that time Jim got himself locked in a cell?" Jenny eventually scoffed.

Dyson made a discreet chuckle as he nodded along, the memory pushing through the heartache. "How long was he in there?"

"Didn't we leave him in there all day? And what about..." Jenny snorted and slapped the table, chinking the handful of cutlery Mary had returned to arrange. "What about the time Gary smashed up the DCI's car?"

"Did he?" Dyson's eyes spread with shock at the news. "I didn't know that! Where was I then?"

"Oh, I can't remember. Out being Supercop, probably." She pulled a face at him, and a surge of unwanted laughter hit them both.

It died right there on the spot when Mary placed a ceramic dish containing an incinerated pie in the middle of the table. The crust was charcoal black, appearing as if it had been torched with a flamethrower. Mary hovered, volleying a nervous gaze between Dyson and Jenny. For a moment, they just stared at it, unsure of what to say.

"Um...shall we get a takeaway instead?" Dyson finally said.

CHAPTER ELEVEN

Khan's Mercedes X55 swept through the darkened Essex countryside. The xenon headlights expunged the blackness, revealing twisted autumnal trees that reached at them from the sides of a narrow road while the windscreen wipers swept away a returning drizzle.

Still on a high from the praise the criminal had heaped on him, Karim kissed his teeth and motioned outside at the reflected shards of rain caught in the light. "Bumbaclat weather, innit?"

"That'll be your global warmin'," Khan replied routinely.

The criminal didn't really care for the precarious state of the planet. If he was going down, fuck it, why shouldn't everyone else die too? He was worth ten of them—them that obeyed the law and led their boring little lives on a diet of spiralling debt and reality TV. That said, the constant shitty weather had really started to irritate him. He had always imagined dying somewhere hot with the sun on his face, surrounded by a bevy of beauties weeping at his passing, not looking up at grey pissing clouds encircled by armed pigs as would probably be the case.

"Ain't warm though, Mr Khan." Karim shook off his concern and looked over at his Svengali. "Where're we going?"

"Those weapons you saw today, I bought them from a scumbag arms dealer called Benny the Bullet. We, um…we argued over the price and I kind of shot him. To death. He's in the boot. I need to bury him before he, you know, gets all stinky and stuff starts leakin' out. I was hopin' you'd help, what with me injuries?

"To dig a grave?" Strangely, Karim beamed from ear to ear at the prospect. "Yeah, man. Sweet. I ain't never dug a grave before."

"Your enthusiasm has not gone unnoticed, Aziz, believe me." Khan buttered him up with a wagging finger, his undamaged eye focused on the detailed 3D holographic sat nav projected onto the windscreen. There was a minor dirt track coming up on the left that led to a clearing amongst the trees. It was the perfect location. "This'll do."

He swung the car onto the path, bouncing it through rutted potholes thick with muddy water. The Mercedes parked up, the headlights bleaching the area to display the small clearing the map had shown.

"Go and find yourself a nice spot," Khan instructed his apprentice, exiting the car and making his way to the boot. He opened it up to reveal nothing but a shovel bought earlier in the afternoon. Contrary to what he'd told Karim, there was no body inside.

Meanwhile, the kid had located a suitable area and was testing the ground with the heel of his Nikes. His knowledge of gravedigging was sparse, but it seemed a good choice. The earth was soft but not too muddy and would be easy to turn over with a good—

"Spade," Khan said, appearing behind him out of nowhere and handing him the shovel. There was a devilish glow about his bandaged, swollen face, underscored by the glare of the headlights. It unsettled Karim and caused him to let slip a gulp. "Get on with it then. I'm gonna wait in the car. And make sure it's deep enough. We don't want some cunt's dog diggin' him up now, do we?"

———

However atrocious the pie appeared, it had tasted divine, the meat within tender and succulent. Heartily consumed with a basic accompaniment of chips and peas that Mary had cooked without burning, the meal was further enhanced by several more glasses of wine until the bottle ran dry.

Once it dawned on them that Mitchell, Knapper, and everyone who had died since the Ripper's escape would live again, the laughter began to return. They were only *temporarily* dead, it was decided. All that it took to 'unfuck the situation,' as Dyson had drunkenly put it, was for the Americans to get their shit together and fix the time machine. Then someone could be sent back to recapture the Ripper *before* his murderous flight from Bernstein and Simmons. It was a lifeline for them to cling to in a sea of desperation, something to be celebrated with the fruity little red Dyson had brought from a kitchen cupboard.

Jenny's head rolled to one side as she stumbled to the punchline of her police-related joke. "…so the traffic cop pulls this guy over and says: 'Well, I guess today's just not your lucky day.'"

Dyson bellowed with intoxicated laughter. Mary grinned away, equally drunk, laughing more as a pleasantry for a gag she didn't understand. She reached over, dousing the glasses she gathered with red wine. She missed Dyson's completely and soaked the table with a slurred "*Whooops.*" He waved the accident away and moved his glass closer. While Mary tried again, successfully filling the glass on her second attempt, Jenny looked at him with a lopsided grin.

"This is like that scene from Jaws."

"What the devil is a Jaws?" Mary asked innocently.

Jenny explained how it was a movie about a killer shark that terrorised a small American beach resort, adding how it was one of her favourite films of all time. She decided it best not to tell Mary the tale of how her and Dyson had watched it together one night, cuddled up on the sofa, before slipping off to her bedroom to thrash about beneath the sheets like the shark's victims had done beneath the waves.

"There's this bit where the hero, Chief Brody," she said instead, "is sitting at his dining table with his wife and this shark expert, Hopper, and they're all getting blind drunk."

"Hooper," Dyson groaned, correcting her with an exaggerated eye roll.

"Hooper! Thank you, Barry Norman. Anyway, they get absolutely bladdered and decide to go out and find the shark. D'you remember, John?"

Dyson gave her a drunken nod, his head extending way beyond its intended stopping point. "Who am I then? Brody?

"*Noooo*, you'd be the shark expert."

"Richard Dreyfuss? You're taking the piss!"

"The shark's the Ripper, making you the expert. See how this works?"

"So, who am I?" Mary asked, dry washing some sobriety over her face in an attempt to play along.

"You'd be Mrs Brody."

Mary looked to Dyson for guidance. "Is that good?"

"Well, she didn't get eaten by the shark so I suppose that's a bonus." He reached for his wine glass and looked at Jenny with a pleading grin. "Please can I be Chief Brody?"

"*Noooo*… I'm Brody!"

"*I'm Spartacus!*" Dyson cried out.

"Wrong film, Supercop," Jenny winked.

Accepting his casting, Dyson grinned. "Fuck it, whatever. Get to the point, Jen."

"The point is…" Jenny straightened up and paraphrased a line direct from the film. "Why don't we have one more drink and go out and look for that shark?"

The mood instantly shifted. Dyson glanced at Mary. She clutched his hand for support, and he returned to Jenny, making a deliberate shake of his head. "I'm out, Jen. We're off to Japan in—"

"Japan!"

"Japan, yes. Tomorrow." He glanced over at the clock on the kitchen wall to find it was gone midnight. "Make that today. I'm not going shark hunting now."

"What?" Jenny instantly sobered at the prospect of his departure. "You're walking away? John… But you can't just *leave*."

"And what's the point of me being here? Huh? Listening to my friends die as this place falls apart, knowing there's nothing I can do about it." He returned the squeeze Mary had given him, the couple presenting a united front. "I'm sorry, Jen. But we're leaving."

What followed was a moment of the most powerful silence Dyson had ever endured. Jenny stared at him, her mouth moving while she thought to construct some reply.

"There's something else I have to tell you both," he said with a deep breath before she found her words. He paused to allow the gulp that fluttered in his throat to subside. "This business with Khan and my old man. Well, it turns out that Alan and Heather Dyson weren't my parents…and that I was adopted."

"*What!*" Jenny choked. "Who told you that?"

"John?" Mary added, her grip increasing on his hand. "Why on earth didn't you—"

"Solly Goldmann." Dyson waited for Jenny to remember the name from the one time she'd met the counterfeiter. "They adopted me as a baby, apparently. After Claire was born, mum found out." He scoffed at that. "*Heather* found out she couldn't have any more kids, so they adopted one. Me."

"Bloody hell, what are you gonna do?"

Dyson shrugged at Jenny's question. "What can I do? I'm thirty-six, and they're both gone. Regardless of what Khan claims Alan Dyson did or didn't do, they gave me a great life as a kid. But now, on the 'Shit I Have To Deal With' scale, it's not exactly way up there, is it?"

Another shrug followed, casual and relaxed, as if Dyson was reflecting on some trivial matter. He had resigned himself to the bombshell Goldmann had dropped. It had come as a shock initially, but its impact had softened over the hours the more he'd thought about it.

Dyson raised his glass and took an unhurried swig. "It's a story for another time."

As graves went, it was very well dug. Eager to further impress, the kid had toiled long and hard to get it just right. The edges were straight, and the thick viscosity of the earth made the sides impressively smooth. It was well over the regulatory six-foot-deep for graves; Karim taking on board Khan's advice about a dog or some other woodland creature digging up the occupant soon to be planted inside.

Covered in muck, his tracksuit and Nikes pretty much ruined, the kid rested on the shovel at the foot of the grave while he waited for Khan to finish his inspection and give his seal of approval.

"That's outstandin,' Aziz," Khan nodded away. "Ten outta ten." His bloated face made an awkward wince, and he appeared almost embarrassed by what he said next. "It's a shame really."

"Shame, Mr Khan?" Karim asked, nonplussed. "What's a shame?"

"To have to do this." Khan reached into his overcoat and pulled out an automatic.

"Mr—!"

He shot the kid in the face from point-blank range before he had a chance to beg for his life, the deafening gunshot forcing a flock of sleeping birds into squawking flight. The force of the impact made Karim's head balloon into a ridiculous shape as the pressure of the bullet driven between his eyes made his skull pop at the seams. The projectile exiting the back of his head on a tide of meaty gunk to bury itself in a tree behind, Karim's eyes continued to watch Khan, betrayed and horrified, the glow of excitement at working for the criminal fading fast. His body swayed and then toppled back perfectly into the hole he created.

"'Partin' is such sweet sorrow,'" Khan snorted, bastardising Shakespeare's famous line from *Romeo and Juliet* for his own needs.

It wasn't at all. He didn't give a tuppenny-ha'penny fuck about the kid and was glad to be rid of him. Karim had become just another casualty in his plan to unleash merry hell on Whitechapel's police. The kid had served his purpose, and now there was no more use for him. Blowing up the two detectives right outside the farm had been a masterstroke if ever there was one, but it had also been Karim's undoing. The last thing Khan needed was a wannabe gangster, picked up on one of the police station's external CCTV cameras not rendered useless by Mathews' bomb, pissing his pants and cracking under interview to throw the proverbial spanner in the works. Khan wasn't done yet, not by a long shot. He was just getting warmed up.

"Yeah," Khan chuckled as he grabbed the shovel before it toppled after Karim. "I buried Benny a couple of days ago. He's just over there." He pointed at the earth a few feet away, where a slight mound protruded from the autumn leaves. "He's your neighbour."

As if woken by a distant gunshot, the prime minister surged forwards in bed with a gasp. He snapped on the bedside light to brighten a surprisingly small and modest bedroom: the residence above the United Kingdom's seat of government wasn't famed for its generous floor space.

The blooming of the light stirred Lucy Vaughn. The attractive mixed-race woman at his side rolled over and cracked one eye at her husband. "David?" Her voice croaked but soon settled into its usual cutglass elegance. "It's two in the morning. Is everything alright?"

Vaughn gazed down at her, his dark face fixed with a lethargic smile. But there was little wit or warmth behind it, causing Lucy to pull herself up into a sit and pinch the sleep from her eyes.

"What on earth is the matter?" she asked through the yawn that forced its way out.

"What must a man do to maintain his reputation, Lucy?" he mused. "And which is more important, said reputation or his life and the lives of countless others?"

Lucy shook her head and held back the second yawn that tried to escape. She took Vaughn's hand in hers. "You're speaking in damn riddles again, David."

"I denied President Garrett a request today; for the sake of my reputation. A denial which Garrett claims could have catastrophic repercussions."

"You spoke to President Garrett?"

"He was here."

"Garrett's in London?"

"In this very house. It is a long and unbelievable story."

"Well, what did he…" Lucy's question faded to be quickly replaced by another. "Did he threaten you?"

Vaughn made a genuine laugh at that. "On the contrary. I had him by the balls." He stared off into space for a moment, tracing the floral patterning of the wallpaper Lucy had chosen upon moving into Number 10. His face had clouded with the utmost seriousness when he looked back at her. "Am I a good man, Lucy?"

"Of course you are, darling!" Lucy chirped as her face grew wary. "You are the most loyal, loving, and honest man that I have ever known. David, what's this about?"

The prime minister reached over to a landline phone set on his bedside table. Similar to the phones found in hotel rooms, it was set with a multitude of coloured buttons, one of which Vaughn plunged a finger onto. As it began to purr against his ear, he looked at his wife with a dour expression. "Remember that sentiment. Because your darling husband is about to shatter your precious illusions."

The call connected, and Vaughn grabbed Lucy's hand tightly. The force of his grip reminded him of when they had flown back from last year's G20 summit, the plane hitting major turbulence over the Pacific. He had felt as sick then as he did now, the contents of his stomach bubbling and desperate to escape.

"Good morning, Rachid. I'm sorry to disturb you," he said to the nightshift operator on the Downing Street switchboard. "Can you connect me with Sir Alistair Furnish straightaway? Thank you." Vaughn replaced the handset and pulled the creases from the Deputy Dawg t-shirt he wore as if making himself presentable.

"Oh, dear God, David," Lucy teased, playfully smoothing out her silk pyjama top in a dramatic manner. "Look at you, like a guilty pupil before his headmaster. It's a phone, you fool. The old buzzard can't see you."

With a tough council estate upbringing under his belt, there weren't many people who could intimidate the prime minister. The French premier had tried during their last meeting, furious at a diplomatic expulsion, as had members of the English Defence League, who surrounded his car, calling for his death or resignation. The current Commissioner of the Metropolitan Police Department was a different story, however. Scottish of origin, Sir Alistair Furnish was a giant of a man in both stature and reputation, a fearsome beast who could burn through sheet metal with the intensity of his stare and wither a man with just the tone of his voice.

Before he could offer any form of defence to her teasing, the phone rang back, eliciting a silent prayer from Vaughn as he reached over for it and cleared the knot from his throat.

"Sir Alistair, please forgive me calling you at such an ungodly hour, but I have a matter of the highest importance to discuss. One of your detectives, John Dyson… Yes, the suspended officer. I have it on good authority that he will attempt to leave the UK for Japan later today, I presume from Heathrow. I need him found and stopped. He is to be brought to me immediately, where I shall attempt to construct a way out of the position that I find myself unwittingly plunged into."

He listened to the deep Scottish grumblings at the other end of the line, pulling the phone away from his ear a couple of inches and wincing at Lucy as she glared at him with surfacing anger.

"Thank you, Alistair," Vaughn said glumly into the handset before setting it back down.

As soon as he did, Lucy launched into professional mode. A prominent human rights lawyer famed for her voracious defence of the well-being of criminal suspects and victims of human rights violations, she was detested by many of the same people who hated him. Lucy had hit the headlines for providing legal counsel to several warlords tortured during capture after the Egyptian War of 2024. Her subsequent victory at The Hague's International Criminal Court earned her few fans: the men were vicious war criminals guilty of slaughtering entire villages in the Sinai Peninsula who many believed were deserving of their mistreatment. It was not a belief that Lucy shared.

"David, what the hell are you doing?" she cried, snatching back her hand to climb from the bed and distance herself from him.

"And there lies the reason for my anxiety, multiplied three-fold. The beast of Loch Ness, your expected but fully justifiable response, and the terrible, terrible secret which Garrett has entrusted to me."

Lucy glared away his defence. "That *police officer*, and I use those words loosely, viciously attacked an unarmed, terminally ill suspect. *During a recorded interview*. There can be no recourse or reprieve for such barbaric actions."

Vaughn looked up at her, his eyes filled with solemnity while he considered an appropriate vindication. He had no desire to terrify his wife with the information that Garrett had divulged—God only knew how it had terrified him—but he was equally reluctant of sending her deeper into a rage either. In the end, he recalled a quote from the long-dead utilitarian philosopher Jeremy Bentham, in some pathetic hope that it would appease her. "'It is the greatest good to the greatest number of people which is the measure of right and wrong.'"

The desired effect missing by several miles, Lucy growled at him and yanked her dressing gown from the back of the door. "Oh, piss off, David!" she yelled caustically, storming from the bedroom and slamming the door shut after her.

Vaughn huffed deeply and sank back into bed. He killed the light, plunging the room back into darkness. "Thank you, Mr Dyson."

Khan cruised the dark and deserted streets of Whitechapel in his Mercedes. His eyes alive and aglow with fevered intent, the damaged one still no more than a slit, he sought something particular in his reconnaissance.

Before filling in Karim's grave, he had unwound the bandages around his distended head and tossed them down on the kid's body. Shocked to discover that those bastard doctors had shaved his head completely bald during his treatment, the loss of his beloved ponytail had struck Khan hard until he'd stared into the driver's mirror and considered how much meaner and ruthless he appeared in the gaudy radiance of the dashboard.

The caramel glow of streetlighting bloomed and died within the car as Khan drove, his gaze occasionally flickering from his search to the dogeared Jack the Ripper book slung on the passenger seat.

"Come on, where are you?" he muttered impatiently, looking from pavement to pavement for what he sought.

A mocking smirk crossed the criminal's lips as he slowed to gawp at the big blue tent erected over the closed-off Vallance Road. The twisted remains of the police car were contained inside—probably what was left of the barbequed pigs who had driven it too. He was surprised the high street had reopened so soon, knowing how the bacon liked to cause traffic chaos at any given opportunity.

Once clear of the pedestrian crossing in the middle of the road, Khan swung the car around and crept back for another look. He did so for no other reason than it was giving him wood, to imagine those two pig detectives torn apart by the force of Karim's explosion.

"*Boooom*," he sang softly as he accelerated away and got back into his search.

Khan drove past the empty pavements where the market stalls would sell their knock off wares, past the Royal London from which he had discharged himself, past the grime and filth and the blue and green glass cube that was the library. He indicated to turn left into Cambridge Heath Road and drew to a stop at the traffic lights, his head turning this way and that, the few early morning pedestrians who prowled the streets of little interest to him.

He was after something more *specific*.

"Come on, come on..."

The second the lights changed, the Mercedes hummed under Khan's frustrated foot. He raced along the deserted road, past the huge Sainsburys where he once chinned some cunt for giving him a disrespectful glance. Blocks of grubby flats and shops slipped by as a continuous blur of nothingness until he was met by a roadblock guarding the tented remains of another of Karim's bombs, forcing him to throw the car into a road on the right.

And then he saw it. Up ahead in the distance.

Khan slowed the car and pulled over against the pavement.

"Perfect," he purred with nefarious purpose. Fixated on exactly what he was looking for, he reached over and opened the glovebox.

Wrapped up in a winter coat, Ginita Nahar trudged across the uneven tarmac of the quiet street. Reaching the pavement, the young Asian woman entered the courtyard of a low-rise apartment block. The building had seen better days; the collection of cars congregated around it in the car park littered with rubbish looking similarly neglected.

Beneath a pink Shayla headscarf, there shone a pretty olive face lit up by the glow of her phone screen. The headphones Ginita wore assaulted her eardrums with some manufactured pop drivel from the charts, her head bopping wearily in tune with the beat. It had been a long shift at her uncle's convenience store where she worked, but at least she'd had her sounds to lift her spirits. Music was her guilty pleasure, but Ginita would be sure to hide her headphones as soon as she was through the front door in case her father was still awake and slumped in front of the television. He would call her music *haram*, meaning it was forbidden in the Islamic world. She found the whole religion thing deeply contradictory. He could watch his stupid TV shows, ogling at the scantily clad women and chuckling like an idiot, yet she couldn't listen to her favourite bands or singers?

Ginita stopped at the battered front door of one of the ground floor flats and pulled off a small backpack. She unzipped it to fish through the contents for her door keys, tutting and cursing in Urdu as she sifted through her accumulated junk.

As she fished, not yet getting a bite, the shape of a man in a hooded grey coat slid from the shadows behind her. If she had seen him, the first thing she would have noticed was the long kitchen knife clenched in his gloved left hand, reflecting the street lighting. But she didn't, and nor did she hear his approach with Harry Styles' crooning in her ears.

Ginita found her keys and commenced the lengthy process of finding the right ones. As well as the three for the front door—it was Whitechapel after all, and crime was rife—there was a set of keys for her dad's Nissan Micra that he would let her use now and then, and an assortment of keys for her uncle's shop that was worthy of a prison warden. The first of the three located, she reached out to fit it into the lock. She was moments from warmth, just seconds from sticking the kettle on and rushing upstairs to use the toilet while it boiled.

She felt a sudden tug on her headscarf, a handful of her hair grabbed in the process. Her head was yanked back to expose a protruding, trembling windpipe. Before Ginita could collect her petrified thoughts and even contemplate screaming, her assailant tore the sharp knife that appeared before her bulging eyes through her neck, delivering a fatal blow. Skin and muscle rent apart like a split in the earth during a violent earthquake, blood ejected with such force as to drum against the door, drenching it as the rain had. On an inhuman spluttering of wet air, Ginita's legs buckled and gave out, twisting her involuntarily as she fell away to paint the whitewashed brickwork with a downwards arc of red.

Flopping onto her back, Ginita stared up at him as her life continued to jet and gurgle from the devastating wound. As she started her journey towards death, right there on the cold, damp floor outside her home, her attacker lowered himself next to her and flashed a sickening smile of white teeth. She concentrated on the face concealed within the fabric of a hood. It was an abomination, swollen and disfigured, tinged with purple and yellow…or was that the focus she frantically fought to keep twisting what she saw? Then, with a gasp that sent a spray of crimson spluttering into the air, it hit her with the shock and speed of the blade's cut. *She knew him.* She knew her attacker!

But…but…that didn't make any sense. He was a local businessman and something of a local celebrity—that's how she knew him. But he wasn't the killer of innocent women. She would speak his name and ask him why he had done what he'd done if only the knife hadn't stolen her ability to speak. Ginita screamed his name inside her head, desperate for someone to hear.

"*Ssshhh…*" her killer soothed in a voice that offered little comfort. He reached up and put a gloved finger to his lips. "That's it. Off you go, off you go, off you go."

The last thing Ginita's brain would try to process, the last image she would ever see, was that of Frankie Khan joyously licking her blood from his fingertips.

CHAPTER TWELVE

Carl 'Carlos' Robinson lumbered down the stairs of the rented three-bed semi, his movement reminiscent of a primate first experiencing the ability of upright walking. The wooden treads thudded and creaked under his colossal weight as he navigated the cardboard removal boxes that obstructed his descent. He cursed and swore at their placement and scratched at the back of a big, fat head that grew straight out of his mammoth shoulders. As his focus grew, he could see the silhouetted shape of a man behind the frosted glass of the front door.

It was just gone eight in the morning when the knocking had started, smashing him from his sleep to fear the worse. He had grabbed the small Walther PPK he kept under his pillow since their escape from London and staggered from the bed. Lauren, his wife of four years, told him not to panic; it was just the IKEA delivery she'd ordered—if he woke them kids up, she would have his bollocks on a plate she warned as he'd stuffed the gun in the pocket of the dressing gown he wrapped around his flabby, naked physique.

The caller knocked again. *Tap-tap-tap*. It wasn't the incessant hammering of the Old Bill that he'd experienced many times before, that much was for sure. They would've had the door off its hinges by now with the red battering ram thing they used on such jobs, the property swarming with coppers as they poured in like a flood.

Probably is *just a delivery then*, he told himself as he reached the bottom of the stairs and felt the gun for reassurance.

For a man of such a formidable size, Robinson had been a nervous wreck since fleeing from his ex-boss. The fucking headcase wasn't one for giving up and accepting defeat graciously, and he had wondered if the criminal would try to seek some sort of violent retribution for their desertion. Khan was a man as evil as he was devious and cunning, and nothing was taboo or off-limits to him. He relished in the pain and anguish of others. It made him hard, he had once joyfully confessed. The admission had scared the shit out of Robinson; that a man could find sexual satisfaction from hurting people. He was no angel himself—he had done some horrible shit in his criminal career. He had killed for Khan, but it was always with respect for his adversary, limiting their suffering whenever possible and doing what he'd done because life had made him a wrong 'un and because it paid well, but never because he enjoyed it. He had watched with concealed horror when Khan had made some naked, tattooed faggot who he believed to be a police grass drink a bottle of some highly potent acid, laughing as he died in agony and then shooting his lawyer dead and talking about starting a war with the police. That was when he knew it was time to go. That was when they all knew.

Since arriving in Manchester, anyone who happened to look at Robinson the wrong way, or any car that followed him for more than 100 feet, brought him out in a tropical sweat and put him on high alert, making him grip his

Walther and wonder if Khan had sent them to put a bullet in him.

Robinson had been as careful as a man deserting the clutches of a lunatic in record time could be. They took only what they could fit in the Transit van he went out and stole the night that everyone decided enough was enough. His brother lived in Burnage and helped him to find a decent property in which to lay low until he could source a new identity for the family. If one mistake was made, it was the shopping trip to IKEA, where his stupid cow of a wife had used her credit card and given their address for delivery, rather than dipping into the suitcase of cash they left London with and insisting on collecting the order as he'd instructed her. But he was probably being daft and overcautious. Khan didn't have the wherewithal to trace credit card transactions.

Did he?

"Hold your fuckin' 'orses!" the big lump mumbled in his sluggish London accent as he stumbled forwards. He undid the deadbolt and unlatched the security chain to wrench open the door.

It wasn't raining in Manchester, and the sky was brightly lit, the blinding sun behind the visitor and the slate rooftops of the houses opposite. It took a moment of intense eye-scrubbing for the figure to turn from backlit silhouette to three-dimensional human form. When he finally did, a stick-thin man with a pirate's eye patch grinned at him.

"Morning, fucko!" he greeted, bringing down the claw hammer he produced out of nowhere on top of Robinson's head before his sluggish hand could pull out the gun. An instant warm wetness flooded his face as his vision turned red, and he lost focus, the sound of Lauren and the kids screaming the only thing he could hear.

. . .

Carrick stepped into the house, followed by Ringo, Chang's Chinese guardian. Ringo closed the door and gave Carrick a single nod; he knew the drill by now. As he took to the stairs and tore up them like an oriental whirlwind, his brothers, George and Paul—John was in Parkhurst for assaulting a police officer—burst in through the back door. Like their sibling, they were both huge, brawny units and men whose facial expressions signified that they not be messed with. As they charged up the stairs after Ringo, the shrieking of the woman and kids soon falling silent, Carrick mused how they must have ruined their poor old mum's fanny on the way out, before returning to his victim on the floor.

Carrick awarded himself a congratulatory nod at felling such an impressive lump with one blow. The said lump, dazed and not half as impressive now he was laying on his back with his dressing gown splayed open to expose a tiny, flaccid cock, clawed at a Walther PPK he tugged from his pocket. Rolling his eye, Carrick stamped on his hand until the fingers broke, reaching down to untangle the weapon from his twisted digits and tap it on and off his blood washed cheek.

"Look at you, you lairy cunt. Who d'you think you are, 007?"

The operation to capture Khan's thugs was going well. Splendidly, in fact. Fuelled by a bag of Charlie Carrick kept for special occasions, they had started their quest in Scotland; Carrick figuring it best to begin with the farthest target on the list and work his way back down the country. After flying up to bonnie Scotland the previous evening, they stole a large refrigerated meat truck from a trading estate outside of Inverness. It was ideal for what Carrick wanted, the rear compartment set with hooks and a pulley system to hang and manoeuvre the carcasses of animals. The company logo spray-painted over and the number plates replaced, they began their search. Scotland heralded two of Khan's ex-employees—five in total once the associated family members were subdued and bound with thick cable ties and hung up in the back of the lorry. By the time they reached Manchester, the truck was starting to get crowded: five of Khan's men and their families strung up and stewing in their own fear to create an ungodly stench of shit and piss that warranted a good dab of Vicks VapoRub to go anywhere near.

There were two in Manchester: Robinson and a big fucker called Trevor Willis, the latter getting a direct hit from Carrick's hammer after abandoning his wife and kids and taking off across a field to evade capture. The hammer had sailed through the air with the precision of a cruise missile and clonked him right on the back of the noggin, impressing even Ringo, who had high-fived him on his accuracy. They would move on to Sheffield next, then Birmingham, then a village just shy of Nottingham. The quest would finish in South Wales, where Khan's number one, Steven Calder, was holed up according to Chang's research. It was a lot of driving, but Carrick had the Chinese Beatles to share the load, the coke to keep them going, and the promise of a handsome payday was always good at keeping workers working. So far, all had been apprehended with the minimum of fuss or fight, with no witnesses or calls placed to the relevant police departments. Only one of the men on Khan's list—Carrick forgot which one—had managed to launch any form of successful counterattack, striking Paul in the gut with a humdinger of a punch that had sent the Chinaman into a rage and caused him to snip off every finger of the hand that struck him with a pair of pruning shears he'd found.

Ringo, or one of his brothers—they all looked the fucking same to Carrick—appeared at the top of the stairs with an old woman trembling in a wheelchair. He was grinning while his captive shook uncontrollably in her seat, her desperate screams denied exit by the sock stuffed in her mouth. The grin increased as he tipped the chair and sent the old girl crashing down the stairs.

Carrick winced as she tumbled, a mass of spindly arms and legs, pointing Robinson's gun lazily at the sobbing woman as she came to a painful stop at his feet. "Don't fuckin' break none of 'em, know what I mean?"

The Chinese Beatles, as Carrick dubbed them, seemed to enjoy the violence as much as he did, although he drew the line at hurting kids, and he'd had to rein the brothers in a couple of times when they started to get slap happy.

Another woman came flying down the stairs, naked but for her panties. She crashed down on top of the old woman, and Carrick could tell by their identical, terrified expressions that they were mother and daughter. While he ogled the fine pair of natural tits Robinson's missus possessed, George and Paul descended the stairs, each carrying a wriggling child desperate to elicit a scream through the duct tape clamped over their mouths.

Carrick stuck a *Gauloises* between his lips and motioned a thumb back at the front door. "Pull the truck on the drive. C'mon, let's get a fuckin' wriggle on."

Police tape cavorting on the fierce squall that raced down Doveton Street, half a dozen uniformed police officers held back a large crowd of camera crews and concerned locals brandishing their phones.

Away from the cordon, outside of an apartment block desperate for refurbishment, half a dozen SOCO worked over the crime scene in their white Tyvek suits, the returning rain mocking them with a good drenching while they marked potential evidence with yellow numbered tags and a photographer snapped away where instructed. Against the wall of the building, a blue tent had been erected. It was a sight that was becoming all too familiar in Whitechapel.

Inside the tent, Debbie stood alone wearing a mask and a set of white overalls, looking down glumly at the cold, pale body of a young woman. She was lying on her back, her headscarf partially torn away. There was no blood; the rain had removed all trace, leaving only a deep, vicious trench ploughed through her neck.

Similarly attired, Raymond entered the tent, his own coveralls struggling against his gut. He pulled an unseen face at the sight of the victim and spoke, raising his voice against the downpour thrumming on the roof. "What have we got, Shaw?"

"Ginita Nahar, boss," Debbie answered, relaying the sparse information she'd learnt since arriving on the scene herself. "Twenty-three. She worked at her uncle's all-night shop over on Massingham Street. FME wasn't prepared to give an estimated time of death, what with the rain and such. But the poor cow's probably been here most of the night."

"Who found the body?" Raymond asked routinely.

"Her dad. Imagine that, boss. Opening the door to go and get a pint of milk and finding your daughter…" She shuddered to a stop, the scenario too dire to contemplate. "Uniform did a quick door to door on arrival, but this is Whitechapel. 'See no evil, hear no evil.'"

The Welshman cocked his head to one side and rasped at the stubble prickling behind his mask. "No mutilations."

"Boss?"

"There are no mutilations."

"But he didn't have the same opportunity he did with Trisha Noble. Outside, no privacy, constantly looking over his shoulder."

"Never stopped Jack the Ripper, did it?"

Debbie considered life in 2030 a whole different ball game to that of Victorian London but decided it best not to voice her opinion.

"No CCTV, I'm guessing?"

Debbie shook her head gloomily. "No, boss. Not even a Ring doorbell. The little scallies round here nick 'em and put them on Gumtree. Oh..." Debbie looked at him with news to share. "Oh, I saw one of Sinclair's lads at the nick. Apparently, the explosives officer tasked with watching the vehicles yesterday had buggered off for a piss without waiting for relief. Jim and Gary died because..." She became visibly angry, taking a moment to compose herself. "Heads will roll, he said."

Raymond offered nothing. No signs of compassion or words of comfort for her fallen colleagues. In police work, emotions were something best left in the locker room at the start of a shift, but after losing two close friends only the previous day, she had expected the bastard to say something. Instead, he just motioned for her to leave the tent. Following her back into the rain, he glanced warily at the hordes of Asian faces watching them from the four floors of balconies above.

"Right then," Raymond said. "Next."

Her face was anything but beautiful pressed against the glass, the fear it reflected only heightened by the cascading rain and the occasional flashes of lightning. Mary pushed away another wave of hangover-induced nausea and stared out at the *thing* sitting beyond the window.

Dyson had called it an 'aeroplane' in that offhand way he took for granted the marvels of his time. It—they—there were many of them, coming and going—appeared so minuscule whenever she gawped at them moving between the clouds, but on the ground and close up, they were immense, beautiful, and ultimately terrifying. White and emblazoned with swirling colour, the one before them had a large BRITISH AIRWAYS painted along its wedge-shaped body, its wings swept back like a diving hawk's. Mary wondered how such an ungainly contraption could ever get off the ground to fly so high. In her day, God had granted flight exclusively to birds and insects, and it was not something man was gifted with the physical attributes to achieve. Yet, this beast would whisk her across the world at close to 1000 miles an hour, so the transparent imagery magically projected on the windows informed waiting passengers, all while producing zero carbon emissions—whatever that was. None of it meant much to a Victorian traveller in time, trembling in a sickened daze, and waiting to be transported to a land she found as equally mystifying.

Japan. She hadn't even heard of the place until Nelly Jacobs, a fellow prostitute famed for her toothless blowjobs, had regaled her and several of the other girls in The Ten Bells as to how she'd sucked off a funny little sailor from there once.

In the distance, another of the metal birds climbed into the air with a roar befitting a wild beast. Mary shuddered as she watched it vanish, swallowed by the eternal greyness of the clouds, the hundreds of other people who either stood or sat all around them, indifferent to its disappearance.

Dyson took her hand and gave it a reassuring squeeze. "Safest way to travel."

"That's easy for you to say, Mr 2030," Mary grumbled, the confident look she forced herself to make crumbling as she stared behind him to where two uniformed policemen carrying big guns came striding towards them. "John…?"

. . .

Dyson turned as they drew to a stop. He had always found the officers of the Metropolitan Police Department's Aviation Security Operational Unit (SO18) to be a particular kind of miserable whenever their paths had crossed, and the two standing before him appeared to be no exception. It was probably the repeated hardship of watching over eighty-five million passengers a year that Heathrow handled either reunite with loved ones or jet off to the sun, while they remained stuck on terra firma, dealing with the criminals and traffickers who kept them forever busy.

"John Dyson?" one of them enquired.

"Yeah, that's me."

"Come with us please, sir."

"But we're about to get on a plane," Dyson protested, conscious of the intrigue the scene was creating amongst his fellow travellers.

"Not anymore, I'm afraid. Your luggage has been removed, and the tickets refunded to your account."

"What? You can't do that." The unblinking expressions they returned told otherwise. "Well…where are you taking us?"

"I'm afraid that's classified at the moment, sir."

The two-minute drive to Headlam Street had taken closer to fifteen with the early morning rush-hour traffic, commuters using the minor side streets as rat runs to lessen their journey time. A phone-in on LBC regarding the Ripper copycat and the police's lack of progress had infuriated him as he drove, the Welshman arguing his defence passionately to the deaf ears of the presenter and various callers.

On arrival, Raymond navigated the curious crowds, parting them with furious blasts of his horn. He parked up next to several police vehicles already in attendance, dancing their pulsating blue lights all around. Outside another rundown block of low-rise apartments, a second SOCO team were battling valiantly to erect yet another blue tent over a body lying next to the battered metal bins that served the building. He trudged to his boot and slipped into his second set of coveralls of the day.

After signing the visitor's log held by a thoroughly waterlogged PC, his biro cutting through the sodden paper and ruining the form, he wandered over to Jenny, Tecoup and his Crime Scene Manager, Brian Lane, already attired in their own coveralls and talking with a couple of uniform beneath the canopy of the entrance to the flats.

The uniform making themselves scarce, Jenny held out something for him to take: a Student Union card wrapped in a clear evidence bag. The card displayed a small photo of a smiling Asian girl.

"Narinda Patel," Raymond read from the card.

"On her way back from a night out with friends, guv," Jenny informed him. "Single cut to the throat."

"Our very own Double Event, huh?" Raymond said grimly.

He remembered reading the Wikipedia page for information on the Jack the Ripper murders of 1888. For a Murder Squad detective, his knowledge of the subject was surprisingly sparse; his rationale always being that there was enough current homicide without fantasising over old cases from years ago that could never be solved. The Ripper—the *real* Jack the Ripper—had killed two women in one night, his reading told him. Frustrated at being disturbed during the first murder of Elizabeth...*Somebody*, by a man with a horse and cart, he had gone and sought out a second victim in

Mitre Street. Had his copycat done the same here, interrupted and forced to flee from one only to seek out the other to continue his maniacal work? But, if that were the case, why wasn't one of them chopped to pieces?

"Why isn't one of them mutilated?" Raymond asked no one in particular.

Tecoup pushed himself off the wall and stepped up to offer a simple theory. "Maybe he was disturbed at both?" he suggested with a shrug.

Before Raymond had a chance to counter the claim, a long roll of thunder rumbled in the distance, the sky flashing weakly with electrical discharge.

Atangba wandered over to join the conversation, glancing up at the grey heavens, his usual grinning face sombre and speckled with glistening rainwater. "Looks like this shit is going to get worse, not better."

He was referring to the weather, but the Welshman thought it an appropriate statement given their current situation. "It will do, unless we hurry up and catch this bastard," he muttered with a chill.

"Boss?" Debbie asked.

"Look around you, Shaw," Raymond instructed, unable to believe she couldn't see it herself without prompting.

Debbie looked over the crime scene. The installed cordon was keeping any further foot traffic from stumbling into their investigation, but from every window, doorway, and balcony, haggard Asian faces, either Bangladeshi or Indian as was the majority demographic of the area, stared, silently watching the enquiry unfold. The police had neither the authority nor resources to dispel curiosity or shoo people away from their own windows. It had been an identical situation at the site of Ginita Nahar's murder.

"Use your head, Shaw. Two dead Asians in a predominantly Asian area. After your own DI beats the living shit out of another one? They're a different culture, with their own beliefs, living in their own tight-knit communities. They don't go around singing the praises of the police at the best of times. If we don't get this bastard soon…" He shot her a condescending look. "Excrement hitting the spinny thing?"

Well and truly schooled, Debbie nodded but said no more. The Welshman huffed at her ignorance and turned to his CSM.

"Go with the bodies, Brian. Get them to pull their finger out, and call me when you get something."

Lane nodded and shot off into the downpour. Raymond watched him go and wandered towards the address given for the victim, peeling away his hood and mask to expose the baffled expression stuck to his fat face.

"He wants to copy Jack the Ripper," he said to himself. "He tears Trisha Noble to pieces, but not these two. Why is that?"

CHAPTER THIRTEEN

"Because this is not the work of your Jack the Ripper copycat," Doctor Susan Turner, the Home Office Forensic pathologist announced with her faded Scottish lilt.

"*Excuse me?*" Raymond choked.

Her clothing cut away and bagged for examination, Narinda Patel lay supine on the stainless-steel examination table between them, her body a naked grey husk mottled purple at its extremities by the settling of what blood remained inside. She had been a pretty girl. A good kid, determined to crawl from the filth of Whitechapel and make something of her life, her distraught mother had extoled proudly when questioned, insisting that she showed Raymond an album packed with photographs of her daughter. A non-smoking teetotaller who didn't dabble in drugs like many of her peers, she had been an excellent student, destined to follow her dream and become a teacher. A victim like his wife, Raymond had considered while the mother shook and sobbed, Narinda had been undeserving of such a brutal end.

Turner lowered her mask and looked hard at Raymond

while he struggled to find some scathing retort. "Detective Superintendent, I haven't even begun the examinations of these two women, but I can tell you just from a cursory look at the knife wound that this is not the same killer. Trisha Noble's throat was cut from left to right, same as the real Jack the Ripper victims in 1888." She pointed to the gruesome wound around Narinda's neck with a gloved finger. "This poor woman's throat was cut from right to left, and I'm willing to wager that it's the same story for Ginita Nahar. Unless your investigation is the victim of extraordinary coincidence with two separate killers striking on the same night."

"That wouldn't surprise me in Whitechapel," Tecoup grumbled through his mask.

Raymond glared at him and struggled to find something to counter Turner's claim with but only succeeded in moving his mouth open and shut. He looked around the room for some sign of support in the masked faces that stared back. Tecoup, Lane, Turner's assistant, the forensic photographer, and the uniformed officer there to confirm the body's identity, all bore the identical look of bewilderment.

He had hoped that Lane managing to work some magic with the coroner and securing two special post mortems pronto, was a sign for a turning of the tide. The fresher the corpse, the more chance of heralding some forensic evidence and catching a break, he always believed. But what Turner now proclaimed only compounded the situation.

The location had changed from Poplar to East Ham given the former's backlog of work; the mortuary a modern contrast from the grim and dark dinginess of Poplar's laboratory. The room was large and airy, the walls spotlessly magnolia under a bright fluorescent glare. There were chairs provided for queasy spectators, positioned sardonically in full view of the drainage channels in the floor for the blood of corpses to flow into. Like Poplar, the air was thick with disinfectant; as useless at disguising the reek of death as it was there.

The Welshman turned up his nose and tried again, clutching at straws moving in a force nine gale. "So…so… he's changed hands?"

Without a word, the pathologist picked up her phone and tossed it to Raymond. He caught it easily. In his right hand.

"I'm thankful your catch is better than your charm, Detective Superintendent." He scowled at the pathologist as she took back her phone and explained. "You did your VapoRub ritual on arrival and have since scratched your nose twice, with your right hand. I know because I watched. Therefore, unless he's ambidextrous or mixed-handed, I would discount your theory. We always favour our preferred hand in any situation. Plus, look at the mutilations."

"But there are no mutilations," Raymond protested.

"Exactly! And that is why I don't believe he did it…your Jack the Ripper copycat. Ach, there's no ferocity here. None of the maniacal, wanton destruction shown to Trisha Noble. He never set out to rip her to pieces. He wanted in and out, as quickly as possible."

Raymond stared at her for a moment, dreading the words that were making their way into his mouth. "Doctor Turner, you're actually telling me I've got a copycat, copycat, aren't you? That's what you're saying, isn't it?"

"Aye, Detective Superintendent, I believe it is."

Volleying between Lane and Tecoup, Raymond clenched the edge of the examination table, his head sinking with despair. When he eventually looked up, his voice was feeble, the desolate and defeated expression he wore behind his mask channelled entirely through his tempered gaze.

"Well, that's just fantastic."

A situation he certainly hadn't envisaged when rising with the hangover from hell earlier in the morning, Dyson sat in the Terracotta Room of 10 Downing Street. He had expected to be well on the way to Tokyo by now, reclined and relaxing while trying to allay Mary's Victorian fear of flying. Instead, the couple were driven at breakneck speeds across London, blue lights flashing, their secret destination only disclosed to be Number 10 as the police car screeched into Whitehall. They were frisked by security and given visitors' passes, instructed that they were to wear them for the duration of their stay and how any deviation from that would be treated as a security breach and dealt with accordingly. Mary was led away by a short, friendly woman with the promise of refreshments; Dyson taken to the impressive splendour of the Terracotta Room and told to wait, his not so welcoming usher informing him that the White Room, Number 10's primary reception area, was currently in use hosting a party of dignitaries from Equatorial Guinea.

He drank his tea, presented in a surprisingly cheap cup and saucer, listening to the rhythmic ticking of the carriage clock that stood on the ornately carved white marble mantlepiece. The walls painted a warming terracotta, giving the room its name; the floor space was bigger than his entire apartment, with ceilings high enough to cause a nosebleed. Decorated with famous artworks on loan from the Government Art Collection, Dyson tried to work out who was who in the gallery of portraits, but had little success.

One hour passed, then another, Dyson pacing the immense Persian rug stretched over the floor and examining the statuettes and ornaments that adorned the various side tables edging the room. He stared from the windows, impressed by the impeccable grounds, until his thoughts grew darker than the clouds above, and he returned to deflate onto one of two green floral sofas that faced each other to reflect on an uncertain future. Before he could dwell too long, a pair of white double doors accented with gold leaf flew open at one end of the room, and the prime minister himself swept in with a hurried pace.

Dyson gulped, his cup and saucer chinking as he lowered them to the coffee table between the sofas and rose. Regarding the premier with suspicion as he took giant strides towards him, he wondered why he'd been brought before him. It wasn't the practice for suspended police officers to be interviewed by government officials—let alone by the prime minister himself.

Opening his mouth to offer a greeting, Dyson extended a hand.

"You've caused me a sleepless night, Acting Detective Chief Inspector," he said curtly, glowering at his digits as if they were infected until his expression relaxed. "And I do so enjoy my sleep."

He grasped Dyson's hand and shook it vigorously, signalling for him to return to the sofa, something somewhere between a scowl and a smile crossing his face.

"I will make this extremely brief. I will talk; you will listen." Vaughn spoke rapidly, sitting opposite and crossing his legs. "I will make a statement in the Commons later today that I have instructed Sir Alistair Furnish to suspend the enquiry against you by the Directorate of Professional Standards officers until such time as this madman in Whitechapel is caught. I will argue that due to your extensive knowledge of the 1888 murders, you are an essential part of this investigation and are to be utilised only in a consultative capacity. You will, however, retain your rank and status. Covertly, you understand. I will dodge the bullets and bile of my detractors while praying to the man upstairs that you can conduct yourself in a manner more fitting said rank and status. I will not divulge the extent of your time-travelling involvement in the case, nor shall I mention your—"

Dyson's eyebrows jumped halfway up his forehead. "You know about—?"

"I talk, *you listen*," Vaughn reiterated, awaiting Dyson's confirmation by way of a single nod. "This is an unprecedented measure, Acting Detective Chief Inspector, and one Sir Alistair strongly advised me against taking, but needs must. Is this an acceptable solution to you?"

"Why...why are you doing this?"

"It is against my better judgement, I can assure you of that. But it would appear you have friends in some very high places."

They shared a knowing look. It was evident that the president had put pressure on Vaughn to offer Dyson some sort of reprieve or stay of execution.

"In addition, I have instructed Sir Alistair to make available to you anything that you might require to bring this case to its swiftest conclusion. The officers who brought you here will take you to meet with him after leaving here." He looked the reinstated detective dead in the eye, his tough veneer cracking for a single moment to reveal something Dyson had never seen on the political hardman's face before. It was fear. Just for a moment it lingered until Vaughn cultivated a smile to push it away.

"Find Jack the Ripper," the prime minister said, adding as an incredulous afterthought under his breath, "Words I never imagined I would have to utter." He stood to smooth the creases from his trousers and present his hand. "Get Garrett his precious blood and end this madness. Do not fail."

"Sir," Dyson replied, a reinvigorated firmness to his grip as they shook their farewell.

And with that, Vaughn turned and was gone, sweeping away as quickly as he'd arrived.

The police car that had ferried Dyson and Mary from Heathrow to Downing Street now drove along Horse Guard's Parade heading for New Scotland Yard. Dyson had insisted on walking the short distance, but the two sour-faced SO18 officers had refused, one of them offering a rare smile and proclaiming that a couple of hours sightseeing in London beat patrolling the airport any day of the week. Strangely silent since meeting Vaughn, Dyson had laughed, more out of kindness than with any merit for the quip.

Mary reached over and took his hand. "Whatever's the matter?" she asked. "You've barely said a word since meeting that man."

Dyson thought for a moment and then tilted his head closer to her. "Do you remember that piano in The Ten Bells?"

A fond smile blossomed on her lips. "Of course I do. I danced a merry jig to it too many times to forget. Why do you ask?"

"Because I think I'm being played like it."

"What does that mean?" Mary whispered.

"It means something's not right here. There's something they're not telling me."

"Who?"

"Garrett…and now Vaughn."

"What could it be?"

"I don't know," Dyson muttered grimly as the BMW swept up against the pavement, the world-famous revolving sign of New Scotland Yard on their right. "But I'm gonna find out. One way or the other."

The refrigerated truck bombed along the M4 motorway with Paul at the wheel, hypnotised by the swishing of the windscreen wipers. It was a tight, uncomfortable squeeze with four of them vying for space. Carrick, being the slimmest, sat squashed up against the passenger door, cursing and spluttering his displeasure while Ringo and his brothers prattled away in excited Cantonese.

Fuck my life, Carrick thought as he struggled to retrieve his phone from the pocket of his trench coat. He dialled —"Oi! Shut the fuck up!"—and listened to the ringing as the cab fell silent. "Evening, Francis," he said into the phone. "Which clever bastard d'you reckon is on his way back from Wales with a truckload of ex-Khan employees and family members?"

He listened to Khan's ecstatic reply, pulling a cigarette from the packet on the dashboard to roll between his fingers.

"Yeah, it's been a *loooong* day, know what I mean? But we've been on the whizz, and the traffic was good." Carrick scoffed indignantly. "Course they're not damaged. Not permanently, at least. Yeah, yeah, I'll bell you when I'm back in the smoke. I bet you can't wait to see 'em." He ended the call. "You sick fuck."

Carrick chuckled and stuck the cigarette between his lips. The day had gone like clockwork. On one of those rare occasions when the UK's traffic system had worked exactly how it was supposed to, it had transported them from one end of the country to the other without a single hitch. There was zero police involvement, and the one witness who had stumbled across them carrying their targets from their home in Nottinghamshire had been knocked into next week by George's fists, Carrick doubting whether the poor old sod would even remember his name once he woke up…if he ever did wake up. Steven Calder had proved *troublesome*, the black bitch with him even more so, but the Chinese Beatles gave them both a good spanking and they soon behaved.

Before Carrick could light up, his phone rang again. He looked at the screen and saw it was Chang. "It's Weedy Wong," he said, looking across to Ringo as he answered. "What you got for me?"

The *Gauloises* ignited to flood the cab with a thick plume of smoke, George growled and muttered something derogatory in Chinese.

"About Ackerman?" Carrick made a series of growing nods. "Good work, Charlie Chan. We're on our way back, be about a couple of hours yet, know what I mean?" He beamed, ecstatic that everything was coming together. "Just make sure you put the kettle on."

Hunched over, his chin bristling with stubble, Raymond pinned a couple of high-definition photographs of the bodies of Ginita Nahar and Narinda Patel to a whiteboard containing a sparsely detailed timeline of their murders.

His day had been long, most of it taken up by the victims' special post mortems, while his team spent their hours canvassing the local area for witnesses. Their search had found no one. Not one witness had any light to shed on the murders of Ginita or Narinder. The news had sent Raymond into a furious rage, his mood already ruined by Turner's proclamation that not only did they have a right-handed Jack the Ripper copycat at work, but *he* had a left-handed fan himself.

Raymond let the shock expletives in the incident room drain away before continuing. "So, there we are. I hope you all have understanding wives and partners because we're round the clock from now on. Twenty-four hours a day, seven days a week. We don't sleep until we have this bastard in custody!"

Pulling free from the oozing slouch he'd fallen into, Henderson shot him a scowl. "My wife wants me to transfer out," he said. "As soon as possible."

Raymond returned him a contemptuous stare. "When the going gets tough…"

Henderson made a brazen show of looking over the dwindling detectives. They weren't what anyone would call a formidable team. "There's nine of us left, guv! That's it. Nine. Jerry, Paul, Jim and Gary. They're all gone. And…and so is Dyson too. *They are all gone.* I can't keep burying my friends like this. We're getting bugger all back-up from the Yard, in the way of resources or manpower. My wife's scared, guv. She wants me out of here, she doesn't want our boy growing up without his dad."

"You need to stay focused, Henderson," Raymond bit angrily. "And we need to shut this bastard down—these bastards now if Turner's right. ASAP! The press are pissing in their pants over this. They're flying in from all over the world to cover it!"

Saunders confirmed the claim with a fatigued nod. "I saw some Italian broadcast rig setting up this morning."

"That's nothing," Detective Constable Leon Price responded as if it was becoming a competition. "I saw a Japanese news crew yesterday!"

The media could be a powerful ally during a major investigation. Their coverage could provide a formidable conduit between police and public, generating valuable information that could lead to an arrest. But they could be a dangerous enemy, too, often misrepresenting the facts, either intentionally or not, to make the story more appealing to their audiences, and so hindering an enquiry rather than helping it.

They also had the tendency to turn on an investigation like a pack of wild dogs if it failed to produce the expected results and call for change. Raymond had already faced the wrath of the tabloids following his disastrous press conference.

Raymond thought about his glorious career going down in flames with a shudder and then moved on. "I've got us a slot on Sky's *Crimenight* regarding Trisha Noble's murder. Apparently, they'll be here later this week to film their reconstruction."

Crimenight had grown to take the place of the long since defunct *Crimewatch*, a BBC show that had highlighted serious crimes and brought them to the public arena. Heavily frowned upon by many police departments, *Crimenight* was considered glitzier and geared more for entertainment and titillation, with its 'Crime Doesn't Pay' segment, in which hapless criminals failed spectacularly on captured CCTV, and its 'Hot Cop of the Week' portion. The Welshman hated it, much preferring the good old days of *Crimewatch*. It had portrayed the crimes with the seriousness they deserved, and he had always found Kirsty Young the consummate professional...and somewhat alluring with her sultry Scottish brogue. But despite his aversion to the format, *Crimenight* had aided the police departments of the UK immeasurably over the years. Only the previous month, its appeal into the dreadful murder of two small children in Sheffield had uncovered a key witness who proved instrumental in wrapping up a five-month enquiry by the South Yorkshire Police Department. The year before that, in an extended special spanning two nights, it documented how a random tip-off to the show's website had finally led to the solving of the much-publicised disappearance of Richard John Bingham, aka Lord Lucan, the murderous aristocrat who had vanished in 1974 to become part of British folklore.

"Right," Raymond continued, finger combing his thinning hair into order. "Somebody give me some news. Some *good* news! Where are we with hospitals and surgeries?"

Tecoup shook his head, his deep Glaswegian tired and empty. "Not a damn thing, guv. No one's seen bugger all. We're still at it, but it's not looking good."

"Unbelievable. I want that list of possibles we got from HOLMES gone back over again. We've missed something somewhere, I can feel it."

Jenny groaned and caught Raymond's eye. "Sir, with respect, Barry's right. This is insane. We're stretched to the limit here. We just haven't got the bodies for this."

"We do now!" a voice called out from the swinging doors of the incident room.

The entire room turned to see Dyson stride in, a line of eleven men and women following in hot pursuit. All neatly attired, there was a fresh spring to their step and an air of relaxed composure radiating from them; the polar opposite of the crumpled suited, exhausted despondency of Raymond's overworked team.

"*John!*" Jenny cried out, scrambling out of her seat until she caught the Welshman's disgusted glare and froze in place.

Dutifully reserved, the remaining detectives hovered awkwardly, clutching their armrests, in two minds whether to approach Dyson or not. Most settled on a discreet and welcoming nod for their superior.

"Well, well, well," the Welshman growled, his jaw tightening as he fought to contain his growing rage. "The Commissioner's office told me you'd be back. I have to say, I thought it was a sick joke. Yesterday you were a pariah, the most reviled man in the Met. Yet today, what are you…the Pied Piper of Scotland Yard?"

Dyson ignored the dig to approach Raymond, gesturing to the detectives who were beginning to mingle and introduce themselves. "Twenty bodies, sir. Fresh meat, just what we need."

"Really? I count eleven."

"The rest are on their way. Furnish drafted them in from various branches and surrounding—"

Raymond stormed off without giving Dyson the chance to elaborate, tearing his phone from his pocket as it began to ring. He crashed through the double doors, only slowing when safely out of earshot. He took a moment to stew, stomping the corridor before answering.

"What is it, Pat?" The flickering of a begrudging smirk struggled to take hold while he listened to Carrick. "The Blind Beggar, twenty minutes. I need a fucking pint!"

Killing the smile, Raymond finished the call and turned to find Sinclair hovering behind him, the look of disgust he wore mirroring his own perfectly.

"We just got told to drop the charge against Dyson," Sinclair uttered. "It came direct from the Yard." He looked hard at Raymond, fast approaching boiling point. "Something stinks in Whitechapel, guv. And it isn't just those fucking curry houses!"

———

"Dyson's clean," Carrick declared from behind his pint. "Financially, at least."

Raymond's face slackened at the news. Not the result he had wanted to hear, but given Supercop's bullet-dodging abilities, it came as little surprise. He toyed with a beermat and huffed a sickened look over the pub.

The Blind Beggar was quiet compared to their last visit, and the Welshman began to wonder if people were purposefully avoiding the area in case they fell victim to the upsurge in violence. They sat at the bar this time, the table they occupied before taken by a group of rowdy builders, immune to Carrick's threatening stare.

"Are you sure?"

"My boy did a deep dive into his finances." He pulled a thick ream of paper from the pocket of his suit jacket and slapped it on the countertop. "Bank statements, going all the way back. Dyson's got 673 grand in the bank, split between a current account and a high-interest savings account. Fucker probably don't even need to work!"

He said that last part with spite, like a man without a pot to piss in. He took a moment to sup his pint while Raymond gave the bank statements a quick once over.

"There's no suspicious activity within the accounts. Salary goes in, bills come out. The dosh came from his old girl after she shuffled off in 2020, one of the first-ever Covid stiffs in London. As far as I can tell, the money originated from property investments Dyson Senior made years ago. You know: buy cheap, sell high? If the money was bent, it's not due to anything your Dyson did."

Raymond grumbled and tossed down the paperwork. Along with it went any thought of Dyson; it would only irritate him to dwell on. Instead, he turned to Ackerman, the supposed FBI agent. "What about the other matter?"

"Oh, his name's Brad Ratski," Carrick announced casually.

"Okay." The pint glass hovered at Raymond's lips. "And…?"

"And nothing, Bill. That's it. He's like God or Muhammed, know what I mean? He don't exist. He's a fuckin' spook. My boy has checked *everything*. Everywhere. Apart from…"

He took a folded sheet from inside his suit jacket and flattened it out on the tacky surface. A printed email between

President Garrett and the head of White House security, it authorised executive-level clearance to one Brad Ratski.

The barmaid who had pulled him up before for daring to hold his unlit cigarette approached and tried to take a surreptitious look at the email. "What's that?"

Carrick leant forwards over the bar and beamed. "None of your fuckin' business; that's what that is." As she kissed her teeth and sauntered away to serve, he returned to Raymond. "Issued in 2029, shortly after Garrett won the presidency. My boy hacked the White House—the shit I could tell you about Elvis and Area 51!"

"Get on with it, Pat."

"Other than this, there's no record of a Brad Ratski anywhere in the US. No birth certificate, driver's license, no school records, no medical history, no…what do they call it, social security number? Nothin' with the IRS. *Nothin' with anyone.* There are ninety-six Ratskis in the land of the free. None of 'em our Bradley. But this guy is issued a top-level security pass to the White House. Access all areas. He can take a dump in Garrett's personal shitter if he—"

"Then how…" Raymond interrupted, thinking carefully about his question. "Then how does a man with no birth certificate obtain a passport to enter the country?"

That brought a shrug from Carrick. "He hasn't got a passport. Not that my boy could find."

"Same question: how does a man with no passport enter the UK?"

"Maybe he came in as diplomatic baggage?" Carrick joked, although it didn't seem that outlandish a suggestion given the circumstances. He unfolded another sheet of paper and laid it on top of the first.

It was a colour photograph showing a promotional shot of the presidential entourage standing on the South Lawn of the White House. Ratski was there, at the president's side. Stern-faced in a sea of smiles.

"Every one of these wankers is identifiable. They all have history and leave a paper trail. Garrett, Secretary of Defence, Secretary of State, yada, yada, yada… This aide…" Carrick started to stab at various faces within the photo. "This weedy looking fucker got himself a DUI charge when he was eighteen. This one here had an abortion when she was fifteen—this one witnessed her own mother's murder when she was a sprog! I can tell you any fuckin' thing about anyone in this picture. All except this bastard."

His bony finger plunged down on Ratski's face.

"Well…well…" Raymond fished, "what if he's Canadian?"

"What, and gets an access all areas job with the US government? Come on, old man, you can do better than that. He ain't Canadian, Bill. My boy checked."

The Welshman took a hefty swig on his pint. "And no one questions this? That a guy with no passport or past is strolling around with the most powerful man in the world?"

"On the contrary, my friend. You dig around enough on the internet, you can find shit. There was a Reddit thread of over 300 posts devoted to discoverin' his identity when the photo was released. Serial masturbators in their mummy's basements mostly, 'Who is this mysterious man?' kind of shit."

"Was?"

"Yeah, someone shut it down quicker than you can say conspiracy theory, know what I mean? But not before someone screen grabbed the original post. That's—"

"How your boy found it." Raymond nodded along, drawing a small circle slowly in the air. "And this all brings us back nicely to Dyson. He's implicated somehow. And he's in deep enough to have someone save his arse from the DPS."

"He's beat the charges?"

"The DPS have been told to drop it." Raymond banged his fist on the counter and made the pints jump. "I spoke with a friend at the Yard. Furnish dragged him over the coals for using Khan as a punchbag—you could hear him screaming from the canteen, by all accounts." Carrick cringed at the thought while Raymond surged on venomously. "Then he proceeds to offer the bastard what equates to a blank cheque to wrap up this Ripper enquiry. Naturally, he asked for the bodies that I was denied by my DCS….and he got them! I know a few of them—they're good coppers. But that's not the point. There was other stuff too, I don't know what."

Carrick shrugged and savoured his pint while he thought. "Well, you know what they say, mate. If you're losing ten-nil at half-time, you might as well forget it and fuck off down the pub. Know what I mean?"

Raymond scoffed at the notion. He wasn't the kind to accept defeat quite so easily.

CHAPTER FOURTEEN

With the golden sheen of streetlamps providing the only light, Ratski sat hunched over the desk of his shabby rented office, the door closed to allow him some privacy from the agents outside. He poured over his phone, lost in the image of the vivacious blonde staring out at him, as stunningly beautiful as he remembered her, despite her coating of grime and muck.

"God, I miss you so much," he croaked.

The image vanished—the woman taken from him as she had been in real life—replaced by an animated handset and the words DYSON CALLING and accompanied by Petula Clark's *Downtown.* Ratski sighed and swiped his thumb across the screen.

"Detective Dyson, what a pleasure to have you back," he said mockingly. "How was your vacation to Heathrow?"

Dyson fought the urge to tell the ball-breaker to fuck off and parted the blinds of his glass-walled office to ensure the main CID area was still as empty as when he entered.

"What happened to the Ripper's knife, Ratski? Tell me you didn't do anything stupid like give it to Bernstein and Simmons before he escaped?" The detective listened while Ratski told him that wasn't the case. "Good. No, just keep it safe." There was another pause while Ratski asked what he was doing, Dyson pulling a face like it was so obvious. "I'm doing what you wanted me to do. My job."

Dyson tossed his phone down on the desk and left the office, moving with an invigorated hustle along the corridor. He ploughed through the double doors into Raymond's incident room and skidded up next to Jenny stood at a filing cabinet, sifting through a stack of dusty files.

"Jen, check with uniform to see if there were any break-ins or burglaries, incidents of shoplifting, something like that. Post-Harford, but before Trisha Noble was killed, where a knife was stolen. Seven to eight inches, very sharp.

"And why am I doing this?" she asked.

He moved a couple of inches closer to lower his voice. "Ratski still has the Ripper's knife, but he's got hold of one from somewhere. If we...can..." He dried up and tilted his head to one side, listening.

"What is it?" Jenny whispered.

Her question was answered by the deafening whirling thump that exploded overhead, shaking the windows of the incident room. Detectives spat coffee and obscenities, dashing over to peer up at the darkened sky. Dyson and Jenny followed, craning their necks as the familiar blue and yellow tail boom of a police helicopter slipped above them.

"I think it's going to land!" Jenny yelled above the racket.

"I know," Dyson responded with a knowing smile.

The downwash of the rotor blades was so powerful. It forced Dyson into an undignified scuttle as he struggled through a ferocious storm of rain and roof chippings towards the monster, his suit jack fighting, desperate to climb over his head and fly away. There was no time to stop and admire the sleek, sweeping beast with its striking blue and yellow paint job—it was hard enough just to keep his balance the closer he got.

The huge yellow 'H' painted on the reinforced flat roof was faded and peeling due to age and lack of use. At enormous expense, Whitechapel police station had been constructed with a helicopter pad, the original intention to post permanent aerial support in the capital to counteract the spiralling crime rate from a closer location than it took the National Police Air Service (NPAS) to reach from their airbases in North Weald in Essex or Redhill in Surrey. But as the country's finances took a steep nosedive, the idea was scrapped, much to the relief of the local community who had vociferously protested the plans.

Dyson pulled open the door and climbed into the rear seat on the left side of the helicopter. As he slammed it shut, the noise dissipated to no more than a comfortable rumbling, the detective pleasantly surprised by the quietness of the interior. Things had obviously changed a lot in helicopter design since he took one along the Grand Canyon a few years back.

As the company bumph proudly boasted, the Airbus EC150d was the quietest, most fuel-efficient, and environmentally friendly helicopter available on the open market. Twin-engined, with a cruising speed of over 180 miles per hour—159 knots if you preferred the aviation equivalent—and a ceiling of 18,000 feet, the NPAS operated four of them around London. Each crewed by three civilians, they were call signed India 96 through to India 99.

The man in the blue jumpsuit and white helmet he

scooted up next to detected his amazement and said in a voice only slightly raised against normal conversation: "Best soundproofed chopper in the world. Well, on the inside anyway. Nevertheless…"

He extended a finger and motioned to a headset hanging above Dyson. The detective slipped on the cans and positioned the mic, any remaining noise completely disappearing.

"Acting Detective Chief Inspector John Dyson?" His voice delivered with crystal clarity, his neighbour grinned and thrust out a gloved hand.

"That's a mouthful," Dyson said as they shook hands like old friends. "John will do."

"Tactical Flight Officer Two. Tony Peretti—*Tony!* Welcome aboard India 98."

Dyson couldn't make out much of the man behind the bulbous helmet and the *Top Gun* sunglasses he wore, but he seemed pleasant enough, his cheeks rosy and sprinkled with freckles.

"Aside from radio protocol, we've no airs and graces in this baby, John. The fat bastard in the driving seat is Richie Markam. Ex-RAF, so obviously his shit don't stink. We call him Duck because he'll fly you in and out of a space that's as tight as a duck's arse."

Duck laughed. He didn't turn but raised a hand as a sign of welcome, a Glaswegian accent that would give Tecoup's a run for its money assaulting his ears. "Ach, dinnae mind that wee fucker. Hi, John."

Dyson returned the greeting, noticing that he really was exceptionally large, the zip of his jumpsuit broken and split open around the waist.

"And next to him," the tactical flight officer continued, "is Crispin Allerton, or TFO One. He's Duck's co-pilot in case his heart gives up from all the shit he eats. He runs the cameras and searchlight—I run avionics, navigation, and comms. Crispin's a bit of a stuck-up twat, daddy's an MP or something, but he's alright in small doses."

They swapped hellos, the TFO ahead of him sounding just as his colleague had described him as he corrected Peretti: his father was a councillor. The detective couldn't see much of him from his position, apart from a few sprigs of ginger hair that poked out from the base of his helmet.

While the men continued to bicker playfully, Dyson darted over the interior of the helicopter. Duck and TFO One sat before a state-of-the-art flight console adorned with multicoloured screens and a headache-inducing array of buttons, dials, knobs, and switches laid out like a banquet. A heads-up display projected an abundance of data onto the curved windscreen, instantly stumping the detective and making him appreciate Mary's nervousness at the sight of the airliner at Heathrow. Allerton held what appeared to be a wireless games controller. It was what he would use when airborne to control the fifty-million candlepower Nightsun searchlight and thermal imaging cameras.

"So, what's the story, John?" Peretti asked in his headphones. "Is this anything to do with that wacko chopping up women we've been hearing so much about? Our instructions were vague to say the least, but our skipper claims we're on a temporary detachment to Hotel Tango?"

Dyson nodded along as he spoke. "I requested a helicopter to be stationed here until we catch—"

"They *gave* you a helicopter!" Peretti exclaimed. "Just like that?"

"*Jus' like that!*" the pilot repeated, trying his best to sound like a Scottish Tommy Cooper.

"Pretty much."

"Well, shit. They must be desperate to catch this guy."

"Yeah, you could say that," Dyson muttered as casually as

he could.

"And what would be our role, John?" Allerton asked.

"If we get a sighting, we can have you up in minutes. Now we've lost our surveillance room—"

"Aye, heard about that," Duck interrupted grimly.

"—you'll be our eyes. Worst case scenario, we can get you up at night to have a fly around and see who's about."

"And when we're not needed?"

"I can always find you something to do," Dyson said with a devilish smirk.

All three seemed to like the idea of that, Duck even trying on a rank for size. "Detective Inspector Markham. Aye, I like that."

"*You're nicked, my old son!*" Peretti played along, making a gun with his fingers and jabbing them in the back of Duck's neck.

"Don't get too excited. It'd just be manning phones and making tea."

"John, we spend every working day stuck in this ten-million-pound tin can," Allerton lamented, finally turning in his seat. He looked much younger than he sounded, his face pale and thin with a nose that looked like it had been broken in a rugby scrum. "We look down at the viciousness that people do to each other every day. Up here, it's not real, it's like a video game, and we're isolated and immunised from it in our own little bubble. But it would be an absolute blast for us to get our feet on the ground for once, so to speak."

Peretti chuckled along and reached forwards to squeeze Allerton's cheek. "Bless him. He's like our own little onboard Aristotle." The tactical flight officer turned back to Dyson. "Buckle up then, guv. We'll be serving refreshments once we reach our cruising altitude." He gave the back of Duck's seat a hard kick. "Take us up then, fat boy."

The pilot nodded. A final pre-flight check of his instruments, and he toggled his mic and spoke. "Heathrow Control from India 98, seeking permission to leave MPD Whitechapel, over."

Permission granted, Duck pulled on the collective. The engine tone increased to a gentle hum as India 98 lifted with a slight jolt. The helicopter shuddered and rattled in the wind, rain snaking across the glass. Whitechapel began to shrink as they climbed into the night. Starting to whistle, Duck feathered the cyclic, and the helicopter banked right and sped along the A11, heading east.

"WHO THE HELL DOES HE THINK HE IS!"

His pudgy face turning as red as the blood on the crime scene photos hung up in the incident room, Raymond slammed his fist down on the nearest desk and immediately regretted it. His heated question found no answer, the detectives peeling themselves away from the windows to resume their allotted tasks in silence. He knew exactly who John fucking Dyson was!

Arriving back from meeting Carrick in the nick of time to see the helicopter shoot skywards, the Welshman had detonated with the force of one of the previous day's car bombs. It was Dyson—of course, it was Dyson—with another of the gifts bestowed on him by the Commissioner.

Raymond stalked the carpet and attempted to walk off his rage before his heart gave out, but he caught Debbie and Mohammad exchange a contemptuous eye roll, and another wave of blistering anger swept over him. Breath chugging like a train through gritted enamel, he clawed someone's personal radio off the window sill.

"...bloody well show him," he grumbled, fiddling with the knobs for India 98's frequency, intent on calling Dyson back. Only then did he realise the radio was dead, the battery like him, drained and exhausted. He launched it across the incident room with all the energy he could muster to shatter it into multiple pieces on the floor.

"Um, Detective Superintendent Raymond?" a timid voice asked.

Raymond spun, his trench coat twirling. A uniformed policewoman stood in the doorway, staring at him with eyes like saucers. Clearly a probationer, she looked horrified by his aggressive display.

"What!"

"There's, erm…there's someone to see you downstairs, sir," she stumbled. "She says she's your wife."

Lost and alone, Maggie Raymond paced the small front office she'd been put in while she waited. Oblivious to the posters warning about drink driving and phone theft, tears bit at her hollow cheeks as she picked at the frayed edge of her coat, unravelling the thread for it to dangle and sway.

"Maggie!" Raymond rushed in and collided with her, his wife sucking him into her arms to cling to as if drowning.

"Oh, Bill."

"What on earth…?" His voice muffled by the shoulder he was forced against, Maggie's sobbing increased as he tried desperately to escape, but it was like fighting intense magnetism. Finally, he succeeded in breaking free, horrified by her hysterical, twisted countenance and the reasons behind it. He gripped her hands in his, her pain instant and contagious. "What is it, my love? Is…is it Sue?"

"It's…it's Karen. She hasn't come home. She's missing, Bill! She hasn't…hasn't come home from school. I've been so worried."

His eyes crashed shut, the throbbing aching in his hand forgotten in a heartbeat.

Karen had died of *leukaemia* in 2016. But Maggie's Alzheimer's, as devious as it was destructive, had convinced her that she was still alive: a precocious child into pop music, preparing for her mock GCSEs, and just discovering the finer qualities of boys. It was unbearable enough to suffer the anguish of losing a child, but to not remember that pain and lose them again and again was another level of cruelty entirely. It wasn't the first time Maggie had suffered such trauma, and Raymond knew it wouldn't be the last. Her condition was deteriorating, Sue warned when he'd last spoken to her. Maggie was beginning to wander away from home, escaping like a fugitive to prowl the streets with no understanding as to why. Only a couple of days ago, Raymond had found her tending the grave of the daughter she now believed to still be alive. The brutality of that fucking disease knew no bounds.

When Raymond spoke, his voice quivered on the verge of collapse. "Karen…Karen isn't with us anymore, Mags. She's with the angels, so she is. I'm so…I'm so sorry, my love."

"No! No, no, no. Why would you say such a thing? Why would you lie to me like that? She went to school this morning—*I saw her!* Don't you say that. Don't you ever say that!"

Raymond turned away, only to round on her spitefully. The pressure of juggling such a high-profile investigation and caring for a sick wife too much to bear, his face darkened as he exploded with venomous rage.

"She's dead, Maggie! She's fucking dead, you stupid woman! You can't keep doing this. Not now! I can't…I can't handle this as well. I am hanging by a thread here!" Raymond scrubbed at his face, banishing the tears before they came. "And…and you shouldn't be in Whitechapel. Don't you understand? It's dangerous!"

It suddenly turned very hot in the little office, Raymond's heart beating a heavy accompaniment to the growing embarrassment and loathing he felt for his outburst. In all their years together, he had never spoken to her with such viciousness. He watched her as she weakened, sinking into a chair next to the table. She stared down at the tiled floor, sniffing and snorting until her empty gaze returned to him.

"What's wrong with me?" Maggie cried.

The Welshman dropped to his knees like a subject before his queen. "You're ill, Mags." He squeezed her hands tightly, desperate to find some glimmer of positivity among the terminal despair. "Once I get this Ripper bastard, I'll retire," he swore solemnly, his lips curling with sadness. "I promise you, my love. The Job's not what it was—it's finished. And… and if it's a choice between looking after you or looking at the dregs of humanity across an interview room, *I choose you.* We…we can take that cruise, like we spoke about?"

"I'm scared, Bill." A wayward hair slipped across her face, Raymond reaching out to reposition it with the most loving of touches. His hand remained in place to cup her cheek.

"*Ssshhh…* It's going to be alright, my love. I'll have a car run you home and let Sue know you're safe. Okay? Just promise me you won't go wandering off again. Promise me. Please?"

Maggie said nothing as she started to sob again.

"We'll have to call it a day soon," Duck said, cocking his head back in Dyson's direction. "We've gotta get back to base."

"I thought you were staying?"

"Aye, we are." Duck patted his instrument panel respectfully. "But this big bastard doesnae fit too well in the local BP or Texaco."

"And you certainly wouldn't want to put unleaded in it," Allerton laughed. "Why don't you join us and sample the heady heights of North Weald? We have an exceptionally well-stocked vending machine in our mess room if you're feeling peckish."

Dyson shook his head politely. "You'd better drop me off; the Prince of Darkness will be going mental. You're coming back later, right?"

"Did you hear what Aristotle here said, guv?" Duck thudded a playful fist into Allerton's arm. "We're not likely to miss the hunt for wee Jackie boy, are we?

There was a calm serenity to Whitechapel when viewed from the air. From the helicopter's thousand feet altitude, the troubles on the ground seemed more than a million miles away. It appeared so peaceful, with only the soft thrum of India 98's rotors providing a gentle, soothing heartbeat. Golden arteries of street lighting stretched as far as the eye could see, the slow-moving headlights and brake lights of vehicles their flowing lifeblood.

After two and a half hours, nothing had been found. Dyson hadn't expected to strike gold on the first night, but that didn't ease his disappointment. Allerton would stiffen now and then, hopes rising as he blasted the streets with his searchlight, zooming in on the various cameras at his disposal only to reveal some innocent individual scurrying through the deluge.

The crew made small talk and joked while they flew, the detective too preoccupied with other considerations to fully immerse himself in their banter. His mind flip-flopped and bounced from the prime minister's involvement and his ominous goodbye of 'Do not fail' to thoughts of the Ripper and the lies and broken rules since his escape. He thought of those who had died; friends and colleagues and the blameless victims of the killer he brought back. He thought of the incoming shitstorm from Raymond when he found out about India 98 and his unauthorised flight. The Welshman had reacted like a grounded teenager when Dyson had returned to a hero's welcome, leading his new band of detectives to join the fight. He doubted whether the reaction would be any better when he learnt that the Met's Commissioner had effectively *given* him a helicopter. But mostly, Dyson thought of Mary: lifesaver and lover, and the one true positive in the whole sorry mess.

It was Allerton that broke him from his mental ping-pong, raising his hand above his helmet and pointing to the left. "John, what's that down there?" his voice said in the headset he wore.

Dyson peered through the rain while the searchlight beam washed over rooftops, following the light as it settled on a four-storied cube of redbrick dilapidation shrouded in scaffolding. It stood on the apex where Durward Street met Winthrop Street, the Whitechapel Sports Centre and tube station its closest neighbours.

"It's a Victorian schoolhouse. They turned it into apartments in the late 90s, but a fire gutted the place a few years back." He explained how the flat roof had been the school's playground; space considered a valuable commodity in Victorian London. "Why, what have you got?"

Allerton motioned to one of the screens in front of him. "Movement inside," he said slowly. "Hasn't been there until now."

Pulling himself forwards on TFO One's seat, the detective peered at the screen ahead of him. It was hard to read the image at first, the building appearing as a transparent grey block with the boarded-up windows a total black. But the

FLIR thermal imaging camera the NPAS employed was an impressive piece of kit, peering right through the walls of the building and presenting it in all its three-dimensional glory. As Duck swung the helicopter nearer, Allerton zoomed the camera in. Dyson began to understand the image as it cleared, noticing something moving within. Something on the second floor. Something red and orange.

The heat signature of a human.

"Someone's down there!" Dyson gasped.

Next to him, Peretti worked at the small desk he sat at, tapping away at the keyboard to transfer Allerton's feed onto his own screen and give Dyson a more comfortable view. He expanded it with his fingers and made a thoughtful stroke of his chin. "Looks like a bloke to me."

Dyson confirmed TFO Two's suspicions with a nod. He noticed something else and pointed. "What's that there? On the ground floor?"

Peretti swiped the image around the screen until it settled on another shape. In the near centre of the building at street level, something grew and shrank, changing shape and dancing amongst the greyness, constantly fluctuating from orange to red to white.

"Is that a fire?" Dyson asked.

"Looks that way to me, aye," Duck said, his eyes flickering from sky to screen. "Classic heat signature. Looks like someone's set up camp down there."

The detective thought for a moment. "Can you put me on the roof?" he asked, already feeling for his Glock.

"You wanna go down there?"

"I'm not much use up here, am I?"

"I cannae land, John," Duck explained. It was dangerous, especially if the building had been ravaged by fire. Regardless of the Victorian's phenomenal engineering abilities, he doubted whether they had designed the roof with a tonne and half of helicopter in mind. "I can hover, give you a couple of feet?"

"Fine. I need a torch and a radio."

"Miles ahead of you." Peretti grinned, slapping a Maglite and personal radio into Dyson's hand. "Radio's good to go. You'll come straight through to us."

India 98 descended and moved into position, hovering over one edge of the roof. Rain and debris whipped up in the maelstrom danced and shone in the headlights, tinkering softly against its bodywork.

"We'll get back up on standby and hang around as long as we can," the pilot said in the headphones as Dyson pulled them off and threw open the door.

Duck had certainly earned his nickname, Dyson considered as he stepped out, the helicopter hovering less than six inches off the roof. The force of the thudding blades overhead slammed him into the rough surface. He screwed shut his eyes from the vicious flurry and waited for India 98 to pull away. As it did, he pulled his Glock from its holster and switched on the torch, drawing a white line over the roof. Settling his breath, Dyson scurried over to a turreted brick building that housed the internal staircase.

"Dyson from India 98 for a radio test, over," a voice crackled.

"Strength's good, R-5. Situation?"

"He's stopped, probably the noise. Still on the second floor, over."

"All received. Maintain radio silence. Dyson out."

He threw a thumbs up at the beast and tried the door. Of course, it was locked. He could channel his bodyweight through his shoulder and launch himself repeatedly at the door until it gave way...or he could take the easy option and use the thundering of the helicopter to his advantage. He aimed his gun at the lock and fired, the silent gunshot blowing a neat hole through the mechanism. The door scraped over a blanket of burnt embers but opened without too much protest. Dyson moved inside and started gradually down the stairs, broken glass cracking underfoot. Hands linked, he held the gun and flashlight as one, traversing them left and right, up and down. The stairs creaked under his weight, adrenaline surging through his body as he descended, while his heartbeat rose to clatter in unison with the thumping of India 98.

Down and down he went, cautiously, past blackened walls and scorched paintwork. Reaching the third floor, he found what had been a communal hallway linking the apartments, a gaping hole in the wall exposing the remnants of lives too damaged to salvage: the rusted springs of a sofa, the shell of a microwave oven. He offered the light around briefly and carried on with his descent.

Entirely devoured by the inferno, the second floor was littered with cinders that crunched like fresh snow. Dyson swung the torch into the floor's hallway and entered what remained. The skeletal framework of smashed partition walls created a maze littered with debris, causing shadows to dance wildly.

Dyson edged towards the remains of a door, pushing what was left of it open with his shoe. The torch brightened on what was once a spacious living room and kitchen. Empty now, the furniture reduced to charcoal and springs, a rusted sink hung in mid-air supported by two copper pipes and a dozen cracked tiles where a wall had once been. Several other doors led off to more shattered rooms, all of which would need to be searched.

With a glum nod, Dyson entered the room and immediately screamed.

CHAPTER FIFTEEN

"Dyson from—98. Repeat, Dyson—India 98. *Come—, John.*"

A hand reached out, guided only by the screen light of his Apple Watch shining out from inside his sleeve. Grubby fingers clamped around the radio and thumbed the talk button.

"India 98 from Dyson, receiving," the detective groaned, pulling himself into a sit. "Don't tell me you heard me scream from up there?"

"Negative. We saw you drop on—screen. The floor—way, right, over?"

Dyson winced while he deciphered the message. Its screen cracked and broken, the damaged radio hissed madly, the words that did come through heavily distorted. He assumed the voice was Peretti's as he was the communications officer but couldn't be sure.

"I don't think there was a floor…not where I was standing," Dyson said into the radio, picking himself up to sway on an invisible wind. He staggered and felt his ribs with a painful "Fuck!" The light from his watch dying, Dyson pulled up his sleeve to jiggle his wrist until it came back on.

"Dyson—India 98, —are—injured? Anything damaged, over?"

"Only my pride," he muttered to himself, rattling the dead torch and clicking the radio's talk button. "Yeah, your torch. And the radio's going mental. Where am I? What floor?"

"You're on the—floor, over."

"India 98, repeat message. I didn't get that."

"Say again, you're on the first—"

Dyson pieced together the information: he was on the first floor. A fact confirmed by the burnt hole in the ceiling high above, just visible in the radiance of his watch before it faded again. He scrolled through the watch's menu and found the flashlight function. The screen lit up, the glow nominal but better than nothing. Discarding the broken torch, Dyson moved his arm around to cast the light over the floor, searching for his Glock.

"—from India 98. He's—your way. Repeat, heading—way, over."

The sentence came together to hit him like a brick. "He's heading my way!"

Dyson dropped to his knees and painted the watch all around, the quest to reunite with his Glock driven by a desperate urgency. He ran an outstretched hand over the rough surface of the floor to find it littered with glass and other things that stabbed and poked…but there was no gun.

There was no gun!

Radio protocol abandoned, Peretti cried out. "Fucking move! He's—straight—you! Approaching from—north—!"

"Shit!" Dyson turned back and forth on his knees. North? Or was that northeast? Northwest? And which way was it? He sucked in a breath and held it, listening to the heavy footfall crunching towards him. Each step more desperate than the last, the acoustics of the ruined building made it impossible to determine from which direction the approach came.

"Get—fuck out—there, Dyson!"

The detective ploughed through debris frantically until the familiar polymer grip of his Glock brushed against the back of his hand.

"—right on you! Dyson!"

As the unseen figure drew closer, the direction of his advance becoming vaguely apparent, Dyson snatched up his gun, but it didn't move. Not more than six inches. Something was holding his arm in place. The watch screen highlighted a length of burnt electrical cable wrapped around his forearm.

Black amongst black, nothing more than an obvious looming presence, the figure stopped on a crunch of embers. Dyson passed the gun to his free hand and brought it to bear, but that only shone the light away from whoever had arrived.

And then he spoke: a ghostly voice surging from the darkness. "Who are you?" the unseen figure bellowed, his voice accented by a heavy Eastern European inflexion.

Dyson blasted out the held breath and deflated. Unless the Ripper had taken a crash course in English since his arrival in 2030, it wasn't him. He finished unravelling the cable from his arm and stood to shine his watch forwards, illuminating a crooked, old man who appeared far less imposing in light than he did hidden in the dark. Dressed in the scruffy costume of the streets, he emitted a thoroughly unpleasant fragrance of body odour and rotting fish, a set of big yellow teeth shining through a faceful of thick, bushy beard.

"Who the hell are you?" Dyson snapped, his nose wrinkling at the stench.

"I ask first," the vagrant said again. "Who are you?"

"I'm the bloody police!" Dyson grabbed up the radio as the figure scuffed and pawed at the floor. "India 98, false alarm. It's not him."

"I am live here," the old man announced proudly before launching into jumbled tirade of pigeon English. "My name Aleksander Kowalski. This where I live—this my home. My home, not yours. You trespass. That will not please my friend. Oh, no. No, no, no. He no like police. Better for you to go now."

Dyson froze. "What did you say?"

"My friend does not like—"

"Dyson!" Peretti interrupted frantically. "There's—else in—with you."

"Say again, India 98."

"He was behind—fire! —couldn't see—from—angle. John, we—to go. We're running—fumes!"

"My friend is here!" Kowalski cackled wildly, his little body rocking with glee.

"Say again, India 98," Dyson spat into the radio.

As if to deliberately mock him, the radio delivered India 98's final sentence with perfect clarity before dying with a splutter of static. "There's someone else in there. He was behind the fire. John, he's coming straight for you!"

His vision shifting in and out of focus to paint everything in a lurid, unnatural colour, the Ripper crashed through the door of the Tsaritsyn brothel. Breath deep and rasping, he clenched one bloody hand across the gunshot wound in his gut, the other desperately gripping the lesions in his neck to stop the life flowing out of him. He careened drunkenly back towards his black steed, still stood where he had dismounted, awash with kaleidoscopic rays as the new day pushed over the city's rooftops.

"Halt!" an authoritative voice cried out in cold Russian.

The Ripper snapped his head in the direction of the voice—a movement that nearly sent him toppling to the ground in his injured state.

Two men shimmered and grew from the shadows of Tsaritsyn. The first, an adolescent constable with a face full of acne. He looked no more than a boy, wrapped in a police overcoat two sizes too big for him, his heavy revolver held weakly as he approached the Ripper with nervous caution.

The other man walked slower, his speed set by a pronounced limp. The cane he carried cracked a rhythmic beat on the cobbles as he advanced. He was an emaciated husk of a man, old and spiteful, wrapped in a long coat with fur collars. A fox fur ushanka atop his head, a thick moustache hung down to his jowls, framing the unforgiving sneer that betrayed his utter ruthlessness.

"I am Detective Inspector Druzyak of the Tsaritsyn Criminal Investigation Department," he announced in a voice colder than the air. "It would be in your best interest to surrender, for I will not see you escape this city."

While the young policeman moved to grip his pistol with both hands, Druzyak spat on the floor and pointed his cane at the two men who had waited for service in the brothel cowering on the street corner.

"These whorefuckers made claims against your conduct and told of screams and gunshots and how a constable entered, yet to return. What crimes have you committed in that house of sin?"

The Ripper said nothing, weighing up the men with a calculated stare: a frightened boy and a cripple. The constable looked as experienced with guns as he was with life itself. The detective was lame but merciless. He knew men like him well enough. Callous bastards who took pleasure from the pain of others.

His gaze shifted to the horse. Even with his body wracked by unrelenting agony, the Ripper felt sure he could reach his ride and gallop to freedom before either of them were able to shoot him dead. Capture meant certain death: the Motherland's judicial system would hang him for murdering a constable and two sailors of the Imperial Russian Navy. Escape was the only option.

"Oh, you want this beast?" Druzyak smirked.

He shambled across the cobbles towards the steed. No stranger to human interaction, the Ripper's horse shook itself lazily and stood firm as he approached. Without a moment's hesitation, and in a move that brought a perverse pleasure to his face, Druzyak took a revolver from within his coat and put a bullet straight through the side of the horse's head. The steed released an unholy shriek as one side of its head opened with a deluge of red, its legs buckling and kicking as it dropped into a heap that caused the ground to tremble.

"No!" the Ripper gasped, glaring at the detective with a look of death.

Druzyak cackled and let his gun slip away. The Ripper's inhuman gaze fell on the boy, causing him to gulp and the revolver to wilt. In a turn of speed that surprised even himself, the killer used the constable's break in concentration to take off with a stumbling run.

"Get after him!" Druzyak yelled, raising his revolver and firing a salvo of shots at the fleeing Ripper. The bullets buried themselves in the brickwork as the constable raced in awkward pursuit in his oversized uniform, the detective limping along behind him.

The Ripper slipped into a narrow alleyway between the brothel and a shop that sold meat and vegetables, bouncing from one wall to the next, his coordination struggling to maintain balance. Another gunshot ringing out to blast shattered brick inches from his head, he lurched into an overgrown yard, manoeuvring abandoned detritus that littered his path to throw himself over a low picket fence.

Police whistles beginning to shriek, he peeled his face from the cold, wet mud to see a giant Russian Bear Dog tearing across the yard towards him. The killer clawed at the dirt to stand, but the hound pounced and slammed him back down. Muscular, wrapped in matted, shaggy fur that stank of shit, its fangs bit and snapped inches from his face. A death machine, desperate to taste the flesh of the intruder, the breed was used for hunting the black bears of the Motherland; a man with a bullet in his belly would be an easy feast. Holding the hound back, his grip flagging, the Ripper fought to retrieve the bayonet from the confines of his coat, plunging the blade repeatedly into the beast's flanks until it yelped and skulked away. The bayonet still embedded in its side, the hound collapsed in the corner of the yard, its life ending with a mournful whimper.

The Ripper staggered up, collapsed, climbed again, and charged on, only burning adrenalin and a desire to hold Katerina in his arms again driving him onwards. He ploughed along the side of the house, using the wall for support, stumbling out onto a street of furrowed mud.

A single two-storey dwelling stood ahead, alone on the very edge of the city and surrounded by a smashed fence and tall grass. No more than a shell, the house had been left to ruin, the roof caved in and open to the elements, its windows black and empty of glass. A thick forest of twisted trees stretched out behind it; the still dark core untouched yet by daylight.

He threw a look back and raced up to the entrance of the house, driving himself straight through a flimsy wooden door with little resistance. The room was cast in the glow of dawn, crisscrossed with shafts of dull light bleeding through gaps in the slatted walls and yawning windows, the musty stench of dry decay as thick as the dust stirred by his arrival.

The Ripper settled his steam train breath, a moment of lucidity causing him to curse his decision to enter the house. He was trapped! His eyes went over every corner and crevice for some means of escape and weapon with which to assist it. There was nothing but a small broken table and a wooden bucket of long-forgotten hand tools. From the back of the room, a narrow hallway led to what was probably a kitchen. He found a curtain on the floor and tore it in two. One piece he wrapped around his neck to stem the blood loss, the other he balled up to stuff between skin and shirt for the same reason.

"Who lives in this shithole?" the Ripper heard the detective ask the young policeman as they drew to a stop outside. He slumped back against the wall and listened to their conversation.

"Nobody, Detective Inspector, sir," the boy replied. "The widow who resided there passed many years ago. People say it is cursed with spirits and will not enter."

"Do you believe in spirits, Constable?"

"I do not, sir,"

"Very good. Then in you go."

"Sir?"

"Go and bring him out, boy."

They were coming in. The Ripper pushed off the wall and stumbled over to examine the contents of the bucket. More men could be heard arriving, summoned by the incessant peeping of police whistles.

"You men," Druzyak commanded. "Position yourself at the rear to prevent this scoundrel's escape."

At least two Slavic voices gave affirmative responses, one adding: "I bring news from The Love House, Detective Inspector. Constable Yenardin is dead, sir. Along with other bodies. All slain by this monster!"

"Very well."

The Ripper heard boots thud on the wooden porch, a shadow moving between the gaps in the door's planks.

"Constable?" Druzyak called out to the boy.

"Yes, Detective Inspector, sir."

"Alive or dead, it matters not."

The young constable gulped and pushed on the door, instantly terrified when it swung open with ease.

"Shit," he croaked out a plume of cold breath.

It was Yuri Valerie Kenenko's first week as a policeman of Tsaritsyn. Too sickly for the statutory conscription that had seen his friends leave the city in their droves, it was only his father's acquaintance with Captain Borishov at the police station that secured him the role of constable. His father had told him it would make a man of him, and he had been desperate to turn his disappointed stare into one of approval. The training was nonexistent: a revolver, cutlass, and an ill-fitting uniform, in which the last occupant had been killed, thrust into his hands, Kenenko told nothing but to oversee the prevention of crime and uphold the law of Mother Russia.

The boy stepped inside the house to find the room empty. "This…this is the police!" he cried out weakly. "Better you…you surrender yourself now…for both our sakes."

"Get on with it, Constable," Druzyak huffed lazily from the safety of the fence. Kenenko turned to see him loading an elaborate pipe with tobacco.

"Lame bastard!" he hissed, too quiet for the detective to hear.

Kenenko dragged a sticky layer of cold sweat from his baby-face and crept across the room, every step bringing an unwelcoming groan or creak from the unsteady floorboards.

Heading into a thin passageway at the end of the room, he found a staircase that twisted up to the floor above; the treads collapsed and impossible to climb. He moved on and stopped at a small kitchen. As bare as the other room, the rusted remains of a cast-iron stove stood partially rotted through the floor and smothered by ivy.

A creak came from behind that he hadn't caused. Kenenko spun, crying and gasping, his eyes bulging with fear at the fast-moving shape that flew out of a cupboard door in the hallway.

"No!" the constable yelped as he felt a thud and the sudden warmth of his own blood.

Sucking on his pipe, Druzyak looked up to see the constable shuffle out of the house onto the porch. Minus his revolver, there was a small, rusted wood axe embedded through his cap, securing it to the top of his head.

"He…he has my pistol, Detective…" the policeman muttered, falling forwards into the dirt.

The detective sighed; the boy's death an inconvenience he could do without. Druzyak limped up to the house, stopping short of entering. He had no intention of meeting the same fate as the constable. Looking around, his cold eyes spied a dented metal container used for the storage of lamp oil next to a pile of chopped wood. Druzyak lifted the canister to discover it contained a sloshing liquid inside. He pulled it up into an awkward hug and popped off the cap to sniff the contents. That caused him to smile.

"Constables?" he called out.

"Yessir," came the joint reply.

"One of you return to me this instant."

Footsteps swished through the grass, one of the policemen emerging from the side of the house to stand to attention. His eyes shot down nervously to his dead colleague.

"Don't worry about him. He's just dead." Druzyak dismissed the boy's passing with an uncaring jut of his eyebrows and thrust the paraffin container at the constable. "Take this and pour it all around."

"All around, Detective Inspector?"

"The house, you imbecile."

"What do you intend to do, sir?"

"I will not lose another man this day, even one as hopeless as this boy. We'll set a fire and force him out."

The constable took the container and began to douse its contents along the base of the building, disappearing around the side. It took less than a minute for him to return, join the trail, and toss the canister away.

In that time, Druzyak had pulled a small brass lighter from his pocket. It had been presented to him on his discharge from the Russian Army, after the bullet from a Turkish musket had blown his leg apart and made him worthless to the Motherland's fighting machine.

"Twenty years, and all I have to show for it is this fucking lighter," he moaned with resentment, unscrewing the cap to spark the flint. A tiny flame grew and danced on the breeze. Never a man to undertake a task when there were subordinates to do it for him, the detective handed the lighter to the policeman. "Burn it!" he sneered, hobbling away.

The constable nodded and lowered the lighter to the trail of paraffin. With a fiery whooosh *that caused him to fall back, the flames spread and raced away in both directions to circumnavigate the house. It had been a dry, hot summer in Tsaritsyn, and the abandoned dwelling caught quickly, the fire taking hold to climb and devour the wood and surrounding grass.*

"Stand ready," Druzyak called out. "He will flee or burn; I give not one shit which."

The Ripper sat by the burning metal drum, staring intensely into the flames while the memory faded.

He shook himself alert and glanced up at the thunderous racket coming from above. Kowalski had taught him the name for the beast that brought the sound of war: *helicopter.* He had seen many in 2030, fliting about in the skies like bugs. On leaving the small room where they had met, the killer had watched aghast as one descended from the heavens to land on the glass monstrosity next to the hospital that remained from his time. The old man had cackled madly and told him they were not to be feared. It was a form of transport for ferrying the sick and dying for medical treatment. Draining the drink Kowalski had provided him, the Ripper tossed the metal container into the fire and watched the red and white paint darkened to black. It was called *Coke Cola*, the old man had informed him, along with a litany of other words he had taught in his native Polack tongue and limited English.

While annoying, his prattling voice riddled with insanity, Kowalski had shown him only kindness since their meeting. Mothering him like a hen, he had provided sustenance and shelter and redressed his wound daily to prevent infection. He had replaced the trousers he'd cut away with another pair, similar to those he shot the vagrant for. They were called *jeans*, the old man had explained. Occasionally, Kowalski would offer him the use of his *mobile phone*, the device clutched by these people as if their lives depended on it, using it to speak to others and access something called *the internet.* Did the killer need to contact someone, Kowalski would ask, holding out the thing for him to take. The Ripper declined, only Katerina coming to mind. She was dead now, he accepted, the realisation so much more painful than the damage caused by the train. It would cause him to weep when alone, while Kowalski earned his minuscule coin begging outside the railway station where the trains moved beneath the streets.

The place the old man had brought the Ripper under cover of darkness he remembered from 1888. It was a schoolhouse on the corner of Buck's Row, an intimidating cube of red brickwork that he would pass on his daily commute to and from the foundry. Empty now of children and destroyed by fire, Kowalski had made a home for himself in one room that had escaped the inferno relatively unscathed. He kept the room lit with candles and the occasional fire to warm his bones, the flickering light provided exposing a table and chair at which to eat and two sofas, unlike anything he remembered from the Motherland. There, they would sleep and sit, Kowalski regaling him in limited Russian with tales of his life before the streets. Like the Ripper, he had been a soldier, a medic for an unknown army called *NATO*. After that, he came to England to work in construction until his constant drinking soured the marriage to the wife he still idolised. When Kowalski asked him about his past, the Ripper would refuse to respond. How could he tell the old man the events that had brought him to this future Whitechapel without sounding madder than him?

The Ripper tensed at the sudden scream and snatched up the revolver at his side.

While the helicopter caused him little concern, the heavy thump that followed the shriek did. Instantly chilled despite the warmth of the fire, he listened, tuning out and disregarding the throbbing of the metal machine to focus on the footsteps and scuffs coming from above. Where was Kowalski, he wondered, cocking the hammer of the gun silently. He had left to relieve himself and was yet to return.

After a long while, the sound of the helicopter began to dull. Ghostly voices grew to reverberate around the burnt shell. The Ripper tilted his head, blocking out the crackling of the fire and listening hard. He heard Kowalski speak, heard him cackle with laughter. The killer stood, staring up at a ceiling etched with soot, the extra height improving the clarity. There was another man. He sounded angry. He sounded…

"*Der'mo!*" the Ripper spluttered, his breath growing to become an animalistic snorting.

It was *him*. The bastard who brought him to this place!

CHAPTER SIXTEEN

The helicopter gone, all Dyson could hear was his heart drumming a frantic beat against his aching ribs and the taunting cackle of the old man.

"*You are fucked, my friend*," Kowalski sang madly, hooting with delight.

"Story of my life," Dyson snapped, shining the light from his watch onto the crazy face. "Your friend, what does he look like?"

"*Jak śmierć*," the old man replied flamboyantly.

"What the hell does that mean?"

"*Like death*. He is like death. As cold as its embrace." The cackling stopped, and Kowalski grew serious for a moment. "When he look at things Man take for granted, it is with fear and wonder. He is not from here, I suspect."

"Sounds like I need to meet your friend."

"That is good, that is very good," Kowalski said, his laugh returning to crack his beard in two. "Because he stand right beside you."

Dyson spun—the wrong way—a sledgehammer of a fist rocketing into the side of his head out of nowhere. The blow caught his ear, splitting it open on a tide of blood and driving a high pitch ringing deep inside. He stumbled away, his disobliging legs collapsing him into a groaning heap among the cinders and glass. Dyson lay stunned for a moment, listening to the clanging, Kowalski's maddened amusement, and a frenzied wind that grew to tear at the building, howling like some demon that only nightmares brought.

A boot blasted out of the void into the side of his skull. Head wrenched to the side, Dyson rolled away, shocked and breathless, clawing at the ground with desperate fingers, only to feel himself lifted by some invisible entity. Held aloft as if weightless, a foul and fetid breath washed over him. Gun lost in the crash, he pulled back his fist and unleashed a punch too uncoordinated to land.

"*Zachem ty privel menya v eto adskoye mesto?*" the Ripper snarled from the blackness, asking questions he couldn't answer. "*Chego ty khochesh' so mnoy?*"

Lifted and sent flying again, Dyson crashed into an awkward heap of flailing limbs. Feet rushed towards him, crunching debris to deliver a kick that thundered into his stomach like a gunshot. Dyson rolled, praying his gun would somehow find its way into his hand. His collars tightened, and he was yanked into the air. The heavy fist that thudded into his jaw sent him airborne, skidding across the floor. The Ripper scooped him up and pulled him close, blasting him with that awful reek as something cold pushed against the side of his temple.

There was nothing but a curtain of agonising black, but the detective didn't need light to tell he had a gun at his head. He cursed his stupidity for entering the building alone. That was Dyson: foolhardy and impetuous to the end…and this might very well be his end. While the catalogue of scrapes and sticky situations he'd gotten himself into over the years was long, he doubted where anything was as monumentally fucking dumb as this. He opted not to recall a specific example, considering instead how the Ripper had him at a serious disadvantage. He was blind compared to a man born into Victorian gloom who had lived amongst shadows and had no doubt had time to become accustomed to the darkness of the old school.

"*Skazhi mne! Skazhi mne, ili ya tebya zastrelyu!*" the Ripper sneered, dousing him with that awful stench again.

"I don't know what you're saying, you carrot-eating fucker!" Dyson cried, thrusting his knee upwards to where he hoped the Ripper's balls would be. He hit the jackpot. The killer howled with pain and let the detective slip from his grasp. Dyson set off running, stumbling through an invisible obstacle course until he smashed into something hard with a resounding *boooom*.

The corrugated sheet he impacted toppled forwards, landing on the scaffolding shrouding the building with a thunderous clatter of metal. The coldness of the night bit Dyson as he lay dazed, the rain slapping down to sooth his wounds. He looked up, staring down at the junction of Durward Street and Winthrop Street. Pretty blue lights washed and danced, the distorted voices of friends and colleagues calling out, their combined arsenal all aimed up at the hole he had ejected himself from.

Over frantic cries of "Armed police!" a hand clamped around his ankle and yanked him back inside the school. Dyson tried to claw his way back, his nails screeching along the sheet metal, but he was too stunned, powerless against the Ripper's strength. The killer dragged him to his feet, and the detective got his first good look at his adversary since the night they returned to 2030.

Bathed in a psychedelic mix of streetlight gold and police car blue, the Ripper stood strong and unmoving, as muscular and imposing as remembered. The full head of unkempt hair was gone, unevenly hacked off and shaved away, the beard and moustache likewise. Only the cold, merciless stare remained, the look of death that Dyson would remember until the day he died. He only hoped it wouldn't be yet.

The Ripper wheeled Dyson around and forced him into a chokehold, stabbing the gun back against his temple hard enough to draw blood. With a deep, feral snorting, he dragged the detective back into the blackness, unfazed by the gloom and fully aware of his surroundings. The killer descended the stairs, dangling his hostage in front of him. Once the ground floor was reached, the Ripper drove Dyson forwards at an incredible speed, crashing him through a sheet of corrugated metal that covered the entrance of the building. The metal peeled back on Durward Street, flooded with police.

"Remember this, Buck's Row?" Dyson choked, struggling to breathe and close to losing consciousness. "Where…where you killed…Polly Nichols." He managed to drive an elbow back, but the blow was feeble and only made the Ripper tighten his grip.

The killer hissed something alien in his ear and dug the revolver tighter into Dyson's head. Forcing him into an awkward shuffle, he parted the gathered police as Moses had the Dead Sea. They fell back, powerless to act, their faces engraved with frustration and fury. The Ripper's gun was cocked, the hammer pulled back and ready to fire. It would only take the minimum of pressure from a dying muscle spasm to drive a bullet into Dyson's head at point-blank range. The risk was just too great. For the same reason, no one attempted to tackle him once he passed. It was a genius move: the killer had made himself untouchable.

Dyson felt nothing. No fear, no panic. To die with the Ripper would be a deserving end for the deaths that had followed the killer's escape and the suffering he had brought to Whitechapel. His mind somersaulted, thoughts of Mary left alone clashing with Ratski's strict instructions. The Ripper was not to be harmed. But… Dyson shook his head, the gun cutting deeper into his flesh.

Fuck Ratski! And—

"Fuck you!" he sneered at the Ripper, stopping dead on the tarmac and digging in his heels to prevent his escape. Dyson's face an inferno of rage, he pushed back against his captor. "*Shoot him!*" he croaked angrily, pleading eyes darting from policeman to woman. "Fucking shoot him! Do it!"

Not one of the assembled police officers heeded his order. No one moved, not an inch. The Ripper snarled and pressed him forward a few steps.

"I said, *shoot him!* Take him down. Now!"

Still nobody complied, the weight of causing his death too heavy a prospect to bear. Several lowered their weapons and stepped back. A uniformed sergeant, his Glock supported on the roof of a squad car, stewed with frustration until he laid down his gun. Another lowered the grip of their automatic, the gun dropping lower than Dyson's chances of survival.

"He's gonna kill me anyway," the detective begged. "Shoot him. Somebody take the fucking shot!"

Heads shook ardently to reject the plea. The Ripper restarted Dyson, pushing through his protest and staggering him through the police lines. Debbie slipped past on his left, close to breaking. Jenny, opposite, screwed shut her eyes and refused to look despite him growling her name. Past Atangba…Tecoup…Saunders, Dyson's eyes darted from face to face, gun to gun. The Glock welded to Detective Constable Leon Price's hand rattled ferociously. Dyson nodded against the Ripper's grip for him to do what had to be done.

"Leon, I am *ordering* you to shoot him."

Price's face crumpled like a car in a crash, and he turned away to deny his superior's request, revealing Raymond stood behind, the last in line. His own features as contorted and furious as Dyson's, he hissed through gritted teeth as the detective was driven past. "You stupid fucking bastard."

"Shoot him, sir!" Dyson turned his head the best he could, the immense pressure on his windpipe distorting his voice into something inhuman. "*Kiiill…hiiim…!*"

No, Raymond shook in response; he wasn't prepared to do that.

The Ripper spun his bullet shield around and hauled him back along Durward Street. At the corner of Whitechapel Sports Centre, where a broken-down fence separated it from a block of low-rise flats, they left the road to trample through a patch of overgrown grass that led to a car park. The police held their positions, hesitant to follow, Raymond screaming into his personal radio for the return of India 98 while they waited for the gunshot that would sound Dyson's demise.

"How the hell did we miss this!"

Stalking the large office, Ratski stopped to vent his rage. With a ferocious roar, he lashed out and kicked a litter bin across the room. The assembled Secret Service agents stood their ground, unmoved by his fury, rubbish fluttering in the air.

The ball-breaker's taut, pasty face flickered with embarrassment at his pathetic display, but only for a second. "Somebody say something!" he screamed.

The usual police chatter that filled the air since set-up was silently absent, the fact that no one had noticed for over forty minutes angering Ratski almost as much as the loss of the feed.

Over at the refrigerator-sized computer servers, two agents worked away on their hands and knees. The panel removed from the middle cabinet, another agent lay half-buried inside as though he was in the process of being eaten. Wrapped in looms of wiring, he held a penlight in his mouth, shining it on a circuit board he was holding.

"You people are supposed to be at the top of your game," Ratski continued, restarting his skulking. "You assured me this equipment was reliable!"

"Ah, fuck this shit, man," one agent groaned, maddened by their treatment. He turned on his heels and stormed towards the office's double doors.

"Get back here!" Ratski shouted, following him in hot pursuit.

"Hey, fuck you, man!" the agent cried from the doors. "Fuck you and all this bullshit. I answer to President Garrett and fucking Callahan, not some two-bit weasel cocksucker like you!"

Ratski drew to a stop, hit by a wave of awkwardness. His jaw tightened and then relaxed as he shook his head and answered weakly, too quiet for the agent to hear as he smashed through the doors and stormed off. "It's classified..."

The agent stuck within the tower wriggled his body free and reached back inside to flip something. With a resounding clunk, everything lit up like the Vegas strip, the sound of computer boot-up sequences and panicked police transmissions filling the air until he dialled down the voices to a suitable level.

"The gear's fine," the agent explained casually, rolling down his sweatshirt sleeves and trying his best to placate the ball-breaker. "It's the shitty voltage in this building—needs a major rewire. Plus, we're running 120-volt equipment through a 240-volt step-down. Shit fluctuates and—*blam*—blows an internal breaker or fuse. These babies are wired in series; one goes, it takes the rest with it. We tripped out and lost the feed, that's all. Relax."

Ratski's awkward wave was swamped by a tsunami of rage, the agent's blasé attitude infuriating him. "You lost the feed…? You *lost* an opportunity to get this bastard because of your incompetence. You told me this equipment was reliable!"

"I told you, the equipment's good, man!" the agent responded, not quite so calm.

Ratski strode across the office and dragged the agent up by the scruff of his neck. It was no easy feat; the agent was near twice the size of the ball-breaker with a face that had seen the horrors of war. Nevertheless, Ratski was consumed by a rage that couldn't be dampened. He gripped the agent's neck and pinched, steering his staggering spasms across the room and slamming his face into the windows that looked down on Whitechapel Road. The glass rattled in its frame, the impact significant enough to send one set of blinds crashing to the floor.

"Get your fucking hands off me!" the agent protested.

Unafraid, Ratski glared at the agents who began to rush forwards in defensive mode and pressed his victim's face tighter against the dirty windowpane. "What do you see, Special Agent Dipshit?"

The agent had no choice but to look across at the heavy presence of police vehicles swarming up and down the street, a police helicopter clattering high above, scorching the rooftops with its searchlight.

"I see cops, Ratski. Lots of fucking cops!"

"Cops! That's right. Mourning another loss while they hunt the bastard responsible. A job you were brought in to assist me with!" Ratski broke off his attack to push the agent away. "Now, I don't give a good goddamn about another dead cop. That is inconsequential. But Dyson's death, if he is indeed dead, further erodes our chance of success here. And that is not an option, believe me. I really wish—I *really* wish—you all had the clearance to appreciate... what... that...means."

The burst of physical exertion had taken its toll. Ratski puffed, leaning on the window ledge for support. He plunged a hand into his pocket and pulled out his medication to tear the lid from the bottle and shake a pill into his trembling palm.

"Then how about you declassify this bullshit and tell us?" the agent said, massaging the back of his neck. "How about you tell us what's so special about this John Doe that you're so desperate to get your hands on? Huh? Huh, Ratski? A Jack the Ripper copycat? Really?" He scoffed, turning to his colleagues for their backing.

The support arrived by way of a chorus of affirmations and unanimous nodding. Another agent stepped up, inches from the ball-breaker.

"What the hell, man?" he mocked, the nods continuing behind him. "Are we—what are we...helping the cops? In competition with them? What is this shit show we're involved in, Ratski?"

Ratski said nothing; divulgence wasn't an option. He glanced across at the police station. On the second floor of the concrete façade, the overweight detective from the Murder Squad stared along Whitechapel Road, forlorn, his face torn between annoyance and despair, an image that echoed Ratski's reflection countenance perfectly.

All eyes on him, Ratski finally turned and wandered back to his office. "Make sure this doesn't happen again," he said quietly, shutting the door after him.

Hands sunk deeply into pockets, Raymond pulled away from the windows of the incident room and huffed. If there was a man on God's earth who looked more defeated and desperate than he did right now, the Welshman wanted to meet him. To compare notes and share a pint.

He glanced over at Jenny perched on the edge of a desk, cradling her phone and willing it to ring with information about Dyson. Apart from her, the room was empty. Tecoup and Price were busy interviewing Kowalski, everyone else out helping in the search for Dyson and the suspect who had dragged him away.

"Anything?" Raymond asked.

Jenny shook her head, glancing over to the doors as Price entered.

"Mad as a box of frogs," he exclaimed, pulling up the nearest seat to dry wash his face.

"The tramp?" Raymond asked.

"Yes, guv. I dunno, we've got him on assisting an offender, but he's got some serious issues going on upstairs." He stopped to tap the side of his head. "Whether anything would stick or not is another matter. You gotta feel sorry for the poor old sod. I reckon he was lonely."

"Sympathy is reserved for the innocent, Price, not those who harbour suspects and pervert the course of justice." Raymond sighed again. "What else did he say?"

"Not much. He said he stitched up a laceration on our boy's leg and kept him medicated with out-of-date drugs he'd nicked from the bins behind Boots. It would check out with the dates. Kowalski claims not to know his name or anything else about him. He said he was always quiet and barely said two words, and when he did, it was only in Russian."

"Russian?"

"Kowalski's granny came from Volgograd…something like that. So he knows a bit of the lingo."

"First thing in the morning, get on to Hereford House and speak to Janice," Raymond instructed Price. "She's been running HOLMES for me. Get her to add Russian to the search parameters; see what that brings up."

"Guv," Price responded with a nod.

Raymond laughed, although humour was the last thing on his mind. "Bloody marvellous, isn't it?" He sank into a chair of his own, the three of them creating a triangle of hopelessness. "They couldn't catch him in 1888…and we can't catch his fan either. Sorry, *fans.* Incredible. Forensics, fingerprints, DNA, HOLMES—helicopters…" He threw a lazy finger up at the irritating still thundering overhead. "All the stuff that the Victorians never had and…*we still can't catch him.*"

Neither Jenny nor Price answered; both far too concerned for Dyson's welfare to acknowledge the Welshman's maudlin ramblings.

"He's running rings round us," Raymond concluded, his head sinking away as if his batteries were drained of power. It was only the sound of running footsteps that caused him to look up again.

Debbie blasted through the doors and skidded to a stop. Out of breath, her eyes glassy, she stood teetering on a ledge between grief and joy. She struggled to get the words out, but nothing would come. Settling her breath, she coughed and tried again.

"They've found John!"

CHAPTER SEVENTEEN

It was a wonder that he hadn't been stopped. Being pulled over by the traffic pigs, high as a satellite, with a bag of the finest Colombian marching powder on the passenger seat, a carving knife in the glove box, and an automatic handgun stuffed down his pants would have certainly caused some *complications*. Driving like a blind man, enough of the white stuff coursing through his body to kill a horse, Khan had managed to get from London into the darkened Essex countryside without hindrance or without crashing. The car he'd stolen, a Tesla Model 9, had autopilot, but he was in no fit state to figure out how to work it.

The criminal hadn't nicked a car since he was a kid; the procedure nowhere as easy as he remembered it. In the end, he waited for the owner to return, shattering his jaw into multiple pieces with a good swing of the jack and prying the key from his quivering hand. The act had given him almost as much of a buzz as killing the two Paki girls. That had made him so hard that he'd had to knock one out in his Mercedes as he relived their final moments, recalling the look of fear and terror stamped on their pretty faces as they died.

The Mercedes was gone now: burnt out in a car park in Hackney. It was a shame—he loved that motor. But it was too well-known as *his* car. If the bacon managed to rustle up some witnesses to the dead girls, it wouldn't take them long to put two and two together and get 'Khan.' He still had so much to do, so the car's loss wouldn't be for nothing.

After several minutes of bouncing through brutal potholes—in hindsight, he should've stolen a 4x4—the thick forest parted to expose a stark clearing of flat earth. It wasn't the same place that had seen the nocturnal burying of Karim and Benny the Bullet. Tonight's adventure would require something even further from civilisation. Out in the wilds of Essex, where there were rumours of inbred families and a handful of people who still lived without the luxuries of the modern world. Other stories told how the area had been the site for witchcraft and ritual sacrifice back in the 1960s, and the way the bent and gnarled trees stood fearful of encroaching on the space made him believe there was some truth to the tale. Khan wondered what horrors the trees had witnessed over the centuries and how they would compete with what they would see tonight.

The Tesla hummed to a stop. Khan threw open the driver's door and nearly fell out onto the wet autumnal leaves that were heavy on the muddy ground. He could smell the sea on the air, brought in on a fierce squall that caused the old trees to whisper like an expectant audience.

It was a perfect spot for a reunion.

My boys! Khan thought with a malevolent ripple of excitement as he unfurled himself to his full height and brushed the creases from his suit. He plugged a thumb into each nostril to suck up any excess Charlie before staggering over to the refrigerated truck that was already parked up on the edge of the clearing.

"Fuckin' state of you," Carrick rocked with laughter,

leaning against the cab. "You look like how I normally wake up, know what I mean?"

The criminal gave a dismissive sweep of his hand, his eyes fixated on the prize. Carrick launched himself off the door, intersecting his approach to block his path.

"*Whoooa!* Not so fast there, Speedy Gonzales. I think you owe me a bit of bunce first." He gestured at Khan's nose with a waggle of his finger. "And you've got your dinner all over your hooter, know what I mean?"

Scouring at his swollen nose, Khan stumbled back to the Tesla while Carrick lit a cigarette. The criminal returned moments later with the sports bag taken from his office and the kitchen knife that had taken Ginita Nahar and Narinda Patel's lives.

"Count it if you want," he mumbled, slapping the bag into Carrick's gut and recommencing his approach on the truck.

He circled it like a vulture would its prey, taking in every exquisite contour of its tattered bodywork, his hand brushing against metal and plastic while his mind tiptoed through vicious thoughts of the havoc he would wreak on those within.

"You ain't froze 'em to death like a box of fuckin' fish fingers, I hope?" Khan motioned up at the refrigerator unit.

"Do I look like a cunt?" Carrick said, wandering over to join him.

Khan looked the bent pig up and down, stood there in his leather Gestapo coat and pirate's eye patch. "Maybe just a little bit, Pat. Know what I mean?"

Settling the bag by the back wheel, Carrick grumbled through the cigarette stuck between his lips and unlatched the two large doors at the rear of the truck. With a hefty tug, he swung them open to reveal the contents, gagging and coughing at the stench that rolled out from within.

Khan peered inside, undeterred by the fug of shit and piss. "That's fear, that is, Patrick. Pure, primal fuckin' fear."

Illuminated by several dim light bulbs were thirty-five people. Crammed inside the back of the truck, most hung suspended from the meat hooks that had carried the carcases of animals. All bound and gagged, many still in their night-wear, some had passed out due to the ordeal, while others moaned like the undead. The men, his boys, those who knew what Khan was capable of, fought desperately against their restraints as he stared in at them.

"And they're all there?" Khan asked Carrick, his grip on the knife tightening as he pulled himself up into the back. "I ain't gotta do a headcount, I hope?"

"Course they're fuckin' there," Carrick protested, chugging on his *Gauloises*. "Told you that, didn't I?"

The truck started to rock as the struggling increased. Khan pushed his way through the bodies, setting them off like some perverse Newton's cradle, weaving his way through to the back of the truck, to where a dozen children ranging from toddler to teenager were chained up against the wall. Their expressions uniformly terrified, their faces were streaked with dirt and tears. Khan bent and grinned, sending their parents into apoplectic defensive mode, fighting and thrashing to protect their offspring.

"*Helloooo...*" Khan cooed, cupping the face of the nearest waif. "It's Uncle Frankie."

No more than an angelic five-year-old, her face buckled at his touch, and she promptly wet herself.

"Dirty little..." The reassuring smile he projected cruelly vanished as he snatched back his hand, replaced by something cold and uncaring. "Not long now, kiddies. And don't forget...as you're on the way, remember to ask your daddies why." The criminal sprang to his feet and started to search through the truck. "Now, where's Chardonnay? Chardonnay

Maitland?" The bodies swung and struggled until Khan found his goal: a pretty twenty-something shaking with immeasurable fear. "*There she is!*"

Roger Maitland, Chardonnay's gorilla-sized thug of a father, strung up next to her with his trophy wife, moaned and writhed, frantic for the freedom to protect his daughter.

"Hello, Rog," Khan said casually before returning his attention to the girl. "I was payin' for all your university fees, d'you know that? To give you a better life—the start I never got. I was good like that; I'd help any of this lot out. They'd have never found a better boss than me. Until your old dad here…"

He poked Maitland in the gut with the tip of the knife. The thug thrashed about frantically to free himself, but it was all for nothing. As well as the bindings of ropes and cable ties that suspended them from the meat hooks, each adult victim was bound by the feet to the floor to prevent them from lashing out. Once Maitland realised the game was up, he began to sob, tears etching down his face.

"…and the rest of these *spineless fuckin' bastards* decided to betray me."

With an indignant scoff, Khan sank the knife into Maitland's gut. The thug screamed against the tape; his cries held in while his blood flowed out. Khan thrust the blade all the way up to the handle until the thug's eyes widened further than any man's he'd ever seen before. So impressed was Khan that he rewarded his victim with a complete 360-degree turn of the blade and then pulled it out. Maitland's body sagged as the blade came free on a tide of red, his head slumping down to his chest.

Maitland dead or dying—Khan didn't care which—he turned and smiled drunkenly at his victim's sobbing wife and daughter. The criminal winked at Chardonnay and blew her a kiss. "Anyway, your funding's cut," he said matter-of-factly, drawing the blade through her throat and dancing his way clear of the erupting arterial spray. "Oh, I am gettin' *soooo* good at this!"

While Mrs Maitland choked on the vomit she spewed against her gag, Khan ran his fat, glistening tongue along the knife's edge and caught sight of Carrick's disapproving stare. "Fucksake..." he heard him grumble from outside.

"Now!" Khan clapped his hands and wagged his ringed fingers with deliberate theatrics. "Where's me old mucker, Stevie?"

He pirouetted and pranced through the bodies like he was on the dancefloor until he found Calder. Sherelle hung next to him, choking on her tears, the duct tape covering her mouth thick with snot.

"There you are, Stevie!" Khan chirped as he reached over and kissed Sherelle gently on the forehead. "And the lovely Sherelle too. Hello, darlin'. You alright?"

The criminal tooted with laughter and danced his blade up Calder's neck. Over tight, scarred flesh, he tickled the bloodied steel until he slipped it under the tape wrapped around his head and sliced through. Tearing it away with his fingers brought an instant torrent of abuse.

"—gonna fuckin' kill you, you mad bastard! You're insane! I hope that tumour makes you suffer, and you die in fuckin' agony, you evil shitcunt!"

Khan placed a finger to his lips and made a long *shuuu-uush*. He waited for Calder's rage to diminish before speaking. "D'you remember the first time you came to my house for tea? We must've been, what...five or six?"

"Fuck you, Frankie!"

"I think we had them crispy pancake things that were all the rage. Yeah, I'm pretty sure it was. Anyway, me old mum, God rest her soul, she said she thought you were lovely. '*Oooh, he's such a nice boy, Frankie*,' she told me afterwards—said she thought you were gonna be my best friend. And…and she was right. You were. You were, Stevie. My bestest buddy. *In the whole wide world.* You remember we did everything together? Right little tearaways. Got nicked when we were fourteen for torchin' that teacher's car. What was his name…? The one that used to touch up the girls and have a crafty hand shandy under his desk? I fuckin' loved you. I held you *so tight* when the cancer took your old man, and you…you did the same when my…you know."

Khan gave Calder a trembling smile tinged with emotion. He reached out and patted the cheek of his number one until his damaged features transformed into a hideous visage.

"And then this fuckin' bitch—" The criminal spun on Sherelle and thundered the knife into her gut. She unleashed a scream ferocious enough to tear apart her gag. "—drove us apart with her constant fuckin' shit!"

Calder and Sherelle's screams grew to become one excruciating howl as Khan plunged the blade in over and over. He felt his groin harden to concrete as the light began to dull in Sherelle's eyes, and she heaved up a thick, congealed wad of blood.

"*You're better than Frankie fucking Khan, Stevie,*" he impersonated the dying woman spitefully, punctuating every word with a thrust of his knife. "Bet she said that, didn't she? Didn't she? Huh? Dirty crack whore wog. You could've done so much better than that."

"You drove us apart! *You!* You had it all, but it wasn't enough! You and this fuckin' war with the police! You're evil, Khan! *You're the Devil!*" While Khan took the insult as a compliment, Calder looked over at Sherelle, her head sunk against her chest, oozing a long red rope towards the floor. "Baby? Sher? Sherelle!" An inferno blazing in his eyes, he snapped his head back to Khan and exploded with a ferocious roar. "I AM GONNA FUCKING KILL YOU!"

Khan ruffled Calder's hair and then took a perverse moment to tidy it again. "Nah... No, you're not. Not in this life."

He looked over terrified faces, some pleading for forgiveness, some wishing they could free themselves to rip his throat out. The vile stench within the truck had swelled, his violent display emptying bladders and bowels and psychologically damaging the crying, snivelling children for what was left of their miserable lives.

"You remember the last thing I said to you on the phone, Stevie?" Khan asked Calder.

His number one responded by pulling back his head and trying to headbutt the criminal in one final act of defiance. When Khan stepped out of striking range, Calder spat in his face instead.

"I said I was gonna burn you alive, didn't I? All of you. For your treachery." A mocking smile grew while his victims howled in one agonising voice. Khan swiped the glob of spittle from his cheek and smeared it down the filthy t-shirt Calder wore. "I've never been one not to make good on a promise, have I?"

Without another word, Khan barged through the bodies and jumped down from the truck to be met by Carrick's appalled face. "Frankie?"

"What?"

"There's kids in there, mate."

"You ain't my mate. You're a bent copper; that's what you are. You're a stray dog at Frankie Khan's table, whimperin' for the scraps that I throw you. Now, take your money and fuck off, Pat."

He trudged back to the Tesla and returned a moment later with a metal jerrycan full of swilling liquid. As he fumbled with the lid, his coordination clumsy and addled by cocaine, Carrick pulled a small Walther PPK from his pocket.

"Well, fuck me," Khan sighed, rolling his one good eye at the one-eyed man. "What, you think I got them 'ere for a get-together? A good old shindig? Party hats and streamers? Don't be a fool. You knew the fuckin' score from the start. Now, I'll say it again, once more... *Take your money and go.*"

Carrick shook his head and cocked the gun for effect. "Just let the children go, Frank. That's all I ask. Do what the fuck you want with the rest. But you ain't into murderin' little kids, know what I mean?"

Khan laughed and dropped the jerrycan at his feet. "Or you'll shoot me?"

"If I have to." He waggled the PPK for Khan to see. "I took this from one of them lumps in there. It won't come back to me."

His Italian brogues scuffing and kicking through the leaves, Khan turned on the spot, the frustration building. He stared at the truck, at Carrick, at his victims...his gaze finally settling on the gun. "They've seen your face, *Patrick*."

"That don't matter. I'm Foxtrot Oscar, mate. I'll take that 200 grand, add it to whatever else I've amassed throughout my glitterin' career, and I'll get the fuck out of Dodge, somewhere without an extradition treaty. Maybe I'll go to Thailand like everyone thinks McGruder did."

"McGruder..." Khan muttered with a growing nod, his cunning grin lost on the detective. That sounded like a very good idea. "Well, I have to hand it to you, Pat. You certainly picked a fine time to develop a moral conscience. Go and get the little bastards then, you spineless pussy."

"It's the right thing to—"

"Just get on with it!"

Carrick pulled himself into the back of the truck. "Come

on, kids," he called out, stomping towards the back and disappearing from sight.

That was Khan's cue. His drug-fuelled mind clearing enough to facilitate the move, he leapt forwards, grabbing the left door first and then the right. "Oh, Pat, you disappoint me," the criminal cackled at the ease with which the deception was achieved. With a deafening clang, he slammed both doors before Carrick could fight his way back.

Inside the truck, hammering fists started to pound against the doors, Carrick's muffled voice steeped in fear. "Frankie! Please, mate, please. Let me out!"

Khan ignored his plea. He had promised to burn them all, and burn them all he would. His boys would reassess their betrayal while they watched their kids die in screaming agony, and another burning pig was nothing short of a bonus.

"Frankie…Frankie, please…? Fuck the kids! Do what you want with 'em! Please, mate?"

The criminal tripped over the sports bag and landed face down in the mud. He climbed back to his feet, tutting at the state of his shoes to kick the bag away a couple of feet. The money was irrelevant. He would let it burn; he didn't need it. Khan lifted the jerry can and popped the lid with a metal clunk. While he started to circle the truck, dousing and spraying it with fuel, his deranged mind thought of an appropriate song to complement his work. A drunken rhythm growing to his step, he began to screech his way through a terrifying rendition of *Light my Fire* by The Doors.

Carrick and the captives—a band name in its own right if ever there was one, Khan considered—provided a dreadful wailing accompaniment as he orbited the truck and returned to his start point. Petrol mixed with damp foliage and North Sea air created a noxious blend that burned his nostrils while he danced and frolicked to a safe distance, drawing a line of accelerant after him. Khan tossed the jerrycan away to crazily improvise John Densmore's rousing drum crescendo. Once bored with that, he dropped to his knees and brought a lighter from his pocket. The flame sparked, his eyes aglow in the flicker.

"*Come on, lady, light my fire*," he sang, getting the lyrics wrong. Khan lit the petrol and watched with glee as the flame snaked across the ground towards the truck. "Try to set the world on fire."

WHOOOMP! The truck was quickly engulfed in a raging inferno. Gag-breaking screams erupted from within. Khan collapsed back into the dirt, awash with orange and never more alive. The sound of petrified children screeching their little lungs hoarse was something that no one should ever have to endure, but Khan revelled in it! He felt his cock strain against the front of his trousers. It was harder than Sherelle's life had been before Calder had rescued her. He would put the erection to good use when he was somewhere safe where he could revisit the event in his demented head.

With a square, alien sun hanging overhead, a bizarre blue rain began to fall all around. Punctuated by a jarring soundtrack of electronic beeping and distorted voices, the deluge swept in on torrents, merging and knitting together to form an inexplicable wall of cobalt that grew all around.

From out of nowhere, the Ripper shifted into focus. He stared down, his granite stare intense and terrifying. Then, he smiled widely and asked in a concerned tone: "How do you feel?"

Dyson crashed back to reality with a heavy gasp. His back arching, he tried to claw himself away, one hand instinctively reaching for the gun in his empty holster. When he looked back, the Ripper was gone, replaced by a young-looking Asian man in a white doctor's coat, attempting to hold him down.

"Whoa, relax," the doctor soothed. "Relax, it's fine. You're in A&E, at the Royal London."

The detective sank back onto what he now realised was a hospital bed and scoured the hallucination from his eyes. Now lucidity was returning, he could see that the blue rain and the alien sun were the partition curtain of a hospital cubicle and a light fitting recessed into the ceiling above. His head protested as it processed the information, the base of his skull and neck the epicentre of the pain. Dyson grimaced at the constant hammering inside his skull and edged himself up gingerly onto his elbows to look down his body. His suit was torn and wet and smeared in places with blood and muck.

"I'm Doctor Bhattacharya," the doctor introduced himself in eloquently accented English, his words delivered on an exhausted smile. He made some notes on the clipboard he held and fielded his opening question again. "How do you feel, Detective?"

"Exactly like I did when I woke up on New Year's Day, only without the fun of the night before." Dyson winced and looked back at the thin slit of a window running along the wall behind him. It was still dark outside. "How long have I…?"

"It's just gone midnight, 24th of October," Bhattacharya said and scribbled something else. "You've been out for a good few hours.

"What happened?"

"You were found unconscious by your colleagues. You've got a lump on the back of your head the size of a golf ball, a couple of fractured ribs, and some other superficial injuries, but there's no permanent damage. If I were a betting man, I'd say your suspect clocked you on the back of the head with his gun." The doctor took Dyson's wrist and counted his pulse silently. "Can you recite the months in reverse order?"

"Yeah, can you?"

"*Touché*. Do you remember anything?"

"I remember…" Segments of memory slowly assembled in order: the helicopter…the school…Kowalski…the Ripper… But there was no recollection of what happened after that. Dyson shook the timeline away, something far more important dawning on him. "How am I still alive? Why didn't he kill me?"

"Are you complaining?" Bhattacharya asked with the cock of one eyebrow. "Let's try and sit you up."

Dyson complied, squirming with discomfort. The doctor shone a small penlight into his eyes, peering in as if he could delve right inside the detective's head while he mulled over the question of his survival.

Bhattacharya appeared far too young to be a doctor. A thick mop of black hair sat atop the glasses he wore, his eyes exhausted and marked by the dark rings the long hours of a junior doctor's shift caused. The obligatory stethoscope and ID lanyard around his neck, the lapels of his white coat were decorated with a childish collection of badges and pins, ranging from those professing his love for the NHS to Snoopy and a Blue Peter badge.

"Touch my finger and then touch your nose," he instructed. "Quick as you can."

Dyson performed the test admirably.

"Coordination's good," the doctor responded, making another note. He looked up and smiled, announcing something completely out of leftfield in a suitably dramatic tone: "'*Beware the wrath of a patient adversary.*'"

"Sorry?" Dyson croaked.

"John C Calhoun, US Vice President in 18…something

or other. I dabbled in US political history while most of my peers were dabbling in drugs."

Dyson scowled at the mention of US politics. "You should've done the drugs."

"No comment," the doctor said with a subtle cough, releasing Dyson's wrist. "What I meant was maybe it wasn't your time? Or he didn't deem you worthy of a bullet? Maybe in the same way rational people need somebody to love, he needs someone to focus his hate on. To keep him on his toes?"

"*What?*" Dyson spluttered with a noise somewhere between a cough and a chuckle. "That's a bit poetic, isn't it?"

"Thank you. My wife tells me I make a fantastic spaghetti bolognese too. Then maybe you were just incredibly lucky? Or he was out of bullets and played you all like a fiddle?

"I…I can't remember."

"What do you remember? Did he say anything?"

"No. Well…yes. But it was all in Russian. D'you know any Russian?"

"*Nyet,*" Bhattacharya grinned. "If I did, would you remember it for me to translate?"

"*Nyet,*" Dyson countered with a grin of his own.

The doctor rested his clipboard on the bed and theorised some more. "Maybe you're approaching this from the wrong angle, Detective. For whatever reason he spared you—and just be thankful that he did—you should embrace that. From what I hear, you're the first person this Ripper copycat has encountered who he hasn't butchered. That's certainly something to cherish."

Whatever the reason for him surviving the encounter, there was little time to sit and dwell on it with the killer still out there. Dyson pushed through the roadworks in his head to slip his legs over the side of the bed.

"What do you think you're doing?"

The cubicle spun like a roulette wheel until Dyson's feet touched the floor and the brakes applied, nearly pitching him through the curtains. He wobbled with embarrassment and clung to the bed for dear life.

"That'll teach you!" the doctor snapped, his smile soured by the detective's stupidity. "You're not going anywhere, I'm afraid. I'm keeping you in overnight for observation."

"Nah, I'm all good." Dyson baulked at the idea, releasing his grip on the bed. "I don't like hospitals."

"Nobody likes hospitals," the doctor exclaimed. "I don't like hospitals, and I work in one."

CHAPTER EIGHTEEN

Ignoring the sleeping detective slumped over his desk and the other one who sat head bowed, staring mournfully into the bottom of a coffee mug, Doctor Amanda Hasted made her way along the progressive build-up of information on the two whiteboards that stood against the wall of the incident room.

She trod daintily past scribbled descriptions, statements, and gruesomely detailed pictures of the bodies who had died at the hands of their mysterious suspect, all vying for space with a large map of Whitechapel marked with coloured crosses, circles, and areas of green shading. She found it both enthralling and unsettling: a side of police work she rarely got the opportunity to witness. Amanda had often admitted if she were to live her life again, she might have gone into frontline policing rather than lurking in the shadows providing forensic support.

She was a scientist for Glaxwell Industries, or the Forensic Science Service, as it was still nostalgically referred to. The independent, privately-owned company provided background forensic support to the police departments and government agencies of England and Wales, utilising the world's most cutting-edge technologies and the brightest of minds. Amanda's particular speciality was the scientific analysis of textiles and materials, pulling the minutest of detail from within the weave or fibre of clothing in the pursuit of evidence. It was a job far more exciting and enthralling in reality than it sounded on paper—especially when it threw up the curveballs and surprises such as the one that had brought her to Whitechapel.

Amanda stopped and glanced up at the newspaper headline someone had affixed to the top of the whiteboards where they met. JACK'S BACK! was all it said. Printed by one of the tabloids to stir interest and titillate its readership, she allowed herself a wry smile, doubting its author, or the detective who placed it there, had any idea how astute the words were. She tilted her head to one side, appraising an Efit of the suspect like it was a work of art in a gallery.

"Hello, Jack," Amanda muttered quietly to herself with a soft Lancashire lilt before packing away her interest and straightening out of the tired, early morning slouch she'd slipped into to stand tall. Footsteps were approaching.

A short, balding fat man bowled through the doors and drew to a stop. Amanda noticed how the white shirt beneath his open trench coat and suit jacket was stretched around his gut to near breaking point. He ignored her and went straight to the sleeping detective to kick his chair.

"Wake up, Henderson!" he boomed in a broad Welsh accent as the man jumped back to startled life. "This isn't the House of Lords; you don't get paid to sleep." He moved on to bang on the desk where the next man was still peering into his cup. "When you refill that, I'll have my usual."

Only then did he acknowledge Amanda's presence.

"And you are?" he grumbled as he peeled himself out of his coat and smoothed his remaining hair into place.

Amanda crossed the room and sorted through the contents of her coat pocket for her credentials. "I'm, um… Doctor, er…" Her fishing elicited an impatient sigh from the man. "Found it!" She flipped open a little black wallet and held it up. "I'm Amanda Hasted from the FSS. I'd like to speak to Detective Superintendent Raymond."

"Would you indeed?" He pointed at her wallet. "That's an Oyster card."

"Oh, I'm sorry. Wrong one." Aware of his tightening jaw, she found the right wallet and presented it for him to see. "Doctor Amanda Hasted, here to see Detective Superintendent Raymond."

"I'm Raymond. FSS doing house calls now, are they?"

The doctor had made her mind up: she didn't like him. It was his grating Welsh baritone and the air of arrogance and rudeness he projected. Senior Investigating Officers were very busy people, she appreciated that, but manners and common decency cost nothing. Amanda felt her stomach turn, doubting whether the news she'd brought would be well-received. She looked over at the double doors as another couple of yawning detectives trudged in. "Maybe we should go somewhere more private?"

Raymond flopped down behind the desk of Dyson's small office and gestured for the woman to sit. As she did, making a song and dance out of taking off her coat and hanging it neatly on the back of the door, the Welshman decided he didn't much care for her.

With a round, moon-shaped face and a brutally short hairstyle he thought too boyish and radical for a woman of science, Raymond wondered if she was a lesbian. She certainly looked the sort, wearing a man's suit with matching tie and exuding some earthy, wooden scent that was more *pour homme* than *eau de lady*. Whatever way she swung, she knew her stuff; he knew that much. She had written several articles for *The Job*, the Met's own in-house publication. Usually full of bullshit propaganda about how glorious life was in the MPD, her pieces highlighted the vital background work the FSS provided in support of an investigation, using previous case studies as reference. The Welshman had found them well-written and informative but heavily laden with waffling technobabble. It boiled his piss how these scientist types were incapable of speaking in plain English. A lecture delivered in scientific mumbo-jumbo was the last thing he needed right now after less than two hours of sleep sprawled over Dyson's desk. He just wanted the meat, not the gravy.

"Under normal circumstances, Detective Superintendent," Doctor Hasted began, fumbling with the latches of the briefcase she pulled onto her lap, "you're right; the FSS doesn't do house calls. But I believe what we've discovered is of enough importance to warrant a face-to-face explanation. Shall we start with your Ripper letter?"

Raymond nodded impatiently, making a deliberate show of looking up at the wall clock. "Can we try and keep it to language that I'll understand?"

She ignored his request and announced confidently: "The letter is fake, Detective Superintendent."

Raymond twitched at the news. That wasn't something he was expecting to hear. "But he mentions the missing part of—"

"Please..." The doctor held up a hand to stall him. "The ink on the letter you received is virtually untraceable. Over 300 companies throughout the world use it. Adding them together, there are approximately nine and a half million pens with the same red ink in the United Kingdom. But, as I said, it's irrelevant because the letter is fake. In fact, from the other information I've learnt, I would go as far as to say I could name the individual responsible for creating it."

"*What?*"

She ignored his flabbergasted retort. "Now, the clothes you sent were particularly interesting."

"Yes, Victorian copies," Raymond harrumphed. "All part of his deluded Jack the Ripper fantasy."

Doctor Hasted smiled sympathetically at him and opened her briefcase, reaching inside to withdraw something from within.

The first exhibit.

She slid a clear evidence sleeve across the desk to the Welshman. Housed within was a small piece of discoloured cloth with some faded writing evident on its surface. Far too faint to read, he lifted it to the light and squinted.

"And what is this?"

"It's the tailor's label from the jacket you sent to Lambeth. The writing's Cyrillic. Russian. Anoshkin Clothing, it translates to." She reached back into her briefcase to supplement the label with an enhanced image, the writing easier to see but equally unintelligible. "They were only a small affair, making clothes for the poor in Baranavichy, a small town southwest of Minsk. The business was handed down through the generations, father to son, etcetera, etcetera. The last I could find, it was run by two brothers at the start of the war. They were both killed by the Nazis in June—"

"That's all very sad, Doctor, but if we could skip the history lesson and return to my case?" Raymond held the enhanced photograph aloft. "So, this is vintage? The jacket's an original?"

"Um…" Doctor Hasted drew a slender hand across her face. "Well, yes, it would seem, but… Okay, this is where it gets tricky. When we carbon-dated the jacket, the results showed that the wool with which it was made only stopped producing 14C three years ago."

"Three years!" Raymond puffed up his cheeks and blew. "Really, Doctor Hasted, I'm not sure I understand—"

"You might do if only you'd stop talking and listen." She looked at him with a fearless scowl until he relented and gestured for her to go on. "Our new machines are state-of-the-art. Accurate to within five years in 500."

As expected, she began to explain how the radiocarbon dating technique worked. Raymond already knew the ins and outs of the process but let her continue, using the time to try and piece together what she had already told him with a subconscious scratch of the head.

Carbon (C) is a non-metallic element that occurs as part of all organic compounds. It is, in fact, one of the basic requirements for life itself, appearing in plants as cellulose and in animals as starch and sugar. Carbon is made up of three naturally occurring isotopes. Atomically weighed, they are called 12C, 13C and 14C. Only about one million millionth part of Carbon consists of 14C. Unlike the other two, 14C is radioactive. When a living organism dies, it no longer takes in 14C. It then decays at a constant rate; therefore, the number of atoms present in a sample after a period of time can be used to determine its age.

The theory that all organic matter contained radiocarbon was first proposed by Professor Willard Libby of the University of Chicago in 1946. By the close of 1947, he had published a paper giving details into his experiments detecting radiocarbon in living matter. By 1960, when he was awarded the Nobel Prize in Chemistry, he had successfully achieved measurements on samples of known and unknown ages.

The early days of carbon dating came with drawbacks. The results weren't always accurate, and the early gas proportional and liquid scintillation counters required a sample of significant size. However, with the advent of the accelerator mass spectrometer, the radiocarbon atoms could be separated from the smallest of samples and dated: a process that had led to the controversial holy relic, the Turin Shroud being unmasked as nothing more than a mediaeval fake in the 1980s. With the arrival of the Yashima/Phillips KX9000s, which the FSS employed, the margin of error was almost non-existent, with a reading, as the doctor had said, accurate to five years in 500.

"All the clothes you sent to Lambeth were made between three and ten years ago." Doctor Hasted paused and gave him a look to indicate that she had finished.

"So...so...they're copies?"

"All the garments were made between three and ten years ago," she stressed. "And all are natural, with absolutely no manmade fibres."

Raymond pushed back into his seat to wonder what that had to do with anything, or what anything she had said so far actually meant. Despite the early hour, he wished there was some whiskey remaining in Dyson's bottle to help wash down whatever it was this woman was trying to say. "I'm not sure I understand what exactly it is you're saying, Doctor."

"Let's move onto exhibit two, shall we? These next items were found in the inside pocket of your suspect's jacket."

"I'm sorry." Raymond held up his hand. "There was nothing found on the garments sent to Lambeth."

"No, because no one checked." She placed a copy of the form that had accompanied the clothing to the FSS on the desk for him to see. "There was no exhibits officer listed on the lab form, so they were probably just bagged and tagged without a proper in situ examination. Probably just an oversight. It's happening more and more these days."

While Raymond ignored the paperwork, seething in

reluctant acknowledgement of her claim, the doctor returned to her briefcase and pulled out a dog-eared piece of white card, again contained within an evidence sleeve. Raymond reached out and took it, his eyes instantly spreading with shock as he exploded with a ferocious cough.

It was a grainy black and white wedding photograph, the thick card clean and crisp except for a few creases. A bride and groom stood arm in arm, resplendent before an old wooden church with a painted onion dome. He wore a full-dress military uniform; she, a modest white gown that made her beauty shine.

"You recognise him, don't you, Detective Superintendent?"

The picture trembling in his hand, Raymond found himself unable to answer. The confusion that had descended on him like a pallet of bricks muddled his brain, preventing the words he desperately wanted to spew.

The bride, the church, the wedding, it was all insignificant. But the groom… He stood an imposing figure, thick and muscular, with stern, unforgiving eyes that seemed to follow Raymond as he took in every detail of the pristine uniform. It was unlike anything worn in combat for years, reminding him of the depiction of Russian troops who had fought during the Crimean War. Over a pair of riding boots and dark britches, the groom wore a tunic decorated with braided ropes and extravagant epaulettes. A curved sabre hanging at his side, a tall fur hat sat askew his head, dressed with feathered plumes and insignia.

Still incapable of speech, Raymond shifted through the junk on top of the desk and pulled out a creased copy of their original Efit. He flattened it out and compared the images side-by-side.

It was the same man!

The Welshman laughed, the rocking of his rotund body

forcing the words to flow. "It's him! Jesus Christ, it's him! He had one of my men at gunpoint—I was as close to him as I am to you now. *It's him!*"

But then he thought about it, and the smile died on his lips. It couldn't be the same person; the photo was years old. Unless…

"Is this one of those dressing up photo things you do at amusement parks?" He cast his mind back to when he and Maggie had visited Alton Towers one weekend in the early days of their relationship. They had entered a plastic Wild West saloon set to dress as a six shooter-toting sheriff and a bordello girl for an astronomically priced photographic keepsake.

"No, I'm afraid not." The doctor allowed the dumbfounded detective a moment to reflect on her rejection. "When we dated it, we discovered it's fourteen years old."

"Fourteen years…?"

"I did some research. Mainly off the record, far exceeding my FSS remit. The church was in the village of Bezhibsk, western Russia." She pointed to a small sign on the whitewashed wall surrounding the church and then produced an enhancement from her briefcase. "It was destroyed by the Germans during Operation Barbarossa. That was the codename given to the invasion of the then Soviet Union."

Raymond's mouth moved silently. Question upon question lined up for release; some rational, many not. After a while, he managed to grab one and spit it out. It seemed the most logical under the circumstances. "What the hell is going on here, Doctor?"

Doctor Hasted sat back and drew in a deep breath, readying herself for the next bombshell. "His name is Gregor Zolkov," she announced with a conviction that froze the air in his chest.

"Gregor..." Raymond whispered, the surname lost beneath a wave of confusion.

"Zolkov. Well, Gregor Feodorovich Zolkov. In Russia, the middle name is patriarchal, the *vich* meaning 'son of.' In this case, Feodor Zolkov. Gregor Zolkov was a native of the village of Zlemensk, born in 1844. We managed to enhance his insignia enough to determine that he was a captain in the Leib Guard. They were the personal protectors of the Russian royal family. Tough buggers, by all accounts. Their selection process was brutal. Zolkov disappeared in 1885 after killing a couple of policemen, a brothel madam, and two of her clients in the city of Tsaritsyn. Modern-day Volgograd, Detective Superintendent."

Raymond tore himself away from the comparison shaking in his hands to stare dumbfounded at her. "How did you...?"

"It wasn't easy. The Russians were no help, despite numerous requests to their embassy. I don't think our relationship has ever fully recovered after them bumping off Litvinenko and poisoning the Skripals. Oh, and the little matter of nearly starting World War Three in Ukraine. But..." She reached back into her briefcase. It was time for the third exhibit.

A single sheet of paper slid across the desk, tearing Raymond from his scrutiny of the photo. It was a colour photocopy of an aged sepia ledger written entirely in Cyrillic. There was a glut of nineteenth-century dates, but other than that, it was unreadable. Raymond scrunched up his face as he tried to understand whatever it meant.

"The Russian military digitised all its old army records for prosperity a few years ago and made them available as an online database," Doctor Hasted explained. "There're no state secrets or anything beyond the Cold War, but it was very handy in this instance. What you're holding there is part of Zolkov's military service record. It mentions personal details such as date and place of birth, when and where he fought...and how he was court-martialled in absentia following the murders in Tsaritsyn and his subsequent disappearance."

By the time the Welshman looked up, Doctor Hasted was waiting with the next piece of the puzzle. She placed an envelope on the desk and let him examine it. Sealed in an evidence sleeve, it was rumpled and worn but otherwise in good condition. The address on the front read:

9 CANNON PLACE
WHITECHAPEL
LONDON, ENGLAND
G. ZOLKOV

"Why is...is it written like that?"

"That's how Russians used to write their addresses. Back to front."

She slid the accompanying letter across the desk. Sandwiched in another sleeve, it was written in beautiful Cyrillic script by a woman's hand. Over that, she laid a printed translated version.

The Welshman read, his lips moving silently.

My dearest Gregor,

Even after three years, words cannot convey the sorrow that still pains my heart at your leaving. But that sadness has become marred by the monstrous crimes that you have committed—offences which I have only recently been made aware of. How could a man I cherished more than life itself perpetrate such atrocities?

In your last letter, you asked me again to leave St Petersburg and join with you in London, to live in the squalor to which you have been forced to become accustomed, that we might be reunited. But you are not the beautiful man I married, and I have little desire to leave Russia and journey across the seas. I have since found that beauty again in the arms of another. He is kind and loving and has taken over the upkeep of our house. Therefore, I decline your request, and I should ask that our correspondence cease and that you do not contact me further to save me from additional anguish.

I hope you can find peace amongst your apparent turmoil and that God will be merciful with his judgment upon you.

Katerina.

"One hell of a Dear John letter, wouldn't you agree, Detective Superintendent?" the doctor said when Raymond finally looked up. "Look at the date?"

Raymond did as instructed, his eyes flickering between the original and the copy. "*Avgoost* is Russian for August?"

"That's right. August 1888. But when we dated it, we found out it's less than a year old. I did some checking. Nine Cannon Place was a lodging house back then, obviously long gone now. I searched everywhere; it took me an absolute age. In the Whitechapel Heritage Museum, I found the register for the second half of 1888. It really was a stroke of luck. Most of these lodging-houses didn't even know how many people they had living in them, let alone keep records. Gregor Zolkov was a resident between the 29th of July and the 9th of November. There's a very strange entry for that last day. Apparently, Zolkov was taken away unconscious by a man who told the owner of the house, a Mrs Drabbit, that he was a policeman. He dragged Zolkov outside and stole a Hansom—"

"Get out, Doctor," Raymond interrupted. He gathered up her findings and tossed them across the desk to her. "And take all this *shit* with you."

"Detective Superintendent!"

"I don't know what this nonsense is you've brought me today, but I can't accept whatever it is you're trying to sell me. Russian soldiers born in 1844 becoming serial killers in London—in *2030?* No, I'm sorry. I deal in fact, not fiction. There's only one explanation here, Doctor Hasted. Your state-of-the-art machines have gone spectacularly bloody wrong."

"No, no, they haven't! I repeated the tests on two separate machines—both specifically recalibrated prior to testing. Each time, the result was the same. All my findings were verified by my colleagues and—"

"Those results are wrong!" Raymond palm-slapped the desk and glared at the doctor. "I refuse to accept this…this *fairy-tale*. Your results are flawed. Plain and simple."

Her face flushed an angry shade of red. "The only *simple* thing here is your ignorance in the face of scientific evidence!"

"Just go. Please. Before I'm forced to contact your department head of whatever forensic shitshow you're working for."

"Detective Superintendent Raymond." She took a trembling breath. "Sherlock Holmes once said—"

He recoiled in response and exploded a sigh. "*Oh, pleeease!*"

"'When you have eliminated the impossible—"

"'—whatever remains, however improbable, must be the truth.' I know what Sherlock Holmes said! And he was as fictitious as this bullshit!"

Raymond closed his eyes for a moment to settle his

breath, hoping she would be gone when he opened them again. She wasn't. *Dear God, it's easier getting rid of damp!* he thought.

"I haven't finished yet," the doctor pleaded.

"You mean there's more of this shit? You…you have another mind-blowing revelation that a simple man like me won't be able to grasp? You've got a cherry to top your crazy cake?"

"Yes. Yes, I do." She nodded with uneasy confidence. "I believe Gregor Zolkov is the *real* Jack the Ripper."

CHAPTER NINETEEN

Five hours behind and 4734 miles from Whitechapel, the jungles and rainforests of Venezuela's *La Gran Sabana* region were alive with a rhythmic symbiosis of sound that had played since the dawn of time. Over a backing track of a billion unseen raucous insects, frogs croaked amongst the fetid leaves and rotting husks of dead trees, accompanied by the song of multicoloured birds and the deep baritone caws and wailings of howler monkeys from the twisted branches of the giant kapok trees. But, in this particular area, on the southern slopes of the monolithic Ptari-tepui, there was something else hidden within the nocturnal racket. Something fast and rhythmic and not part of the complex biodiversity nature had installed.

Something man-made.

Night within the sweltering rainforest was impossibly dark, the bright luminescence of the constellations lost beneath the thick, impenetrable canopy of foliage above. Thin daggers of white moonlight plunged down to earth here and there, offering little but a faint reminder of the sheer ruggedness of the place. A landscape of tortured rock formations, high and flat tepuis with precipitous sandstone walls, twisted rivers gouged into the earth, waterfalls, and vast cave systems formed during the planet's birth scarred the surface, making it one of the harshest environments known to man. But beyond its stark brutality and absolute beauty, there were noticeable irregularities if you allowed your eyes to focus in the obscurity. A straight line here, an unusual glow there.

There was a camp. Concealed by camouflage netting and guarded by the silhouettes of armed men, swallowed and born from the bellies of trees they patrolled. Strung up hammocks swung in the warm breeze, clothes likewise, dangling from vines. The dying embers of a fire glowed in a pit, circled by vacant camping chairs, enjoyed now only by the squadrons of critters that swooped and fluttered around the smouldering fire.

A light sparked amongst the gloom. Flickering orange, it lit the campsite briefly to expose the source of the unnatural sound. A diesel generator the size of a small car purred away next to a tent filled with equipment and empty bunks. Cables writhed from within, slivering off to enter a gaping fissure in a nearby wall of sheer rock. The glow faded to leave only the crackling tip of a Lucky Strike.

His pasty, east coast complexion baked to the colour of a native by its relentless sun, Tyler Lundahl was no stranger to South America. A veteran of CIA incursions, he had visited most of its twelve sovereign countries in his twenty-two-year service: mainly under the cover of darkness while parachuting from the back of a C-130 without the need of a passport. This certainly wasn't the first, off the radar shit his South American Taskforce had been assigned, and he was as accustomed with covert entry and exit strategies as a tourist was with duty-free shopping. In fact, illegal dabbling in the continent ran in Lundahl's family: his father had been a big player in the Iran–Contra affair, stuff the old man still didn't like to talk about. And what Lundahl Junior had done throughout his career in the region was highly classified, and would remain so for many years to come.

Lundahl smoked his smoke and rested against the fat belly of a ramón tree. He watched as a jaguar curled its lithe body between the spindly vines that hung down by a bubbling stream, a twitching capybara held between its jaws. He felt the camouflaged AR-15 slung across his midriff for reassurance but doubted he'd have cause to use it. In an environment such as this, you were more likely to be killed by a frog the size of your fingernail or fall into a hidden crevasse, your body smashed on the rocks below, than you were eaten by a big cat.

He glanced over as Zack Finn sidled up with a practised military gait. Covered, like him, with a greasy sweat and emitting a foul heat-induced body odour, both wore grubby shorts and tees with ballistic vests and night vision sunglasses, courtesy of a joint venture between the Department of Defence and Rayban. Both were shaven bare beneath their baseball caps, more due to the damn heat than any regulation.

Finn was from Californian winemaking country and spoke with the lazy tongue of a habitual stoner. But he was a first-class soldier and could go from chilled to combat-ready in less than a single heartbeat. "Damn this freaking heat, Ty," he rolled. "Get me back stateside and put a cold one in my hand."

Lundahl agreed with a series of nods that sent perspiration raining from his square-jawed face. He motioned over at the jagged tear in the sandstone wall, not twenty feet from where they stood. "Today's the day, so Biggs says."

"Motherfucker said that yesterday." Finn kissed his teeth and spat, further marking his annoyance by ripping a leaf from the nearest vine and pulling it apart piece by piece.

"Have faith, brother," Lundahl cackled with a smoky laugh. "You'll be back in time to read the kiddies their bedtime story."

"Whatever you say, boss man." Finn plucked the cigarette from Lundahl's mouth and helped himself to a drag.

"Hey, get your own," Lundahl protested with comic outrage, snatching back his smoke. Theirs was a close relationship; more akin to brothers than boss and subordinate. The men parted with a marine fist bump, Lundahl wandering over to the split in the wall and stepping inside.

As what light there was in the rainforest petered away, the opening became a natural, winding tunnel, a string of motion sensor festoon lights strung along the wall snapping on to light his way. Descending a downward path of crisp shale, Lundahl ambled past a rockface encrusted with protruding shards of shimmering quartz and cascading rivulets of water stained gold by plant tannins. Deeper and farther he trudged, whistling lazily and clicking his fingers in tune until the tunnel took a sharp left then curved back around on itself to open into a cave the approximate size of a decent house in a good neighbourhood. He stopped to shield his eyes from the light blasting from multiple floodlights set up along the rough walls, the gaps between each filled with stacked plastic drums of sulphuric acid.

Six bare-chested, glistening brutes in hardhats, full-face respirators, and nothing more than shorts and boots worked at several strategic points within the cave. The heat was breath-taking; the work even more so.

Each team of two worked at a designated position, where tomographic imaging surveys revealed the deposits of what they sought to be richest. One ran an ultrasonic lance over the rockface, each pass effortlessly and silently shattering the sandstone and crumbling it to the floor in fist-sized chunks. When the ground was heavy with debris, his partner would move in and collect it in nothing more high-tech than a bucket, lugging it across to the centre of the cave to a machine reminiscent of some huge piece of plant from a factory production line. The length of three cars, its shiny red surfaces were dotted with threatening stickers that warned of loss of limbs, chemical burns, and electrocution to the untrained operator. The bucket emptied into the machine's hopper, the deposit was sent into a series of crushers, pulverisers, and grinders to reduce it to a grainy sand which could then be chemically leached of its precious content. The silence of the ultrasonic lances was more than compensated for by the absolute din created by the contraption, the accompanying acidic stench caused by the leaching process as disgusting as it was necessary. At the end of the production line, below a small stainless-steel spout from which the finished product fell as a fine grey dust, sat a metal box of the approximate dimensions of an American pool table.

But it was no ordinary box. Its walls, base, and hydraulically operated lid were all six inches thick—for a very specific reason—and a complex digital touchscreen, moulded at one end, gave the weight of its contents and a host of other information in a threatening red. As with most colour indicators in life: green was good, red was bad; the payload not yet reaching its required mass despite its heaped mound reaching up beyond the sides. At each corner of the casket was a muscular robotic leg, similar to a dog's, complete with a clawed foot for navigating rugged terrain. Each limb was connected to a mass of sensors and gyroscopes fitted to a domed head that protruded from the opposite end to the screen, decorated by some prankster with a chalked on smiley face. The Autonomous Cargo Quadruped—Paul, as it had been christened for no other reason than its pool table size—had been designed by Boston Dynamics as a packhorse for the world's most inhospitable landscapes, and there were none more unfriendly than what lay beyond the cave walls.

While the production line clanged and banged, Lundahl let loose a sigh on a thick plume of smoke. Despite its continuous, twenty-four-seven operation, the work was slow. For every US ton of the finest Venezuelan sandstone processed, less than half an ounce of the mysterious element that had brought them illegally into the country was extracted.

Lundahl waved over at a solitary man who stood at the foot of the coffin like a relative desperate for a loved one to rise from within. Wearing a respirator, he pawed nervously at the baseball cap in his hands, his eyes transfixed on the casket's ominous red display.

"Today's the day, right, Chester?" Lundahl called over to him, sucking on his cigarette and wiping the sweat from his face. "Tell me we're out of this shitbox sauna today?"

Doctor Chester Biggs gave a cautionary nod and pulled the mask from his head with a sucking sound as the seal broke. His nostrils widened at the bitter taste of acid as he gagged and coughed, then hollered back. "Oh, we're close, buddy. I mean, *real close*."

Biggs' doctorate was in geology, and his appearance was one of scientist over soldier, with his tufty scruff of greying hair, scrawny little arms and legs and overweight civilian paunch. But Biggs was something of an anomaly: a scientist bred in CIA captivity. He was as comfortable in the operation of an AR-15 as he was with any of the unfathomable, high-tech devices Lundahl had seen him use in their time in the cave. In fact, the old boy could fieldstrip an assault rifle quicker than any man he'd ever seen. Lundahl had wondered why the CIA needed geologists on their books. It turned out it was for missions just like this: the stripping of hostile foreign nations of their natural resources.

Lundahl grimaced as one of his team dropped another bucket of smashed rock into the hopper for it to clatter and crunch under the 3000lb weight of its first set of jaws.

"You said that yesterday," he shouted above the racket, taking a final puff on his Lucky Strike and flicking it away. "Finny says you're a motherfucker." Biggs cackled in reply while Lundahl strode across the cave, a cagey grin growing on his own face. "So, how about it, Chester?" he yelled. "How about you tell me now?"

"This again?" the doctor said with a groan, deliberately accentuated over the crushing of rock.

"Yeah, this again."

Lundahl knew not to ask questions, but there was something about this mission that had set alarm bells ringing before they even left the tarmac back at Andrews Air Force Base. Clandestine operations were generally just that, arranged in the shadow of absolute secrecy, but even they involved an army of personnel to oil the cogs and ensure it went off as it was supposed to. Pre-mission briefings in conference rooms at either Langley or the Pentagon would outline every heartbeat of the task. Those meetings would be attended by a legion of personnel: CIA directors, admirals, generals, analysts, planners, lawyers, and a whole host of government aides answering to either the secretary of defence or the president himself. But this one had been very different.

Lundahl was led into a secure coms room at Langley by his direct superior, General Tuck Williamson. Williamson then left—he didn't have the clearance to remain—and an encrypted conference call was initiated between a sour-faced American who looked like shit, and an elderly, balding US scientist, who looked healthier than his colleague despite his age. Neither had introduced themselves other than to give the prerequisite clearance codes for the conversation to begin, but Lundahl had noticed the old man was wearing a name badge on the chest of his blue jumpsuit that read CENTRICH. He made a mental note of that as they gave him specific latitude and longitude coordinates and instructions to assemble his best team. A CIA geologist would accompany them as mission specialist, and all the equipment they would require would be found on-site. They had been where they were going before, Lundahl reasoned. And that was it. Briefing over. They were wheels up in two hours. Destination: Venezuela.

He had used one-hour-thirty-seven minutes of that time performing his allotted tasks, assembling his team and gathering armaments and supplies. Lundahl's squad were a well-oiled machine, and everyone knew their role, leaving him the time that remained to placate his nagging curiosity by asking a pretty analyst who he'd dated for six months to run a background check on the name Centrich. Despite her hesitation, Marcy had done so on the promise of dinner on his return. She still had a thing for him.

Leonard Centrich, his name turned out to be, had left Dulles International Airport for London Heathrow on the 7th of October; his fare paid for by a company called Rust Futures. It was shell corporation, Marcy had speculated, detecting many of the tell-tale signs. His ticket was issued as part of a block booking of six. All first-class, all the ticket holders, like Centrich, were quantum physicists or academics in fields which Lundahl had zero understanding of. They were all top of their game, apparently. Whatever that game was.

The flight was cleared to use Guyanese airspace and, as the C-130 Hercules had approached the border of Venezuela, it swooped low to avoid detection, hugging the ground like an old friend to land at a disused airstrip in the heart of the *La Gran Sabana* region. The men disembarked, and the plane was airborne again in less than ninety seconds. The rest of the journey would be on foot, through some of the cruellest terrain God had seen fit to dress the planet with. Two days later, they had arrived at their designated location and got to work. Their extraction was supposed to be easy by comparison. 'Charlie point,' as it was termed, was a clearing less than two klicks from camp. They would hustle up with the cargo, and a Chinook would arrive to get them the hell out of there before the Venezuelans even knew they stopped by.

Lundahl plunged his hand into the casket. Whatever *it* was, it had absolutely no weight and caused some strange tingling sensation to his skin. He watched it run between his fingers, pouring more like a liquid than powder.

"*C'mon.*" Lundahl gave Biggs' withered old bicep a playful slap. "How about you tell me what this shit really is?"

"Every day, you ask me the same question, and every day the answer's the same. You can keep this up all the way back to Langley, but my answer isn't going to change. I can only tell you what they tell me. Which is zip. I just don't have the clearance, buddy. We mine it; they dine it."

"But you're a goddamn geologist, Chester."

"I'm a level-three clearance mining geologist, and this isn't my field of expertise. I may be many wonderful things, but a chemist is not one of them. Some suit or general at Langley, or someone higher up the chain in Garrett's administration knows what this is, but it sure as shit isn't me. I was brought here to read the topography data of previous excavations and tell you meatheads where to dig, that's all." Doctor Biggs gave Lundahl a sympathetic look before turning deadly serious. "I can tell you one thing, though... This stuff shouldn't exist."

"What do you mean?"

"Exactly what I say. Okay, cast your memory back to fifth-grade chemistry..." Lundahl did so reluctantly while the doctor's explanation began to increase in speed and complexity. "There are 118 elements on the periodic table. Only ninety-four of those are naturally occurring, the rest being synthetic or man-made. Nothing with an atomic number greater than ninety-nine has any use outside of scientific research because they have such short half-lives and have never been produced in large enough quantities."

"*Riiight...*" Lundahl said slowly, like a man who had flunked his sciences.

"Each element is numbered one through to 118, from hydrogen to oganesson; their ranking denoting the number of protons found in the nucleus of each atom. Now, all matter in the universe: your AR, the trees, Paul here, Gomez over there, that bucket of bolts C-130 that brought us to this hellhole, ice cream, your mom, her dog, your Chevy, everything—*everything*—is built from those ninety-four naturally occurring elements. For instance, hydrogen and oxygen create water."

"H2O." Lindahl rolled his eyes. "Yeah, I know that much."

"That's right. Two hydrogen atoms and one oxygen, *ta-dah*, water. The human body, on the other hand, is made from a sweet little cocktail of oxygen, carbon, hydrogen, calcium, phosphorus, potassium, so on and so on, all the way down to infinitesimal traces of strontium, iodine, copper, and my personal favourite, molybdenum. We are a literal walking, talking cake mix of elements. Anyway, my point is the existence of this stuff means that the periodic table is wrong. There are now 119 elements. It's naturally occurring because we're—"

"Digging it out of the ground."

"That's right, we're digging it out of the bedrock. But as to where it sits on the table, I don't know. If it had six protons, it would be carbon; if it had seven, it would be nitrogen. It's that clear. But I don't know the make-up of this because it's classified, and—"

"You don't have the clearance," Lindahl groaned.

"That's exactly right, my friend. It's a metal of some description as far as I can tell…maybe a semi-metal. But all I really know for certain is that it's important. To somebody." Biggs shrugged. "Other than that, I am as much in the dark about this shit as you, my friend."

"You know it's for a bomb, right?" Lundahl declared, throwing out his own theory. "We all know that much. You might not wanna admit it, but we all know. Man's greatest achievement is coming up with bigger and better ways to fuck itself up the ass. All the iums end up in bombs."

"Iums?" Biggs smirked at that.

"Yeah. Pluton*ium*, uran*ium*, polon*ium*…" Lundahl tossed back the remaining powder and watched it swirl and settle in the box. "*Venezuelium*."

As Doctor Biggs looked embarrassed by his own ignorance of the new element, two things happened in relatively quick succession as if directed by some omnipotent power with a flair for perfect timing.

The display on the casket turned green and started to chime softly. It was a beautiful sound after being stuck down in the belly of the Earth for almost two weeks. Biggs damn near jumped for joy, smashing his hand down on the nearest emergency stop button on the production line. As the gears shuddered and ground to a halt, he whistled and drew his finger across his filthy throat when the men turned to look over. The doctor and Lundahl stepped closer like nervous lovers, Biggs reaching out to pull him into a crushing bear hug.

"That's it, buddy. We're done."

Lundahl wanted to share the celebration, but there was a shit-ton of donkeywork to do first. He pulled himself free from Biggs' embrace and started to bark orders. "Gomez, Floyd, get this shit sealed up and run pre-walk diagnostics on Paul. I want this metal dustbin ready to move topside ASAP. Ferddin?"

One of the workmen lowered his lance and swept the sweat from his ugly face to give a disciplined reply. "Yessir!"

"You, Jones, Slavin and Erickson tear down the camp and get it stowed down here in two hours."

"Yessir!"

Lundahl clicked his fingers and pointed at another of the workers. "Constantin, get on the uplink. I want heavy extraction from Charlie point at zero-five-thirty local."

Before Constantin could even contemplate moving, the second thing happened, and unlike the box's chirping, it was not a beautiful sound.

Gunfire erupted from outside the cave. It punctuated the joy, killing it stone-dead, bouncing off the walls to send the workmen scuttling to replace their tools with assault rifles. Even the good doctor pulled an automatic from the back of his shorts. To experienced soldiers, they all knew there were two very distinctive guns at play: their own ARs carried by the men patrolling the jungle and the antiquated rattle of Kalashnikovs.

"Jesus Christ!" Lundahl gasped as the gunfire died away as rapidly as it started. He turned to the doctor and delivered the order he had hoped never to have to give. "Arm Paul and blow up the Venezuelium!"

The thick walls of the specially designed casket were filled with high explosives for just such an eventuality. Another fact that had spiked Lundahl's interest in the element had been Uncle Sam's absolute unwillingness to share it with anyone else—even if that meant destroying it.

Biggs nodded with regret, but before he could move to the illuminated screen and initiate the sequence, the clatter of multiple boots surged into the cave, hidden behind glaring flashlights and preventing them from fixing on a target to open fire.

Lundahl squinted over as Ferddin roared and decided to try his luck anyway. But military altercations rarely ended up how they did in the movies, and the man was cut down in a stream of lead from multiple sources before he'd even got a single shot off.

"*Suelta tus armas—suelta tus armas!*" the invaders screamed, thrusting their AK 47s forwards like spears.

Drop your weapons. The Americans all knew enough Spanish to translate the message and were left with little option but to comply. They let their guns fall away and clatter to the ground as soldiers from the National Army of the Bolivarian Republic of Venezuela flooded into the cave, fanning out until Lundahl and his team were completely surrounded. Clothed in jungle fatigues and topped with contrasting red berets, their grim faces were painted in striking green and black camouflage, all except for the overweight individual who swaggered to the front wearing a lieutenant colonel's uniform.

"*Bienvenido a Venezuela,*" he said with a shit-eating grin that exposed a mouthful of yellow teeth.

CHAPTER TWENTY

Bleached red by an ominous shepherd's dawn, a frenzied murder of crows sat atop the burnt-out remains of Khan's wrath. Drizzle pit-a-pattered on what was left of the truck's melted fibreglass roof while lazy plumes of residual smoke drifted sombrely. The birds cawed madly, pecking and stomping while summoning the courage to swoop within to feast. Two hungry foxes sat watching with cunning eyes, drawn by the stench of death and the prospect of their next meal.

The cab was gutted. Nothing but skeletal metalwork and oxidising seat springs remained; the memory and mess of Carrick and the Chinese brothers completely erased. Looms of burnt electrical wire snaked across the floor of the interior on a carpet of shattered windscreen glass. The refrigeration unit that had been mobile prison to Khan's men and their families was scoured black by smoke, with jagged breaches here and there where flames had eaten through to offer brief glimpses of the nightmare within. From one hole, the head and upper torso of a victim protruded awkwardly. Char-coaled beyond recognition, its mouth was caught in the unimaginable rictus of a dying scream, its bony fingers still clenching at the wall for escape. At the very back of the truck, one of the doors Khan had slammed with such vengeance was nearly burnt right through in one corner; nothing but a fragile wall of crazed cinders surviving the furnace.

A big, greasy crow, crooked with age and twisted with frustration, swooped down to settle at the base of the door, poking at the wood with its beak for entrance to the prize inside. Suddenly, it froze, twitching and bobbing its head until something caused it to flap its wings with a squawk and fly to the safety of the surrounding trees. As if connected by some avian sixth sense, the rest of the murder took flight to join their companion. Their heads dancing with rhythmic investigation, they watched the truck, observing with glassy obsidian eyes, while the foxes stood and began to prowl its perimeter.

In a move that defied comprehension and denied the Essex wildlife their coming feast, a fist exploded through the remnants of the door, shattering the embers. Its flesh burnt and blistered and coated in oily fat and blood, the hand punched and clawed chunks of ruined wood away from the base of the door, desperate for freedom.

Someone had survived!

A man on a mission, Raymond charged along Whitechapel High Street, ignorant of the fellow pedestrians he ploughed through. Their heated protests and the rain that drenched him to the skin were inconsequential, the comical gait his stout little legs produced as he surged along outweighed by the cold, stone glare he wore.

He could think of nothing but the bullshit tales told by

the woman from the FSS: fanciful nonsense created by an unstable mind or some twisted ploy to make a name for herself. But behind the ridiculousness of her claims, there had been nothing but absolute truth and conviction on her face. He had seen enough insincerity and guilt in his time to know the signs. But what she had told him made absolutely no sense, no matter how many times he replayed it in his head.

"Yes. Yes, I do." She nodded with uneasy confidence. "I believe Gregor Zolkov is the real *Jack the Ripper."*

"Well, of course he is!" Raymond threw his arms wide and cackled with borderline hysteria. "Madam, I'm no expert—like your good self, obviously—but I would have thought a 200-year-old serial killer might be a bit past his prime to start—"

"He isn't 200-years-old," Doctor Hasted sighed.

"Then how do you explain this ridiculous claim of yours?"

"There's only one logical explanation that I can find…" The doctor made a look like she was about to throw up or confess to murder. "Time travel."

Raymond listened as the clouds groaned and released a well-timed clap of thunder. He stewed for a moment, facially undecided whether to explode with rage or laughter. He reached for his temple to soothe a vicious pounding that had suddenly started to grow inside until he could contain it no longer. The first option selected, he glared at the doctor and erupted with the intensity of the outside storm.

"Time travel!" Raymond flew into the air, the chair he forced himself from skidding backwards and slamming into a shelving unit full of files. "That's it, get out!"

"Calm down, Detective Superintendent!" Doctor Hasted followed his lead and sprang to her feet, thrusting her

outstretched hands as if he was a beast ready to charge. "I realise how utterly preposterous this must—"

"Calm down? Calm down!" A slap insufficient this time, Raymond punched the table in anger and caused the glass walls of the office to rattle. "You feed me a line like that and expect me to calm down?"

The doctor wheeled around slowly on the spot, glancing up at the ceiling and mouthing for someone somewhere to give her strength. She completed her revolution and straightened up. "Have you finished?"

"Have I—?"

"Have you finished!" she screamed, a fury coming from nowhere to hit him like a thrown brick. "Have you got it all off your chest? Concluded your rant?"

Shocked into silence by her outburst, Raymond's eyes bulged, his features continuing to protest for him. The veins in his neck straining to near bursting point, he buckled back into his chair, exhausted both mentally and physically by the interaction.

"Say what you have to say," he said, motioning her back into her seat.

"Thank you. If you took something, the letter, for instance, if you took a one-year-old letter from 1888 and brought it forward to today in some kind of time machine and then carbon-dated it, it would still be only a year old. Theoretically, you would skip the 142 years between those two points in time like that."

Their gazes locked. Doctor Hasted lifted one hand to click her fingers purposefully, indicating the speed she assumed one would travel.

"Both the letter and picture should be brown and worn with age, but apart from a few creases, they're in perfect condition. The same applies to the clothes. Given what we know, that is nothing short of impossible. Therefore, I strongly believe the only rational explanation is that Gregor Zolkov is the real Jack the

Ripper and has somehow found himself in the twenty-first century."

Gregor Zolkov is the real Jack the Ripper, *the Welshman told himself, mulling over the statement while trying to defuse the ticking bomb inside.*

In all his years with Homicide and Serious Crime Command, he had heard some pretty outlandish claims and revelations from the Forensic Science Service, but none of them had ever been comparable to this. He thought briefly of Malcolm Rubens, a vicious rapist who had preyed on the women of Romford until his arrest and conviction. The bastard had supposedly perished in a house fire only weeks after his release from prison…until the FSS found traces of his DNA at the crime scene of a brutal rape and murder several years later. Rubens, it transpired, had been in debt to local loan sharks and thought faking his death would clear his obligation. Then there was the time his team picked up a case where a mother had made allegations about her husband raping their five-year-old daughter. A medical inspection discovered the girl's hymen to be broken, indicating the possibility of rape on someone so young. However, the forensic examination that followed found traces of Daucus carota*—carrot to the layman—in samples taken from the girl's vaginal cavity. Presented with the evidence, the mother soon confessed to attempting to incriminate her husband so that she could be with her lover.*

Raymond's stare broke, and he brushed at something on his trousers before returning with a pursed smile. "Well, thank you for coming in, Doctor. I'll be sure to take your findings into consideration as and when the case progresses. Now, if you'll excuse me…"

"But Detective Superin—"

The bomb exploded, blasting words like hot shrapnel. "Get out! I have never heard anything as fucking ludicrous in my entire life! You come in here, with...with tales of time-travelling serial killers—that time travel is your only logical *explanation!"*

"Will you shut up and listen to me, you stupid man!" Doctor Hasted countered, her blast dwarfing his. "We have an ex-Russian special forces soldier who murdered a bunch of people in Volgograd and then—!" Realising that Raymond had done as requested, she gulped awkwardly before continuing. "And then flees to London to live in Whitechapel, and who is abducted *on the morning of the last Ripper murder."*

"Get out, Doctor," the Welshman said quietly, dismissing her with an exhausted sweep of his hand. "Please, just go. I am too old and too tired to argue anymore. You come in here and expect me to swallow stories about a Russian soldier—one of the king's personal protectors no less—who builds a time machine—"

"I never said he built a time machine!"

*"Who builds a time machine and comes forward in time because, you know, a change is as good as a rest. Well, let me tell you, Doctor Hasted, I don't know what you've been smoking, but I'll be contacting your superiors regarding this. This whole thing, the clothes, the letter, and the photograph, it's just some elaborate hoax this bastard has concocted as part of his sick fantasy. Now, if you please...*get the fuck out of my office!*"*

Accepting defeat with a derisory snort, the doctor shot into the air and shovelled her evidence back into the briefcase. She turned for the door, wrenching her coat from the hook. "Have you ever read Tales of An East End Bobby *by Andrew Melvin?" she asked, her hand quivering on the handle.*

"No, I have not," Raymond sneered in reply.

"Then I suggest you do. Especially the fourth chapter, Stranger Than Fiction." The door opened and slammed shut, and Doctor Hasted from the Forensic Science Service was gone.

. . .

And she would be gone if he had his way. *You mark my words!* Raymond grumbled inwardly.

But it was the cryptic recommendation Doctor Hasted had left him with that brought the Welshman to Whitechapel Library. Something about her closing statement had nagged at him like an old war wound. He didn't believe a word about her absurd time travel explanation. That was just...*impossible*. But there had been some other vital piece of information she'd wanted to impart until prevented. Over the cup of tea Price had finally delivered, the seed of curiosity had sprouted and took life until he could fight it no longer.

"The real Jack the Ripper," he said indignantly as he pushed through the swing doors of the glass-fronted library.

Raymond ignored the garish interior with its bright neon colours and red rubberised flooring that squeaked underfoot as he waddled over to a curved information desk. Passing drenched mothers and children and people lounging in comfy chairs reading from books and newspapers, he approached the frumpy old librarian sat behind the counter. Wrapped in a thick cardigan to protect her from the obvious chill within the building, the woman was engaged in an animated phone call, complaining in the most irritating of tones about the library's heating, or rather, the lack of it. It hadn't worked for three days now, apparently.

"And Bert reckons it won't be fixed till next week," she droned, ignoring his arrival. "I don't mind telling you, if I get another cold, I'll be straight on the phone to my solicitor."

Raymond slapped his warrant card down on the frosted glass countertop, and she responded by turning her swivel chair away from him. She glanced back as he made a deliberate cough and held up a finger for him to wait. His patience already paper-thin, that was enough for him to reach over the counter and end the call for her.

"Call them back," he said, waving his identification in her face. "Tales of An East End Bobby?"

"Who do you think you are?" The librarian pulled the cardigan in around her body and glared at him like death itself.

"*Tales of An East End Bobby*," he repeated, punctuating every word. "*Do you have it?*"

She huffed and muttered something under her breath, stabbing at the keys of her computer terminal. "*True crime, second floor*," she said with identical pronunciation.

The book was not found without incident.

Five minutes of fruitless stalking of the true-crime section caused Raymond to curse the library's chaotic, haphazard arrangement. The small library he kept at home, mainly consisting of crime fiction and travel guides to places he and Maggie had visited, was arranged by genre and displayed in neat alphabetical order. The fact that a public library couldn't do likewise only added to his frustration. Their shelves were arranged with anything but a potential reader in mind. There were books discarded on top of books, books put away spine first, and books shoved away upside down.

When the required book was finally spotted, Raymond backtracked to its place on the shelf only for some cocky little bastard with dyed red hair and a face full of piercings to pounce on it first.

"I need that!" the Welshman cried.

"Tough shit, Grandad. I got it first, so jog on." The boy gave him the finger along with a smarmy grin.

Raymond flipped open his warrant card and gestured to the hovering digit. "And this tops that, so unless you want to get arrested for obstructing an active police investigation, hand it over and bugger off."

The cocky little bastard weighed up his options. Not wishing to get himself arrested, he kissed his teeth and complied reluctantly. Raymond snatched the book from his grasp and hurried away to an empty table.

Tales of an East End Bobby was plain and faded with a cracked leather cover and worn gold lettering embossed over its front and spine. Sinking into one of the table's hard plastic chairs, he opened it and checked the front matter. First published in 1902, what he held was the 1955 edition. Poor old Andrew Melvin was long gone by now, Raymond thought, either spewed out of a crematorium chimney somewhere or ending his days as worm food.

He flicked through the pages with enough impatience to cause the paper to flap until he found chapter four. As told by Doctor Hasted, it was titled Stranger Than Fiction and seemed to consist of the weird and wacky tales policemen encountered in their early twentieth century careers. There were unbelievable anecdotes: ghost stories, UFO sightings, and the recounting of mysterious happenings, all made by police officers of the East End. He skimmed through the tale of some sick individual caught having 'inappropriate relations,' as the author put it in the delicate parlance of the day, with his dead father's corpse while wearing a ball gown. Sufficiently disgusted, Raymond moved on, past tales of bank-robbing conjoined twins, spectres and flying saucers, speed-reading through words here and there until he saw one that made him stop and turn back a page.

Whitechapel.

Sitting the book down on the table, the Welshman began to read. His brow crumpled as he tore through the words, lips moving silently until his mouth fell open and remained that way. He felt his breath flutter and his heart pound as he raced through the story, consuming it like a much-needed meal. When finished, Raymond looked up and stared over the faces of other readers dotted throughout the floor, half expecting the smartarse doctor to leap out on him and declare how she'd told him so.

"*Jesus fucking...!*" Raymond finally spluttered, Christ abandoned as his features completely collapsed.

CHAPTER TWENTY-ONE

With a warm and convivial smile, Joseph Weintraub, Vice President of the United States of America, welcomed the weary men and women who filed silently into the White House Situation Room.

Garrett's senior by three years, Weintraub was sharper than a comedian's wit, possessing a shrewd alertness unclouded by age. His appearance, however, loitered on the questionable borders of an ageing playboy, desperate for a return to better times. The 'Hugh Hefner of Capitol Hill' as Weintraub was sometimes known—something he took as a compliment instead of the intended critique—he was always impeccably dressed by DC's best outfitters, his hair was plentiful and as black as Pennsylvanian coal, his teeth the best porcelain money could buy. With skin tanned a Mediterranean ochre, it was a package that had broken many hearts in his younger days. The muscle honed and carried with such pride in his youth slackened and consigned now to memory and photographs, he still kept himself in shape, fighting the sedentary lifestyle that the later years brought by running five miles each day and rowing the Potomac when the Secret Service and weather permitted.

Bathed in a peculiar glowing light, the president sat immediately to Weintraub's left at the head of the long, polished conference table that dominated a low-ceilinged room, its walls covered with pastel suede and mahogany panels fitted with multiple flat screens and video conferencing cameras. The vice president watched his dear friend with fondness as he greeted those who entered like a father welcoming his family home to Thanksgiving supper. Previous White House protocol dictated that the president was the last to enter and everyone was to stand for his arrival, but Garrett had done away with many of the traditions and conventions he deemed unnecessary upon his inauguration. Like them, he was just a man, made of flesh and bone, he argued. He was not a god or royalty; his omnipotence bestowed him by the ballot box, not some divine intervention or birthright.

In order of seniority, the summoned members of Garrett's cabinet and selected White House staff arranged themselves around the table as they had done on countless occasions before. If they were passed on the street, any one of them could be considered innocuous and innocent enough to be mistaken for a doctor or accountant were it not for their Secret Service shadows. The three women present wore smart, brightly coloured business suits; the men similarly attired in greys and blues by Armani and Tom Ford. None wore ties; their shirts open a couple of buttons to show bare and weathered skin. It was 05:15 in Washington DC, so the digital clocks set in the walls at various locations indicated. An ungodly hour to be dragged from bed, let alone to struggle with the intricacies of a Windsor knot. Ties would come later when the working day officially began.

Arranged with water bottles and glasses placed with military precision, the table was quickly dishevelled by the files, folders, and personal belongings of those in attendance. Curiously, there was not one smartphone present: electronic communication devices were barred from the room and had to be turned in outside, each phone assigned a yellow Post-it Note with their owner's name and placed inside a metal-lined wooden box that had once been a cigar humidor.

The last to enter was an impeccably dressed four-star United States Air Force general, who was wearing a tie, the chest of his dark blue tunic decorated in multiple lines of coloured bars. General Charles Kimsey, Chairman of the Joint Chiefs of Staff, saluted the president and vice president and removed his peaked cap to reveal a head as bald as his grandchild's. He sat with a regimented stiffness into the comfy leather seat halfway down the table and straightened the creases from his uniform.

The loading of the room complete, the doors were closed. Business could begin.

Weintraub looked across at Casper Bruin, the President's National Security Advisor, and gave him the nod he required to begin.

Bruin, the youngest man in the room at forty-eight, the short crewcut he sported a throwback to his days in the US Marines, pulled his heavy frame over the table and spoke in a low Louisianan twang. "Mr President, Mr Vice President, I'd like to apologise for the early morning roundup, but the Watch Floor has picked up something of concern. Something I considered important enough to gather us all for a preliminary sitrep."

Located in the basement of the West Wing of the White House, the Situation Room was a 5,525 square-foot intelligence management centre that consisted of large and small conference rooms—they were assembled in the larger of the two, the John F. Kennedy Conference Room as it was officially known. There was a Watch Floor, Surge

Room, offices, and a multitude of secure phone booths, impervious to surveillance equipment and prying ears, designated Superman tubes. Created in 1961 by the then National Security Advisor, McGeorge Bundy, at Kennedy's behest, to monitor and deal with domestic and international crises, the centre was extensively remodelled in 2007 to bring it into the digital age and increase its abilities and capacity. Run by an apolitical staff equally comprised of members of the intelligence community, Homeland Security, and the military, it ran twenty-four-seven, collating and fusing more than 2000 pieces of information every day. When an incident deemed necessary, the National Security Advisor could organise an emergency briefing for the National Security Council, as he had done now.

"We're getting some troubling reports coming out of Venezuela," Bruin continued, "regarding the capture of an unknown number of US nationals on their soil."

"*What?*" Garrett's Secretary of State, Chip Alsaidi, spluttered, recoiling in his plush leather chair.

"That's ridiculous!" the hulking figure of Jacob Lang, the Secretary of Defence, protested, his look as cold as stone. "We have no current authorised operations in Venezuela."

Weintraub watched Doug Romain, Director of the CIA, shift his gaze along to the president, an evident air of guilt about him. Garrett responded by meeting his look with an awkward nod, rasping a trembling hand across his face as if to disguise the slip. But it was enough for Weintraub to make the connection.

"You were aware of this, Mr President?" Weintraub asked. "Thank you, Casper," he added, allowing Bruin to recline back in his seat.

"I was, Joe," the president admitted. "And I had hoped for it to remain that way. Doug acted on my personal request, providing personnel directly to myself and Brad Ratski."

Weintraub suppressed the urge to roll his eyes at the mention of *that* name and instead scanned the assembled faces as a wave of disquiet went around the table. His look returned to Garrett and became questioning.

"I'm afraid it's classified," the president replied with a notch of bluntness.

"Classified?" Weintraub climbed to his feet and started a slow pace of the table. He stopped behind the Secretary of Homeland Security, Mel Wilson. She was a beautifully stern-faced woman in her fifties, and Weintraub could smell the gentle waft of the Chanel No5 she always wore. "Sir, I've assembled our National Security Council in this room. There should be nothing *classified* beyond anyone present."

"With respect, Mr President, should this not have been a matter discussed prior to…" Alvin Walter, Secretary of the Treasury, took off the tortoiseshell glasses perched on his nose and squeezed at the bridge as a mark of bewilderment. "What the hell were they doing in Venezuela, sir?"

Garrett deflected the question with one of his own: "What is the current situation?"

"It's all radio chatter at the moment," Weintraub explained, "but it appears said US nationals were apprehended by the Venezuelan Army in possession of some unknown natural resource they'd mined from the bedrock in the *La Gran Sabana* region. They've suffered an unspecified number of casualties and have been flown to Caracas for interrogation."

"Can we…can we get a lid on this?" Garrett asked, his breath labouring.

Bruin answered. "Of course we can, sir. We can instruct an immediate blanket to all press and media outlets. But it's only a matter of time—"

For reasons known only to himself, the president made a deliberate scoff at that. It was enough to cause the whole table to turn to him and for him to shake away their interest and gesture Bruin to continue.

"As I was saying, Mr President, it's only a matter of time before these folks are paraded through Caracas for Venezuelan TV as another example of US imperialist aggression."

Arnie Hector, the Director of National Intelligence, took up that baton from Bruin. He stared at the president from below two ridiculously bushy eyebrows reminiscent of Leonid Brezhnev. "And make no bones here, Mr President, the fallout from this could be huge. Excavating natural resources from foreign soil, without that nation's authority... Damn, we're the bad guys here. It would be a delicate enough situation if they were allies, but a nation that sees us as an enemy aggressor."

The president nodded in regretful agreement. He paused for a long moment while he composed his next words, his expression appearing desperate to divulge more. In the end, he asked only what their options were.

"We don't bow to pressure from the Venezuelans or the international community if and when the shitstorm hits." The vice president glanced around the table and counted the agreeable heads. There were enough to give him the confidence to proceed. "To do that would be a sign of weakness. If we truly want this stuff, whatever it is—if we truly need it—then by God, we'll take it. By any means necessary."

General Kimsey nodded along in enthusiastic agreement. His words came as a scratchy East Coast growl: a permanent reminder of the bullet that had clipped his larynx during Operation Desert Storm. "I can have a SEAL team prepped within an hour. Our intel is solid, and we have a good idea where they're being held." He opened up a leather dossier he brought with him and referred to several satellite images of a sprawling metropolis set in a lush valley steeped by rundown barrios. "Despite the years of Moscow's investment, Venezuelan air defences are poor, and their ground troops are no match for—"

"Jesus, Charlie!" Garrett gasped with horror. "You want to *invade* Venezuela?"

"No, sir. I'm talking about a tactical incursion. Surgical. In and out, minimal casualties. That's all."

The president looked around the table, his mouth ajar as if some terrible revelation had just been realised by him alone. He withered and began to look physically sick until he stiffened to shake his head sternly. "No…no, I will not authorise that. This matter…this matter must be resolved…diplomatically."

"Mr President, are you okay, sir?" Monika Weston, Garrett's White House Chief of Staff, asked, her pretty face pinched with concern. Garrett nodded her worry away as his breath grew deeper.

There was a moment of uncomfortable silence apart from the president's panting and the muted ringing of multiple telephones coming from other rooms. Weintraub cleared his throat, and all eyes turned to him.

"Can I have a moment alone with the president?" he asked the room.

Of course he could. He was Vice President of the United States. Chairs swished over the royal blue carpet as everyone stood dutifully and headed for the exit.

Weintraub offered the same friendly countenance with which he had greeted them. He waited until the door clicked shut and then looked over at the president still sat at the head of the table. But there was something about his expression this time. The change was startling, like a chrysalis's metamorphosis into a butterfly. But, whereas the rebirth of *Lepi-*

doptera life was considered wonderous and beautiful, there was little beauty behind the vice president's transformation; the kindness of his smile distorted into something darker and much more calculated.

"Mr President… Bob." He smiled, his voice heaped with saccharine compassion. "You've served this nation far greater than anyone could've asked of you. You've accomplished more in your short tenure in this old house than many presidents do in two terms. But I believe, and I am not alone here, that it's time for you to consider handing over the reins. With this *haemolytic anaemia*, you're simply too ill to execute your duties effectively. And those duties are only exacerbating your illness. It's a vicious circle."

Weintraub shot a surreptitious glance at the circular plaque on the wall behind Garrett's head: the Seal of the President of the United States. His eyes glowed for a moment while he imagined himself sat beneath it.

"And I say that with the heaviest of hearts, as your greatest friend and ally," he concluded.

"My greatest friend…"

"This cloak and dagger BS in London has gone on for too long now. And now you're authorising clandestine missions into—"

"You told me to go!" Garrett cried weakly, thrusting a shaking finger at his vice president. "You! It was *your* idea, Joseph. Remember that conversation? I trusted you. I certainly didn't expect you to plot a goddamn *coup d'état* in my absence."

"*Coup d'état?*" Weintraub continued to exude his sugary smirk. "My one concern is for this great nation, Robert. You're signing checks for this secret operation you're conducting hand over fist. A figure that equates to over nineteen billion dollars in black budget expenditure."

The president stared at him open-mouthed, crestfallen at his words.

"I checked, Bob. *Nineteen billion dollars.* To save one life? Covert missions into hostile nations? For what? For what, Bob? How does Venezuela figure in your cure?" Garrett's tight-lipped refusal to answer caused Weintraub to shake his head. "I'm sorry, but I can't allow this folly to continue."

"Why…why are you doing this?"

"Because you're weak, Bob. You've always been weak, even before your illness. I was the one with the political influence, and that's why you chose me as running mate. Your dependency on this Ratski is unsettling, to say the least. This mysterious *special adviser* or whatever you call him. A man with zero political experience but top-level clearance? A DC nobody. And yet the only one fully within your confidence on this matter. People are asking questions of your motivation. The American people are asking questions of their president's absence. How this once great orator now refuses to make public speeches…probably because the political decoy you've employed sounds more Billy Ray Cyrus than he does Robert Garrett! If your deception were to become public knowledge—for a president who ran on a manifesto of absolute transparency and honesty—the damage to this administration would be devastating. I can't continue to cover for you on this. Not at the detriment to the United States."

"Then what…what do you intend to do?"

The vice president hardened at the question and took a moment to answer. "Regrettably, I will have to take steps to have you removed from office under the 25th Amendment."

Created in the dark days following John F Kennedy's assassination and amid escalating Cold War tensions with the then USSR, the 25th Amendment was designed to address the serious lapses in the Constitution's provision for presidential succession. For a document of such significance, it was set out in just four small sections and committed to only two sides of a single sheet of paper. The first section gave implicit instructions that, in the event of a president's removal from office through death or resignation, the vice president would automatically become leader. The second dealt with the appointment of a new vice president after the enactment of the first clause—something Weintraub hadn't even considered yet. Section three regarded the temporary, willing transition of presidential power, *pro tempore*, to the next in line in constitutional succession through illness or short-term incapacitation.

Section four was the big one. The removal of an incapacitated sitting president who refused, or was unable, to evoke the third clause. It allowed for a vice president, together with a majority of the president's cabinet and members of both Houses, to declare the president 'unable to discharge the powers and duties of his office.' If a majority was secured, a vice president would become 'acting president,' not president, while the incumbent remained in power, albeit powerless and in name alone. The use of section four had been discussed during Ronald Reagan's second term when it was considered he was becoming lazy and inept and losing his mental grip on the real world; and again, on multiple occasions, during the rocky tenure of the forty-fifth president.

"You want...want to throw me under the bus, Joe? After everything...everything we've been through together?"

'*In order to become the master, one must first pose as the servant,*' Weintraub thought, not even he callous enough to voice the fitting quote by Charles de Gaulle. Instead, he widened his smile for Garrett. "I'll give you a little time to think about it."

The president looked over at Weintraub, the constant hurt of his *haemolytic anaemia* doubled by deceit. He slammed his fist down, his gnarled, skeletal hand passing straight through the table.

"Fuck you, Joe!" Garrett snarled through gritted teeth. His body shimmered for a single second as the strange light that bathed him glowed and faded, his holographic image, projected live from London, vanishing from the seat.

In the panelled study of Arizona One, Garrett reached out for his oxygen mask and clamped it over his mouth with a violently shaking hand. He scrubbed at the tension and let his racing breath settle, staring down at the dozen high-definition cameras facing him, arranged in a semicircle on a concave rig. The small attached monitor of the Yumshima DXT44 Holographic Conferencer that had displayed Weintraub's deception with such clarity now showed only a sea blue screen, the words NO CONNECTION floating around in no discernible direction.

"You've always been a bastard, Joe," the president mumbled into his mask, grabbing his phone and working through the menus.

Whether he was a bastard or not, Weintraub had always been the yin to Garrett's yang, the bad cop to his good. Headstrong and impetuous, the proponent of sledgehammer tactics over the president's more measured and pragmatic approach, it was with a degree of hesitation that he was chosen to run on Garrett's ticket. He had political expertise by the bucketload; something that many pundits and voters believed the hopeful president, as an outsider, lacked. A DC veteran with over twenty-six years' experience as state senator for Iowa, Weintraub had intimate knowledge of the workings of federal government and an established foreign policy track record that was as impressive as it was long. But despite his glowing list of accomplishments, he was not without his critics, many of who believed him too conservative and gung-ho for modern-day politics. The First Lady had never much cared for him, finding him aloof and unlikeable, and there had never been a better judge of character than Helen Garrett. How the president wished now that he had listened to her advice.

Like Garrett, Weintraub had served in the United States Air Force, a fact that had given them an instant connection as they shared fireside tales after the marathon hours on the campaign trail. But whereas the president had flown helicopters in the various conflicts America always seemed to become embroiled in, Weintraub had controlled remotely piloted aircraft—the USAF hated the term 'drone'—safely ensconced in an air-conditioned cubicle at Creech Air Force Base. He had flown the General Atomics MQ-9 Reaper unmanned aerial vehicle under the call sign of 'War Hawk,' awarded for his cold and calculated observance of a situation, waiting for the precise moment to strike. His skills became legendary in the mess hall chatter of the USAF. On one occasion in the spring of 2002, when tasked with taking out a convoy of senior Al-Qaeda members in Afghanistan, Weintraub's drone suffered a complete weapons failure. With the high-value target set to escape and American lives put in danger, Weintraub took the unauthorised decision to crash his 5.25 short ton bird into the convoy, exploding its payload of Hellfire missiles and vaporising the targets but destroying sixteen million dollars' worth of hardware in the process. His superiors had looked upon his actions with both reverence and disgust: the financial loss of the aircraft eventually outweighing the initiative he had shown to get the job done. In the days before social media, it had taken a campaign by friends and family to bring the story into the public arena; President George W. Bush himself stepping in to save Weintraub from court-martial for the wilful destruction of government property.

"Hawk," Garrett scoffed with utter disgust.

It seemed so appropriate now. A man in constant awareness of his surroundings, Weintraub's eyes had only ever been focused on the next rung of the political ladder. The old DC adage of 'The vice president is only a heartbeat from the Oval Office' had never seemed so startlingly apt. Another quote came to mind, one as equally pertinent given his friend's treachery.

"'You want a friend in Washington? Get a dog,'" the president recited bitterly. Sickened by his naivety, he looked at his phone and dialled, whipping away the mask as Ratski announced himself on the other end. "Brad…" Garrett panted. "I believe…I believe it's started."

That was all he said. It was all he needed to say.

CHAPTER TWENTY-TWO

The greenhouse was the size of a five-a-side football pitch and in desperate need of repair. The wooden framework irretrievably rotten, white paint flaked and peeled away with neglect to layer the floor like the last snows of winter. Many of the filthy panes of glass were cracked or broken. Only the thick rolls of loft insulation that covered the building, held in place with a patchwork of blue tarpaulins, kept the interior dry and free of the rainwater that drummed on its taut surface. The lagging also helped retain the heat produced by the strategically placed heaters, humidifiers, and blinding hydroponic lighting, creating the tropical environment required to cultivate the jungle of lush, flourishing cannabis plants arranged in neat rows. There were over 600 plants in total, all as tall as a man, with colas (the flower) the size of a child's fist that provided some of the best *shit* in the whole of Essex. The insulation served another purpose: to mask the infrared signature emitted from the greenhouse from the police helicopters that would occasionally swoop over the Essex countryside looking for setups just like this one.

A man in a grubby white dressing-gown, flip-flops, and nothing much else meandered between one of the many rows with the hunched, head down plod of a habitual stoner. In the fingers of one hand, he held a smoking joint, while the other brushed and caressed the iconic seven-lobed leaves he passed.

He reached into the pocket of his robe and pulled out a small remote control. *Listen to the Music* by The Doobie Brothers began to blast from the speaker system he'd installed to promote growth. His plants loved music, and it helped them produce some killer buds. Today, it was San Jose's finest; maybe tomorrow he would play them some Stones or Led Zepp. Occasionally, he would put on some obscure global shit: Tuvan throat singing or one of Puccini's overrated operas—but never that manufactured pop drivel that the kids loved. His babies hated that shit as much as he did. A rhythm grew to his step as he got down to the music, gyrating and clicking his fingers as he sucked on his spliff.

Haircare a triviality he could do without; his locks were long and flowing, his beard as thick and dark as Jesus Christ's had apparently been. His look was achieved more through a lack of personal hygiene than any conscious decision to base his image on the western world's interpretation of JC. Both were handsome men with kindly features…except that Jesus had never worn Rayban Wayfarers at any time in his short life, from what his drug-addled memories of religious education could recall. But his appearance had earned him the pseudonym of 'Doctor Christ,' developed over the years as his reputation had grown. He adored the moniker, and it was definitely way cooler than the name his parents had bestowed upon him on entry into the world: Jeremy. Jeremy Dwayne Wigmore. That was a godawful name to saddle a child with, he had always considered with spite.

Unlike his stupid name, the 200-acre arable farm Tony and Patricia Wigmore, farmers by tradition, had left their only son upon their untimely demise had been the best thing they had ever given him. The land had long been abandoned and returned to nature, but the haul he made from his greenhouse crop allowed him to make a comfortable living, supplying the gangs of Essex with their high potency weed while practising the side-line he offered to an exclusive clientele.

While Doctor Christ danced and bopped through his plants like some 1980s disco nightmare, he failed to hear the door at the end of the greenhouse screech open and slam back shut with the rattle of glass. Too preoccupied with the air guitar he'd started to strum, his tempo so disorientated he could have been playing a completely different song, he didn't hear the scuff of a shoe on the stone floor.

It was the pervasive stench that struck him first. An aficionado of weed and its many distinctive variants, Doctor Christ had grown and sampled strains that smelt of ammonia, piss on a pavement, floor cleaning solution, cabbage, sweaty pussy, pine forests, crushed black pepper, musty armpits—the list was endless. But he had never experienced anything like what assaulted his nostrils now. It was similar to barbequed pork that had been overcooked and left to fester.

Doctor Christ danced to an awkward stop and sniffed the air for clarification, pulling a disgusted face at what was returned. He reached for the remote and killed The Doobie Brothers, an instant chill clawing up his spine as he became aware that he was no longer alone. Someone was standing right behind him, a ghastly agonal breathing rasping throughout the greenhouse. It wasn't the police, he felt certain. Not unless it was a lone officer who had just run ten miles with terminal asthma. With a gulp that ballooned at his throat, he turned. The sight that greeted him would never be forgotten, a fact cemented by the hellish, high-pitched scream he unleashed. Doctor Christ stumbled back and fell into his plants, snapping two off at the stems.

A couple of feet from where he lay, something nightmarish stood before him, swaying like a stalk in a breeze. If only for the briefest of moments, Doctor Christ wondered if it was some creature conjured by his own brain, pickled by the psychoactive properties of the tetrahydrocannabinol he consumed in copious amounts. He tore away his crooked Wayfarers to scrub at his eyes, desperate to erase the abomination, but the thing still remained.

It appeared so pathetic as it stood there shivering, its arms pulled up in front of its body to protect what was already destroyed. Naked, except for a few clinging remnants of clothing fused to the skin in several places and a muddy pair of shoes and socks, the majority of its upper torso was charred and horribly burnt. Descending from ruined to red raw to painful blistered pink, the legs remained relatively untouched by flame. The thing shuffled forwards and extended its hands in a pleading motion. "Help me," it was saying without words, its lips burnt away to create a permanent clenched-teeth grimace. The man's head—Doctor Christ had decided it was indeed a man—was blackened and crisscrossed with a network of jagged red trenches where the burnt skin had cracked to expose the tender flesh beneath. Its hair was all but gone, incinerated to leave only a few scraggly tufts sticking up here and there. One eye twinkled weakly under the hydroponic lights, the other one empty but for a glob of raw gristle that swung from the socket.

The 'doctor' part of Christ's name came from his previous profession as a veterinary surgeon. He was a damn good vet until the incident that had seen him struck from the registry of the Royal College of Veterinary Surgeons for professional misconduct. Before that event, he had treated enough domestic pets or farm animals torched by nasty drunken fuckers to know this creature had suffered a similar fate. His quick visual inspection of the man had revealed just one thing: it was a miracle the poor bastard was still alive.

"Here we go again," Dyson muttered under his breath as he knocked on the glass door of his own office.

Raymond sat reclined behind the desk, staring intensely into space, lost on some contemplative plane. After another knock, he glanced up and beckoned Dyson to enter.

No doubt summoned to receive a carpeting for his helicopter stunt, Dyson ached at the prospect. He had survived his encounter with the Ripper reasonably unscathed, apart from the constant throbbing in his head, a plaster across his nose and ear, and a couple of dressings hidden beneath his suit. There were two fractured ribs, but they didn't hurt as long as he remembered not to breathe too deeply. After leaving the hospital, Dyson had trudged home through the rain, only to collapse into Mary's arms and sleep like the proverbial baby. She had silenced his alarm when it sounded and let him sleep for a few more hours, her innocent act of kindness making him late for the bollocking of a lifetime.

Dyson limped inside the office and closed the door with a gentle snap. When he turned back, the Welshman was beaming up at him with a deliberate smile. For him to be smiling at all was unusual, but there was something buried deep beneath whatever it was that amused him.

"Morning, sir," Dyson said with the lacklustre enthusiasm of a child facing his headteacher.

"Only just," Raymond scoffed, looking at his wristwatch. He waved his hand, motioning for the detective to sit.

"Sir." Dyson slipped into the chair opposite and braced himself for the explosion of pure Welsh fury that was inbound.

Instead, Raymond pulled on his bottom lip and returned to introspective mode, staring up at where the wall met the ceiling like it contained the answers to every question ever wondered by Man. After what seemed an age, he glanced over at Dyson. "Why did you join the police?"

"Sorry, sir?"

"I'm just interested, that's all. Why did you join?"

Dyson thought of the man he believed was his father until Goldman's bombshell had blown apart the illusion. He had joined to be like Alan Dyson, but after the counterfeiter's news and the devastating tale Khan had told, he wondered if it had all been for nothing.

"I wanted to play football," he lied, recalling how two gangly legs and uncooperative feet had cut short that idea before it ever became a serious contender.

Clearly disinterested, Raymond brushed his answer away. "I was all set to work in the mines. 'Welsh coal, best in the world,' they used to say, even though the mines were shutting down all over the place. I'd watch my da, this wide-eyed, hero-worshipping little whippersnapper, while he'd hack his guts up every night, spewing this thick black shit you could grease an axel with down the sink. Black lung, it was called. Terminal and horrible to watch. But I still wanted to do it: to stand proudly next to him at the coal face."

Raymond paused, his unsettling smile turning to one of affection.

"One day, my mother bought me one of those cheap detective novels. Picked it up at the church fete, she did. I was hooked. It was an escape from the inevitable future that would surely kill me, same as it did my poor old da in the end. I'd hardly ever seen a policeman up until that point. Our village didn't even have a station; it was that small. The nearest was in Pontypridd. Anyway, I couldn't get enough of the books. I ate them up! Chandler, Chesterton, Conan Doyle, Agatha Christie—all the big guns. And then I began to wonder…could I become a copper? And that was that; my fate was sealed." Raymond gazed across the desk. "Do you read much, Dyson?"

"Probably not as much as I should."

"I read a great little book today. Well, part of it anyway. Let me…" Raymond reached into the desk drawer and pulled out a book with a faded cover. "Let me show you. I had to hit the librarian with a Section 19 to get this. I don't have a library card for Whitechapel." He tossed the book over to Dyson. "Here, read from where I've marked."

Section 19 of the Police and Criminal Evidence Act allowed a police officer to seize an object or possession if it was believed to be stolen, at risk of damage or destruction, involved a crime, or could be considered evidential.

With that in mind, Dyson eyed him curiously as he took the book. It was years old, its red leather cracked, the gold embossed title stamped on the cover distressed and hard to read. He opened it to a page bookmarked with a scrap of paper and began to read.

UNBELIEVABLE OCCURRENCE

A strange story recounted to me was that of Detective Sergeant Sidney Carmichael of Whitechapel Police Station. The date was November the 9th, 1888, Carmichael remembered it well as it was the day Jack the Ripper's final victim, Mary Jane Kelly, was discover—

. . .

Dyson took a sharp intake of breath until his ribs protested. His heart quickening, the book started to shake as his hands suddenly turned clammy. He stared back at Raymond, his mouth falling open. The Welshman responded with a devious chuckle, gesturing for him to carry on.

He said that himself and Detective Inspector Frederick George Abberline, the policeman responsible for the Jack the Ripper investigations no less, had become involved in a chase for a stolen Hansom cab. They found it abandoned and almost smashed to pieces in Colbart Street, Whitechapel. The two detectives disembarked from the cab in which they themselves were travelling and searched the immediate area on foot.

Inside an empty warehouse, they found the thief, who Abberline recognised from a previous encounter as one Robert Garrett. He was together with a woman, and a man who was lying unconscious on the floor. The man and woman were holding hands and obviously acquainted. Abberline smashed one of the panes of glass with his pistol and opened the window. They climbed in and confronted the thief, but he produced a knife from his pocket and put it to the woman's throat. Carmichael went to the window to blow his whistle to summon assistance, but the man warned Abberline that he would kill the woman if Carmichael blew it, pulling the woman tighter to him to demonstrate his intentions. Ordered to return, Carmichael suggested to Abberline that they should rush the thief and overpower him. But before they attempted to do so, the man became agitated and told the woman that something had gone wrong. She responded by saying, 'No, John.'

. . .

Dyson gulped and looked helplessly at Raymond as if he were drowning.

"Read every word, *John*."

With little other option or chance of reprieve, he returned to the passage.

It was at that point that the incident took a devilish turn when the reprobate's demeanour changed from dread to determination, and he demanded the detectives' guns, handcuffs, and money. Fearing for the woman's safety, Abberline agreed, and the two policemen were shackled by their own restraints. It soon became apparent, however, that the man and woman were in cahoots. With Abberline and Carmichael incapacitated, the dastardly pair made good their escape, dragging the unconscious fellow with them and stealing another horse-drawn vehicle outside the warehouse. Carmichael became visibly distressed as he recounted what happened next.

An incomprehensible light bloomed within the building, appearing out of nowhere. Brighter than the sun itself, it shattered all of the building's windows and made such a dreadful hullaballoo. After the light had faded, Abberline instructed his sergeant that they should remain silent about the incident as he feared for their futures with the police and for their pensions.

Carmichael did just that, carrying the secret until divulging it to me. He described the thief in some detail. 'His name was John, as I have stated, although Fred knew him by another name. He was tall; some ladies would say handsome, with an unkempt beard and hair, and his hands were badly cut and bruised. I think maybe he had been fighting.

There was more, but Dyson had read enough. Sickened, he closed the book and gawked dumbfounded at the Welshman.

"Well, well, well. What a pickle. Let me tell you what I think I've managed to deduce, and you can fill in any blanks for me." Raymond rocked back and forth in his seat, relishing in Dyson's discomfort as he made a tight nod. "You, the world's leading authority on Jack the Ripper, or at least the only one who's a serving police officer, was sent back in time—I can't even believe I'm saying this—to 1888 by someone in the US government, probably this Brad Ratski. Oh, I know he's not Michael Ackerman, by the way, so you can save your defence. You go and arrest Jack and bring him back to October 2030 for some batshit crazy reason? How's that sound for starters?"

"Pretty good," Dyson whispered. "Although, it was the president himself who recruited me. Ratski's just some glorified gofer."

"You met President Garrett?"

Dyson confirmed that he had. There was little point in attempting to build a lie out of the truth with such damning evidence quivering in his hands. But more than that, it felt cathartic to have the secret aired, the crushing guilt that had saddled him since the Ripper's escape finally easing.

"You come back, and Jack escapes, killing Bernstein and Simmons, the two Secret Service agents who were being used to ferry him to…a secure location? Now, Jack's smart, Jack realises he's going to stand out like a bacon sandwich in a mosque dressed like Bert the chimney sweep. So, he finds George Harford and kills him for his clothes."

"I think that's about it."

No, that wasn't it. Raymond shook his head vigorously, concluding his summing up at an accelerating, breakneck pace. "You mean apart from him not showing up on dabs and DNA for obvious reasons, slaughtering your local junkie scumbags, having another costume change, and then getting back into the fine art of Rippering by making poor old Trisha Noble victim number six!"

He stopped his rocking and looked hard, the next words out of his mouth the ones that had eluded Dyson since the whole sorry mess began.

"His name is Gregor Zolkov, by the way."

"*Gregor...!*" Dyson blurted out, too astonished to even finish the name.

"That's exactly how I responded!" the Welshman smirked. "Ex-Russian special forces, would you believe? One of the tzar's own personal protectors. It turns out Gregor disappeared from Russia after going on a killing spree in 1885."

"How...how do you know all this?"

"Oh, I can't take the credit for this outstanding bit of detective work, unfortunately. Clever little cow from the FSS pieced it all together from stuff she found in his clothes. I threw her out; I didn't believe a single word she was saying. You wouldn't, would you? *Time travel?* She left me a final fuck you in that book. Her trump card, so to speak. And that's the only thing I can't figure out... How she linked the book to you and Zolkov, and I'm far too pig-headed to phone her to apologise and ask."

Raymond paused to poke a menacing finger at Dyson.

"The bigger question here is...what the hell do we do about you? You've constantly lied through your teeth, withheld information, and I've probably got you on falsifying evidence."

"Pardon me?"

"The letter, Dyson, the letter. The letter you wrote to tie the cases together and stop us wasting valuable time. Nice touch; you had me fooled. But not so much Amanda Hasted of the Forensic Science Service. No doubt she got your name from the crime scene logs and made the connection to the John in the book. Bit of a leap, but—"

"Guilty," Dyson relented with a sigh. He opened his mouth to add something else but decided it better not to mention framing Wayne Sonnex for the murders of Mickey Houghton and Ronnie Palmer.

"I assume," Raymond continued, "that this is all top-secret stuff, and Garrett, believing you the best man for the job, went cap in hand to our eager to please government to save you from the clutches of the DPS?"

"It was the prime minister," Dyson confirmed. "I was summoned to Downing Street."

"The prime minister." The Welshman nodded appreciatively. "You're becoming quite the friend to world leaders, aren't you? And since this newfound ability of yours to pull helicopters and policemen out of your arse, shall I also assume that any further attempt I make to have you removed from the case and suspended will be brick-walled by your new chums?"

"Look...*sir*. My one concern is getting this bastard. After that, you can do what you want to me. But I can't have any more women dying like Trisha Noble. I...I can't live with that on my conscience."

"Because you brought him back?"

"Because I brought him back. I was gonna run—I was ready to leave the country—but they pulled me back in. So, I'm back in...and I will not quit until we catch this bastard."

Raymond watched Dyson for a long moment until his finger, still aimed forwards, drifted down to point at the book. "Who was the woman?"

"Mary Jane Kelly," Dyson said, answering Raymond's next question before he could ask it. "She wasn't a victim; they got that bit wrong. It was another girl in Mary's room. Mary helped me. She saved my life."

His eyes narrowed with suspicion, Raymond's finely tuned ability to read people striking gold. "Dear God, you brought her back, didn't you? You fell in love with her, and you brought her back."

"I did."

Inflating his cheeks to purposefully blast out the flabbergasted air between his lips, Raymond made some unintelligible grumbling and let gravity sling him forwards in the chair. He reached down behind the desk to produce a full bottle of scotch and a couple of paper cups. "I said I owed you one."

The Welshman spun off the cap and poured out two generous measures, handing one over to Dyson. He sipped from the whiskey, covertly watching Raymond while he rasped at his chin, trying to piece together the last part of the jigsaw.

"But why do they want him?" he mused between sips. "The Americans? Why bring back Jack the Ripper?"

"Because Garrett's dying, and they need the Ripper's blood to save him. They both have the same ultra-rare blood group."

Raymond choked on his scotch, spluttering an errant dribble down his chin. "And they couldn't find anyone else?"

"Oh, they did. One who was sicker than Garrett, and the other one Ratski managed to kill while trying to kidnap him."

Both men rolled their eyes together in incredulous, synchronised harmony. Raymond cleaned himself up and grew quiet, almost embarrassed to ask his next question. "So…what's it like? Travelling through…you know? Time travel?"

"Instant," was Dyson's first response. He thought some more as he savoured his whiskey, peering into the cup for answers. "Noisy. Painful. Hot! You arrive feeling drained and sick to your stomach, but it soon passes."

Raymond nodded along, enthralled by the explanation.

He thought for a long time before speaking, rolling the paper cup back and forth in his hand. "Look, I am an unlikeable old bastard. I can be infantile, petty, and generally unpleasant. I know that—I know what they say. I never got it until now; God knows there's enough real crime out there to worry about. But Jack the Ripper? It's the Holy Grail to a copper: *the one that got away.* I can appreciate why you did what you did. I would have probably done exactly the same given the opportunity if I were twenty years younger and as many pounds lighter. Therefore, we need to bury the bullet or whatever it is they say and work together. We get Zolkov, Garrett gets his blood…and I get to go home to my wife. Deal?"

Dyson sat forwards, straightened by the bewilderment he felt. "Wait… You're not going to crucify me?"

"What would be the point? You're protected. Like it or not, I just have to accept that." He extended his arm over the desk to Dyson. "So, do we have a deal?"

"Deal," Dyson said with a widening smile, the paper cups sealing the contract without the reassuring chink of glass.

"Just tell me one thing," Raymond asked with a groan, his lips quivering into an unnatural grin that grew to become a rousing laugh. "Tell me it's not a big blue police box?"

The joke missing by a mile, Dyson blinked, struggling to accept that the Welshman had taken the news so well. He had expected fireworks and shouting, blood and tears—anything but amusement. Yet there he sat, howling with a bout of uncontrollable laughter that caused his whole body to convulse and wobble. Dyson started to chuckle along, cautiously at first, wary that he was being led into a trap.

"It's not the TARDIS, unfortunately," he snorted. "And the bloody thing's broken too, hence why someone doesn't just go back and fix this mess."

"Broken!" Raymond threw his head back and roared some more. "You couldn't make this shit up, could—"

Mohammad crashed into the office without even a knock. "We've got a witness!" he panted excitedly, eyes quickly volleying between the laughing detectives. "To Ginita Nahar's murder."

CHAPTER TWENTY-THREE

The large room at the back of the farmhouse that Tony and Patricia Wigmore had used as a dining room had been converted into a hotchpotch surgery and operating theatre. Doctor Christ had little need for a dining room. He never entertained, not in a social capacity at least, and the old pine table in the kitchen was more than adequate for the Pot Noodles, takeaways, and prepacked sandwiches on which he lived.

Clean, with walls a soothing pastel blue—a complete contrast from the rest of the pigsty he inhabited—the room held all the tools required for the preservation of life: all bought from eBay or pilfered from local hospitals at his request. There were monitors for vitals, defibrillators, and stainless-steel cabinets and drawers crammed full with scalpels and supplies and every imaginal piece of kit needed for the wounds he would treat. Then there was the stuff that he had fashioned himself; converting something useless and unneeded into something worthwhile and necessary. The dining table, for instance. It remained in the centre of the room where it had stood throughout his life. But now, it stood higher, its legs elevated by Doctor Christ's rudimentary carpentry skills to provide a comfortable operating table; its surface covered with a tight waterproof membrane to wash away the blood of patients when required. The lighting above, essential for his delicate work, came courtesy of the rectangular light box that had hung over his local pub's pool table until the mysterious burglary that had seen it stolen. A hospital bed positioned opposite the room's big window dressed with floral curtains afforded excellent views across the Essex countryside. A nice touch for his convalescing patients, the image of tranquillity was only spoilt by the ripping sound that the cheap linoleum flooring made underfoot, constantly sticky from the nose-searing cleaning fluid he used.

The man who had stumbled into his greenhouse occupied the bed, watching as daylight retired through the windows to become a weak red smudge on the horizon. Lower body covered by a sheet and blanket, his scorched chest rose and fell in a staggered, painful motion, accompanied by a sound Doctor Christ found reminiscent of Darth Vader's dying moments. A gauze dressing covering the missing eye, the nose and ears were all but gone—something Doctor Christ had been too terrified to notice during their initial meeting. The permanent, teeth-bared expression magnified to manic proportions by an oxygen mask, the vision brought back the nightmares that had plagued his troubled youth. It was a wonder he'd been able to function confronted by such a monstrosity. But function he did; doing all that he could to stabilise his patient and make him comfortable. A network of electrodes connected whoever the hell this was to a monitor that displayed his struggling vitals, while tubes fed a concoction of pain relief and saline solution into a forearm canular.

Perched in a wheelchair by the door, Doctor Christ looked up from the A4 notepad balanced on his lap and watched the man with a mix of pity and revulsion. He took a long, final draw on the blunt pinched between his fingers and stabbed it to death in an overflowing ashtray on the floor.

"Can you hear me? Nod if you can."

His good eye blinking away from the window, the man in the bed turned his gaze to him and complied.

A lifetime of cannabis abuse had transformed Doctor Christ's voice from one crafted from the best education his parents could afford into a hyperactive slurry of verbal diarrhoea, peppered with the nuances that a junkie's lexicon always seemed to favour. "Good news first, man. I'm a doctor, well, a vet. Veterinary surgeon? You know, like where you'd take your dog? I mean, I was. I *was* a vet, but I got struck off for…for doing something I wasn't supposed to do with one of my patients."

He stopped only to improvise a loose fist, sliding the index finger of his other hand in and out of the tunnel created.

"I know, dude. Disgusting, right? It's wrong and all kinds of fucked up, but I figure you're not in any position to get up and throttle me, so I feel okay telling you. Honesty is the best policy and all that. So, the RVC struck me off, and now I grow the best weed in Essex, and serve the traveller community and criminal fraternity's medical needs when there's good reason for them not to involve hospitals and the authorities. So, in that respect, you came to the right place."

Doctor Christ drew a long breath, his expression becoming grim. It was time for the bad news. "Um… I mean, I'm not going to sugar-coat this, man. That's not my style. I wouldn't do that to a patient. That's not what I do. Medically speaking, and chances of living to a ripe old age, you are what we in the medical profession like to call *fucked.* I mean, like big time."

He glanced down at the notes made during his examination after finally getting his patient into bed. That, in itself, had proven a monumental task: he had been far too stoned and uncoordinated to go carrying bodies around. Instead, he tried to drag the man until he'd felt the skin loosen around his wrists and feared it might come away like a well-done lamb shank. Left with little other option, Doctor Christ had huffed and puffed and manhandled him into a wheelbarrow padded with an old duvet for delivery.

"Dude, I'm gonna keep the medical lingo to a minimum. Most of my previous patients never understood it anyway and just purred or licked their balls anyway." He laughed; his patient didn't. "You have a mix of first and second-degree burns to the torso, arms, upper legs, and head. Sunny point number two: you have severe smoke inhalation, and your lungs are shot to shit. You've got some serious scorching of the larynx, so I'm afraid your karaoke days are over. I don't know if you'll ever be able to speak again, man. I'm afraid your old chap's gone too. Sorry, dude. I've had to fit a, you know...a catheter. *Downstairs.*"

Doctor Christ squirmed at the grin seared across his patient's face, knowing it was anything but an expression of happiness.

"You've put me in a bit of an awkward position if I'm honest. I know, I know, not your intention. It's cool. I can't phone the authorities about you due to my little ganja plantation I've got going on out there. And I...I can't drive you to the hospital and leave you outside because some robbing little shit stole my wheels last week. I got seriously baked and popped to Tescos for some lemon ice cream and peanuts to quell the munchies, and it was gone. Bastards! Look, man, like I said, I won't bullshit you or give you a load of toffee. I think you'll be dead by the morning—it's a fucking miracle you've lasted this long. Sorry. RIP and all that, man. Or...or I can give you a nice little dose of pentobarbital to, you know, end your suffering. It's what we use when it's time for your pooch to cross the rainbow bridge. It's quick and peaceful, man, and I can give you a decent burial out in one of my fields. You won't be the first—it's like a pikey graveyard out there! I'll play a bit of music and say some nice words."

The man shook his head at Doctor Christ's offer.

"Hey, man. Gunshots and stab wounds are my bag. I can keep the pain away with morphine and any amount of other shit, and…and I can keep you basted like a turkey in Silvadene, but I am not a specialised burns unit. And right now, that's what you need."

His patient raised an arm a few inches off the bed that left a stained outline on the sheet and pointed at the notepad.

"You want…?" Dr Christ tore of his notes and wandered over to place the pad within easy reach, slipping the pen between what was left of his fingers with a sickened grimace.

The pen shook as he dragged it over the paper, his handwriting resembling the famous image of Guy Fawkes' signature after torture for attempting to blow up parliament. Doctor Christ craned his neck as he wrote. It took him a moment for his drug-hindered brain to decipher the jagged, shaking lines.

CAN YOU KEEP ALIVE? the message read.

"Keep *you* alive? Fuck, man, you want to live? Like that?"

The pen trembled and moved again… TO KILL WHO DID THIS.

"I dunno, man. You're at a heightened risk of infection. That's the danger with burns victims, you see? *Infección.* I dunno, I just…I don't know. This stuff here," Doctor Christ threw a hand wide over his surgery, "it would be like trying to fight a house fire with a water pistol. Sorry, I shouldn't have said that. Sometimes I say some stupid stuff. One time,

I went and promised this old dear her cat would be fine after its ovariectomy. Guaran-fucking-teed it. She was crying and shaking and shit, all this snot coming out of her nose. I gave her a big hug and told her Rosy… Was it Rosy? Ruby—*Ruby!* I told her Ruby would be fine. It was a routine procedure, nothing to worry about. Dude, the fucking thing was stiff as a board the next morning!"

By the time Doctor Christ had stopped waffling and looked down again, the man had written 100 GRAND YOURS!

Never one to miss a potential payday, Doctor Christ licked his lips at the thought of a hundred big ones. "*If* I can keep you alive?"

His patient responded with a single nod.

Doctor Christ thought about the challenges involved. It would be a herculean task and require specialist equipment, and there would be no guarantee of success. He made himself look down at the mysterious man in the bed. "Who the fuck are you, dude?"

CALL ME BURNIE, the man wrote.

"At least you still got your sense of humour," Doctor Christ scoffed with a reluctant shake of his head as he accepted the challenge. "Who the fuck do you wanna kill, man?"

The front door flew open to reveal Khan's grinning face.

Surrounded by a glowing aura of orange street lighting that accented his bruises to create a menacing visage that no smile could disguise, the criminal thrust a hand through the rain that poured down on him for the homeowner.

"Good evening, Mr Anwar," he said, greeting the stout

Bengali man standing in the hallway in his most proficient and warmest voice.

Dressed in the post-shift remnants of a bus driver's uniform, a burning cigarette stuck between his lips, Ravi Anwar scowled through the smoke, statuesque and unmoving.

"You'll have to excuse my appearance," Khan said, his grin slipping just a notch while he retrieved his unwanted hand. "I was recently the victim of horrific police brutality."

"I know, I see you on the telly," Anwar replied in blunt and broken English. He smirked fearlessly at Khan before his eyebrows dipped and his look turned to one of repugnance. "What do you want, Khan?"

"You had a loan from a business associate and myself several years ago," Khan explained. "I'm just taking the opportunity to revisit some of our most valued former clients to see if we can't offer a very competitive follow-up service."

"Yes, I remember. You is a bloody loan shark!"

"I prefer the term *crisis funding* myself. Might I come in?"

Anwar scoffed and made a nonchalant shrug, turning to plod back along his hallway. Khan entered and closed the door, making a mental note that he had touched the handle. That would need addressing before he left.

"Nice place you have here, sir," Khan lied, pulling a disgusted face at the dingy hallway littered with shoes and abandoned clothes. He stopped to examine a framed family photograph stuck to the peeling wallpaper. It showed Anwar hugging a big fat thing who was obviously his wife, a grinning child sandwiched between them. All three appeared to be having the time of their lives, relaxing on a beach somewhere.

The wife and kid ignored, Khan concentrated on Anwar. He was a big lump of receding muscle in his mid-forties, with a head of unkempt hair and a terrifying stare that probably scared his passengers half to death. The criminal remembered him from the loan he'd taken out when his boiler had exploded and flooded the shithole he called home. Anwar had been a good payer, always on time, with only one occasion where he had needed to be *reminded* of his commitment.

"Perfect," Khan muttered to himself, completing his perilous trek along the hallway into a filthy living room that looked as if it had suffered a recent burglary. They lived like animals, these people, like pigs snuffling around in shit, unworthy of his presence. But his presence would serve an essential purpose. "All alone are we, sir?" Khan asked casually, hiding the revulsion he longed to display.

"My wife is at work."

"Excellent."

As Anwar turned away to stub out his cigarette, replacing it with a fresh one from a packet on the mantlepiece, a baseball bat slid down from inside of Khan's coat sleeve, dropping with the gravity of its weight into his hand.

"I've just finished work, so let's make this snappy," Anwar said, putting a Silk Cut between his lips and fiddling with a cheap plastic lighter.

Khan settled the bat into a comfortable two-handed grip and raised it high, careful to avoid hitting the hideous chandelier overhead. The weapon hovered for a moment, and then he brought it down as hard as he could on Anwar's head, the pronounced *clunk* it made condemning the man to death before he even had the chance to light his last cigarette.

Anwar shuffled around; a look of shocked disbelief smashed into his face. A thin bead of blood came rushing out of his hair to course down his face, the hardened stare fading from his eyes. He whimpered, desperate to speak the word his brain no longer had the capacity to produce.

Khan spoke for him. "Why?"

He pressed the end of the bat into Anwar's chest and pushed him backwards, felling him like a tree and crashing his rigid body through a glass coffee table onto the floor.

"You're collateral damage, me old son. But don't worry, your death won't be in vain."

Anwar's crime and reason for the brutal assault: to bare more than a passing resemblance to the suspect the pigs were after; the one the papers were calling the 'Jack the Ripper copycat.' The likeness was uncanny, and Khan had heard through the local grapevine how Anwar had been stopped several times by the bacon on suspicion of being the killer. That made him an unfortunate and unwilling bit player in Khan's revised plan for war.

The criminal shrugged off his victim's agony as he twitched and shook, chinking the glass he lay amongst, and considered his performance. Khan had expected to kill him with one blow, fantasising on the drive over about Anwar's head exploding as if he'd swallowed a grenade. But this was the real world, and it was a blessing that it hadn't gone down like that. That would've showered him in claret and muck and hindered his escape. Plus, it would've ruined his favourite suit.

"Oh well," Khan sighed as he weighed the bat up and got himself comfortable. With a silent scream so as not to alert the neighbours, he delivered another blow to the front of Anwar's head that caved in his face and popped one eyeball from its socket. Anwar stopped moving, his head swelling as blood trickled from both ears and nostrils. Khan poked his head with the bat and found it soft like a deflated football. "Job done!"

The criminal took a moment to rearrange the growing erection in his pants and tossed the weapon down on the sofa. He pulled a pair of gloves from his pockets and snapped them on. They weren't the nytril ones the pigs wore, but bright yellow Marigolds used for washing up. Sniggering at how ridiculous he probably looked, he began to stalk the living room, sifting through the junk for Anwar's house phone. Target eventually found under a pile of old newspapers on the settee, Khan lifted the receiver and cleared his throat, tuning his voice from Cockney snarl to terrified Asian and reciting from the script developed in the car.

"Police! Help me. Please come quick!" Khan smarted, unimpressed with his delivery. He paced the room, stepping over the body, mouthing his lines silently before trying again. "Police, help me!" he said with a little less Asian. "Police, help me!" he said with a little more. "I've been attacked!"

Another lap of the living room, and Khan was happy. He dialled the emergency services. As the phone purred in his ear, he reminded himself of the fingerprints left on the bat and the door handle.

It was the same drab little office where his wife was shepherded into after arriving at the police station only the other day. Shadowed by Dyson, Raymond pulled a face on entry as he tried to remember when exactly that was. It seemed a lifetime ago now, his perception of time fractured by exhaustion and his mind muddled by the unbelievable information that had just come to light.

This time, there was no Maggie waiting to leap into his arms. Instead, a minuscule woman sat hunched at the room's solitary table, picking nervously at the seam of a paper cup of hot tea. Raindrops on the weatherproof coat wrapped around her skeletal body glistened with life under the glare of the fluorescent lighting. The face that turned at the detectives' arrival contained no such exuberance, ploughed with the deep lines that age had brought and deepened further by recent trauma. The woman ran a trembling hand over her face, smearing the traditional vermilion bhindi of the Indian subcontinent from her forehead, and stood to offer a timid, wordless greeting.

Hair as grey as slate, her sari as plain as she was, the woman was hurtling towards her seventies if she hadn't already got there, Raymond evaluated. He motioned her back into her seat and rounded the table to take the chair opposite. While his shirt took up the strain against his bulging gut, Dyson followed to sit at his side, offering their witness the warm smile absent from the Welshman.

Apart from revealing the reason for her lateness in coming forward, her initial call to the incident room was scant in any detail. It had taken an afternoon of painful clockwatching until the witness arrived to spill her potential beans; the breakthrough that had so excited Mohammad delayed due to her shift at one of Whitechapel's few remaining factories and a manager unwilling to allow her to leave early to help the police with their enquiries. Remarkably, Raymond had opted not to storm her workplace and threaten her boss with obstructing an investigation. There was no suspect in the cells, the clock ticking down on the twenty-four hours they could be held without charge or an authorised extension. The Welshman used the lull to update his decision log—the document he was duty-bound to keep as SIO that detailed his actions during an investigation and why he had taken them—while giddily interrogating Dyson about his trip to 1888. Now, with the witness cowering nervously before him, any lingering questions for his time-travelling companion were filed away for a later date, and Raymond slipped firmly back into detective mode.

"Seeta Choudry?" he asked, gruff and instantly impatient. He dipped his head to catch her eye. "I'm Detective

Superintendent Raymond of the Major Investigation Team. This is Acting Detective Chief Inspector Dyson of Whitechapel CID. We'd like to ask you some questions regarding the call you made to the incident room."

Dyson pulled out a notebook and pen from inside his suit jacket and sat poised and ready. It was the junior man's job to take witness statements.

"I am sorry for coming to you so late," she began with a weak nod, her voice as heavy with emotion as it was with Bengali heritage. "I had no idea… I only heard when returning home to Whitechapel. I have been away, attending my brother's funeral, and…and…I didn't see the news until…" Her face crumpling with distress, she approximated the height of a child with a shaky hand. "I knew Ginita since she was very small."

"Okay," Raymond said brusquely, nodding her along, "just tell me what you saw."

"I live in the flats opposite where Ginita was…was…"

Her reply halted by the massive gulp that pushed against her throat; she stopped to dab her watery eyes with a scrunched-up tissue. Raymond's jaw tightened at the delay, only softening a fraction at the 'Go easy on her' look Dyson shot him.

"I couldn't sleep. I had just found out about my brother. A heart attack, at only forty-seven. I went to the kitchen to fetch a glass of water. I look from kitchen window to see a man walking toward Ginita. She is standing at her door, looking in bag for her keys. At the time, I…I…was upset. You know, my brother? I did not think too much about it. I didn't see him…kill her."

"And…?"

"I returned to bed and try to sleep. I wish now that I had —" She stopped at Raymond's sigh, watching him fearfully as his shoulders plunged with obvious disappointment.

"And this was the night Ginita was murdered?" the Welshman probed.

The witness nodded sadly and sniffed. "Yes, sir."

Raymond waited a moment for her to settle herself before opening fire with a bullet fast salvo of questions: "Did you see his face at all, Mrs Choudry? Can you describe him for me? Was he carrying a knife? Did you see a weapon?"

Overloaded, she shook her head and fought off another ripple of emotion clawing at her throat. "No, I am very sorry. I saw him only from the back."

Dyson stopped writing and looked supportively at her. "Do you remember what he was wearing, Mrs Choudry?" he asked her, his tone calm and everything Raymond's wasn't.

The witness snorted away her upset and raised a spindly arm with the speed of a clock's second hand to point at an Efit of their suspect stuck to the wall along with a host of other wanted reprobates.

"Like that," she said. Chilled by the image, she turned away and let her eyes slip shut. "He was dressed *exactly* like that."

Raymond and Dyson swapped puzzled glances. Something was very wrong.

CHAPTER TWENTY-FOUR

With Mrs Choudry thanked and escorted away by a uniformed PC, Dyson and Raymond reclined against opposite walls outside the office as police and civilian staff meandered between them.

"Turner's wrong then," the Welshman grumbled, launching into a vicious tirade. "This *is* our boy! He's just changed hands. Bloody woman! Four grand a pop she's charging for an SPM, and she can't even get the hand right! I told her—I said to her, so I did: *he's swapped hands*. There was that one down on the south coast last year. He cut their throats, same as this, but everyone he did, he'd change hands, just to bugger up their investigation. Sussex PD was running around in circles for months."

"I'm not so sure," Dyson countered, contemplating the witness's adamant claim of the killer's clothing with a shiver that rattled down his spine. She was convinced that Ginita's murderer and the man portrayed in the mugshot plastered throughout Whitechapel were one and the same. Doctor Turner, however, had claimed the fatal blows struck to Ginita and Narinda had come from a left-hander, as opposed to Trisha's right-handed attacker.

"What do you mean?" Raymond asked, his brow rucking up like an old rug as he peered across the corridor.

"I mean..." Giving a slow-moving civilian a friendly nod in the hope of hurrying her along, Dyson dropped his voice a couple of octaves. "He hasn't changed hands, guv, because this wasn't Jack the Ripper. Jack the Ripper didn't change hands. I was there, remember?"

"Yes, but you didn't—" Raymond stopped and waited for a stout sergeant texting on his phone to pass. Far less patient than Dyson, he almost reached out to shove the man away. "*You didn't see him plunge the knife in!*" he hissed after the sergeant had gone.

Dyson prodded his gut where the stabbing in 1888 had left its mark. "I was kinda busy not dying."

Raymond made an extravagant roll of his eyes at the excuse, but there was little of the previous malice behind it. If anything, there was a dull glimmer of mischief and a softening to his ruddy features. There had been a subtle change to their interactions since the Welshman had discovered the truth. It was slow, like the thawing of permafrost or the speed it took Neptune to revolve around the Sun, but it was there. The aggressiveness of his tongue had dampened too, and he hadn't once called Dyson 'Supercop' since he'd learned of his time travelling escapades and the fact that the man they were pursuing was the real Jack the Ripper.

"Look," Dyson huffed, quickly adding "sir"—they weren't best buddies quite just yet. "Whoever killed Ginita and Narinda, it wasn't Gregor Zolkov. Therefore, Turner's right."

"But you just heard Choudry say that he was wearing the same clothes."

"So what! So what, guv? I could go and buy those exact

same clothes from a market stall outside or half a dozen places online. He's got our Efit as a reference. This wasn't Jack, and it isn't some screwed up, devoted fan copying him to get off. Look at the victims. Both Asian, both killed with a single right to left cut, no mutilations." Dyson paused, sickened by the disturbing idea that he had allowed himself to conjure. "This is someone deliberately targeting the Asian community to rain down some unholy shitstorm on us."

Raymond watched the conviction on Dyson's face as it paled, his own countenance twisting with dread. "I told Shaw the shit would hit the fan over this. I didn't think anyone would be mad enough to purposefully throw it!"

While he simmered, dragging a shaking hand through his patchwork of retreating hair to defuse the imminent detonation of Welsh fury, Dyson snatched his phone from his pocket as it started to ring.

"What is it, Barry?" he snapped, turning back to Raymond as his mouth fell open on receipt of the latest disclosure from Henderson. Judging by his horrified expression, now blanched the colour of snow, it was not good news.

A smouldering joint of immaculate construction resting on his bottom lip, Doctor Christ surveyed the mysterious Burnie from the doorway of his surgery.

In the midst of some frightful dream, his patient twitched and shuddered. Ruined flesh basted in as much *Bacitracin* and *Silver Sulfadiazine* as Doctor Christ could get delivered from his local pharmacists, Burnie lay wrapped in multiple layers of special burns gauze, finished off by a tight swaddling of crisp white bandages to resemble a freshly bound Egyptian mummy.

As tightly as the dressings were wound, Doctor Christ's

fingers were crossed even tighter. There was a hundred grand at stake, and the money he'd invested in treating Burnie so far would be truly down the shitter if he were to succumb to his injuries without disclosing the money's location.

On top of the financial outlay, there was the associated intrigue of the man's arrival. Doctor Christ liked a good mystery as much as the next cannabis growing ex-vet, and there was none better than a horribly burnt stranger stumbling onto his land in dire need of help. BBC Essex, playing on the old analogue radio in the kitchen, was alive with the news of a burnt-out truck discovered in some nearby woods, packed full with blackened and twisted corpses. It didn't take a detective from Scotland Yard to deduce that Burnie had somehow miraculously survived the inferno. There were children in the truck too, so the newsreaders sombrely informed. That part of the story had shaken Doctor Christ to his core; the thought of those poor little mites watching as their bodies were ravaged by flame sickening him enough to forego his lunch. He could only hope that they had perished from smoke inhalation or asphyxiation, as was generally the case with those caught in ferocious blazes.

Who Burnie was, was the burning question. Doctor Christ had thought long and hard about who his patient and his truck mates must have pissed off to get themselves barbequed alive. It was obviously drug-related. The drug gangs of London and the home counties were notoriously brutal when faced with anyone trying to muscle in on their patch. Only six weeks ago, a headless body was dumped outside Specsavers on Basildon High Street. The victim's hands shackled behind his back, a cardboard plaque had been tied around his chest to warn others about messing with the gang responsible: the gang responsible who were still currently being sought by the Essex Police Department.

What if it were them, Doctor Christ thought with a

nervous draw on his spliff, the calming effects of his weed doing little to dispel the worry biting at him. If news of Burnie's arrival, treatment, death, and burial got out, would the medical care he had administered be seen as some form of collaboration by the evil bastards guilty of flambéing the truck and its occupants? Doctor Christ certainly had no desire to end up like a burnt chicken drumstick, and just the thought suddenly caused his body to quiver and buzz. It took his muddled mind a long moment to realise that it was a phone vibrating in his pocket and not his body convulsing out of fear of repercussion.

He fumbled the old Nokia burner phone he kept for the business side of life into his hand and stepped outside the room. Doctor Christ coughed away his concern and shut the door, answering as cheerily as possible. "Yo, Peter, my man! Did you get it?"

The caller, Peter Seller, was renowned in the Essex underworld as a guy who could get his grubby little paws on anything and, as his handle suggested, sell it on, usually with a nice slice of profit added on for himself. But Seller owed Doctor Christ a big favour for pulling a nine-millimetre slug out of him that had blown apart one testicle and left him an octave higher than before the deal that had gone sour. So, this time, his services were on the house.

"You're a frickin' superstar! Yeah, we're square now. Drop it off, and I'll roll you a fat one." He sucked on his doobie and listened as Seller gave him an ETA. "Respect, dude."

Never had Dyson and Raymond been so united. Married in concealed confusion beneath their disposable masks and hooded Tyvek coveralls, they stood together against a wall of grubby flock wallpaper, their heads cocked in unison at the sight before them.

His name was Ravi Anwar his wife had confirmed upon returning from work to find her home crawling with police. The cause of death was unknown, but everyone was in agreement that he had suffered some devastating blunt force trauma to the head. Even the FME, who had already been and gone, abandoned her usual reluctance to offer any speculation or opinion to agree with the general consensus. The body lay crashed through a glass coffee table, the speed of its descent leaving the victim surrounded by an aura of thick, glistening shards. Limbs akimbo, Anwar's head was inflated to a size of a Halloween pumpkin, the features hideously inverted by the impact, the surrounding olive skin bruised a sickening yellowy purple. One eye dangled from its optic nerve to rest on his cheek, unsettling anyone who made unintentional contact. A sizable puddle of dark clotted crimson accumulated below the swollen head, another formed in the concave depression that had been his face.

Identically attired, Debbie sidled over to the frozen pair and waggled the phone she was clenching for the Welshman to see.

"Got it, boss," she said quietly so as not to disturb the painstaking examination of the three SOCO officers crawling around on the floor. "Bow C&C just emailed over a non-evidential working copy."

Raymond tore himself from the sight and reached over to take the phone.

"Didn't hang about, did they?" Dyson remarked as he watched the exchange.

"Their inspector owed me a favour." Raymond congratulated the Met's Command and Control for the speed at which they had expedited the release of the 999 call that had brought the police to Anwar's door while fiddling with

Debbie's phone. It usually took days, if not longer, to get a copy of such a recording. "Right, here we go."

Several seconds of silence were followed by the bored, monotone voice of a female police operator. "What's your emergency?"

"Please help me!" a terrified male cried out. The voice was shrill and panicked, undoubtedly Asian. The fearful timbre to his voice caused even SOCO to stop and listen. "I've...I've been attacked!"

"Okay, sir," the operator replied routinely over the sound of a keyboard being struck. "Stay calm for me and give me your details."

The voice coughed and spluttered. "I am Ravi...Ravi Anwar. 34 Buxton Street, White...Whitechapel. Please come quick! I've been attacked... By a policeman."

"A policeman?" There was an audible gasp from the operator. "Are you sure?"

"Yes. A Detective Inspector Dyson. He...he told me his name."

Dyson glanced over at Raymond and shook his head, muttering "Bullshit" under his mask.

"I want you to stay calm—"

"Please hurry!"

"The call's been dispatched, sir. We'll have officers and paramedics to you shortly. Why did this police officer attack you? Can you tell me?"

"Because he said I am his...his suspect. Jack the...the Ripper. He said he will...kill...me..." The voice faded with a thick gurgling sound.

"Sir? Sir...? Sir!"

Debbie motioned to her phone and reclaimed it from the Welshman. "That's all there is."

As SOCO got back to work, Dyson pointed at the house phone sitting neatly on the arm of the sofa about six feet from the body. "Righto. He dies mid-call, gets up to put the handset back on the phone, then lays back down on the floor and dies again. *Come on*."

"This is ludicrous!" Raymond agreed with a forceful nodding. "The time this call came through, you were with me. We were interviewing Choudry."

Dyson drew grim and pulled away his mask to share his bleakness. "That won't matter, guv. Not once the media gets hold of this. Especially after my run-in with Khan."

"All I hear is that bastard's name. *Khan, Khan, Khan*."

Raymond stomped off and beckoned for Dyson to follow. They picked their way gingerly through the messy living room and back along the narrow hallway. The street outside was heavy with loitering police, the cobbles and brickwork slick with watery blue light splashed from the gathered vehicles. But something was missing. Confused exhaustion at Anwar's dying message prevented the detectives from noticing it at first, and when they did, neither felt particularly compelled to comment.

It had stopped raining!

The great deluge that had pounded London for weeks now had finally petered to a stop. Shredded and torn apart, the whitening clouds above moved at a brisk pace, allowing glimpses of moonlight to bathe them as they peeled themselves free of their coveralls. They walked in silence back to the unmarked pool car they had screeched up in. Dyson, hands sunk deep into his pockets, his scrunched-up coverall under one arm, was lost in troubled contemplation—it wasn't every day someone tried to frame you for murder, albeit poorly. Raymond stared skywards, appearing to either beg for some heavenly intervention or just reacquaint himself with the sight of the long-lost stars.

"Tell me the Americans can sort this mess out?" he finally asked Dyson, ducking under a string of fluttering police tape and working his way through the wall of curious residents who stood gathered. "Otherwise, I'll be stuck in Whitechapel until the day I die."

"That's the plan, guv. Once they replace the Venezuelium."

"The what?"

Dyson ignored the questioning look Raymond cast, something else catching his eye. As they drew closer to a dark blue Vauxhall Astra parked at a precarious angle half on and off the pavement, faded double yellow lines running beneath it, he became aware of something flapping under one windscreen wiper. It appeared some overzealous traffic warden had pounced on the pool car and slapped a fixed penalty notice on it.

"*Jesus Christ!*" Dyson spluttered angrily, his blasphemy loud enough to pull Raymond from his brow furrowed consternation.

"Bloody little Hitlers!" Raymond cursed, rueing the day traffic wardens were introduced. "I'd like to have a bloody time machine, I don't mind telling you!"

What he would use it for wasn't shared, Raymond speeding up to an ungainly waddle to tear the ticket from the car. On closer inspection, he discovered that it wasn't a parking ticket but a printed flyer produced on yellow paper to look just like one. It was a great marketing ploy, Dyson considered, noticing there was one affixed to every car along Buxton Street. A parking ticket was guaranteed to be removed and studied, rather than just swished away by the wipers securing it.

"Oh, bloody brilliant. Listen to this…" Raymond held up the slip of paper and read as if he were rehearsing for a part in a theatrical production, stressing where highlighted portions of bolded text indicated. "'Citizens of Whitechapel! The police have lost control. They *do not* care about your safety. They are guilty of *racially motivated thuggery* and *murder*. Meeting to be held at the Whitechapel Sports Centre at nineteen-hundred hours, 26th October 2030. Your concerned friend and fellow resident, Frankie Khan.' Him, *again!* This piece of shit needs shutting down. Now! He plasters enough of these around town and stirs up the natives with his bullshit; he'll cause a war. You mark my words!"

He mashed the paper into the balled-up coverall he was clenching and scrunched it all together. About to launch the whole lot skywards, he stopped at the grin that crept across Dyson's face.

"What are you smirking at, Dyson?"

"Khan. He's screwed up. Read it again." Before the Welshman could untangle the flyer from his coverall and do so, Dyson repeated the line he wanted, hammering home the word that had caught his attention with deliberate emphasis. "'They are guilty of racially motivated thuggery and *murder*.' Murder, guv. He means Anwar. He can only mean Anwar. But his death isn't public knowledge yet. So, how does Khan know about it unless…?"

He stopped to allow Raymond the honour of finishing the sentence. In this new era of *détente*, it seemed the least he could do. Beady eyes blinking, the Welshman stared at him hard until Dyson's amusement became infectious, and his lips curled into a smile.

"Unless he was responsible!"

Wanstead Flats had never enamoured itself to the hearts of the public in the same way the picturesque Hampstead Heath to the west and Wimbledon Common to the south had. Barren and featureless, a blot more than a beauty spot, the 334 acres of open grassland to the south of Epping Forest had once been the venue of a famous eighteenth-century livestock market and celebrated Easter fair. Commoners were free to cut peat for fuel for centuries, and cattle were allowed to graze the land until the outbreak of BSE in the mid-1990s, when the practice became forbidden. Utilised during the Blitz as the site of a massive anti-aircraft battery, 'the Flats,' as it was known locally, had ended the war as a place to train allied troops for the Normandy landings and a site to house German POWs. These days, it was touted, somewhat overenthusiastically, as the perfect retreat for Londoners wanting to escape the city and enjoy outdoor sports, picnics, and 'experience a breath-taking natural vista on the capital's doorstep.' But what its website and those who sang its praises failed to mention was its less than salubrious side.

Located next to a murky body of water that boasted two islands rich in wildlife and discarded litter, the Alexandra Lake car park had been a notorious haunt of doggers: perverts and degenerates who would watch willing exhibitionist couples get it on in the warm confines of their vehicles while they gathered around to *entertain* themselves. That tradition had ended abruptly in 2028 when one amorous couple were butchered by the female party's husband arriving unannounced to find his wife not only in the heated throes of an affair but allowing a sizable crowd to observe their wild fornication. In a story that had made the national news, he had murdered both of them with a shotgun, along with several of their audience who were too slow to escape the weapon's range with their trousers around their ankles. Since then, the doggers had deserted the car park for safer pastures, their spot claimed by local drug dealers as a safe place to conduct a quick deal.

With the exception of one car, a muscular looking BMW 10 Series, the car park was deserted at midnight. Khan's stolen Tesla pulled in off Aldersbrook Road, lined on one side by expensive and impressively modernised Victorian mansions; the Flats opposite. It passed under the canopy of trees that bordered the parkland, crunching over crisp shale into the rain-flooded car park and sailing to a stop next to the waiting vehicle. Both driver's windows lowered simultaneously, three big bastards dressed in tracksuits and drenched in gold staring threateningly from inside the BMW. They appeared identical, as if cloned from a master copy kept somewhere safe. Heads shaved to near baldness, each man sported a catalogue of black ink tattoos around their meaty necks and over their shovel-like hands.

Russian fuckin' mobsters, Khan thought with a hidden groan, feeling for the automatic stowed down the side of his seat.

Only the driver spoke. "Frankie Khan?" he asked in treacle thick Slavic. He leaned forwards in his seat to expose a roadmap of scars over a rock-hard face, smiling a mouthful of twenty-four-carat dentistry that shone in the inadequate lighting the car park provided.

"You Viktor?" Khan answered abruptly, unafraid. Russians appreciated directness, so he had heard once, and this was no time to pussy about.

"Who else you expect?" Viktor replied.

"You got what I asked for?"

"Relax, my friend. I got." Viktor patted a moulded case the size of a microwave oven sat on his passenger's lap. "You have required funds?"

"Course I 'ave. What d'you take me for?"

Viktor didn't answer, but Khan doubted whether the reply would have been complimentary. The big lump jostled the box off his companion and fed it through the limited space between his body and the steering wheel. As he huffed and puffed and struggled to guide the case through his window, Khan considered how it probably wasn't his greatest idea killing Benny the Bullet when he did. He would've located the wanted item with much more ease than it had taken him to trawl the dark web for a London-based supplier, pissing about in a car park in the middle of the night like a junkie desperate for a hit.

"State of art," Viktor said with his best sales patter as the box finally left the BMW. "Same as what US Government use. Very good shit, easy-peasy to set up. Just follow instructions."

The criminal took the case and reversed the process onto his own passenger seat. Once safely stowed next to him, he plucked a weighty carrier bag from the footwell and handed it to Viktor. "Two hundred grand, as agreed."

"I don't need to count this, I hope?" Viktor asked, cocking a suspicious eye at Khan.

"I don't give a fuck if you count it or not, you Russian cunt; it's all there."

Viktor scowled and bared his gleaming teeth, obviously offended. "Ukraine."

"What?"

"I am Ukrainian cunt, not Russian." He faked a disgusted spit and took a cursory look over the contents of the bag. "Pleasure to do business with you, Frankie Khan." With nothing more to say, Viktor winked and floored the BMW, spitting up gravelly waves as he tore out of the car park to become a distant memory within seconds.

"Ukrainian cunt," Khan chuckled, patting the case as Viktor had. He did a blissful little wiggle in his leather seat at the thought of the fun he would have with the purchase. It would come in very handy. Very handy indeed.

But what on earth was it?

CHAPTER TWENTY-FIVE

The Sun was shining.

Providing little heat on the cold October morning, its reappearance seemed trivial in comparison to recent events and the tightening blanket of death and misery cast over Whitechapel. But just the sight of the star brought an energised spring to Raymond's step as he hurried along Vallance Road with something resembling a smile stuck to his face.

It wasn't just the improvement in the weather that raised his mood from the usual crushing sombreness. As the Sun had brightened on another day, Raymond had risen after a night of minimal sleep, haunted by thoughts of Gregor Zolkov and Frankie Khan and the merry hell both were wreaking, to find the *old* Maggie returned to him. Full of beans and with little sign of her Alzheimer's, she had beavered away in the kitchen, singing like the morning birds to make him a simple breakfast of tea and toast. He had hated to leave her so reinvigorated, only the fact that he was now hunting the real Jack the Ripper tearing him away. Raymond hugged her tightly, doubting whether the fleeting, nostalgic glimpse of the woman he'd married would remain until he saw her next…whenever that would be. It had been the most pleasant surprise, one that set him up for the day ahead, and he refused to let thoughts of her returning degeneration sour it. Not even the tortoise slow commute from Bromley to Whitechapel, or the fact that he'd had to park half a mile away from the police station on finding its underground car park chockfull, could erase his uncomfortable smirk.

He had laughed off his wife's jokey retelling of the old 'You can't polish a turd' idiom to dress in his best suit and whitest of shirts, adding a silk paisley tie Sue had got him for Christmas. It would be a horrendously long day, and he needed to look his best. The Welshman was due at Sky's Elstree studios in the evening to film the live portion for their *Crimenight* broadcast. The reconstruction of Trisha Noble's murder had already been filmed and edited, so the producer had informed him with an early morning phone call to go over the running order and what would be expected of him. His career charted by multiple appearances on *Crimenight* and its BBC forerunner, *Crimewatch*, Raymond knew well enough what to expect. From a slim detective sergeant with a boisterous mane of hair appealing for witnesses to one of the last major bank robberies in the UK to the overweight bastard he'd become for his first MIT case, he was probably more familiar with its mechanics than the smarmy looking gobshite who currently presented the show.

As Raymond hustled towards the junction with the high street, he could see the assembled members of the media laying siege to the police station, jostling and pushing against the crowd control barriers Chief Superintendent Horbury had ordered installed. They crowded the pavement like fevered Black Friday shoppers desperate to get a bargain, every day their numbers swelling. Amassing from all over the globe, their outside broadcast vans and trucks, fitted with aerials and satellites powerful enough to reach distant planets, added to the rush-hour gridlock and parking woes while waiting for the next development or titbit of gossip. When it failed to arrive, they would just make up their own stories. Everything from Trisha Noble had been a secret prostitute working from home to the perpetrator of death and destruction being a rogue Murder Squad detective. They had already hounded Trisha's husband out of town with their unrelenting harassment, forcing him to escape to an undisclosed location with his parents.

The Welshman slowed to consider his options. Should he fight his way through the throng and risk being recognised as the head of the investigation or duck inside via the underground car park? He watched as a voluptuous Spanish reporter led by a reversing cameraman made her way towards him, gesticulating wildly with her hands while telling the folks back home all about '*El imitador de Jack el Destripador*' in breathless and passionate Spanish.

"*Jack el…el…Destripador,*" Raymond fumbled in terrible Castilian.

He had heard just about every translation of his quarry's name since the furore had grown like the tumour in that bastard Khan's head. He was *Kirisakijakku* in Japanese, *Jack lo Squartatore* in Italian. The French called him *Jack l'éventreur*, while the Korean reporter he'd witnessed only the other day had almost sung the name as *jaeg deo lipeo.* Perhaps the most unsettling rendition, given that someone was now specifically targeting Asian victims to stir up racial tension, was the Bengali presenter from one of the local community channels who had called him *Jyāka dyā ripāra*, adding an unknown diatribe of venom as he glowered heatedly at the police station. A young Bangladeshi PC Raymond had collared translated the tirade as 'The police are useless and incompetent to stop the slaughter of our people.'

The reporter strode past. Unaware of his status, she continued to rattle away in highspeed Spanish, her high heels clicking an accompanying rhythm on the pavement. Amused, Raymond turned to follow her departure until his attention was drawn to another of the yellow flyers slapped to the windscreen of a nearby car. Determined not to let anything ruin his mood, he stymied the anger that bubbled and grew, releasing the pressure as a deep, growling hiss.

"*Khan...!*"

No fan of the police and their drug hunting helicopters, Doctor Christ had little sympathy for a murdering copper with eager fists. He dismissed the news by puckering up his lips and blasting a contemptuous, sweet-smelling plume across the kitchen. Slowing to drift lazily around a room desperate for a makeover, the smoke caught in the rays of the long-lost friend that splashed through the windows.

"*Hello, sunshine, my old friend,*" he sang with a slur, improvising Simon & Garfunkel's *Sound of Silence* for the Sun's return.

He sat up and killed the TV, and got back into the phone directory-sized instruction manual for the item Peter Seller had delivered. Flipping through the pages to skim read the aneurysm inducing technobabble from here and there, Doctor Christ began to wonder if he had bitten off more than he could chew. He was a disgraced veterinary surgeon who dabbled, illegally, in the removal of bullets and the stitching of stab wounds of Essex's criminal underworld. What he was not was an experienced dermatologist specialising in horrific burns to human skin tissue.

The ex-vet toked on the joint in his mouth and glanced over at the device laid out on the stained pine dining table before him with a mix of awe and trepidation. Procured from the burn's unit of the Chelsea and Westminster Hospital, there were only half a dozen of them in the country, or so Peter Seller had proclaimed as they shared the promised fat one he'd rolled.

The *brains* of the unit—for want of a better word—were contained within a large metal and plastic box fitted with rows of switches and a large touchscreen, still covered in the fingerprints of the surgeon who had operated it last. Several metres of coiled transparent pipework and electrical cable ran from the cube, ending in something that resembled a handgun crossed with a lightsaber. Whereas in the latter, the fiery beam for chopping off limbs would emit to buzz and burn, here, two delicate nozzles protruded at an angle, pointing in on each other.

With a smoky sigh, Doctor Christ pushed the manual away and stood. A mischievous smirk erased his worry as he lifted the device and lugged it out of the kitchen, along a dank hallway, stopping at the door to his surgery. Silently counting down from three to one, he burst through the door and stumbled to an intoxicated stop, brandishing the gun on Burnie laid out on his hospital bed.

"*FBI, motherfucker!*" he screamed in an abysmal American accent.

Burnie shied away, his one good eye flickering with fear while he sent his bandaged arms flaying for a weapon of some sort.

Doctor Christ lowered the gun away with a withering chuckle. "Chillax, dude. It's just a skin gun."

With no voice with which to speak and his ability to cast facial expressions hampered by painfully burnt flesh and bandage, Burnie still managed to produce a look that said, '*What the fuck is a skin gun?*

"A skin gun, man." Doctor Christ tutted with an incredulous stare at his ignorance. "It grows skin, man! And then you spray it on...like paint. You know, like when you mash up your car? I saw it on YouTube once. I had some dude who owed me a big favour *borrow* it from the Chelsea and Westminster, along with all the other bells and whistles I need to do this. All I have to do is perform a series of biopsies of the undamaged tissue of your legs, harvest enough stem cells for this little baby to...to—do what it does. Then I spray the affected area, and it grows skin, man. *It grows frickin' skin!* It doesn't come with any guarantees—and it's gonna hurt like prison buggery with the amount of stem cells I'm gonna have to mine."

He winced at the comparison and looked over at Burnie to see him twirling one dressed hand over and over as a sign for him to hurry up.

"You'll still die, man. Without proper treatment. But it might just keep you alive long enough to do what you got to do." Doctor Christ went on to highlight what he'd learned from the instruction manual's introduction, explaining how the skin gun was developed by Doctor Jörg C. Gerlach at the University of Pittsburgh's McGowan Institute for Regenerative Medicine in 2008 to restore the ruined skin of burns victims.

Scientists had been able to grow skin in laboratories for years, he lectured in his lazy waffle while stroking his Jesus beard. The process was lengthy, and the sheets of skin produced were extremely fragile. Blisters would often form due to secretions, damaging the skin and causing infection. Instead, Gerlach's device used a pneumatic gun to spray stem cells harvested from the patient's own undamaged epidermis. Held in an aqueous solution, the mixture was *painted* directly onto the burn, much like how a graffiti artist would daub his tag over someone's wall. Doctor Christ stopped at that point, apologising with a crooked grin at how terrible his analogies were sometimes. The new method took only minutes, he went on to explain, telling how in the early days of the procedure, the healing time could take ages. The painted area would need to be shrouded by a network of meshed tubes, functioning as arteries and veins, and creating an artificial vascular system, providing electrolytes, antibiotics, amino acids, and glucose to the wound. But with the advent of the drug *Ditacillin*, designed explicitly for the operation to accelerate and promote recovery, and also procured in abundance by his man, recuperation now only took a matter of days.

By the time Doctor Christ stopped talking to look up from the machine like a proud father watching his kid kick a ball, Burnie was holding his notepad aloft, four words scrawled in the centre of the page.

GET ON WITH IT.

"I told you last night," Raymond said to Sinclair as calmly as he could, fearing for his fragile composure. "You need to sort this Khan bastard out."

He had, in no uncertain terms, the DPS detective struggling to keep his eyes open while Raymond raged, Khan becoming just another file in his mounting caseload. Or was that mountain of cases, he had quipped acerbically in reply to the Welshman.

"What can I do, guv?" Sinclair begged with pleading hands. "This isn't even my shit. I came here for a bent copper with a bomb. Not a cop killer with a robot gun, or…or the local arsehole and his man-eating…his man-eating…" Voice faltering to a stop, he took a moment.

No doubt to remember his fallen comrade, Raymond presumed, offering a sympathetic bop of his head.

When Sinclair spoke again, his words came with the soft

effeminacy that had enunciated his arrival in Whitechapel, escorted by a tremor to his strained features. "After Dyson Fury put a chair round this bastard's head and walked away like Mother Theresa, the DPP crapped themselves and deemed Khan out of bounds. Every cop-hating fuckwit from here to the European Court of Human Rights is jumping on the Frankie Khan bandwagon just to jump on us."

Dyson Fury! Raymond scoffed inside. He could certainly appreciate how Dyson's escape from justice would look to Sinclair. He pushed his tongue around inside his mouth and stared over the cautious faces of Sinclair's team of detectives, watching from what they considered a safe distance. "Just—"

"Guv," Sinclair interjected weakly. "I forwarded Anwar's 999 call and previous interviewed recordings of Khan onto Newlands Park for comparison. If we can get a hit on that, *then* I'll go back to the CPS for guidance. But until then, I'm not putting my arse on a plate for a piece of shit like Frankie Khan."

Home to the technical support branch of the Metropolitan Police Department, the Newlands Park laboratory in Sydenham was charged with the handling of audio and video evidence. This included the cleaning up of grainy CCTV footage and enhancement of sound recordings to assist with an investigation. Or, in this case, the comparison of two separate samples to determine if they were made by the same voice.

"Arse on a plate?" Raymond smarted. "This is *your* gig, Colin, whether you like it or not. The Yard has spoken, and we must comply. *Whether we like it or not.* Do you think I like coming out of my office for anything other than lunch? Khan's inciting a riot with this stuff, so he is. The bastard printed a leaflet detailing Anwar's death *before* his own wife and kid knew he was dead." He held up one of the flyers and shook it for good measure.

"Sir, he mentions a murder but doesn't give any specifics," Sinclair protested diplomatically. "That's not even enough to put him on the naughty step. It's circumstantial at best. A good brief would fly you up high and then drop you like a tonne of wet shit with that."

Raymond shook his head and thought about his crumbling serenity. "Where are we with McGruder? For the love of God, you must have something? Take him out with the shotgun if you have to."

Sinclair raised an agreeable eyebrow. Taking Khan out with a shotgun was clearly an attractive proposition.

"Just get him off the streets before he starts a bloody war."

"And how does that look, guv? To the great unwashed. Police harassment? Persecution? Pursuing a dying man on a witch hunt? A respected businessman who's always paid his taxes and gives a shit-ton to charity. A pillar of the community who shot his own dog rather than let it maul your DS to death. Who then gets himself beaten to a pulp by another copper with a grudge. Because as sure as my shit stinks, that is exactly how his legal team will dress it up. Khan will be the victim here, not Ravi Anwar."

"Right you are," Raymond nodded curtly. "Well, you just remember that then. You remember that when Whitechapel goes up in flames." With nothing more to add, he spun for the double doors of Incident Room Two and stomped off.

"Guv," Sinclair called him back reluctantly, huffing like a petulant youth. "Look...I'll put one of my boys in the audience of this bullshit meeting. We'll...we'll mic him up and have a team waiting in a van outside. Khan says a single word out of line and we'll pull him on public order offences. That's about the best I can do."

"Thank you," Raymond said, recommencing his exit from the room.

"I don't know what good it'll do, though. Khan's a slippery bastard by all accounts."

Raymond stopped at the open door and drummed his fingers on the push plate. Glancing back at Sinclair, the smile borne of Maggie's temporary improvement came rushing back. "Everyone's luck runs out one day, Colin."

Today's been a good day, Maggie contemplated as she watched the bright and radiant reflection in the mirror of her dressing table. She finished applying her eyeliner and hooked a pair of plain silver hoops into her earlobes with all the care and concentration it took to defuse a bomb.

"Thirteen I was," she announced once the task was complete, her voice alive with life. "When I got my ears pierced." Maggie gasped a trembling grin, pleased as punch with her recollection as if she'd remembered some complex equation. "I can remember it like…*like it was yesterday!*"

Maggie had gone with her best friend Janice to some grotty beauty salon on the high street misleadingly named Glam R Us. They had bunked off school, both terrified of needles and quaking in their school uniforms while lying to the old bruiser who owned the establishment how they had their parents' permission for the procedure. Her smile flourished with a fluttering pride. That an event, so distant and innocuous, could be retrieved from a brain seemingly so damaged was a feat worthy of celebration. Maggie raised a glass of wine to her mirror image and drank from it, spilling the tiniest drop on the knee-length black dress she was wearing.

"Oh, crap!" she cursed, dabbing at the spill with a cotton ball to erase it.

After Bill had left for another gruelling day at work,

Maggie had spent the hours doing some minor household chores, much to her daughter's annoyance. She had made the bed and hoovered and dusted the house from top to bottom, Sue mothering her mother and ordering her repeatedly to go and sit down while force-feeding her tea and biscuits. Relenting with a hefty sigh, Maggie had sunk the tea and nibbled on a biscuit, phoning her husband to tell him how much she loved him. She listened while he complained how his 'big case'—that was what he called it—continued to flounder and go nowhere before declaring his love for her too, overjoyed that she had been returned to him. After that, she'd sprung from her seat and proceeded to dash outside to cut back her roses for winter before the rain returned, laughing triumphantly at her daring escape from her daughter's care. Maggie cherished these days: when her Alzheimer's released its grip long enough for her to function in near normality. They were brief and fleeting now, but she would grasp them with passionate exuberance, taking each one as if it were the last before the disease consumed her entirely.

"I remember when I met you," Maggie said, her smile turning to one of fondness. She put down the glass on the dresser and picked up her favourite lipstick. "I thought you were so handsome in that police uniform. I never believed in love at first sight, but...well, there you were. Just standing there. I plucked up the courage to speak to you, all tongue-tied and whatnot. I made some lame excuse about directions to someplace I already knew how to get to. You were smitten too, I could tell. All fingers and thumbs. Under the spotlight like one of your suspects."

There came no response from her husband.

"Lazy lump," she called out, eyes flickering behind her in the mirror to slowly fill with sadness. "I can remember when we broke up, Bill. After we lost our baby. Our Karen. I was devastated. We've had our fair share, haven't we? Of tragedy, I mean. Anyway, enough of the past."

Maggie straightened up and smiled away the heartache to pop the cap from her lipstick and dial out the bullet of deep rouge within.

"*Soooo…*" she cooed. "I'll meet you back in Whitechapel after the show, and we'll go for a spot of dinner at one of those amazing curry houses in Brick Lane. It'll be just like the old days." When no answer came, Maggie puckered up her lips and began painting them. "I'm talking to you, William Raymond," she said with a pout.

Sniggering at his silence, Maggie continued to apply the gloss with scrupulous precision, her hand rock steady. Job done, she blew herself a kiss and stood, pulling the creases from her dress to turn and examine the empty bedroom. The immaculately made bed lacking a snoozing body, the door to the en-suite wide open to expose its emptiness, her husband was nowhere in sight.

Maggie was all alone.

The biopsies had been taken. Late in the previous evening, Doctor Christ had sliced three-dozen postage-stamp-sized squares of undamaged epidermis from Burnie's calves to harvest them of their stem cells. Despite the near overdose of morphine he'd administered, it was still a painful procedure and not one the ex-vet would've subjected himself to, favouring instead the compassionate delivery of a bullet through the back of the head or a hypodermic full of blue juice. But Burnie's sheer determination to have his revenge had seen him through the ordeal. The healthy stem cells were isolated from the basal layer of the samples and mixed with a proprietary enzyme solution—derived from pigs and stolen by Peter Seller from the hospital as part of his *shopping list*—in a processing unit (also pinched) that heated it to disaggregate the keratinocyte, melanocyte, fibroblast and Langerhan cells. The resulting cocktail was then added to a buffer solution and left to 'marinade' overnight as Doctor Christ had put it, apologising to his patient how they weren't the correct words and how the weed sometimes made him forget the right ones, but they were close enough. The final step, completed by the subwoofer-sized box attached to the skin gun, was to create the mixture for application: a Regenerative Epithelial Suspension, the manual called it. After adding the required dosage of the *Ditacillin* miracle drug, he was good to go.

It was time to get painting.

Unwrapped from his dressings, Burnie stood naked and exposed in one of Doctor Christ's five shabby bedrooms, his arms jutting out at odd angles that offered the most comfortability. An innumerable mess of raw purple-reds, bulging all over with fat, pustulous blisters, his wretched body was twisted by an unimaginable agony, the remorseless tremor that buffeted him causing the catheter dangling from the burnt nub of his penis to vibrate wildly. Clear plastic sheeting hung from the walls, with more stretched tight across the carpet. The intention was to create a sterile environment, but the scene produced was more akin to a serial killer's murder room or a place where gangsters would dispatch their rivals rather than a place where life would be prolonged.

Long enough to come good on your side of the bargain, Doctor Christ thought as he pawed the skin gun awkwardly, daunted by the task ahead.

He had performed spinal surgeries on cats and dogs, cured horses of cancer, even rebuilt the shell of some unfortunate tortoise run over by a motorbike, but he had never sprayed skin onto a barbequed human to prolong its miserable life before.

"Are you ready?"

Burnie replied with the closest thing to a nod he could. The ex-vet pressed a button set on the top of the barrel, jumping at the splutter of air that blasted out a fine mist of clear solution. He stepped onto the plastic sheeting, aiming the gun anxiously at Burnie.

"Okay then. Here goes nothing."

CHAPTER TWENTY-SIX

The brutal juxtaposition of Victorian dwellings and contemporary boxy apartments went unnoticed to the pretty, mid-twenties woman as she scurried along the pavement of the darkened side street. Wrapped in a long winter coat, underneath a struggling umbrella, she raced past parked cars and under street lighting, the glowing phone pressed against her ear mixed with a face full of tangled, wet hair.

"No, he said it's a good deal, Mum," she explained excitedly into her phone, "with lots of potential to move up in the company. Hopefully, he'll get a nice bonus out of it, at least." She listened to her mother's reply and then answered, her response not nearly as enthusiastic. "My job's *okaaay*. It's Dullsville with a capital D, but it pays the bills."

While the woman scuttled through the downpour to continue her homeward commute, the heavyset figure of a man bled from the shadows behind her. Shoulders broad and strong, his face concealed by the hood of the camouflage jacket he wore, he took a long, slow look over the empty street and then followed.

The woman drew to a stop at a squat cube of uninviting

beige brick. She trudged up a couple of steps to the entrance and pushed through into the darkened foyer of the apartment block. Motion sensor lights eventually snapped on to expose a visitor's couch, a couple of potted plants, and a concierge desk absent of any such custodian. The woman shook off her brolly and collapsed it, grumbling into the phone about the building's lack of security and how they were paying an exorbitant amount of money to live there. Her mother telling her it was time to move, she took to the stairs, the lethargy brought on by the nine-to-five grind slowing her ascent and causing her to grip the handrail for support. Up she trudged, laughing and joking and making small talk until the second floor was reached. She turned out onto the walkway of an atrium, black doors lining all four walls, the open void in the centre of the building plunging down to the foyer and the gym she never used. Passing framed floral prints, she dove her hand into her coat pocket for her keys and yawned. The first key slid smoothly into a mortice lock and turned. A cylinder lock followed, the woman cursing as she jiggled the key in the hole. Finally, it relented, and the door swung open.

"I love you too, Mum," she finished, blowing a kiss into the phone. "That's for Dad. I'll speak to you tomorrow. *Byeee.*" The woman entered, the door closing with the reassuring thud of solid wood and bolts being thrown.

Time passed, filled with the insignificances of everyday life. A car horn beeped outside…a dog barked…a phone rang in one of the apartments. Then, with a scuff of carpet, a shadow slid across the wall, deformed into something inhuman by the lighting. The man in the camouflage jacket came to a stop at the woman's door.

The image froze. A moment captured in time. And then it wobbled and fizzed, and *Crimenight* presenter Nick Kerridge walked straight through the frozen scene as it pixelated and faded away to expose a brightly lit studio, the jazzy *Crimenight* logo suspended in the air behind him. A tiered bank of telephone operators sat waiting to field the deluge of calls they were expecting, Kerridge adopted a grave expression and turned his handsome, made for TV face to camera three.

"What happened next to Trisha Noble is too shocking for our reconstruction to show on television," he said with a seriousness directed through the concealed earpiece he wore. "But a madman stalks the streets of Whitechapel tonight, under the supposed resurrected guise of its most infamous son… *Jack the Ripper*." The name delivered with an exaggerated flair; he let it sink in for a moment before throwing wide a hand and gesturing for someone to approach. "I'm joined by Detective Superintendent Bill Raymond of the Metropolitan Police Department's Major Investigation Team."

Raymond shuffled up on cue. As awkward and clumsy as a virgin lover, he blinked under the glare of the studio lighting. He had done plenty of these before, but that didn't mean he enjoyed the experience.

Greetings exchanged, Kerridge began. "Detective Superintendent, you're on record as saying that this is the worst crime scene you've ever witnessed."

Raymond took a moment to eye up the presenter. Kerridge was far too glib and slick for his liking. With his perfectly sculptured hair, square jaw, and gleaming teeth that could burn out a man's retinas, he came across more like a used car salesman than serious television presenter. He was anything but such a thing, his career having been launched off the back of some grubby reality TV show where he'd gladly masturbated a farmyard animal to climax to avoid eviction for another week. After that particular high point in his fledgling career, Kerridge had been involved in a drugs scandal with a number of topless models and then got himself banned for drunk driving the following week. When watching the show with Maggie, Raymond often remarked how it was a travesty that such a scandalous miscreant had managed to land the gig. But he was only as grubby as the show's vulgar format; Trisha's murder presented to viewers under the distasteful banner of 'Tonight's Top Crime.'

Despite his dislike of the show's design, *Crimenight* brought results. With that in mind, Raymond straightened up and made an earnest dip of his head. "Yes, that's correct, Nick. The ferocity and depravity shown to this poor woman is something I shall never forget."

Kerridge nodded along sombrely for the camera. "Now, it's been stated that there were no signs of forced entry into Trisha's apartment."

"That's right."

"Then how do you believe he gained access? Trisha Noble was said to be particularly vigilant with home security after suffering a burglary only six months before her death."

"That is an avenue we're currently exploring."

"But if this letter that the killer penned is to be believed, then that would mean a security-conscious woman willingly let a deranged killer into her home."

The letter was irrelevant now that Raymond knew Dyson was responsible for its composition. Deciding it for the best not to share that knowledge with Kerridge or the show's 3,500,000 live viewers, he played along and gave the presenter an agreeable look. "That appears to be the case. Although, we—"

Kerridge cut him dead and surged onwards. "And now you believe that there is an antagonist at work—a copycat copycat, so to speak—deliberately murdering women from the Asian community with the sole intention of stirring up unrest against the police."

The presenter's line of questioning caught Raymond off guard. He wasn't expecting Kerridge to deviate from the prepared list of questions he'd been shown before the cameras started rolling. That had not been one of them.

"Um…again, this is an avenue that is under investigation."

"That's certainly a lot of avenues there, Detective Superintendent," the presenter retorted smugly.

Raymond's jaw hardened, his small eyes widening to bore right into Kerridge. "What I'd like to say is, and I can't stress this enough, is how vitally important it is that we apprehend this man as soon as possible. And how important the public are to this investigation."

Kerridge left an elongated pause, more to relish in the Welshman's discomfort than anything else. "And I'd imagine the investigation is being severely hampered by the loss of Whitechapel police station's dedicated CCTV room, destroyed in an apparently unrelated attack by one of its own detectives?"

Beginning to feel like one of the numerous suspects he had questioned over the years, Raymond could only reply with a single nod.

The multiple desks of Incident Room One pushed together to form one long slab of plasticised wood, the detectives of Operation Milton Keynes crammed around watching Raymond's performance, all in various states of exhausted undress. All except for Dyson. He had returned home briefly before the show's transmission to shower, shave, and steal a kiss from Mary, coming back recharged and casually attired in jeans and a hooded top to look anything but the deputy SIO of the investigation. Brian Lane, Raymond's trusted

CSM from Hereford House, was there, as were India 98's crew. Excited spectators to a line of police work they never got the chance to see, they stood against one wall while their helicopter sat dormant on the police station's roof like a slumbering beast. Before each member of Raymond's team was a notepad and phone; everyone poised and ready for the wealth of information they felt sure would follow the appeal.

"Two-nil to the goat wanker," Henderson cackled loudly at Kerridge's snipe, relishing Raymond's televised squirming. He tore a sheet of paper from his pad and scrunched it into a ball, tossing it at the Welshman's image and hitting him square in the face. "That rattled you, didn't it? Welsh twat."

Dyson pulled his gaze away from the broadcast to glance over at him. "Barry?"

"Yes, guv."

"Shut up, mate."

"Yes, guv."

The men and women of Operation Milton Keynes scoffed away the moment of levity and returned to the TV as the presenter's quickfire probing turned from interview to interrogation. "But you would agree, Detective Superintendent, that mistakes have been made during the course of this investigation?"

"I would not, no," Raymond defended.

"And that a detective assaulting an unrelated suspect has damaged the already fragile public support you so desperately need for your enquiry?"

Dyson cringed at the question and shifted in his seat until the faux leather creaked.

"The same detective," Kerridge pushed, "who, as we're now hearing, was involved in the *murder* of a local resident. I think I'd be completely justified in asking what sort of operation you're running in Whitechapel?"

A round of incredulous groans and under the breath

expletives circled the table while Raymond responded angrily on screen.

"Our investigation has been severe—!" he snapped, immediately offering Kerridge a begrudged smile. "Our investigation has been severely hindered by a number of external influences and situations that have arisen—which I'm not at liberty to discuss at present—to wilfully mislead the public and deliberately misrepresent the MPD in a bad light."

"Such as?" the presenter probed.

"As I said, Mr Kerridge, I'm not prepared to discuss those matters at present."

The grumbling of the table died away while Raymond and Kerridge exchanged poisoned glances, each man looking like he might lash out and strike the other.

"Go on, boss," Debbie joked, chewing on a biro. "Knock the fucker out."

"*Live on TV!*" someone else added theatrically, sounding much like an American sporting commentator.

The Welshman did no such thing. Instead, Kerridge turned away and looked directly into the camera to flash his award-winning smile.

"Operators are waiting to take your call!" he cried with the gusto of a game show host, his delivery increasing to the speed of a radio advert's legal warning. "Or you can call the incident room at Whitechapel right now on the number displayed on your screens or by using the MPD's website, social media pages *or* by calling Crimestoppers anonymously." He paused for breath and clapped his hands together to wrap up the show. "Now, before we go, there's just time to announce last week's competition winner—"

"Wanker." Dyson killed the TV and sent the remote-control skidding along the table.

"Which one?" Atangba scoffed.

Dyson responded with a half-hearted smile he didn't want to make while Jenny offered him a genuine and sympathetic one from the far end of the desks. "I thought they were supposed to be on our side?"

Duck, India 98's overweight pilot, looked over at Dyson, clearly in two minds whether to broach the question dangling from his lips with the detective slipping further into despair. "So…what happens now?" he finally asked, his gruff Glaswegian cutting through the fetid air.

Dyson cupped his face with his hands and blew out a long breath, the energy he had returned to the police station with woefully absent. He stared down at his telephone and willed it to ring. "Now we wait."

Hidden deep within the 400-odd concerned residents of Whitechapel who had gathered to hear Khan speak, DPS Detective Constable Anuj Sharma meandered casually as the crowd continued to grow. An experienced undercover officer, inserted as promised by Sinclair, he was there to monitor the situation, relaying any relevant information back to his boss by way of a concealed throat mic he wore. The conversation was one way, with Sharma already giving a whispered appraisal of the approximate number in attendance and confirming Khan's presence.

Thus far, the makeup of the audience was a good ninety per cent Asian, with a few white boys dotted here and there and a rainbow of mixed anxious women loitering towards the back. Asian men, Bangladeshi and Pakistani boys of a similar age as himself, exuded an already ugly mood, spreading contagiously from one to the other on an air of cheap scent and eastern spices. Sharma dressed like they did, in the latest tracksuit and trainers, his baseball cap pulled down a notch over his eyes on the off chance someone might recognise him. Many were already wearing bandanas or scarves over their faces to mask their identities. A worrying development, the young detective considered, given the hatred that had so far been spat in venomous Bengali and aimed directly at the police.

The sports hall of the Whitechapel Sports Centre was mammoth in size, and more than capable of accommodating double, if not treble, the audience that the criminal had drawn. A high ceiling jutted upwards, angled by multiple corrugated wedges fitted with huge glass panels to let light flood in during the day. At this hour, illumination came from a network of fluorescent units suspended from the rafters. Beneath their feet, the squeaky wooden flooring was marked out with a variety of worn coloured lines for badminton, basketball, and volleyball.

The main man himself stood on a raised stage at one end of the cavernous room. Partially concealed behind a wooden lectern he had yet to stray from, he was dressed in a suit Sharma estimated cost more than his monthly pay, every finger covered in the most ridiculous of gold rings. There was no fear behind his eyes as he surveyed the arrivals, only an arrogant pride that he had drawn such a crowd.

"Surely he knows we're here?" Sharma asked quietly, more for his own benefit than for the mic concealed beneath the pulled-up neck of his tracksuit top.

Unlike the locals, Sharma wasn't familiar with Khan. Sinclair had thrust a hurriedly prepared briefing document, complete with various photographs, into his hand and told him to study it before the meeting. The criminal was a grade-A piece of shit, the file told. A cold, calculating bastard who had risen to the top of his game under the guise of legitimate businessman, the young detective found it absurd that he had managed to escape justice for so long.

Before he could dwell too long on Khan's miraculous escape from justice, the lights suddenly dimmed, and everyone moved forwards on a chorus of claps and cheers. Playing his part, Sharma joined in convincingly, whooping and hollering as he had at the last gig he'd attended.

Behind the podium, Khan glowed, his bald head and rings glinting under the incandescent shimmer that bathed him. He straightened his posture to appear statesmanlike, like a world leader about to address the United Nations... until he drew a finger across his throat to silence the room, and the image was broken.

"Here we go," Sharma muttered, tilting his mouth towards the mic.

The hall fell silent, and Khan began with a welcoming spread of his arms. His voice sounded soft and gentle; the East End abrasiveness of the sample recording Sharma had listened to as part of the criminal's file deliberately dampened for his audience.

"Friends, fellow citizens of Whitechapel. Some of you may know me, many of you will not. For too long now, we have been the victims of racial indignation and hatred." He indicated to the lingering bruises on his swollen face. "I have suffered. *You* have suffered. We have bled blood, sweat, and tears for this country...and yet we are treated *less than dogs!*"

An acquiescing cheer resonated around the room, the crowd instantly buying what Khan was selling. Sharma joined in, sticking two fingers in his mouth to unleash a shrill wolf whistle.

Khan gave them a solemn look, driving his speech onwards with passionate conviction and intonating certain parts to gut-punch his message across. "Yes, friends, we have been treated like *animals*, by those we put our trust in. Those that we call upon in our *darkest hour*. Those that have sworn to *protect us*."

At that point, a couple of Asian elders in front of Sharma shook their heads in disagreement and headed for the exit, while the remainder continued to lap up Khan's spiel with approving cries.

"To take from us our beloved—*our most cherished of family members*," Khan carried on. "I'm speaking of Ravi Anwar. Viciously murdered by the same serving police officer who beat me to near death and *who continues to escape justice*. I'm speaking of Ginita Nahar and of Narinder Patel. Beautiful young women, *their whole lives ahead of them*, murdered, they say, by a deranged killer. I'm speaking of my very own parents, their deaths a *deliberate consequence* of the horrendous actions of the corrupt police officers involved. Look at the man or woman to your left." Everyone, Sharma included, did as instructed. "Is he or she the next victim of their brutal agenda? Are you? Will it be *your* parents, *your* brother, *your* sister? How many more must suffer, I ask you? *How many more must die?*"

The audience began to frenzy, the faces Sharma could see in the half-light twisting with rage to drive their angry fists skywards. Expletive-laden shouts filled the pause Khan left. "Fuck the police!" they started to yell, a rhythm growing until the phrase became a unified chant.

"Fuck the police!" Sharma echoed, joining in for effect. Deep inside, the statement terrified him. His dad had always taught him never to underestimate the power of words or the gullibility of the fools who heard them. That had never seemed so pertinent as now. The room was a tinderbox of hatred and resentment, ready to ignite into violence given the right spark.

Khan lowered his outstretched arms to dial down the noise.

"But what can we do? Indian, Pakistani, Sri Lankan, Bangladeshi. Muslim, Sikh, Hindu—those of no or little faith. We are a people united by skin tone but fractured by religion, ideology, and the geography of our heartlands." In a purposeful display of theatrics, he raised one hand and brought his fingers together into a clenched fist to signify unity. "We must put aside our differences and stand as *one*. Black lives may well matter, but let me tell you... *So do Asian!*"

"Christ, this fucker knows how to work an audience!" the young detective spluttered subconsciously, his loose words lost to the ferocious cheering that erupted in the sports hall.

"We must rebuild and repair," Khan cried passionately from his platform, shaking the trembling fist. "If they will not heed our legitimate concerns, then we must resort to other methods, no matter how unlawful. We must come together. We must rise from the ashes of our history, put aside our differences, *to seek our revenge and...*"

He paused for deliberate effect to stare imploringly across the sea of eager faces. And then, Khan exploded with the intensity of a car bomb.

"FIGHT THE POLICE!"

A massive roar of approval detonated in the hall that seemed to shake the building to its foundations. A fold-up chair was plucked from the side-lines and sent clattering to the back of the room, narrowly missing the women who were moving for the exit. Another chair was hurled through a floor to ceiling window that formed part of a glass wall along one side of the room. The majority of the audience started to chant rhythmically. One word, over and over, their voices rising with the temper in the room.

"*Khan! Khan! Khan! Khan! Khan! Khan! Khan! Khan! Khan! Khan! Khan! Khan!*"

The criminal nodded his gratitude and placed a hand on his heart, touched by their worshipful praise.

In the back of a battered Transit van parked along the road from the sports centre, Sinclair and five of his DPS detectives squatted on a collection of folding chairs and milk crates beneath a flickering lightbulb. The picnic table they huddled around sagged dangerously close to collapse under the hefty weight of a radio receiver and a couple of DPS laptops. The bare metal floor was littered with coffee cups and chocolate bar wrappers, and there was a Pepsi bottle left by the vehicle's last occupants that contained some mysterious liquid the colour of fermented piss. The detectives shared a grim bleakness: mostly due to Sharma's worrying commentary and the content of Khan's speech, but partially as a result of their cramped conditions.

A morning of multiple phone calls and form filling had secured the van from the Met's Fleet Services in Lambeth. Upon delivery at noon, by a gruff and greasy overalled civilian, it was discovered to be far too small to accommodate six full-grown adults and empty of any of the surveillance equipment usually installed. The civilian had shrugged nonchalantly at their protests, telling them to take it or leave it but stipulating to Sinclair that it had to be back by midnight. For that reason, the vehicle was christened 'Cinderella' while one of Sinclair's team scrambled about like a madman to cobble together the required equipment to kit her out. After close to two hours stuck inside, the interior stinking of body odour and flatulence and tainted even further by Khan's transmitted bullshit, Sinclair had begun to wish that he hadn't bothered with the van. They could've just as easily parked a couple of pool cars a little farther away out of sight.

"Fight the police," one detective uttered with disgust.

With an equal look of repugnance, Sinclair flipped a switch on the receiver to silence the feed from Sharma's mic.

"That's it," he said, the prospect of another job joining his overflowing plate causing him to sigh. "Let's get in there and shut this freak show down." He snatched up his personal radio and keyed the talk button. "All units from Sinclair. Go, go, go!"

The 'all units' he referred to were the dozen uniformed officers waiting to join the raid. He had positioned a further six near the rear entrance of the sports centre in case they were needed to cut off any attempt of escape. In addition, Sinclair had arranged to have the Territorial Support Group (TSG) on standby. They were waiting in a fleet of Mercedes vans not more than a minute's drive away. In Sinclair's experience, from his dim and distant days of uniform and CID, people at events such as Khan's were, as the saying went, 'All mouth and no trousers.' They would soon bugger off and make themselves scarce when threatened with arrest. Khan, on the other hand, wouldn't be going anywhere. The CPS and their cowardly warnings be damned, the criminal had said enough to warrant arrest for public order offences, at the very least.

Cinderella's back doors burst open, the detectives expelling out onto Durward Street and charging towards the sports centre. On cue, a fleet of vehicles began to skid up out of nowhere, their lights painting the darkness blue. Merging to become one thick clump of bodies, DPS and uniform swarmed through the entrance, crashing through turnstiles and racing along a wide corridor.

Never one to lead from the back, Sinclair ploughed through the glass doors into the hall first. He raised a loud-hailer to his mouth and spoke, letting the machine do the shouting for him. "This is the police! Disperse and leave the area now." A group of women heeding his advice with a collective whimper, he thrust a pointed finger along the hall to Khan. "You, Frankie Khan, remain where you are!"

From his stage, the criminal smirked sardonically at their arrival, while his audience, seemingly at a loss at what to do next, looked to their Svengali for guidance. With the police fanning out to begin their advance, Khan took a breath and spoke. The softness of his sales pitch abandoned; the hoarse roughness of his voice returned. The three words he uttered were delivered with an unforgiving, remorseless chill.

"Kill them all."

From deep within the audience, a bottle was thrown. It sailed through the air and crashed into the wall behind the police line, its shattering the catalyst for the hall to explode into a ferocious brawl. As if acting under one collective consciousness, the crowd became a horde. Men became monsters, roaring and surging forwards in frightening, blistering symmetry. Panicked screams of "Armed police!" ignored, the attackers swamped Sinclair and his men, crashing into them like a tsunami and burying them under their combined weight. Many of the assailants produced blades, steel glinting in the gloom, the guns drawn by the police coming far too slowly to be of any deterrent. Over terrified screams and vicious expletives, a gunshot suddenly rang out. Then another—and another. Then someone, cop or criminal, it was impossible to tell, released a bloodcurdling scream that just didn't stop.

"Get the fucking TSG!" one of the detectives pleaded over the howling, the last words he would ever cry before succumbing to the barrage of steel thrust into his body.

By some miracle, Sinclair survived the onslaught. His tortured face oozing blood, he crawled from underneath a violent scrum of writhing bodies, gripping his Glock for dear life as he staggered through the carnage.

What he witnessed horrified him. This was no crowd to be scattered by threats of arrest alone. They were a feral mob, stoked up and frantic for blood, unconcerned by the consequences. That assumption was confirmed when he witnessed two brutal thugs wrestle the gun from a robust PC's hand, breaking his fingers in the process, and then shooting him dead with his own weapon. Sinclair opened fire on the attackers, blasting their heads apart and killing them both instantly. Dodging punches and kicks from all directions, another assailant pushed his way through, raising the gleaming machete he carried. The detective slammed his Glock into the man's face to break his jaw in two before the blade came down to open him up. Sinclair broke free of the fighting and headed for the motionless Khan. With no intention of attempting escape, the bastard just stood his ground, laughing at the detective's approach and revelling in the violence he'd created.

"I'll wipe that grin off your smug face!"

Sinclair dropped a gear and sped into a run, his arms working like pistons to drive him onwards. The stage reached in seconds, he launched himself into the air like a guided missile.

"You're under arrest!" Sinclair cried. Arms flailing and grabbing nothing, he sent the podium toppling and crashed painfully into the wall behind where Khan had stood.

The bastard had vanished into thin air!

Eyes on stalks, gasping at the impossibility of what just happened, Sinclair looked down at the empty space he was clutching as he rolled over onto his back. Before he could move and contemplate what to do next, a lumbering youth drenched in Nike roared up and smashed a folded seat down on his head. Crimson jetted from the wound, the detective trying valiantly to shield his face from the next blow. He felt his wrist snap, the instant agony causing the gun to slip from his grasp. The boy screamed like a warrior, raising the chair and bringing it down again and again until Sinclair's vision clouded red, and then everything darkened to a silent black.

A natural reaction to Sinclair's flying rugby tackle, Khan stumbled away from the camera unit of the Yumshima DXT44 Holographic Conferencer. It was the same device the US Government used, he remembered Viktor had claimed. Irrespective of whether that was true or not, it had done its job brilliantly. The experience had seemed so real, like he was actually there in the hall with all those morons swallowing up the shit he fed them. But now the machine was dead—*as dead as that fucker Sinclair*, Khan hoped—the words on the attached screen warning that the connection had been lost.

"You clever bastard, Frankie," he chirped, praising his ingenuity with a self-congratulatory cackle that grew to course his entire body.

The last time Khan had visited the Whitechapel Sports Centre was over two years ago—he'd had no intention of going anywhere near it tonight. Experience had taught him that bacon would secrete an undercover pig at the meeting. They were probably on to him by now, either for the two Paki girls or Anwar. Maybe they had even linked him to his barbequed boys by now, by way of an errant clue left at the scene. Regardless of what the reasons were, he was a wanted man and so needed to tread carefully. The device bought from the Ukrainian mobsters had given him the freedom to stoke the fires of conflict without fear of capture.

Khan's actual location was a sturdy double garage in Doveton Street. Packed to the roof with plastic crates and metal boxes in various sizes and shades of green, he stood in a clearing ample enough for the machine to take a 'Full Body Capture,' as the instructions had called it. As Viktor had promised, the set-up was idiotproof. The conferencer did its magic: adjusting lighting levels and deleting the unwanted garage background, and then beaming his likeness—or whatever it did—to the projector unit hidden out of sight behind the lectern, all in real-time.

The lock-up cost him 500 quid a month, but it was money well spent. It gave him a place to store anything he didn't want to be found in possession of, such as the haul of military-grade weaponry he'd gotten from the now dead and buried Benny the Bullet. Rented under an assumed identity, Jolly Ranganathan—some little cunt who had once agreed to be a witness against him until tragically falling down a lift shaft—the garage came with electricity and discretion guaranteed; the owner not giving one steaming shit what went on within as long as he got paid.

Khan's amusement grew to a hearty roar, one so intense that it brought tears to his eyes, and he was forced to lean on a stack of the green boxes to support his hilarity. Despite losing his treacherous former employees, their glorious burning stench still lingering in his nostrils, he would have his war with the pigs. Of that, he was certain. Judging by the number of sirens screaming in the distance, no doubt heading for Durward Street, it had begun already.

The event had taken only the most basic of planning. While a local printer had produced Khan's flyers—free, as a show of support for the families of the two butchered girls—the gang of chain-smoking schoolkids he'd employed had plastered the vehicles of Whitechapel over and over in exchange for enough cash to keep them in fags for a good while. Securing the venue had been an easy enough task. Khan had visited the manager of the Whitechapel Sports Centre at his home in Leyton and sufficiently menaced him into cancelling the wedding reception booked for the Saturday evening and handing over the place in its entirety. After the weedy looking fucker had given him a set of blood-stained, violently shaking keys, Khan had killed him and his screaming bitch of a wife, stuffing them both inside their own chest freezer; for no other reason than the act brought him pleasure. With another couple of drug-dependent morons hired to set up the hall and install Viktor's machine, Khan was good to go. There was no guilt for a sobbing bride and her scuppered wedding plans. The people of Whitechapel were the shit under his shoes, worthless pawns to do with as he wanted. The mugs who took up his cry for revenge were nothing more than foot soldiers. Gullible expendables, too dumb to realise that he wasn't even at the venue, who could be manipulated as easily as clay. The others, however—

"Shit!" the criminal exclaimed, scrubbing his joyful tears dry to weave through the narrow path left between the crates and boxes. "I forgot about the others." He ducked down to grab the bottom of the garage door, heaving until it rattled upwards on its cantilever with a screech.

Outside, a 100-strong mob of hoodlums and thugs lurked, fists clenched, ready and waiting. Dark colours the order of the day…or night, Khan corrected; their garb was a uniform of blacks and browns that would allow them to blend into the darkness. Identities were a mystery, with every face hidden behind either a bandana or some hideous rubber Halloween mask. All that could be seen was a kindred eagerness in their ruthless eyes to get busy. This lot, 'the others,' were Whitechapel and East End criminals either known to Khan or recommended by his pal, Nicky Minter. These were dangerous men, violent thugs mostly, with their own axes to grind against the pigs. A rent-a-mob given a couple of grand apiece for their trouble, they were more than guaranteed to tear the fucking town up. Parked behind them were a handful of stolen cars and vans, all with the driver's windows broken and the ignitions smashed off.

Khan exited the garage to link his fingers behind his back, strolling along their front line and inspecting each man as if he were on parade. The power he felt at that very moment caused a tingling stirring in his loins: these were *his* troops, and *he* was their commander. He stopped at one scrawny example and made an emphasised tut, brushing a sprinkle of cocaine residue off the front of his bomber jacket and zipping it right up around his skinny neck to hide a unique and easily identifiable tattoo.

"Anythin' in a uniform dies tonight," Khan growled, his opening gambit met with a rousing chorus of agreement.

He waited for the euphoric clamour at the prospect of settling old scores to subside before speaking again. When he did, he swept an accompanying arm over the contents of the garage.

"There's more than enough in there for you to 'ave your fun. Take what you want and then load up the rest in the motors. I want it distributed to the frontlines. Coordination through the SafeChat group only. You all joined the fuckin' group, right?"

While they nodded to indicate they had, Khan gave himself another vigorous smirk at his resourcefulness. Since the Tottenham riots of 2011, civil unrest had relied heavily on social media platforms to direct rabble-rousers to trouble hotspots and warn of the whereabouts of approaching pig units. SafeChat, much like Facebook Messenger and Whats-App, used end to end encryption to protect its content, but with the added facility of allowing users to create groups that could be automatically deleted in their entirety from all member devices at a specified time, much to the disgust of the bacon who were left with nothing evidential on which to build any potential case.

"You find fuckers riotin'," he continued, "you tool 'em up and move on. Tool 'em up and move on. Rinse and repeat, rinse and repeat. As well as bein' me special forces, you're also the supply chain, d'you understand?" A second nod spread slowly amongst the pack. "Good. Crack on then."

Khan stood aside and let them get to it. Like the first lucky shoppers at a Boxing Day sale, the horde converged on the opening and fought their way inside. The weapons hungry equivalent of piranhas, they tore the guts out of the garage within minutes, leaving it bare apart from its single dangling lightbulb. Boxes were rifled, handguns handed out, multiple magazines stuffed into pockets. Machine guns and grenades, assault rifles and shotguns, there seemed no end to the criminal's generosity.

One lumbering oaf who appeared not overly blessed with an abundance of grey matter hauled a heavy plastic box as long as he was tall up onto his shoulder only for it to see-saw wildly as he staggered under its weight. Khan recoiled in horror, hoping to God the idiot didn't drop it.

"Not that one!" he ordered, rushing over and waving his hands. "That's mine—and you be fuckin' careful with it!"

"What is it, blud?" the oaf asked, his curiosity stoked.

"None of your beeswax, that's what that is." The piece of paper Khan pulled from one pocket was shoved into the carrier's free hand. "Get yourself somethin' else and take this to the address on here. Got it?"

"I ain't no fuckin' div, blud," the oaf assured him with an offended kiss of the teeth, looking at the address and lurching off towards one of the waiting vehicles.

One crisis averted, another soon took its place. Some cocky little shit carrying dual AK-47s collided with another wielding a heavy M-60 machine gun, its bullet belt worn like a scarf around his neck. Both took issue with the crash and exchanged angry obscenities, pushing and shoving each other until Khan stepped in to pull them apart.

"Don't fight each other, you pair of wankers!" the criminal hollered, fearlessly slapping them both across their covered faces. "*Fight the police!*"

Apologetic fist bumps exchanged, they rushed off together, a camaraderie borne of their collision. Khan watched them go with a proud, protracted smile. The last thing he had expected on a night of such potential bloodshed and violence was to play peacekeeper.

The beam suddenly broke, shattered on his lips by the terrible pain that roared in his head. His tumour was having its say. Fist clenching until the bones popped, he stumbled a step and then regained his balance, forcing the smile right back on his face to nurture it into a defiant laugh. He would not be beaten, not now. Not on the eve of war. His eyes glowed with mischief and malice while he watched the lumbering oaf gingerly slide the mysterious, coffin long crate aboard the back of a stolen pick-up truck.

"Oh, this is gonna be a good fuckin' night," Khan snarled, flicking his wrist up to check the time on his Patek Philippe.

It had just gone nine o'clock.

CHAPTER TWENTY-SEVEN

They were burning him out!

Fuelled by the accelerant he heard that bastard Druzyak speak of, the flames had spread like a disease, consuming the dry, rotten planks that clad the abandoned house he sheltered inside at a terrifying pace. Thick, acrid smoke curled around him mockingly, wrapping him in a hot embrace that scorched his lungs and made each breath harder than the last. Every hacking cough causing the excruciating bullet wound in his gut to protest, he turned on the spot, desperate for escape, desperate for this to all be a terrible nightmare…desperate to return to Katerina.

A man moulded by strict military regime and hardened by war against the Turks and Ottomans and the conquest of the tribes of Central Asia, there was little that troubled the Ripper. He had witnessed men, brothers and compatriots, torn apart by battle, the earth stained red with their blood, unaffected by their demise. It was a soldier's duty to die. But he had seen men burned to death too, their bodies blackened until they crumbled like charcoal and stank of a foulness that could never be forgotten. Following a month-long siege to conquer the Turkestan capital of Geok Tepe, he had watched the detonation of a huge Russian mine to breach the walls of the ancient city. Enemies not vapourised by the initial blast had staggered like screaming human candles, burning spectres taken by an excruciating death.

That was not a fate he relished for himself.

But what could he do? To burst from the door he had entered through would bring a hail of gunfire from Druzyak and whatever reinforcements the police whistles had summoned; a similar fate awaiting him if he attempted to flee from the rear. He clamped his filthy, bloodstained hands against his head and roared with furious frustration, wheeling on the spot, frantic for deliverance. But there was nothing except for a choking kaleidoscope of black and orange all around.

The Ripper froze, stopping so suddenly he nearly stumbled and lost his footing. He peered through the billowing smoke, his scowling gaze concentrated beyond the fireflies of hot embers that swirled and danced around the room. One section of wall to his right, approximately three cubits in length by six in height, remained strangely untouched by the growing inferno.

The killer lurched over to the wall and put a hand on the rough, unburnt planking. The connection brought a surging burst of clarity, manifested by a sharp gasp. He recalled seeing a small outhouse jutting from the side of the building as he dashed for its cover. It had been something too insignificant to register at the time. But it registered now. There was another building beyond the wall. Probably an outside latrine, he surmised. Russian houses didn't have the luxury of indoor plumbing; it was an extravagance reserved for the elite and very rich. Even his own home in the capital, palatial in comparison to his mother's hovel in Zlemensk, had an outhouse built in the small garden where Katerina tended her herbs and roses.

The Ripper slid his fingers between a gap in the wood and heaved with all his might. The plank snapped, shattering like matchwood. He lurched back at the blast of sweltering air that struck his face like a dragon's breath, returning to tear away another piece and then another. Fighting the onslaught of heat, he shielded his eyes the best he could while glimpsing inside the outbuilding.

A maelstrom of fire engulfed the tiny room. The wooden walls burned a ferocious orange, black cinders crackling and glowing. There stood a flimsy door an arm's length away, burning like the walls and rocking on its hinges to let smoke spew into the cold morning air. As suspected, there was a toilet, or rather a hole in the ground covered with shit-stained wooden boards.

He ripped away another couple of slats as the building cracked and groaned, part of the ceiling clattering to the floor behind him on an explosion of fiery sparks. The Ripper took a deep, painful breath and held it, clambering through the hole into the latrine. Instantly, the hem and arms of his long officer's coat caught fire, the hair on his head smouldering wildly. Conceived by a delirious mind, his plan required little of the military precision of which he was accustomed. It was the most rudimentary of ideas: to make an unseen break for the long grass and the forest beyond. It would succeed, or it would not, but he would rather die by bullet than fire.

Cowering from the intense heat, the Ripper burst from the outbuilding, trailing flames from his burning back, and scuttling low towards the grass. Once reaching the limited cover, he threw himself down and rolled until his coat was extinguished. There he lay, panting, wanting so much to hack up the smoke from his lungs. Instead, he listened. Over the dying groans of the house, ghostly voices were carried on the wind, wrapped in the dense curling smoke that drifted amongst the grass. He could hear the curt tones of the detective addressing someone unknown and the idle chatter of the two constables coming from the back of the house. All of them completely unaware of his bolt for freedom.

But then came another voice: shrill and screaming madly. "He is here! Over here!"

The Ripper glared at the source. An old woman, as weak and wilted as his mother but with the voice of a banshee, stood on the veranda of her house, pointing and shrieking for the policemen to see.

"Fuck!" the killer spat, jumping up to accelerate into a flat-out run.

Unseen to him, Druzyak and his constables began to cry for his surrender, their weapons cracking to send bullets in hot pursuit. Lead whistling all around, the Ripper zig-zagged to make himself a harder target until he reached the cover of the trees. Deeper and deeper he raced, the canopy above erasing what little daylight there was to make his getaway a blind dash—one more reliant on faith than judgement.

A protruding tree root snared his boot and sent him flying. End over end, he tumbled down a steep embankment, coming to rest in a thick clump of bracken on a shore of rough shale. The Ripper gasped and looked out over a vast sheet of water as dark as slate. It was the Volga River. Slow and smooth-flowing but colder and wider than a man in his condition could swim.

But...but...the killer blinked at what he saw. Like an angel of salvation, it appeared through the wispy mist that clung to the water's surface, its mechanical heart beating faster than his own. It was something so unexpected, so fortuitous, that the Ripper had to scrub his eyes in case his mind had conjured it to mock him. Thankfully, the vision remained.

There was a boat coming!

A long steam skiff approached, piloted by a lone boatman within a wheelhouse mounted at the stern. Dilapidated and bare of almost all its paint, the vessel listed heavily to starboard, overloaded with a flock of sheep, no doubt on their way to slaughter.

Transfixed by the sight, the killer watched the boat grow closer. Regardless of its condition, he would swim for it and flee along the Volga. He would head for one of the many seaports that served the Russian Empire and leave on one of the tall sailing ships that travelled the world. He would leave the Motherland and then send word for Katerina to join him.

He attempted to stand, only to find himself ensnared by the brambles he had landed in. Claw-like thorns puncturing his flesh, the Ripper fought to free himself, but the heavy wool of his coat held him firm. He could hear the policemen approaching, their heavy footfall snapping twigs and crunching leaves as, out on the river, the boat drew nearer to his position.

With no other choice, the Ripper peeled himself from his coat and left it tangled in the foliage. He pulled off his boots, hopping and splashing down into the river. The coldness of the water cut deeper than any knife, freezing the air in his lungs. He waded out until the black water reached his chest and began to swim. Usually a strong swimmer—he would swim for recreation in the public baths of St Petersburg—he struggled in the icy blackness, his body exhausted and ruined by his fateful mercy mission to Tsaritsyn. Stabbed and shot, he had lost more blood than he thought possible. He had lost his sister, his soldiering profession—possibly even his wife. But if he were captured, he would lose his life at the end of a hangman's noose. So, he swam. He swam like he never had before. He swam until his arms burned and he thought his heart would explode in his chest. Gunshots punctuated his ragged breath, driving him onwards as miniature explosions of water erupted all around.

Another painful stroke and his arm slapped against the wooden hull of the skiff. With the last of his energy, he gripped the gunwale and hauled his heavy body from the water, flopping down among the sheep who bleated with annoyance at his intrusion. In the commotion of his arrival, a couple fell overboard, thrashing about in the arctic depths of the Volga.

"Bastard!" the boatman cried, rushing from his wheelhouse brandishing a rusty billhook as a makeshift weapon.

A brute of a man the Ripper had no desire or strength to

engage with, he pulled the constable's stolen gun from the front of his uniform trousers and held it threateningly to halt the boatman's approach. The coldness of the water caused it to rattle madly in his grip.

"I have killed five people this day!" he roared through chattering teeth, pulling back on the hammer for effect. "Pilot your boat and make it that I am not forced to add to that number."

The boatman gulped. His weapon drooping, he slunk back to the wheelhouse to do as instructed, leaving the Ripper to glance across at the shoreline.

Druzyak stood there, beating the ground angrily with his cane, his face redder than the fire the killer had escaped. Joined now by five constables, two of which struggled to untangle the abandoned coat from the undergrowth, the detective waited impatiently until the garment was freed. When it was, he snatched it from the policemen and raised a pair of spectacles to his eyes to examine the insignia fixed to the epaulettes.

"I know who you are now, Leib Guard," Druzyak shouted across the water to the Ripper, holding the coat aloft. "I will hunt you across all of Russia if that is what it takes for you to see justice. I will find you. And I will see you hang!*"*

True to his word, Druzyak pursued the Ripper across western Russia. From forest to valley, upland to steppe, he never seemed to be far behind; his powers of detection as ruthless as his disposition. His Leib Guard uniform abandoned for the less conspicuous dress of a pauper, the Ripper headed for the bustling port of Archangelsk, where he would board a ship to take him from Russia. He passed through villages and towns, chilled to find hand-drawn posters of his image plastered everywhere that told of his terrible crimes. GREGOR ZOLKOV, they read in heavy Cyrillic, WANTED FOR MULTIPLE MURDER. It seemed there was no escape from Druzyak and the reach of Mother Russia's law.

On one occasion, the killer had taken shelter in the outbuilding of a sprawling farm. After filling his belly with a rabbit caught in a snare and cooked over a small fire, he had drifted into a wretched sleep where he was reunited with Katerina. They made love, and she promised to follow him to the ends of the Earth…until the illusion was shattered by the vicious baying of an approaching pack of bloodhounds. Escaping with seconds to spare, he had run for his life, hounds snapping at his heels while bullets flew all around. Across fields of moonlit wheat, he blasted, submitting to the cold mercy of another freezing river to be swept away to safety.

As his body healed of its wounds and grew stronger, so did his desire to return to Katerina. She never strayed from his thoughts. She was there when he awoke, whether in ditch or dugout, and there when he slept beneath branches or stars, her smile the last thing he would see. In an impetuous act unlike anything he had ever done before, the killer abandoned his goal of Archangelsk and went to St Petersburg in the hope of finding his wife. All he found was their little house surrounded by a mass of police hidden in the shadows awaiting his arrival. The prospect of holding Katerina in his arms fading, he had cursed his foolishness and left the city, travelling north until he crossed into the Grand Duchy of Finland. Annexed from Sweden in 1809 to join the Russian Empire following the Finnish War, it was a flat, barren wilderness of lakes and unending forests that stretched for hundreds of miles. Still intent on finding safe passage from the Motherland, the Ripper headed for the northern port of Oulu, the hub of the region's shipping.

The door crashed open to expose nothing more than a slatted wooden shed in desperate need of repair. The port of Oulu was in decline; the sailing ships that docked and loaded there with cargo for Europe and America old and slow compared to the newer, faster steamships that visited the modern and flourishing docks of Archangelsk and Odessa. It was a fact reflected by the sorry state of the harbourmaster's office.

Positioned above a boathouse on the edge of the quay, the elevated office provided a bird's eye view of the sparsely populated harbour from a row of cracked and filthy windows. Cobwebs dressed the corners, and there was a gaping hole in the roof beneath which stood a wooden bucket. The approach of darkness held off by the flicker of a couple of gas lamps, the shape of a man as decrepit as his surroundings lay sprawled over a rickety desk of handwritten paperwork, an empty vodka bottle next to him.

Druzyak limped in, his cane beating its rhythm on the creaking floorboards. Two uniformed constables followed: one as big as a bear and as seasoned as salt beef; the other, a pathetic weakling still in his teenage years.

"You there, harbourmaster," the detective roared to rouse the drunk, "I am Detective Inspector Druzyak. I have travelled from Tsaritsyn in pursuit of this individual. Tell me, have you seen him?" He offered no proof of his title, instead laying down a printed impression of his quarry before the man.

His skin inflamed by a scaly psoriasis caused by the harshness of cold sea air, the old harbourmaster swatted the flyer away and mumbled drunkenly in Finnish.

With a long-drawn-out sigh, the detective pushed the harbourmaster back in his seat with his stick. "Speak in your Emperor's tongue, bastard Fin."

"Fuck off!" *the old man responded in perfect Russian, pushing away the cane and attempting to return to his drunken slumber.*

Druzyak reached over and grabbed a handful of thick white hair, pulling the harbourmaster's head up to slam his face down into the desk. The old man screamed, his writhing pain only amusing the detective.

"Do I have your attention now?" Druzyak asked.

"What…what do you want?" the harbourmaster yelped, holding his nose to stem the red mess that poured out.

"Have you seen this man?" Druzyak said purposefully, poking the artist's rendering with one bony finger.

The harbourmaster stared at the detective, startled by his assault. He sobered sufficiently to moan about police brutality before putting on a pair of spectacles and examining the image.

Drawn by a local artist in the occasional employ of the Tsaritsyn police, the likeness was compiled from the description Druzyak himself had given. It was staggeringly good; the eyes as haunting on paper as they were in reality.

A ship's bell tolled lazily from somewhere outside while the old man squinted at the face. He burped and coughed, dousing the disgusted detective in stale booze before delivering his verdict.

"I have not seen him, no." The harbourmaster shook his head and tossed the sheet back down on his desk.

"He was last witnessed in a village not a day's travel from here. I have reason to believe he will try and abscond from the Motherland by boat." Druzyak glanced back at the two constables and grinned proudly at his powers of deduction. "It is what I would do if facing the hangman's noose."

"I told you, I have not seen him."

Druzyak limped around the desk to pull a heavy ledger from its cluttered surface. A record of comings and goings to the port, the information was written in scruffy Finnish, unreadable to the detective. "What does this shit say?"

Dabbing his nose with a handkerchief, the harbourmaster snatched the book with a bloody hand. "On this day, April 15th 1886, only two ships have entered Oulu, with but one setting to sail." He pulled a pocket watch from his jacket and held it up until his eyes gained the necessary focus. "The Karjala," he *announced. "Departed not more than two hours past, bound for—"*

"Two hours!" the detective spluttered. He rapped his cane on the floor to show his displeasure.

"But the wind has dropped. It is weaker now than a whore's kiss. She would not have sailed far."

Placated by the news, Druzyak pressed the harbourmaster. "And did this vessel take on additional crew?"

"Who works the boats is not my concern; only that they arrive and depart safely and that regulations are followed," the old man grumbled. Druzyak stared at him threateningly until he relented and gave more. "It is possible. Men come here for coin to work the seas. Sometimes they are hired, sometimes not."

The detective hobbled over to study a faded map pinned to one wall. Oulu was situated on the Gulf of Bothnia, a body of water shaped like a bent finger pointed to the heavens that separated Finland from Sweden. Druzyak traced a digit of his own through the water, past archipelagos of tiny islands and south to where it met the Baltic Sea. Turning onto the Øresund Strait between Copenhagen and Malmö, his finger moved out into the North Sea and then stopped.

"Find me a boat," Druzyak said slowly, a plan forming. He turned back to the two policemen. "And a boatman keen to earn himself a rouble or two. A fast boat, mind. Capable of intercepting this vessel."

"At this hour?" the veteran constable questioned, looking around to indicate the encroaching darkness.

"No, tomorrow, when the ship is halfway to the Americas. Yes, of course now!"

"Yessir," the policemen said together, stomping out of the room and down the steps that led to the dockyard.

Druzyak turned to follow, backtracking a couple of steps to grab a cumbersome brass flare gun and half a dozen cartridges from an open cupboard. The harbourmaster opened his mouth to protest but instantly thought better of it, the detective rewarding him with a mocking pat on the head before leaving.

To Druzyak's delight, the boat the constables secured was a small steam skiff that cut through still water at an impressive rate of knots. To his dismay, however, the hired boatman, a haggard little seadog with a beard as bushy as lamb's wool, had not shut up since leaving port. Happy with his purse, he had competed against the chuffing of the boat's steam engine to regale Druzyak and his constables with facts he considered interesting about the Gulf of Bothnia. He had prattled on and on and on like a tour guide, sharing such riveting details as how most of the northern end of the gulf was impassable during the winter months to all but the hardiest of ironclad icebreakers and how the 450 mile stretch of water was believed to be over 150 fathoms deep in places. Once Druzyak had tired of his jabbering and threatened to throw him overboard and steer the boat himself, there was quiet save for the steam engine and the occasional bark of an unseen grey seal.

Oulu was soon left behind, the few lights that lit the port fading into the eternal blackness that enveloped them. The single paraffin lamp installed aboard the boat proved hopeless at illuminating anything beyond the gunwale; those inside bathed in a weak caramel glow. The bright constellations, so relied upon by sailors to chart their positions, were lost behind a static curtain of stygian cloud from which there seemed no end. Every now and then, they would catch a twinkle of light from a dwelling on the Finnish shoreline, but they had seen nothing for over an hour.

Druzyak sat in the middle of the boat, grateful for the heat emanating from the engine's boiler. He cursed the sea and its briny stench and smoked his pipe, never taking his eyes from where he assumed the black horizon to be. Perched at the bow, the two constables shook violently in their long winter coats, the tops of their heads obscured by raised collars. Behind him, the boatman lounged at the stern, tiller in hand, not in the slightest bit affected by the cold.

"There!" the seadog cried abruptly on a plume of cold breath, sitting up to shoot a heavily calloused hand over Druzyak's right shoulder.

"I can't see any…" the detective began, peering into the nothingness.

"She is there," the boatman announced confidently, his eyes clearly more accustomed to such extremities than Druzyak's.

Sure enough, weak orange lights blinked and grew from the distant gloom, the sight bringing a rare smile to the detective's grim visage. Slowly, so very slowly, the lights rose in strength until a ship formed, a darker silhouette dotted with light materialising from the blackness that surrounded it.

While they honed in on their target, the seadog fed the firebox with coal and started to sing a Slavic shanty. Druzyak groaned but allowed him his indulgence.

"You sailors, old chaps," *he warbled in a deep baritone,* "are youthful fellows. Ey, hey, hey, hey, haw-haw. You are youthful fellows!" *He pumped an arm in tune, looking to the detective to join him in song. Druzyak declined the offer with a look of disgust.*

As the rendition continued, and they drew closer, the ship took shape. Bleached letters grew visible beneath the dull glow of her sternlight: KARJALA. *She was a 180-foot-long four-masted barque, the boatman stopped his singing to tell. A beauty once, she had fallen into a state of disrepair with the drop off in trade to Oulu, he added with a hint of sadness.*

"She is caught in the doldrums," he continued. "Travelling under current alone. If God's breath doesn't return, she'll weigh anchor before Vaasa or be driven upon the Swedish rocks."

"Shut up, you imbecile," Druzyak said, reaching forwards to

snatch a telescope from one of his constables and scanning the deck for the man he sought.

Aboard the Karjala, *sailors in cumbersome whale skin coats toiled the deck, their breath hanging in the air as they worked to catch the weak wind in the ship's slack sails. None that he could see resembled Zolkov. But he was there, Druzyak was certain of that. He could feel his presence, feel it in his very bones. By God, he would stake every rouble and kopeck about his person that it was true. After months of pursuing the killer, the chase was almost at an end. He would have him shackled and transported aboard the skiff before the wind had lifted to a breeze.*

Druzyak shoved the spyglass back at the constable and cracked open the flare gun he had taken from the harbourmaster. Loading it with stiffly frozen fingers, he raised it to the sky and fired. The projectile fizzled and popped as it rocketed into the air, tearing a fierce red cut through the black like a wound through negro skin.

Moments later, a whistle sounded aboard the Karjala, *followed by the frantic ringing of the ship's bell. A light appeared on the stern, a deep voice cutting through the chill in heavy Slavic. "Avast! Avast!"*

While the skiff gained on the floundering ship, the smile returned to crawl across Druzyak's face. "I have you now, Gregor Zolkov."

CHAPTER TWENTY-EIGHT

The Ripper peered out from behind the mizzenmast of the ship to see the familiar shape of Druzyak climb up the rope ladder lowered by the crew and limp aboard. Followed by two constables, their revolvers drawn the moment they found their footing, the detective spoke with the captain as he rushed over with his first mate.

The captain, a man who appeared far too slight for the harshness of life at sea, had introduced himself as Gustav Rahola when agreeing to hire the Ripper at the bawdy tavern that stood on the edge of the Oulu docks. Despite his obvious frailty, he had seemed an amiable, competent enough fellow during their brief exchange, the warnings he gave regarding the tightness of the ship he ran delivered routinely and without the necessary conviction. Fortunately for the killer, one of the ship's deckhands had fallen to his death from the mainsail during their last voyage. The accident had created a vacancy for a 'hard-working man of good moral standing,' as Rahola called it. After the brutal carnage the Ripper had unleashed, he considered himself the furthest thing from such a description, but he was desperate to flee. He had worked the merchant fleets that circumnavigated the globe for many years, the Ripper lied, his fabrication convincing enough for the captain to spit into his hand and seal the deal with a vigorous shake.

Without spittle, a handshake was exchanged between Druzyak and Rahola. What was said between the two went unheard, the words too quiet to distinguish from his hidden position. The captain nodded and turned on his first mate to send him bolting along the deck to the forecastle, where he rang the ship's bell vigorously to rouse the men.

"All men upon deck! All men upon deck!"

As the crew of hardy mariners began to assemble before their captain, the Ripper rasped a big hand across his stone-hard face and considered his options.

The revolver taken from the constable in Tsaritsyn was long gone now, lost during the pursuit of freedom. He carried only a fearsome hunting knife acquired from a cabin he had found and ransacked in one of Finland's endless forests. It was of little use against three policemen armed with guns, and if there was mention of a reward, the crew would soon join to aid his capture. The sea was far too cold to attempt to swim for shore; he would either freeze to death or be shot in the back.

That left only one choice.

It was instantly apparent that Zolkov was not amongst the crewmen assembled on deck. Druzyak shuffled along their line nonetheless, the act of inspecting such a sorry band of individuals giving him a glowing feeling of self-importance. As expected, they were a motley crew of seafarers, as decrepit and exhausted as the ship they served. One had remained head-bowed during scrutiny as if to conceal his appearance, the detective snorting at his insolence to place his cane under the man's chin until he yielded. Eyes that hid some criminal past stared back sheepishly, but they were not those of the murderer he sought.

Druzyak smirked at the sailor and held his gaze: his future in his hands. He whipped his stick away and turned back to the captain. "You said your crew numbered thirty in total?"

"Yes, that is correct, Detective," Rahola replied quizzically.

"Yet I count only twenty-nine," Druzyak said, preening the dangling whiskers of his moustache. "Yourself, your mate here, and these twenty-seven souls. I am a detector of wrongdoers, sir, not an arithmetician, but I can tell you your contingent is plainly lacking by one."

The captain's brow knitted as he performed his own swift headcount to confirm the number. "But…I…I don't under—"

"Begging your pardon, sirs," the first mate interrupted. A weasel of a man, any identifying features lost behind a beard of absurd proportions, he stepped forwards to speak with a grovelling tone. "The new hand we took on in port is absent from deck."

Druzyak pointed his stick at the man. "His name?"

"He did not offer it, sir," the first mate said. "He was employed only to mop and tack, not to become a bedfellow or a comrade with which to share a tot."

"Constables?" Druzyak growled over his shoulder at his men. "Tear this ship apart."

"No!" Eyes widened by the order, Rahola grabbed the detective's arm weakly. "You are welcome to search the main deck, berth deck—my cabin even. Anywhere! But I beseech you, sir, do not permit your men to enter the hold until the hatches can be lifted to allow daylight's air."

Druzyak glared at the captain until he took back his hand. "Whyever not, Captain?"

*"Our cargo can be…*unpredictable.*"*

"Dangerous," the first mate agreed with a nervous tone.

The detective scoffed at their pathetic exhibition of fear. There was nothing Druzyak feared more than failure. "My men will do as I command. I will not see this murdering bastard embrace freedom a day longer." He prodded Rahola with his stick and smiled sickly. "I might yet see you charged with harbouring a fugitive. Dwell on that, Captain."

Rahola's eyes slipped shut, and he muttered a silent prayer, the dread he exuded spreading contagiously to the two policemen.

"If there is a danger, Detective Inspector, sir…" the young constable started with a whimper. "And…and…and there are but three of us against a killer of many. A butcher! Perhaps it would be better to return the ship to port and gather assistance from the Fins?"

Druzyak spun on his heels and slammed his cane into the side of the boy's head with a crack that echoed across the Gulf of Bothnia and sent the cap spiralling from his head. "Do not question my instructions!"

"Sir!" Holding his head, the policeman staggered away in the direction of the forecastle, while his colleague, the bear, stomped away and headed aft.

The young constable snivelled with pain as he crept down the steps that led to the hold. Head still ringing like the Karjala's *bell, he trembled with every reluctant step, the rattle and jangle the gun and paraffin lamp made in his hands challenging the constant creaking the ship's timbers made.*

His search so far had been mercifully fruitless, with nothing more than a scrawny black cat kept aboard to hunt rats found prowling the lower deck. The creature had scared him half to death, and the thought of encountering a killer lurking in the shadows had not offered any comfort. And then there were the frightening words of the captain.

"Do not permit your men to enter the hold," he repeated, his foot touching down and doing what the captain had warned against.

It was the smell that struck the constable first. Somewhere between urine and sweat, it caused him to gag as he lifted the lantern to illuminate the vast belly of the Karjala. *He saw nothing but a sea of large wooden barrels as far as the dull glow would permit. Evenly distributed in a single tier, they appeared neither threatening nor dangerous. However, what did concern him were the thick oak pillars dotted equidistantly throughout the hold that supported the upper decks, each one wide enough for a murdering blaggard to conceal himself behind. The boy swallowed at the thought of inspecting them and the brutality of the detective's wrath if he didn't.*

"Horrible old bastard!" he moaned at Druzyak's assault while beginning to stalk the hold. His heavy boots creaked on the wooden boards as he moved along the narrow gangway set between the casks. "I swear to my sweet mother, I will draw my pistol and fill him with lead, so I will. Detective or not."

His sweet mother would hug him, he considered warmly, pinching the rosy cheeks of his baby face to comfort and molly-coddle him. She had always said he was too much of a kindly soul to become involved in the apprehension of criminals.

"Striking me like a common criminal. How…dare…"

The constable stopped, realising that the creaking of his boots had turned to a crunch, the ground beneath his boots becoming uneven and elevated with every step. He looked down to find the walkway spread with a thick carpet of tiny grey rocks.

Before the constable could bend lower to investigate, the Ripper exploded from the barrel he'd emptied of content like a Jack in the Box. The lid flying off into the air, he grabbed the policeman round the throat and thrust the hunting knife up under his chin, burying it to the handle to penetrate the brain. The boy gurgled and spluttered, his mouth falling open to reveal the blade wedged between his teeth. The killer took the lantern carefully from his hand and placed it on the next cask. Then, with a startling display of dexterity, he clambered free from the barrel and reclaimed his knife, filling the space left vacant with the constable's convulsing body. He found the lid and sealed it back in place, glancing down at the lantern and the spillage with a heavy sigh of—

"Don't move!" a voice boomed from the darkness.

The Ripper snapped his head to see the other policeman bleed from the shadows, his revolver held firm and unwavering. In comparison to the quivering adolescent, this man was a beast.

"Gregor Zolkov," the constable roared authoritatively, "you are arrested for murder. Put down the knife and surrender yourself."

The Ripper regarded him with a calculating stare as he approached. Then, without dispute, he did as instructed. He knelt to relinquish his blade, but instead of casting it aside he buried it carefully by the handle so that it stood vertically in the grey shale that covered the deck.

"Do you know what fills these barrels?" he asked, standing to raise his hands in submission as the constable stomped closer.

"Quieten your tongue, bastard." The policeman ignored the question, the noise of his footfall changing from creak to crunch while he pulled a thick set of iron handcuffs from a leather pouch on his belt.

"Can you smell it, Constable? That gentle reek of ammonia?"

"I don't care what it is."

"You will if you discharge your weapon."

Sufficiently distracted to let his gaze slip to whatever littered the gangway, the Ripper lashed out and grabbed the policeman behind his meaty neck. The beast roared as he was yanked forwards too quickly for him to maintain his balance on the loose, uneven surface, let alone consider opening fire on his attacker. He slammed down onto the deck with a bone-shattering crunch that shook the entire hold.

For a moment, he was still—killed outright, the Ripper

hoped—but then he groaned out a thick breath of dust and rolled onto his back, the upturned knife buried beyond the hilt in his chest. The blade had smashed through the constable's ribs to skewer his left lung. There was no treatment for such an injury; the killer had seen too many men die in excruciating agony on the battlefield of similar wounds. A spluttering rattle growing from within the bear's body, he coughed out on a thick red slobber that slid down his neck. His lips moved, but no words came. He stared at the gun in his grip blankly, the energy to shoot dead his murderer gone from his hands. The policeman looked up with eyes desperate for the pain to end.

"Mercy..." he mouthed, his back arching from a wave of agony.

The Ripper gave the slightest of nods and prised his knife from broken bone to plunge it into the side of the constable's neck, sawing the blade upwards until the carotid artery, jugular, and everything else essential for life were severed on a torrent of red that splattered over him.

The constable dead, his misery at an end, the killer took his revolver and stood, scouring the hot blood from his face to inadvertently create something resembling warpaint. He made for the steps, climbing from the hold to weave along a wood-panelled corridor, traversing his gun from door to door as he passed. Like the cat he had witnessed aboard, a twitching mouse caught between its jaws, he would rid the ship of its troublesome vermin and continue his escape. Only one remained now to be dealt with.

Druzyak!

Slipping out of the stairwell onto the main deck, two bullets slammed into the bulkhead inches from his head to shower him in splinters. The Ripper returned fire, blowing apart the head of an innocent sailor caught in the crossfire and sending the detective scurrying for cover behind a large iron capstan.

Unafraid, driven by a primal determination, the killer stalked towards Druzyak. A deckhand charged at him with a billhook and a scream—the Ripper cutting him down with a gunshot to the face to continue his fearless advance.

While the remaining crew thought better of launching an attack and scattered to the far reaches of the ship, Druzyak popped up from behind his cover to unleash another three shots, one which caught the killer's bicep to knock him back a step. The Ripper glanced down at his wound with casual indifference.

"Lower your weapon and surrender!" Druzyak yelled from behind the capstan, an evident tremor to his voice. "Surrender, and you might live."

The Ripper gave no reply. He stood statuesque on deck. A warrior in red, waiting for Druzyak to make his next move. And when the move came, he was ready.

Druzyak sprouted with a roar and fired.

His reflexes quicker than the detective's, the Ripper dropped and rolled away. He righted himself and aimed fast, putting a bullet into each of Druzyak's knees and one in his gun hand. The roar transforming into a horrific scream that erupted across the Gulf of Bothnia, the detective buckled behind the capstan.

The Ripper stalked his prey, coming to tower over the man who had pursued him across the Motherland. Druzyak appeared so pathetic now, blubbering and muttering as he tried to switch the revolver from his mangled hand to the other. When he succeeded, the gun drifted upwards to find its target. Click, click, click it went as Druzyak's face collapsed with the realisation that he was about to die.

"You've had your six." The Ripper motioned at the detective's gun. "Yet I still have one." He watched the loitering crew, ashen-faced and too terrified to move, and then threw his weapon overboard.

A bullet was too good for a bastard like Druzyak.

A blade, however… The Ripper took the hunting knife from within his jacket and dropped to his knees next to the detective.

Druzyak fumbled in the pocket of his overcoat for something. He tugged the wide barrel of a flare gun into his hand while several brass shells rolled out onto the deck. The blade discarded, the Ripper lashed out and snatched the weapon. A smile cracked on his lips as he broke it open and slid a round inside.

"Let…let me live, Zolkov, huh?" Druzyak begged, his eyes alive with an uncontrollable fear. "Huh? Let me live and… and…and you can flee. Take the skiff—hold the pilot hostage until you reach safety. Kill him, I don't care. Go to…go to Sweden! Across the water. Please…?"

The Ripper stiffened at his pathetic pleading and stuffed the flare gun into his open mouth. "This is for my horse," he whispered as he squeezed the trigger.

The result was nothing short of devastating. The pressure of the flare's ignition blew both of Druzyak's eyeballs from his head on jets of hissing red flame. The detective screamed—but only for a moment—his head inflating like a child's balloon to tear open and spill out a mess of blood, brain and burning phosphorus onto the deck.

As Druzyak's legs kicked their last and fell back, the Ripper grabbed his knife and a handful of cartridges and climbed to his feet. He peered into the shadows and called out. "Captain Rahola? You are safe to approach."

A moment and the Karjara's captain did so, his arms raised above his head.

"Put down your hands," the killer said. "I have no quarrel with you."

"What…what do you intend to do?"

"You will have your men commit these bodies to the water," the Ripper instructed, waiting for Rahola to nod in agreement

before continuing. "You will also provide me with three meals a day, served in the hold, where I shall remain for the duration of your voyage. You know what your cargo is, Captain?"

"Of course I do." Rahola licked his lips nervously. "Guano."

"That is correct. Fertiliser. Birdshit fertiliser. Highly explosive once fermented. It is only by God's good grace that we still stand here now. Therefore, if I see anyone enter the hold who doesn't carry food…" the Ripper waggled the flare gun for the captain to see, "…I will send us all to the next world."

The captain glanced down at Druzyak's exploded, burning head and gulped.

The Ripper turned and trudged back in the direction of the stairs he had climbed. He stopped and looked back at Rahola with an afterthought. "What is this ship's destination?"

"London, sir. The heart of Victoria's Empire."

"London." The Ripper scoffed. He and Katerina had often dreamed of visiting Europe's great cities. "Then it is London where I shall leave you, Captain. That is where I shall make my home."

The Ripper awoke with a heart-thumping jolt. Eyeballs surging, his fingers clamped instinctively around his gun to pull it close.

Those carriages and wagons that wailed and painted the darkness blue were everywhere tonight. *Police cars*, Kowalski had called them. The killer had grown accustomed to their constant shrieking—the sound as familiar to him as cannon fire on the battlefield had once been. But tonight, there seemed so many; the sound so prevalent and incessant. There was something else in the distance, beyond the howling. Something unmistakable to a soldier.

Gunfire.

It came in short, sporadic bursts, faster than anything he

had ever heard.

While he contemplated its origins, he sucked in his breath and nosed the cold air, turning every which way on the soiled mattress that had softened his frightful sleep. What he had thought a lingering memory of his nightmare—the billowing, acrid smoke from that Tsaritsyn inferno—was real. He could actually smell smoke in this horrific, skewed version of the world he remembered. He could taste its bitterness in his mouth, and it clung to him like a layer of sweat. Fire was timeless, but this was the first occasion he'd smelt anything as powerful and profuse in this version of Whitechapel. Troubled by the stench, by the sound of gunfire—by the scream that suddenly pierced the air from somewhere close—the Ripper clambered to his feet and crossed the room he'd claimed as his own.

This place was no different than others he had found. Forgotten and abandoned, ruined by whatever illegal activity had taken place within its walls since its desertion, it was bathed only by the orange hue of the street lighting that streamed through the uncovered windows. There was none of the magical *electricity* stuff the old Polack had mentioned to provide light. Full with broken furniture and junk that was of little use to its current occupant, the apartment stood above an equally forsaken shop that had sold unknown wares. It was located by chance after knocking unconscious the bastard who had brought him to 2030 following their encounter at the old school in Buck's Row. He would have put a bullet through his head were it not for the police who prowled the streets only cubits away, searching for their colleague. A gunshot would have given away his position and ended his own life. Instead, the killer reluctantly spared the time-travelling lawman to slip into the shadows of an adjoining alleyway, where he found a door covered in graffiti that had put up little resistance against his silent assault.

The Ripper peered through the grubby window panes and drew a startled breath, stunned by what he saw.

What he had thought was the radiance of the new-fangled streetlights was the fierce, incandescent glow of a massive fire. Burning somewhere in the distance, beyond the rooftops of the building opposite, the sky was alight with a swirling host of reds and oranges topped by the blackest of smoke. He pushed himself up against the glass to peer along the street. Further along, a deserted carriage left in the middle of the road burned ferociously. While he wondered at the causes of the blazes, something else caught his attention.

A group of gangly adolescent males numbering double figures raced into the street and slowed to a confident, unafraid swagger. These were not lawmen searching for him; that was instantly apparent. Their bodies clothed in the darkest of colours, their faces were hidden behind scarves and ghoulish masks that allowed for anonymity and wrongdoing. Crimes no doubt to be perpetrated with the aid of the fearsome array of firearms they inexplicably carried. There were handguns and rifles the likes he had never seen before, and although each boy fielded the weapon he carried clumsily, inexperienced in its operation, it was still a formidable arsenal.

What was happening in Whitechapel, the Ripper wondered, the thought repeating on his lips to bolster his confusion. "*Chto proiskhodit v Uaytchepele?*"

Before he could dwell any longer on the sudden descent into chaos, a police car skidded to a stop at a crossroads halfway down the road. It remained there for a moment, screaming and swirling its blue lights over the surrounding buildings, its occupants evidently undecided how to respond to the gang stalking towards them. Wheels spinning, the vehicle started to reverse at speed, the lawmen retreating rather than engaging the heavily armed fighters. The horde raised their weapons and unleashed a unified barrage of lead, bullet holes sprouting all over the front window of the car until it lost acceleration and drifted to a stop. One of the constables within fell from his door and attempted to stagger away, but he was soon cut down by a further hail of bullets.

While the pack rejoiced at the deaths, one of the attackers strutted back and stared up at their solo audience. The whistle he made for his companions to join him tore the Ripper from his voyeuristic trance to return the look.

They spoke in hushed tones, eyes flitting up at their spectator until one of them pulled something from his pocket that resembled a small dark ball. He weighed it up in his hand for a moment and then appeared to pull something from it. Some of his cohorts lost their bluster when he did, stepping away or running off as if the object had become dangerous. The boy laughed and cursed them and then hurled whatever it was into the air. With an explosion of glass, the ball smashed through the window and rolled across the floor with the heavy sound of metal.

The Ripper stared at it for a moment, curiously concerned as to what it would do until compelled to dive behind the remains of a broken couch before it did it. Not a second later, the room erupted with a devastating eruption of red-hot flame. The whole world jumped and shook, the windows blown out while a frenzied cheer of bloodlust rushed in.

Dust raining down on him, the killer looked up from where he sheltered. Where the ball had come to a stop was now a gaping hole in the floor. Tendrils of fire licked at the detritus littering the room, taking hold with devastating speed. The thick choking smoke clawed at his throat, burning his eyes, forcing him to crawl unsteadily to his feet.

History repeating itself, the flames of his dreams a growing reality, he had to get out of there.

CHAPTER TWENTY-NINE

After her Uber was turned back on the outskirts of Whitechapel by a burly police officer at an improvised roadblock made from a car slung across the tarmac, Maggie announced to the driver that she knew where she was and would walk the rest of the way. She knew the streets of East London as well as any taxi driver, and even her Alzheimer's had struggled to dampen her keen sense of direction. She would remember quite clearly how to get somewhere, only forgetting why it was she was going there.

It was only on exiting the cab and watching it disappear from the direction it came that she became confused. Not by her location or reason for being in Whitechapel—she was there to meet Bill for a bite to eat when he got back from filming *Crimenight*—but by what confronted her.

Something was very wrong.

Out there in the darkness, there were police cars everywhere. Unseen as yet, their bleating sirens joined with the rhythmic thumping of the police helicopter that circled overhead to create a jarring caterwauling that dug right inside her head. Smoke drifted on streets she hurried down, growing thicker with every turn, carrying with it the stench of fire and petrol. By the time Maggie reached the heart of Whitechapel, she had found a scene straight out of a disaster movie. There were vehicles burning—there were vehicles burning everywhere! Blazes that seemed to originate from abandoned police cars, some on their roofs, had spread to consume the parked vehicles of residents, those fires leaping to ignite nearby buildings. The heat was stifling, sucking the air from Maggie's lungs, and causing her to shield her face. Through her fingers and the shimmering haze, she *thought* she saw several groups of armed men, adolescents judging by their gait, running in the shadows, their faces obscured. But…no, that couldn't be right. Could it?

An inquisitiveness borne out of marriage to a senior detective took over from rational thought to drive her onwards. Like a curious visitor to an alien world, Maggie stumbled past looted shops alive with fire, the conservative black heels she wore crunching over broken glass and scuffing against shattered bricks. The smoke grew in thickness to billow all around her, wrapping her in its hot embrace to sting her eyes and obscure her view, the make-up she had taken such care in applying soon becoming smudged and darkened by soot.

Maggie remembered how her grandmother would tell tales of life during the Blitz when Hitler's *Luftwaffe* had pounded London night after night to smash the great British resolve. Confused by the irrational scenes of destruction, she wondered if she had somehow been magically transported back to the 1940s. Maggie coughed out a scoff at the idiocy of her thought. There was no such thing as time travel. Even as a sufferer of Alzheimer's, she knew that Starbucks and Superdrug, two brands whose high street presence she could see burning ferociously, hadn't existed during the Second World War.

No, this was now!

The boldness with which she had left the taxi eroded by her frightful trek, Maggie stepped off the pavement onto the deserted Whitechapel Road. Even at this hour, when it should've been alive with life, the road as busy as the pavements, there was not a soul to be seen. She clutched her bag and crossed, stopping only to freeze momentarily at a loud chatter of gunfire that punched through the eerie stillness. The shooting stopped, and Maggie rushed across the remainder of the road and pavement to push through the doors of the police station on a plume of pursuing smoke. She coughed and wandered through the deserted reception area with its posters and plastic potted plants, waiting at the next door for the desk clerk to buzz her through to the counter. When he did, Maggie stepped up, her eyes alive with fear.

The desk clerk stood behind the counter, juggling a phone in each hand while another one rung and rung, desperate for attention. "Yes?" he snapped abruptly, returning briefly to one of the phones. "Hang…hang on a minute."

"Detective…Detective Superintendent Raymond…can I see him?" Maggie mumbled, barely able to string a sentence together.

"He's not here, love. You'll have to come back later." He turned his back on her, conversation over, speaking into one of the handsets he was fielding. "It's kicking off all over town, Sarge. I'll pass it onto CAD, but the chopper reckons we've got rioters inbound. A lot of 'em! We're about to go into lockdown here."

"What's…what's going on?" Maggie asked timidly. The desk clerk ignored her question, ending one call and getting straight into the next. "Shall I wait?"

When no answer came, Maggie hovered for a moment, unsure of what to do next. There was rioting in Whitechapel.

For some unknown, incomprehensible reason, there was rioting in Whitechapel, and Bill wasn't there. Where was he? It was him who had suggested going for a meal after he got back from... Her mouth dropping open to quiver at the edges, Maggie choked on a crashing wave of upset. Had she imagined the whole thing? Had he even been there while she'd dressed and put on her make-up? Was the Alzheimer's that had been so dormant finally waking to taunt her and exact its debilitating grip?

"Shall I wait?" she said again with barely a whisper, the tears that bulged in her eyes desperate to flow. Deeply engrossed in his call, speaking now of multiple deaths and casualties, the desk clerk refused to reply. Her body shaking while she fought back the trembling wail that grew from deep within, Maggie shuffled around and staggered back towards the exit.

It wasn't the live destruction of Whitechapel that drew the president's men to a small flatscreen television sat atop a rusted filing cabinet—they had a front-row seat for that from the office Ratski had hired. Oblivious to the increasing crackle of machine-gun fire and ceaseless whooping of sirens coming from outside, the frantic police transmissions from the installed surveillance system going unheard, the Secret Service agents crowded together, their faces etched by a uniform intrigue, captivated by something much closer to home, both geographically and emotionally. Even those sleeping in the improvised dormitory above had gathered, watching what unfolded on the TV with bleary-eyed shock.

"If you're just joining us," the handsome CNN anchor announced grimly, "we're receiving disturbing reports that a US military incursion into the Venezuelan capital of Caracas has ended in disaster with a firefight between US special forces and units of the Venezuelan Army."

The image shifted to grainy video of a gun battle on a deserted street awash with sunshine and smoke. Surrounded by a backdrop of decrepit buildings painted in dull greens and muted yellows lay the shattered remains of a Sikorsky UH-70 Black Hawk helicopter, flames sprouting from its twisted fuselage. Battered and bloody soldiers in full combat dress sheltered behind the wreckage as enemy bullets dinged into the metal, returning fire whenever possible. The footage cut to another source that showed several American soldiers lying dead in a street, blood running from their corpses as Venezuelan soldiers stood guard.

"It's reported," the newsman's commentary continued over video of an excited Venezuelan official holding up a US military identification card to the camera, "that at least three Black Hawk helicopters came under heavy fire while attempting to land in the outskirts of the city near to what is believed to be a military interrogation centre, while a Chinook heavy transport helicopter was shot down over the surrounding jungle."

As he spoke, the constant ticker tape of news stories scrolling across the bottom of the screen changed to read just one headline, over and over: US LAUNCH CATASTROPHIC STRIKE INTO VENEZUELA.

Ratski hadn't been well since the fateful events that had seen him separated from Myra, but tonight, at this hour—whatever that was—he appeared particularly ill. Pale skin glistening with a fine sheen of sweat, his jaw clenched tight enough to snap bone or break teeth, he trudged lifelessly into the office from the grimy washroom out in the hallway. He had just vomited a foul-smelling brew of lunch and dinner into the toilet. That was something that hadn't happened for a while now, not since starting the treatment the president had instructed his own physician to prescribe him following their initial meeting. He swallowed one of the mysterious pills and washed it down with a hefty glug of bottled water, stopping only to narrow his eyes into a dark ringed, infuriated scowl at the sight he discovered.

For some reason, all the Secret Service agents congregated around the TV, not one of them conscious of the panicked voices screaming from the speakers. Whitechapel had exploded into violence, yet they were more interested in something on the television. Their target ran free, and *they were watching the fucking TV!* Incensed by their dereliction of duty, he stopped and hurled the bottle into the nearest trash can. The deafening clatter it made rousing precisely no one, the ball-breaker stormed across the office, determined to chastise them…until he too saw what they did. He pushed his way to the front, worryingly entranced by the footage.

"Live from Caracas," the big African American he stopped beside announced. The agent—Ratski couldn't remember his name—chewed on his bottom lip and shook his head with disbelief. "What the fuck are we doing in Venezuela?"

The last time Ratski had spoken to the president, Garrett was ambiguous, to say the least. He had said, with a noticeable quiver to his tone, how it had started. 'Brad, I believe it's started,' were his exact words. Someone not so aware of the situation might have questioned his meaning, but the ball-breaker knew well enough. He had known his whole damn life: every second of every day hurtling towards that very moment and what was yet to come.

"The ingredients are on the table," Ratski said aloud without thinking, the phrase cryptic enough to draw questioning glances from almost every agent in the room.

"What the hell does that mean?" someone from the back of the throng asked.

Silently cursing his lack of discretion, Ratski didn't reply. There was nothing he could say to these men. They just didn't have the clearance. As if to emphasise the growing significance of a situation that only he understood, one of the televised Black Hawk helicopters, smashed and broken on the Caracas tarmac, exploded in a devastating fireball of aviation kerosene that vaporised the soldiers sheltering behind it.

"Holy fuck!" one agent cried, joined by a variety of likewise invectives while they watched their countrymen burn, helpless to respond.

This is it, Ratski's hurtling mind told him. Unable to tear his gaze from the television, his eyes aglow with flame, he felt sweat punch free from every pore, his gut knotting as another wave of bile rose from his empty stomach.

After a lifetime of waiting, it had finally started. It was happening now.

History in the making.

The chance of a lead coming from Raymond's *Crimenight* appearance diminishing by the second, the detectives of Operation Milton Keynes lined the windows of the incident room, watching in muted horror while Whitechapel burned. The office infiltrated by the sickening reek of cordite and petrol, not one soul spoke, their tense silence interrupted only by the growing sound of gunfire. From their elevated position, they could see fires spreading across the skyline like a pandemic. Through the swirling haze of smoke, across the deserted A11, an older wing of the Royal London Hospital was fully ablaze; nobody in any doubt that there were patients and staff trapped within, either dead or dying.

Duck and the two tactical flight officers were gone—India 98 scrambled to provide an aerial overview of the extent of the violence at the request of the station's chief superintendent, Andy Horbury. Given the title of Silver Commander for the duration of the trouble, Horbury would manage tactical implementation under the strategic command of the Gold Commander, a role assigned to one of Scotland Yard's senior officers safely ensconced in the headquarters' Major Incident Control Room. As SC, as it was abbreviated, Horbury had appointed multiple Bronze Commanders from the police station's upper ranks and the various specialised departments arriving in Whitechapel to restore order, each one given a specific set of instructions.

The reconnaissance India 98 provided made for stark listening, replayed to the incident room via a personal radio discarded on the desk, its volume turned up to the max. The streets were littered with the bodies of fallen colleagues and burning police vehicles, Tactical Flight Officer Two detailed sombrely, giving a grim running commentary of the various gun battles that raged throughout Whitechapel. He told with trembling emotion, reminiscent of the reporter who had described the Hindenburg disaster, how one of the TSG's personnel carriers was blown apart by a shoulder-mounted rocket launcher, the bastard who fired the kill-shot high-fiving his compatriots, while those trapped inside thrashed and burned. Other TSG units had abandoned their vehicles and retreated to the relative safety of the police station; their own Bronze Commander arguing over the airwaves how their flame-retardant overalls and NATO helmets offered little protection against the jacketed rounds and grenades the rioters had got their hands on. The commentary continued, telling of a riderless police horse from the Met's Mounted Branch in Bow galloping along Commercial Road, drenched with some ferocious accelerant and engulfed entirely in flame. From Aldgate in the west to Stepney in the east, there were incidences of looting. A small retail park off Cambridge Heath Road, only recently opened by some minor celebrity, had been stripped bare and torched by a horde of enterprising opportunists who saw the rampaging as an excuse to get themselves a new TV or the latest pair of trainers. Robbery inconsequential compared to murder; what concerned the detectives was what had sparked the insurrection. There were unconfirmed reports that Khan's meeting had turned to violence, and the DPS detectives who had gone in to break it up and arrest the criminal were injured, some even succumbing to their wounds.

The police station was in lockdown, with over 300 faceless, heavily armed rioters amassing on their doorstep, India 98 estimated. Steel shutters were lowered over the ground floor windows and doors to prevent a breach; the upper floors deemed safe, protected by thick bulletproof glass installed during construction. So far, the windows had held, despite the numerous crazed pockmarks left by pot-shots taken at the watching detectives, many of whom filmed the violence on their phones in an evidential gathering capacity. Their faces set with anger and frustration, all had argued that they should be out there, doing *something*. Their role would come later, Dyson reminded them, when the time came to trawl through the collected footage, identify those involved, and then arrest the bastards.

There was a strategy in motion, the hyperactive chatter from the personal radio told. An entire army of TSG units, dispatched from their bases in Alperton, Catford, Chadwell Heath, and Clapham were currently inbound, together with the additional backup of officers from surrounding Metropolitan Police districts. Upon their coordinated arrival, they would move in on the rioters, encircling and corralling them together for arrest. That was the plan, but Dyson had serious doubts as to the ease of the task or their chance of success. This wasn't Brixton, Tottenham, or the Brexit riots that had flared nationwide in 2025. Rioters then had fought with bricks and bottles, but these thugs were armed to the teeth with military-grade weaponry, giving them the ability to shoot their way out of any cordon the police set up. They were well organised too, so a handful of initial arrests discovered, coordinating their attacks via various encrypted social media sites. For that reason, it was decided to cut all cellular phone signals and internet services in the Whitechapel area at twenty-two hundred hours. The order had come directly from the prime minister himself, by all accounts.

The news of the communication kill order had left Dyson just seven minutes to call Mary and check she was okay. The network swamped to capacity; it had taken him over a dozen attempts to get through.

"I just wanted to hear your voice," he said discreetly, turning from the ferocity outside as a police car sprayed with graffiti raced past on the wrong side of the road, its masked occupants firing machine guns indiscriminately from the windows.

Whatever reply Mary gave, it brought the faintest flicker of a smile to his face, pushing away the wretched despondency for the briefest of moments.

"According to our intel—intelligence, sorry—you're well away from the trouble hotspots. The flat's secure and off the main drag. You'll be perfectly safe inside." He stepped away from his colleagues to lower his voice to a forceful whisper. "Look, just in case... Fred's gun is still in the drawer. For emergencies! That's not an invitation for you to go outside and get all Bruce Willis with these scumbags." The detective smirked as Mary asked who Bruce Willis was. "I'll tell you later. I love you, Miss Kelly."

He ended the call, cradling the phone gently as if it was

Mary herself. Dyson thought of Abberline and the pistol he'd taken from him on their escape from 1888. He wondered what the great Ripper detective would make of the calamity that had befallen his beloved town until a huge explosion rocked the whole building.

"Jesus Christ!" Saunders exclaimed, Dyson returning to join him.

A burning fire engine slid down the road on its side, spewing smoke and gouging tarmac. When it finally came to a screeching stop, the battered crew clambered through the shattered windscreen to sprint off in their cumbersome gear, pursued by a dozen rioters armed with machetes and machine guns.

A flicker of movement caused the detective to look away from their hopeless escape, focusing through the swirling miasma to the building almost directly opposite his location. Above a parade of shuttered, turn-of-the-century shops stood an office complex, the original Victorian frontage remodelled into a long stretch of windows to create a jarring juxtaposition of old versus new. Light bled through various chinks and cracks in the drawn blinds that covered every window… except for one. Either missing or broken, the blind's absence highlighted a solitary figure at the window. There were desks and chairs and more men gathered in the background of the office, but it wasn't them that caught Dyson's eye. His arms linked behind his back, this stone-faced observer watched the fire crew run for their lives with a cold, uncaring detachment. That people ogled tragedy with such ghoulish voyeurism was nothing unusual. That was a dark part of the human psyche now: to witness death and destruction with absolute indifference, often filming whatever disaster was occurring to share online for likes or financial gain. Indeed, there were individuals and groups Dyson could see, hanging from windows or lurking on rooftops, their phones held aloft for the best possible angle. But that wasn't what interested him. What drew the detective's eye to that particular man at that particular window was none other than the fact that it was—

"*Brad fucking Ratski!*" Dyson spluttered with enough disgust to turn every head from the inferno consuming the fire appliance.

"John?" Jenny called over to him with a look of concern.

"Guv?" Saunders asked, heralding a chorus of anxious enquiries from colleagues.

Dyson stared at the detectives while they stared back at him. His mouth hung open, a thousand variations of the same thought crashing and colliding inside his head.

Why the hell is Ratski here?

There was no logical reason for the ball-breaker to be in Whitechapel. Not when he should've been at the hotel, at Garrett's beck and call while the leader of the free world clung to what remained of his life. If Ratski needed updates, the bastard had a phone; there was no need for him to personally venture into the East End. But there he was, as bold as fucking brass, in a rental office, surveying Whitechapel as though it were his kingdom. Whatever the motives behind his presence, there was one thing the detective was certain of. There was something more at stake than an escaped, time-travelling serial killer and a pint of his precious blood.

There was something Dyson still hadn't been told.

The acute geographical knowledge that had served Maggie so well abandoned her shortly after leaving the police station. The confidence with which she had awoken that morning appeared now as broken as Whitechapel, Maggie returned to a hopeless creature, confused and dependant on others for her survival.

Her condition worsened by the sickening stench of burning and increasing gunfire, everything became an unescapable sensory overload. Up was down and left was right, and Maggie only knew she was in Whitechapel because the sign of one burning shop had given its location. Streets became identical facsimiles of each other, the smoke thickening to obscure any chance of reading the road signs she staggered past. Her reason for being in Whitechapel had deserted her too, and Maggie could think of nothing other than Karen, her and Bob's only daughter. She was dead now—cruelly taken from them in her infancy. Fractured pieces of memory convinced Maggie that Karen had passed away—she could remember standing at her graveside, weeping as any mother would their child. Yet competing images told how Karen had left for school that very morning, her smile as bright as the summer sun.

"Help me please," Maggie wailed, imploring with open arms the hooded figures who scampered in the darkened recesses of the street.

Armed to the teeth with guns and knives, they ignored her plea. The window of a shop Maggie hadn't heard of in a road she didn't know suddenly exploded in a shower of glass, sending a rolling wave of flame climbing into the air on a chorus of maniacal laughter. The front of a clothing store she shuffled past crashed out and sent her stumbling away with a frightful gasp, two men wearing balaclavas emerging from within, laden with bags stuffed full of ill-gotten gains.

Maggie stared longingly at the police helicopter that thundered overhead, naïve in the hope that it would land and whisk her away to safety. When it did nothing but douse her in blinding white light that blasted over roofs and road, she gritted her teeth to chastise her foolishness.

"You stupid bloody woman! You…you should have stayed in the station—" The sight of a police car skidding around the corner and careening towards her silenced her dissent. "Bill?" she called out, her eyes desperately optimistic. It was one of the big area cars her husband used to drive in his uniform days. Maggie stepped off the pavement and waved her hands as a sign for it to stop.

It soon became painfully apparent that the driver wasn't her husband, and nor did he have any intention of stopping. Maggie fell backwards onto the cold pavement with a stumbling leap. The police car sped on, bathing her in a fierce blue light, while the boy in the passenger seat wearing a tracksuit and sunglasses blew her a kiss.

Maggie clawed at the ground, desperate to right herself. A throbbing pain came from one knee, pulsating in time with searing images that tore through her skull of a child's coffin disappearing into an open grave. She grabbed her head in both hands, desperate to expel the vision, the memory… whatever it was. But the illusion only grew and flourished, thumping, flashing, its increasing intensity contorting her features into a pitiful visage. The mascara she'd applied with such care streaking down her cheeks, she clambered to her feet with the coordination of a drunk and staggered straight towards a large horde of faceless youths who strutted menacingly out of the curling smoke.

Shocked by the speed at which the illusion had deserted her, Maggie choked, frozen with panic. She watched the arrivals with horror while they watched her with humour, nudging each other and giggling at the spectacle. All armed and dangerous, their leader wore a police cap speckled with blood crooked on his head. Maggie tried to find the words, but what were the *right* ones? Should she beg for their mercy? Scream for help? Before she got the chance to do either, the horde roared with one conjoined voice and came charging towards her.

"No, please!" Maggie implored her attackers, bringing her hands up to shield herself.

The gang ran straight past—a wailing woman of no importance to them. One knocked her flying into the path of another thug who pushed her away and called her a bitch. Maggie stumbled and fell back to the pavement of whatever street this was. Tears surging from her eyes, she listened to their receding footfall and pulled herself up into an uncomfortable, hunched sit, rocking back and forth and singing her husband's name with a ferocious tremble.

"*Bill... Bill... Bill...*"

There was nothing but her voice. For a moment, not a gunshot sounded, nor one siren screamed. Even the constant thudding of the police helicopter had faded away to nothing more than a faint rumble. To the terrified woman, her mournful bellowing lasted a lifetime, only drawing to a whimpering stop when she heard the nearby tinker of broken glass. Maggie took a deep breath and held it in her bulging throat while a distorted shadow produced of flame and streetlight grew to crawl over her hunkered body. Summoning what little courage she had left, Maggie looked up, blinking through the tears as she focused on whoever stood above her.

Then, with the frailest of relieved smiles breaking loose across her ruined face, she released her breath as a splutter of air and took the gloved hand that reached out for her.

CHAPTER THIRTY

Dyson's hurried escape from the police station would be conducted with all the finesse of a drug dealer evading a mob-handed bust by the Drug Squad.

Storming from the incident room, Dyson had clawed himself into his leather jacket, furiously fiddling with the zip to fasten it, while pursued by several of his fellow detectives. Ignoring their concerned cries, he'd flown down the stairs to grab a worried-looking duty sergeant peering from a first-floor window at the glowing sky. Sergeant Derek, as he was affectionately known, protested at the interruption, his thick eyebrows jumping in shock as Dyson proceeded to march him down one corridor, then another, stopping at a small single window and instructing him to unlock it.

The front entrance was far too dangerous to flee from, Dyson explained. He would be shot to death or hacked to pieces; the station left vulnerable with its protective shutter raised. For the same reason, he couldn't risk rolling beneath the metal door of the underground car park and making his getaway from there. The location of the window, however, would allow him to drop into a small car park at the rear of the police station that served the neighbouring shopkeepers. From there, he could slip along the covered alleyway that led out onto the high street and use the smoke to his advantage to dash across the street unseen. Well, at least he hoped it would be as easy in practice as it was in theory.

Why he wanted to go outside, Dyson neglected to explain. With a pinched expression that looked like a cross between constipation and toothache, Sergeant Derek asked in the paternal tone for which he was famous: "Are you sure you want to do this, guv?"

"No, maybe you should go instead?" Dyson replied dryly, double-checking his Glock and stuffing it into the left-hand pocket of his jacket. While the sergeant rejected the offer in the most vociferous of terms, the detective felt the gun's polymer grip and adjusted its position to offer the best angle for a quick draw should he need it.

"Just you be bloody careful," the sergeant advised grimly.

"Careful's my middle name, Derek," Dyson quipped, bouncing his head up and down to hurry the sergeant along as he sifted through a bunch of keys worthy of a school caretaker.

"Really, I thought it was fucking idiot." Finding the key he wanted, the sergeant unlocked the window and swing it open.

The burning stench of Whitechapel flooded in to make them both curse and splutter. Dyson coughed away the invasive reek to clamber through the window and lower himself down until he dangled from his shaking fingers.

"Don't wait up," he grimaced through clenched teeth, dropping down the wall and slamming into the hard ground with enough force to jar both ankles and send him sprawling across the cracked tarmac.

He rose unsteadily to his feet and gave the sergeant a thumbs up. Sergeant Derek responded with a disapproving headshake and shut the window. Dyson stuffed his hands deep into his pockets and limped across the empty car park before turning into the alleyway and stopping dead.

"Fuck sake…" His eyes slipped shut for a moment, confronted by a lone miscreant relieving himself against the brickwork. His body thin and scrawny, wearing a tracksuit stolen for someone twice his size, the thug twirled on Dyson's approach and stuffed himself away, exchanging his penis for a gleaming katana lent against the wall next to him.

"Well, look who it fuckin' ain't…" the budding Samurai hissed, peeling himself away from the shadows. The single bulb that shone in the alley lightened on an angry, pock-marked face full of malice and the glistening sores that severe drug addiction caused. "Detective Inspector Shitcunt."

Dyson huffed at the inconvenience, decidedly unimpressed by the swordsman's sloppy display as he proceeded to thrash and cut the air with all the skill of a junkie ninja.

"You remember me, pig? Put me away for a five stretch. I fuckin' told you I'd 'ave you, didn't I?"

His real name and the reason behind his incarceration hidden away behind more pressing matters, Dyson managed to recall one of the string of aliases listed on the Met's CRIMINT database. None of them complimentary; the monikers served to highlight his complete lack of criminal acumen and common sense. Amongst others, there were Dimbo, Retard, and—

"Nugget…" Dyson groaned. "Not now, mate."

"Yeah, now, *pig*." Nugget, as in Fucknugget, stopped his slashing and pointed the blade at Dyson. "I reckon it's time for me to get some revenge."

"I doubt you could even spell revenge."

Before Nugget could disprove the claim, the cogs of his mind visibly turning, Dyson rushed forwards to crack him in the side of the head with his Glock. His would-be attacker dropping into an instant, out-cold heap, the detective kicked away the sword and casually stepped over the body to stalk along the alley and peer out from the end.

From the ground, unprotected by the bulletproof glass of the incident room, the turmoil seemed so much more brutal and foreboding. Beneath the orange glow that hung over Whitechapel, the rioters outside the police station continued to frenzy like wild animals. High on adrenaline, those with guns continued to fire at the building, their gunshots and petrol bombs accompanied by zealous cries of "Kill the police!" Those without weapons tore up paving slabs, shattering them into manageable sized missiles with which to throw, while others attempted to prize the shutters from police station windows with their bare hands. Behind the main throng lurked a ring of curious observers. Not explicitly involved themselves, they huddled in groups, laughing and joking, flitting from place to place for a clearer view to film the carnage on their smartphones.

Masked men and onlookers unaware of his presence, Dyson pulled his hoodie over his head and scurried across the main road without hindrance. There was a glass door set between a chicken shop and a dentist that led up to the office where he'd spied Ratski. An investigation into a burglary on the premises several years ago had left a vague memory of the internal layout imprinted on his mind. The plan he'd hastily concocted to gain access was simple enough— albeit legally questionable without a warrant or any reasonable suspicion of wrongdoing. But that wasn't what worried Dyson and caused his brows to fuse together with uninterrupted concern. He had broken more rules than bones and windows combined over the years and always managed to survive the fallout. He doubted whether another black mark against his name, on a night when Whitechapel was at war, would amount for much in the grand scheme of things.

What troubled Dyson was the ball-breaker's presence in Whitechapel. Why was he up there? Had he so little faith in the abilities of the police that he had launched his own investigation? Was that who the other men in there with him were, US federal agents? Was Ratski *that* desperate to save his president's life to install his own team into Whitechapel? And if so, why? People died, even presidents. It was the one sobering guarantee of life. So, why was Robert Garrett so special?

"There's still something they're not telling you, you fucking idiot," the detective told himself for the hundredth time. "Not even Nugget would be stupid enough to get himself mixed up with this mob," he cursed, ridiculing his involvement.

Dyson pushed the door gently and was glad to find it was neither locked and nor did it creak to announce his arrival. Widening the gap just enough to squeeze inside, he closed it without a sound and looked over the small foyer. There was nothing but a half-lit stairwell and a pile of cardboard boxes stacked in the space beneath. The carpet worn to the thread by traffic, paint and paper peeled from the walls and the overbearing smell of damp fought for dominance against the fires outside.

Pulling down his hood and returning the Glock to his pocket, Dyson made a nod and set to work.

More enthralled by the events on screen than they were with the violence beyond the windows, the Secret Service agents continued to crowd around the television. They gawped with horror as shaky phone footage showed a US military helicopter spiralling out of control and slamming into the ground in a Caracas street. Its undercarriage collapsing, one poor soul in full battledress was flung from the open side door to be ground into a meaty smear beneath the Black Hawk as it skidded along on an eruption of sparks.

"Motherfucker!" one of the agents winced as the video ended and returned to the CNN anchor-man.

"Um, we're receiving unconfirmed reports now that this mission was to release several US citizens apprehended and held against their will. I must stress that this is unconfirmed at the—" He stopped and touched a finger to his earpiece, nodding and going off autocue. "Okay. It's all happening now, folks. Venezuelan Foreign Affairs Minister Jorge Iturriza has just been reported as saying: 'Venezuela has defended itself honourably against a deliberate act of American aggression.'"

"This is some spec ops shit gone sideways," another agent announced.

"You don't say, Einstein," his neighbour replied with a lazy roll of his eyes. "We've been trying to overthrow that shitshow down there since before Chávez blew his porchlight."

It was an accurate statement to make. The history of US-Venezuelan relations was a long and complicated one; the socialist utopia Hugo Chávez had created in the 2000s a constant fly in the ointment of American capitalism and its plans for expansion in the region. When a landslide victory brought Chávez to power in 1998, he took back control of Venezuela's colossal oil reserves—the country had the largest supply anywhere on the planet—increasing tariffs on foreign economic interests and ploughing the money into social programs and raising the living standards of his people. Venezuela flourished, becoming a model that many South American nations aspired towards, a fact that worried many within Washington DC. When Chávez died in 2013—or was the victim of assassination as many believed—the country had already begun to falter due to falling oil prices and sanctions imposed by the US and the West, resulting in hyperinflation, starvation, disease, a spiralling crime rate, and a mass exodus from the country. The rot continued, the West backing the more favourable Juan Guaidó in his bid to overthrow the incumbent Nicholas Maduro as president—they even backed a clandestine attempt to have Maduro physically removed from power in 2020. The plot failed, the Trump administration denying any knowledge or involvement. In the presidential elections of 2024, the country rejected Guaido's capitalist plans for salvation, electing Ernesto Ortega instead as its new leader. The US and its supporters baulked with dread as Venezuela accepted multibillion-dollar investment deals from both Russia and China. In exchange for cheap oil and an increased foothold in South America, Venezuela got a revitalised economy and infrastructure. Everybody was happy…except for America and its allies.

Before the agent could broaden his claims of failed military intervention, the shrill bleat of a deafening alarm shattered the tension.

"That's the fire alarm," one agent scoffed loudly with an icy calmness borne out of his Secret Service training. He wandered over to the windows no more panicked than a man approaching a bar for last call. "The bastards are burning us out."

His reaction not quite as serene, Ratski burst out of his office on automatic high alert. The sternness of his exterior pained by the racket, he grabbed the first agent he could lay his hands on. "What the hell's going on?"

"Fire alarm," the accosted agent barked back, jutting his chin over in the direction of the street. "The shitheads are burning down the whole town."

Ratski released his catch and licked his lips contemplatively while pondering the situation. "Okay… Okay, listen up." The agents complied, turning to face him and await his instructions. "Grab what you need and take a weapon," the ball-breaker ordered, his voice booming over the ringing. "Travel light—you're not going on vacation. Do not engage unless fired upon. I *do not* want an international incident. Go!"

Ratski crashed back through the door into his inner sanctum to grab his coat and the precious phone that held his treasured memories. He re-emerged to dart across the main space and take a gun for himself, stopping only to give the TV a final nervous look.

Commentary obliterated by the alarm, the footage showed a ferocious firefight underway in Caracas, filmed by a trembling civilian sheltering behind a car.

"Shit," Ratski muttered with a distinct shudder, the whiteness that already bleached his skin turning a shade paler.

Once everyone had assembled in the cramped lobby, more men than floorspace, Ratski sent an agent through the door to perform a brief reconnoitre of the surrounding area. No one spoke while he was gone. To those charged with protecting the world's most powerful man, the intense soundtrack of combat and the brain-drilling alarm went unnoticed as a seemingly everyday occurrence.

The scout re-entered to relay his report, reeling off the details with swift, soldierly delivery. "There are no visible signs of fire on the street exterior, but as for the rear…?" Unable to determine that there wasn't an inferno ravaging the back of the building, he cocked an eyebrow at Ratski and left his opening statement as a hanging question. "Regardless, situation is FUBAR. We've got a heavy contingent of wannabe warriors numbering approximately three hundred at our two o'clock armed with AKs and autos. They're happy enough shooting the shit out of the precinct at the moment, but we have law enforcement inbound from the east and west. A *lot* of law enforcement. It's about to get tribal out there, and I, for one, don't relish sheltering in a building that might be about to go up like the Great Fire of London when it does. Suggest we exfil current location and wait out this shitstorm at the designated rendezvous point." To a chorus of muted agreement, he licked his finger and drew a map on the door's dirty glass. "Hospital emergency room is the RVP. If we take the next right—"

"New Road," an agent with better geographical knowledge than him called out over the din.

"Thank you, Christopher Columbus. Swing left here, we can avoid any potential—"

"Just get on with…it…!" Ratski interrupted, his words dying as something caught his impatient gaze.

The scout's jaw tightened with resentment and he nodded, leading everyone outside into a single-file trot along the sidewalk. The ball-breaker lingered until he was alone, the door swinging closed to dampen the ruckus. He crossed the lobby to where a fire alarm call point was fixed to the wall at the foot of the stairs. Recently activated, a dull light flashed in one corner of the small red box. Somebody had entered the building to set off the alarm.

"But there is no fire," Ratski found himself saying, jumping as a petrol bomb exploded off the front of a huge dark shape that crept into view inches from the door.

A slow-moving line of truck-sized armoured personnel carriers stretching across the whole street trundled towards the precinct. Dark blue or black—Ratski couldn't tell under the pulsating light the convoy emitted, reducing everything to a lightning-fast series of snapshots—each APC was emblazoned with nothing but the word POLICE along its side. Bullets and projectiles began to rain down on them, plate steel and ballistic glass preventing any harm to the occupants inside. While the vehicles farthest from view began to slow, the right flank continued to advance, fanning out to surround the gathered troublemakers. With a hiss of pneumatic brakes, they made a coordinated stop, the chugging of their diesel engines united and deafening. Then, under a swelling assault of lead, the back doors of each APC flew open, and swarms of heavily armed, black-suited knights in Kevlar leapt out to take up defensive positions behind their cover, screaming in unanimity to announce their arrival.

Ratski gave the blinking fire alarm a final glance and shook off his misgivings to slither through the door and follow in the direction the Secret Service had taken. Free of the building, he could see that another column of armoured vehicles had arrived from the east. The outer flanks of the two lines meeting, their fenders kissed to create an unbreakable barrier to ensnare their prey. The rioters' response was hopelessly inadequate and, from what little Ratski could see through the gaps between the vehicles, the horde had begun to lay down retreating fire, dispersing along the road that ran alongside the precinct.

The ball-breaker glanced up at the white façade. Beyond the bullet holes and scorch marks, a long string of suited personnel—detectives, he assumed—watched the action unfold from the second floor, their faces matched by an identical bleakness.

A black-suited officer sheltering behind the closest APC shouted at him to leave the area. Ratski complied with nothing more than a nod, picking up his pace to turn into the road the scout had detailed.

Detectives? Ratski mused with a smirk, staggering to a stop to look back.

His cold stare narrowed, going from face to face of the men and women at the windows in search of someone. When that someone couldn't be found, his gaze returned to the office to find its exterior still free of flame. Ratski pushed his tongue around inside his mouth, the nagging feeling he'd felt in the lobby returning to bother him like a familiar tune he couldn't name.

CHAPTER THIRTY-ONE

"Come on, come on, come on!"

Wedged behind the wheel of his BMW by his gut, Raymond waited impatiently in a static queue of traffic at the junction of Middlesex Street and Aldgate High Street. At the request of Scotland Yard, a roadblock had been installed to prevent vehicles from entering Whitechapel and forcing everything back into the city to create nothing short of traffic Armageddon. Like some New York City nightmare, the area was hopelessly gridlocked, the air full with the angry honking of car horns.

News of the rioting had broken over Raymond's car stereo while driving back from the studio, drained by the grilling received from the *Crimenight* presenter. A quick call on the main-set radio to the Information Room at the Yard had confirmed the news report, detailing the extent of the trouble and the resulting road closures. Further cordons had been set up at the top of Commercial Street, across Mile End Road at Stepney Green Underground station, and at Limehouse DLR station on the A13. It wasn't watertight, they never were, especially with the maze of smaller streets and alleyways that intersected Whitechapel, but they would keep the majority of innocent motorists from straying into what the newsreader had animatedly described as a 'war zone.'

Raymond peered between the cars ahead and caught sight of two City of London Police Department officers trying their best to manage the chaos. Both gorilla-sized buggers decked in tight black uniforms and armed with machine guns, neither of them appeared particularly enamoured with their assigned task.

The smallest constabulary in the UK, the CoLPD—C-PLOD as the acronym was humorously rearranged by their Met counterparts—were charged solely with policing the 'square mile' of London's financial heartland. From Farringdon to Aldgate, Clerkenwell to the River Thames, C-PLOD had been involved in several high-profile investigations over the years. The Provisional IRA had detonated two truck bombs during the early 1990s, devastating vast swathes of the square mile, the Sidney Street Siege of 1911 had begun on their patch, and the man they now sought had slaughtered Catherine Eddowes just a few minutes' walk from where the Welshman sat trapped in his car. These days, their lot generally consisted of fraud investigations and cases of violent robberies committed against unwitting tourists who had ventured into the City of London during its hours of deserted darkness. As a good portion of their budget came directly from the Corporation of London, C-PLOD were somewhat protected from the financial woes suffered by other UK police departments: a fact which had spawned a bitter resentment by the Met of their City of London counterparts.

"And they've got better bloody canteens," Raymond said with bitterness, his thoughts turning momentarily to a recent meal he'd bagged himself at Bishopsgate police station and the angry protests coming from his rumbling stomach.

He watched the duo of primates shepherding the vehicles in front back into town with lethargic pointing and sweeping gestures, ignoring the abuse they got in return from fuming motorists. When he got within spitting distance of the policemen, Raymond disregarded their directions and gave them a long blast of his horn to get their attention. He emitted a bellowing, walrus-like yawn and held his warrant card up against the windscreen for them to see. After a brief conflab between themselves, one ambled over, his head tilted, admiring the sleek lines of the Welshman's car as he came.

"MIT," Raymond snapped with his usual cold abruptness. "I need to get back to Whitechapel."

The arriving PC eyed up his identification and exaggerated a wince. "Can't guarantee your nice motor's gonna look like that in the morning, sir."

Raymond didn't care about the car. If some little scrote burnt it down to the chassis and seat springs, the Met would have to supply him with a new one. Cars could be replaced; lives could not. All he could think about were the detectives he'd left behind in Whitechapel. *His* detectives as they had become. Fond was a strong word, and one the Welshman rarely used outside of his wife and daughter, but he had become quite partial to that ragtag mob of CID dicks he'd been forced to adopt into his investigation, even if he didn't show it. They hadn't caught their man yet—they didn't even know who he *really* was—but Raymond knew they wouldn't stop until the job was done. Dyson's detectives were competent and had tenacity and stamina by the bucketload. There were men and women under his command at Hereford House who would go sick at the first sign of a sneeze, yet Jenny Brent had been shot at, blown up, nearly eaten by a pack of murderous hounds, and still she came back for more! Maggie's illness and losing a child to cancer had extinguished any glimmer of belief that there was some virtuous, omnipotent being in the sky doing right by Mankind. Nevertheless, he had still said a silent prayer for Jenny and the members of Operation Milton Keynes when the news broke. He only hoped someone had heard his plea because technology had failed him spectacularly. The mobile networks to Whitechapel had been temporarily cut in response to the rioting, and the phone lines and Airwave radio system had both become casualties when the police station came under attack, so the Yard claimed.

Raymond's worried scowl dampened any further conversation the city policeman considered making. He turned to his colleague and whistled for him to move aside the roadblock. As soon as the metal barriers were dragged over the tarmac, Raymond nudged the BMW through the gap and accelerated away, turning left where others were forbidden. Back into Met territory, Aldgate soon became Whitechapel.

"Dear God..." the Welshman uttered with shock, his beady eyes bulging like saucers at what confronted him.

Smoke, thick and dense and black, smothered the deserted lanes of Whitechapel High Street, hanging immobile on the windless air. From deep within the approaching cloud, muted bursts of deep oranges and reds grew and flickered, becoming a multitude of fires when the smoke swallowed his car. The ground turned into an undulating mess of jutting debris that rocked the BMW and slowed his drive, his hands tightening on the wheel in response. The devastation was immeasurable. Everything was burning. Homes, shops, vehicles, it was like—

"A fucking bomb's gone off!" Raymond hissed, his mind flashing back to those IRA truck bombs that had devastated the City of London until the memory was shattered by India 98 bursting from behind a line of burning rooftops to swoop overhead, laser-like searchlight blasting over the war-torn streets.

A different world from the one he'd left only hours before, a dozen fire crews battled blazes left and right. One tender of weary firefighters doused the dying embers of an inferno that had swept through the Whitechapel Art Gallery; the decorative stone arch that had welcomed visitors to the gallery collapsed onto the pavement in a pile of blackened rubble. Raymond scowled at the sight and shook his head with disgust, recalling how he had taken Maggie there one rainy afternoon during the infancy of their relationship. A parade of shops on the right had been ransacked and robbed, leaving clothes and electrical goods strewn across the pavement, dropped or discarded by looters. A few doors down, the building that once housed the Whitechapel Bell Foundry—a local landmark that stood since 1570 and had cast Big Ben and the Liberty Bell in Philadelphia—was gone: reduced to a pile of smouldering brick and charred wood. Every now and then, he would catch a glimpse of a ghostly, faceless shadow skulking in the gloom, armed with a machine gun or pistol.

"Stupid little bastards!" Raymond spat, his face reddened by flame and rage.

Rioting never made much sense to the Welshman. It was generally committed by those who lived in less than affluent areas, angry enough with society, the government, the police—anyone but themselves—to destroy the neighbourhood and make it even less desirable and unworthy of the investment and regeneration it desperately needed. It was the definition of insanity.

While Raymond continued to groan and gripe, a bullet punctured his back door with a resonant slap of metal that sent a puff of seat foam flying in the air. Intentional or not, he had no desire to find the shooter and question his motives. Instead, he floored the car, its electric motors singing a piercing falsetto as it fishtailed away, tyres crunching over glass and debris until they flapped with multiple punctures. The wheel heavy and unresponsive, Raymond heaved the two tonnes of German engineering awkwardly around a burning ambulance, an upside-down taxi the next obstacle. He clouted the cab's front end and sent it spinning on its roof. The fight continued—Raymond sending a burning industrial waste bin skidding across the road. Zooming past the smoking remains of a police car, he shuddered at the blackened body hanging from the driver's window, frozen in its desperate bid for escape. Unable to determine whether it was man or woman, friend or foe, he spluttered out another incantation that it was no one from Operation Milton Keynes, finishing just as a hulking shape lurched from behind an abandoned vehicle to step out in front of him.

"*Jesus Christ!*" Raymond stamped on the brake and sent the BMW skidding to a stop.

He pulled his head away from the steering wheel and looked up, one hand creeping for the Glock hidden within the folds of his trench coat. The dark form shrank in size and grew in clarity as the smoke lulled to become nothing more threatening than a diminutive policewoman. Uniform torn and bloodied, she swayed and stumbled like one of the undead, her quivering gun raised to point directly at Raymond.

"Turn this fucking car around!" the PC boomed, wide-eyed, a petrified shiver to her tone. "Get…get out of Whitechapel."

Raymond flung open the driver's door and clawed himself out of his seat into a stand. "You need to get inside, now."

He watched her while she shook, her brain desperately trying to untangle what he'd said. Blood oozed from a vicious gash on her head, and it was evident that an even worse, unimaginable trauma had been suffered inside. Slowly, her Glock dipped and dropped down against her thigh. Her brain finally recognising the intruder for who he was, she slackened and gripped the bonnet of the BMW for support, leaving bloody handprints and smears all over the silver paintwork.

"It's you, sir!" the PC spewed with borderline hysteria, a fresh track of tears etching their way down her trembling flesh. "I've…I've found another one."

"Another what?"

"Another woman, sir. She's…she's been gutted. It's him—your Jack the Ripper copycat! It's fresh, and it's horrible…and…and I can't get the picture out of my—" The traumatised policewoman drove a finger aggressively against the side of her head. "Will you come and take a look? The radios have crashed, and…and I can't get hold of anyone."

"*What!*" Raymond choked.

"I said—"

"I heard what you said," he snapped with no more than a whisper, his mouth hanging open when finished to create a pained and clueless look. "In the middle of a riot?"

Raymond ignored the policewoman's fervent nodding, his expression twisting to become as equally disturbed as hers. Whitechapel was in the grip of a brutal outbreak of violence that had no doubt left scores injured or dead, yet the Ripper had emerged from the shadows, onto streets heavy with police and perpetrator, to slaughter another poor soul.

In the middle of a fucking riot! Raymond killed the BMW's motors and pulled his Glock from its holster. "Show me."

After making a suitable space amongst the boxes stacked

below the stairs of the foyer, Dyson had set off the fire alarm and hidden inside the cardboard cave. There he waited while the claxon wailed and an American voice delivered the findings of his reconnaissance. Only when the unmistakable arrogance of Ratski's voice faded and a full two minutes had passed did the detective push the boxes aside and slip out.

He ascended the stairs warily, his Glock held ready in a two-handed grip. On reaching the first floor, Dyson crept along a short hallway, checking the doors he passed to find two empty bathrooms and a sparsely stocked cleaner's cupboard. He stopped at the double doors that ended the corridor and peered through one of the glass panels.

The last time he had been up there, during the break-in that had seen several laptops stolen, the vast room was alive with office life, cooing secretaries giggling doe-eyed at his questioning while their male counterparts watched him with undue suspicion. The office was empty and decrepit now; its better days long gone. Within the grubby magnolia walls were chairs and desks aplenty, all dated and vacant, with filing cabinets and storage units still ergonomically positioned. Against the farthest wall stood three fridge-freezer-sized computer servers. New additions no doubt brought in by Ratski, they were reminiscent of the equipment that had populated the police station's surveillance room before Jerry Mathews had vaporised the whole lot. Similar but not identical, these servers appeared much more high-tech and expensive than what the Met's budget had extended to. Lit up like the Blackpool Illuminations, an endless jumble of cables and wires ran down from each server, taped across the carpet to a host of terminals set up on the desks.

Dyson cocked his head to one side and listened. Voices were coming from inside the room. Mysterious and ethereal, they were the words of many, talking and shouting over each other, competing to be heard above the squawking of the fire alarm. Even more intriguingly, given that the room had been occupied by Americans, the voices sounded like...English accents.

Steeling himself, Dyson tightened his hold on the gun and pushed through the doors, sweeping the weapon over the room until he confirmed it was empty. He smarted at the racket and went straight to the fire alarm control panel, hitting a collection of random buttons until he got lucky and the ringing stopped. When it did, the disembodied utterances became thunderingly loud, coming as one muddled soup of people speaking together to create a calamitous cacophony.

"Hoskins is injured! Need immediate medical assistance —TSG Bronze Command, rioters are in retreat—Units coming in from neighbouring stations to—Hotel Tango from India 98, rioters are dispersing along Vallance Street, still heavily armed—Um, I've got multiple bodies on Goodman Street—*Help us! Help*—!"

"Greg Fanshaw...?" Dyson muttered, recognising one of the speakers as an inspector he knew. He rushed over to the servers and traced the power lead from each tower to a grey industrial switch box fitted to the wall. There was no need for an electrician to tell him what the big chrome handle on the front did. Dyson gripped the lever and heaved. With a heavy mechanical *cluuunk* and the sound of draining power, the voices died on the air and fell silent. Except for one.

"...about to cross live to Caracas," the excitable tone of an American newsreader said, "where President Ortega is due to make a statement to the country's National Assembly."

Dyson eyed up the small TV sat atop an old filing cabinet and did the maths: Caracas plus Ernesto Ortega equalled Venezuela. Whatever was happening in the South American country where the ball-breaker illegally mined his top-secret time travel shit, it was irrelevant. The detective returned his Glock to the pocket of his leather jacket and began to stalk the office while a man's voice began a passionate address in heated Spanish.

He found a desk that held five long rows of neatly arranged Taser stun guns. The adjacent desktop contained a couple of Sig Sauer automatics; their likewise precise positioning indicating that there had been many more. On the pillar that separated the tables, Dyson noticed a copy of their own Ripper Efit stuck to the plaster. Despite the pair of thick glasses that some comedian had added in marker pen, the image was no less unsettling.

"Do you know what's going on here, Jack?" Dyson asked, his face marred by tender bewilderment. Disappointed by the Ripper's lack of response, he tutted and wandered away, weaving through the desks towards the windows and coming to a stop where Ratski had stood.

Disorientating, blinding lights from the TSG's armoured personnel carriers strobed over the high street, causing everyone to move in broken, jerky steps. The shooting had mostly stopped; the majority of the insurgents vanished into the night. There were bodies down there, some moving, some not. TSG were busy rounding up the rioters who hadn't escaped their corral, zip-tying their hands behind their back to lay them face down on the ground.

Dyson's gaze went to the incident room. Surrounded by most of Operation Milton Keynes, Jenny stared back at him. Her face painted with concern, she placed a hand on the glass as if to initiate a connection. "I'm okay," he mouthed slowly. Not waiting to see if Jenny understood, Dyson turned back for the last door left to investigate.

He strode past the television. Venezuela's president continued to enunciate feverishly; the young man's jaw tight with heated emotion as his clenched fist beat a rhythm to the unknown words he spoke.

The door flew open with the rattle of loose glass. If Dyson was expecting to find a jackpot of evidence in what he assumed to be Ratski's command centre, he was bitterly disappointed. Frigidly cold, the tiny room reeked of damp and was bare apart from an old wooden desk, chair, and crooked hatstand. There was nothing on the scratched desktop except for a can of deodorant and a spooled phone charger. Whatever underhand shit the ball-breaker was up to in Whitechapel, he had left nothing evidential on show. The detective huffed and rounded the desk to slide open the first of three drawers. Finding nothing more incriminating than a solitary paperclip sliding around inside the bottom drawer, he moved on to the next. It contained a well-stocked, neatly arranged assortment of stationery. Dyson tore open the top drawer and froze solid at what he found. With a sharp intake of breath, the confusion that had gripped him since spying Ratski at the window went stratospheric.

On top of a neat pile of paperwork was a Metropolitan Police Department warrant card. To the untrained observer, it was just a cheap black wallet, but the detective recognised it for what it was…and it made no sense. The bed of printed emails on which it lay, official despatches topped with the emblem of the White House, became as insignificant as the Venezuelan president's speech drifting through the door. Dyson lifted out the warrant card, his heart quickening as he turned it over in his hand to find the shining silver badge on the flipside. The faux leather appeared new as if it had just been issued; not scuffed and frayed at the edges as his own was, the metal insignia dulled to a dark patina. Back in 1888, he had *borrowed* Sidney Carmichael's identification, figuring it would come in useful to aid his escape. But why did Ratski have one, and where did he get it? He flipped open the warrant card, and the face of the missing probationer, Christopher Haddon, stared back at him.

Full of enthusiastic beans, Haddon seemed likeable enough when Dyson had met him briefly. Desperate to progress, the young PC was hellbent on making detective as soon as possible. But those aspirations were to go unfulfilled: Haddon vanishing during his first solo shift, never to be seen again. Not a single witness had so far come forward to offer any insight, and news of the probationer's disappearance was soon lost beneath the swell of public interest in the ongoing hunt for the Ripper. What little attention the case did generate was mostly negative; one nefarious reporter even suggesting that Haddon was the copycat killer and had fled London before he could be arrested once his hapless colleagues uncovered his crimes.

Dyson scoffed at the notion and shut the warrant card. "Why the fuck have you got this, Ratski?" he muttered to himself, instantly startled by the reply that followed.

"Where's your search warrant, Detective?"

CHAPTER THIRTY-TWO

Raymond followed the policewoman as she limped across the pavement towards Greatorex Street on the left. Usually a vibrant thoroughfare full of bustling businesses and restaurants catering predominantly for Whitechapel's Asian community, the narrow one-way road stood in desolate darkness but for a flickering smudge of orange on the horizon. There had been a power cut, she informed him, probably caused by the rioters. On one corner, before light submitted to dark, the windows of an Islamic bank had been smashed through, its plush leather furniture pulled out and discarded on the pavement.

Given the perilous situation, the Welshman wore no Tyvek coverall as was usual during the attendance of a murder scene. This would be a cursory examination to confirm the PC's claims, nothing more. He would avoid getting close enough to the body to risk any chance of cross-contamination. The corruption of a murder scene by a stray fibre of clothing or microscopic flake of skin could seriously obstruct the chances of a conviction, and it certainly wouldn't be a fitting epitaph for the soon-to-be-retired SIO if he was the one to scupper it.

A cynical huff followed. Who was he kidding? There would be no trial if what Dyson claimed was true. The Americans would be waiting in the wings to claim the Ripper as soon as apprehended, airlifting him out of the country to drain him of his precious blood at some secret, Area 51-type facility. Given the shoulder to shoulder, best buddy relationship between the UK and US, and now that the prime minister was involved, the whole thing would be swept under the very big carpet governments kept exclusively for hiding such dirty secrets. As infuriating as that was, it was out of his hands. Regardless of the outcome, the investigation would proceed as normal—or as normal as it could, given the circumstances. The area would be secured, somehow, and once the unrest was finally brought under control, a thorough investigation would be launched. The FME on duty would attend, followed by Brian Lane and a van full of SOCO, and then the ball could be got rolling on Whitechapel's latest murder.

"She's down here," Raymond's guide said, her voice raised a couple of notches above a whisper to compensate for India 98's distant thudding and the sound of faraway gunfire. She led him along the pavement, glass and debris cracking underfoot, navigating upturned chairs and sofas to stop at a black rectangle of nothingness sandwiched between the bank and a gaudy apartment block. Victoria Lockwood, as the policewoman had nervously introduced herself once the screaming and the gun pointing had finished, jutted her chin down the alleyway. "It runs all the way behind the shops."

Raymond nodded and peered up at the flats until he turned to give the windows above the businesses of Greatorex Street a similar inquisitive look. Both excellent vantage points for potential witnesses, every window was as black as the street, lacking any of the fevered rubbernecking he'd encountered where Ginita and Narinda had met their brutal ends.

Victoria shook her head and answered the question he was about to ask. "No witnesses, sir. I haven't seen a soul. Apart from…" She raised a trembling finger to the laceration concealed by her hair. "I had to hide down here from…*those bastards*," she continued venomously. "That's…that's when I found her."

The Welshman nodded again, a rare glimmer of sympathy behind his eyes. Victoria didn't look much older than his daughter. Whatever horrors she had endured, she was balancing on a knife-edge, and he wasn't going to be the one to push her.

He pulled out his phone and thumbed through the apps until he found the torch. Usually glaringly adequate for such endeavours, the little beam seemed to struggle against the stygian void, taunting his desperate want for light and offering only a spectrum of varying greys. Raymond listened to the sound of running water flowing from somewhere inside, grumbling and screwing up his face while trying to peer through the gloom. He could make out the vague outlines of industrial bins dotted here and there along the alley, an abundance of lumpy round bin bags congregated around each one. But beyond that, it was like looking into a black hole from which even light couldn't escape. Eventually, his eyes were able to determine that there was something else in there. Something laying amongst the rubbish about halfway down. About twenty metres away was a…*shape*. There were no other words to describe it given the lack of illumination. Gun in one hand, hopeless torch in the other, Raymond stepped into the alley and let the blackness swallow him. Victoria let out a deep breath that bristled his ear and followed.

The burning stink that choked Whitechapel was so pervasive Raymond almost missed the subtle accompaniments he was all too familiar with. The smell of blood, like rusted iron or a handful of wet coins, blended with the foul stench of expelled excrement to grow in strength with every step. He pulled a sickened face and glanced back to see it matched by Victoria's. People often released their bladders and bowels when reaching an abrupt end to their lives: a fact that many investigations preferred not to disclose for the sake of the victim's loved ones. He fidgeted with the phone as he drew closer, trying to make it brighter while vocally cursing the contraption and his recent decision to upgrade.

Each step brought slow, muddled clarity. The nondescript shape transformed into a pile of discarded rags, merging and knitting together to become distinguishable as the body of a woman. Supine, her legs were splayed open and twisted unnaturally, her arms limp at the side of her head. Another couple of steps, and Raymond could make out a torrent of black blood doused all over the rough concrete floor, glistening like engine oil in his pathetic beam.

The Welshman shook the phone furiously, sending weak shadows careening all over the walls. "Where's your torch, constable?"

"I…I lost it, sir."

Raymond thought it better not to ridicule her explanation and continued to stalk the corpse. The knee-length black dress she wore was sliced apart from hem to neckline, its torn edges smoothed and laid out with meticulous symmetry on the neatly presented tails of a winter coat. Flesh, as cold and white as snow, clashed brutally with the dark chasm sliced up the woman's front, running from the top of her underwear to between her exposed breasts. In contrast to the neat arrangement of her clothing, organs cut or ripped from the gaping wound lay all around, rejected in haphazard fashion.

Something about her clothes forced Raymond beyond the mental barrier he had told himself he wouldn't cross. It was more than professional intrigue, the body pulling him closer as a magnet would metal. Head tilted to one side, he stared at the abomination, a peculiar feeling seizing him and taking terrible hold.

The vicious knife wound ploughed through the woman's neck was as deep as a Welsh valley, the flesh parted to produce a distinctive V shape all the way down to the spine. Head turned away from him, her features were obscured by a thick spray of arterial blood and a mess of hair, and yet… there was *something* about her profile. Something that forced another involuntary step from Raymond. Likewise, there was something about her hair, dank and blood-soaked as it was, and the single earring in her delicate lobe that sparkled weakly in the light.

"Earrings," he mumbled in a voice different from his usual irascible tone, as devoid of life as the woman before him.

"Sir?" Victoria enquired timidly from behind. "Are you okay?"

Raymond glanced back and found himself unable to speak. The cold breath caught in his throat, and his whole body started to shake as a strange convulsion raced through him like a bolt of electricity. He suddenly felt frail, grabbing hold of the brickwork for support. Victoria pawed the ground nervously in her boots, the wide-eyed gawk he made boring straight through her. Her concern ignored, he slid along the wall, gathering speed until he pushed off and staggered to take up position above the body. What he did next caused the policewoman to gasp in horror, shocked that a detective would do such a thing.

Raymond sat down. He pinched his trousers to loosen the material from his thick thighs and just sank into an awkward cross-legged sit next to the woman. For a Murder Squad detective at the site of a brutal slaying, aware of how crucial it was to preserve the crime scene, it was an unimaginable and inconceivable move. His descent synchronised with a flood of tears that burst free from his eyes, Raymond reached out with a flaying hand and grabbed the body.

"*Sir!*" the PC spluttered, taking an immediate step back from his serious breach of protocol.

Taking a moment to squeeze the woman's bony shoulder, the Welshman dragged her into his lap, painting his trousers a wet crimson. Victoria continued to speak, but her protest went unheard, his heart beating like a thousand drums all at once. The only word he could pluck from her verbal jumble was 'evidence.'

"What about the preservation of evidence?" she was probably asking him, stupefied by his irrational and unbelievable display.

Evidence?

What fucking evidence did he need? The identity of the man who had butchered her with such brutality was painfully obvious. While he might never learn why she had come to Whitechapel—maybe a broken memory had panicked her into making the journey as she did before—he knew without a doubt who had committed the crime.

"It's alright," Raymond murmured softly. "It's okay. She's...she's..."

He turned the woman's pale face towards him. Her cold, glassy stare watched as he stroked a loose hair away and rubbed a spot of blood from her cheek with his thumb. A deep, mournful wail rose from within as he drew the woman into his arms and hugged her. Quivering on the violent judder that charged his body, a rope of saliva slipped from his mouth, hanging there until lost in the matted hair he brushed against his lips and kissed tenderly. He saw Victoria look away, disturbed by his actions, while he choked back the caustic tide of vomit that rose, desperate instead for the words to escape. And then they did—on an uncontrollable howl of raw emotion.

"SHE'S MY WIFE!"

As if roused by a distant scream, Dyson shook off the surprise of Ratski's unheard approach to glare at him standing in the doorway of the small office. Nothing short of hatred, it was the look of a killer, not a cop—a man who had reached the absolute end of his tether and was ready to strike. A nauseating boiling surged through his body as his flesh seared with rage. He looked away for a moment with hopes of dampening the volcano moments from erupting. The caustic words of Ortega's passionate speech bleeding through from the main office did little to pacify him. The man sounded as furious as the detective felt.

"I said—"

"I don't need a warrant," Dyson snapped in reply, his burning scowl returned to Ratski. "Not if I believe life to be in danger."

Ratski gestured with his arms to indicate the emptiness of the office. "Whose life is in danger?"

"Yours!"

The volcano exploded. Unable to control himself any longer, Dyson scrambled over the desk in a frenzied display of dexterity, launching a blistering attack that caught Ratski unawares. He grabbed hold of the ball-breaker and pummelled a fist into his face, smashing the demeaning arrogance from his face and sending him staggering back into the main office. Ratski thudded into the wall with a crack of plasterboard, a beautifully timed cheer coming from the Venezuelan president's supporters.

"What in the—!"

Another sentence went unfinished as Dyson leapt out of the office to grab his prey by the collars and slam him back into the wall. Ignoring the Ratski-shaped indentation in the broken plasterboard, Dyson shook his colleague's identification inches from the ball-breaker's wounded face.

"What the fuck is this!" he screamed. "Where's Chris Haddon?"

"Calm down, Dyson," Ratski countered painfully, desperately trying to free himself from the detective's unbreakable grip.

"Don't tell me to calm down, you Yank fuck! Where's Haddon?"

With an indignant roar of his own, Ratski succeeded in pulling himself free. The move was awkward and sloppy, but he managed to stumble away and compose himself, dragging the blood from his face and dabbing at his bleeding lips with a tissue. He took longer than Dyson considered necessary to pull the creases out of his thousand-dollar suit, straighten his tie, and then shake the dusting of plaster from his hair. Only when he was ready did Ratski turn back, the reply that came in answer to the detective's question delivered so callously that the heat inside of Dyson's body froze to an instant chill.

"He became involved in my investigation, and I had to take the necessary steps to ensure his silence."

"Your investigation? *Your* investigation?"

"Well, we couldn't rely on you, could we?"

The internal seesaw from hot to cold swung back into the red again, and Dyson found his fists clenching reflexively at the snipe. "Where is he? Where's Chris Haddon, you piece of shit? Did...did you kill him? Is he dead?"

"I told you, I took the necessary steps."

"What?" Dyson smarted and let the assumed meaning behind Ratski's words sink in. "You killed him? You *killed* a fucking cop?"

"I took the necessary—"

Taking his own necessary step when dealing with a potential cop killer, Dyson threw away Haddon's warrant card and charged across the space that separated them. The floodgates were open now, a cocktail of adrenaline and testosterone racing through his body to send him way beyond what was considered reasonable force. Fist met face, over and over, until the sickly bleakness of the ball-breaker's countenance became a tenderised mess, and he slipped from the detective's grasp to leave him holding nothing but air.

"You murdering bastard," Dyson growled. "We are fucking done! This bullshit—all these lies. It's over!"

"And…and what…what are you going to do?" Ratski puffed, spitting out a thick wad of blood. "There's nothing you can do to me."

His nostrils flaring with the ferocity of his breath, Dyson started to circle his fallen adversary, his death stare fixed on its target while he massaged the pain from his aching fist. One revolution complete, another begun, he slowed to a stop, the daggers he gave the ball-breaker dulled by a sigh and reluctant return to a more professional stance. Fury had driven him to this point, but it was prudence that took the wheel now.

"Brad Ratski," Dyson said, clearly enunciating every word of the mandatory police caution. "I'm arresting you on suspicion of the abduction of Chris Haddon. You do not have to say anything, but it may harm your defence—"

"Stop this." Ratski pulled himself up into a squat and hacked up another lump of blood and phlegm onto the dirty carpet. "Remember what I told you at the hotel? Pick your fights carefully."

"But it may harm your defence if you do not mention when questioned something—"

"Stop."

"*If you do not mention when questioned—*"

"Stop!"

"Fuck you!"

Dyson rushed forwards and kicked the punch-drunk Ratski back down. He flipped him like a burger, crashing him onto his front to force the air from his lungs. Arms flailing, Ratski fought back, desperate to grab his attacker. Dyson responded by slamming a knee into the small of his back and sending him into a spasmodic shock that stalled any chance of protest.

"Something you later rely on in court. Anything you do say may be given in evidence. *Do you understand?*" Freeing his handcuffs from the clip on his belt, Dyson reached down and snapped one bracelet around Ratski's left wrist.

"Better than you, you dumb bastard," the ball-breaker mumbled the best he could, his face squashed into the carpet. "Do you have any idea what you're doing? Do you? Do you!"

Arresting a foreign government official for a serious crime such as abduction or murder came with a whole tonne of legal implications and an even bigger pile of paperwork. Arresting one who had already killed two drug dealers and was involved in a top-secret time travel project to save the life of the world's most powerful man was something way beyond his comprehension.

Dyson wavered, stuck at an imaginary crossroads between right and wrong. As attractive as the prospect of nicking Ratski was, it would produce more fallout than a nuclear explosion. *Everything* would come out. It was a clusterfuck waiting to happen. The killer would be exposed as the real Jack the Ripper, and Dyson, the man who brought him back to kill again. Mary's true identity would be discovered, and Solly Goldmann revealed as the counterfeiter who had hidden her in 2030. Dyson, a serving police officer, would be hung out to dry: if not for employing the forger's illegal services, then for his part in the unleashing of a serial killer on London's streets. Dyson and Goldmann would probably go to prison, and Mary would be hounded relentlessly by a salacious press eager for an exclusive. At the same time, the more serious journalistic members of the worldwide media would expose the lies of President Garrett and the prime minister, their respective oppositions calling for their immediate resignations.

Or maybe nothing would come out. This was the US Government, after all. With more secrets than staff, it had the reputation of being a ruthless animal that crossed the boundaries between right and wrong without impunity. Assassinations, illegal wars, regime changes—you name it, they were rumoured to have done it. History was littered with America's innocent casualties. A more likely scenario was that everything would be buried to protect the truth, Dyson included, just as Ratski had warned during their altercation at the hotel.

And that split-second of hesitation was all the ball-breaker needed.

He screamed and tore his manacled hand free from Dyson's grasp, throwing it back awkwardly to slam the open bracelet into the side of his head. The blow lacked the strength or coordination for a knockout, but it was powerful enough to lacerate his cheek an inch shy of his eye. Dyson stumbled to a stand, spewing blasphemies and swiping at the stinging wound. By the time he turned back, Ratski was on his feet, twirling like a ballerina to roundhouse a foot straight into his gut that doubled him over and sent him crashing to the floor. Their positions reversed, Ratski began to pace a straight line back and forth.

"Enough! Enough of this," he panted in animated American. "What do you hope to achieve? You want to arrest me—charge me? With what? What do you have? An overworked, underpaid British cop with a story of state-sanctioned time travel and a colleague's badge I could've found in the street and was about to hand in at the precinct? Sure, good luck with that. Remember the cards, Dyson? I'd fold if I were you because you have *nothing!*"

Dyson glanced along his body. Shifted by the impact of his landing, his Glock was protruding from his pocket within easy reach. Before he could consider reaching for it, using it as a tool to placate his attacker, Ratski spied it too, charging with a blur of arms and legs to whip it away. He held the gun victoriously for a moment as if awarded it at a ceremony and then hurled it across the office.

"What do you have?" he repeated, a sardonic winner's smile cracking through his ruddy-faced exertion.

Chuckling at the absurd display of machismo, Dyson pulled himself into an agonised sit and prodded his diaphragm gingerly. Something hurt inside when he breathed, but it was no worse than he'd suffered before, and it certainly wasn't about to dampen his next move. He reached into the other pocket of his jacket for something far more damaging than a bullet.

His phone.

"What do I have?" he said, pausing to work his way through the home screen until he found what he wanted. "I have this."

Starting mid-sentence, Ratski's voice came from the phone's tiny speakers. Despite its muffled quality, there was no mistaking the recognisable tone. "—they couldn't transfuse him. He had a blood group that no one had ever seen before. And so, Bishop's blood as it became known, was discovered the very day the boy died. It's so rare that there have only ever been four recorded instances of it. The boy, an Australian woman who died in 1989, Bob Garrett, the current President of the United States, and…the man we believe is Jack the Ripper."

"You recorded our conversation!" the real Ratski gasped. His body tensing, he gripped the nearest desk for support, staring open-mouthed at the deliberate, shit-eating grin Dyson gave him.

"I did. Strictly speaking, I shouldn't have. Regulation of Investigatory Powers Act, blah, blah, blah. But what's a bit of intrusive surveillance between friends, huh? It's not the best quality as the phone was in my pocket, but our voice recognition boys can work wonders." Dyson waited for a response, but Ratski was too stunned to give one. "Oh, you want more?" he asked, scrubbing through the audio file and stopping it randomly.

"Your main priority is to catch Jack the Ripper," Ratski said on the phone. "Crime detection has moved on significantly. I'm confident you'll have him back in custody within the next forty-eight hours."

"Forty-eight hours. How's that working out?" Dyson ended the recording and slipped the phone back into his pocket. "It's all there. The whole thing. You see, one of the first things I ever got taught as a copper was never walk into a room you don't have a way out of. It wasn't part of the official Hendon training course, more a piece of friendly advice. But I've never forgotten it. Now who has the best fucking hand?"

Instantly sickened, Ratski withered, the no-nonsense ball-breaker suddenly lacking the ability to break anything other than the thin lustre of sweat that grew on his brow. His eyes slipped shut and his head sank to his chest, the folding of his arms and tight pursing of his lips a familiar indication to the detective that he was frantically searching for a way out of the mess. Dyson could almost hear the gears turning inside his head. Electing not to revel in his adversary's discomfort any further, he rose silently and limped away, peering under chairs and behind desks.

"What are you doing?" Ratski whispered, his voice flat and hopeless.

"I'm looking for my gun." Dyson stopped and glanced back. "When I find it, I'm gonna stick it in your spine and *really* try not to blow you in half. Then I thought we'd go back to the nick for a chat and a nice cuppa. How does that sound?"

"No, stop," Ratski ordered.

"Yeah, you said that already."

"I said *stop!*" Unseen to Dyson, Ratski pushed himself off the desk and lurched forwards, his eyes alive with panic. "Don't you walk away from me. Don't you dare!"

Before Dyson could tell him to go fuck himself—which he fully intended to do—a deafening gunshot punched an ear-piercing ringing right inside his head. The shockwave rattling the windows in their frames, he wheeled around to find the ball-breaker holding one of the Sig Sauers. Whether snatched from the desk or pulled from within his jacket, the gun was pointed upwards, a flurry of blown apart ceiling tile drifting down like snowflakes.

"I can't let you do this, Dyson," Ratski said, an energetic tremble in his voice. He brought the gun down to aim it at the detective. "I can't let you expose what I'm doing. If you do, everybody dies."

The sound of more gunfire drew his nervous scrutiny to the small television. Ratski watched, mesmerised by the images. Ortega's speech finished, poor quality phone footage showed a ferocious firefight between two groups of soldiers under the scrolling banner of LIVE FROM CARACAS. The explosion of a rusted jalopy jumpstarted Ratski back to the moment with a noticeable jolt.

"It's happening now, Dyson, at this very moment," he babbled, the gun trembling under his command. "*At this very moment.* You disrupt what I'm doing here, and you—*you*—kill everyone!"

The detective snorted at the absurdity of his claim. Over the years, he had been accused of a catalogue of wrongdoings by disgruntled felons during arrest, desperate to turn the tables and save their own skins. Genocide, however, was definitely a fresh take on the idea and one worthy of some kind of recognition.

"Who the fuck are you, Ratski?" Dyson's gaze narrowed with suspicion. "I mean, really?"

"I'm just like you. I'm just trying to do the right thing."

"Is that what you told Chris Haddon?"

"Chris Haddon is—"

"You're insane," Dyson interrupted, sneering with disgusted.

"Insane? I'm the one trying to stop this madness!"

The cranial gear turning had returned a workable solution. Ratski slipped back into his default setting, straightening his posture and solidifying his grip on the gun. Never had he appeared so unpleasantly determined; his grim gauntness accentuated by the smearing of blood mixed with the glistening layer of perspiration to transform him into something as inhuman as the Ripper himself. Completely focused, he regarded Dyson as nothing more than a problem that needed sorting.

"I can't have you getting in the way," he announced, his voice calm. "I won't allow it."

"Crazy bastard..." Dyson looked at the gun, steadfast and pointed right at him, and smirked out a scoff. "Then you're just gonna have to shoot me, aren't yo—?"

BANG-BANG! Ratski squeezed the trigger and pumped two shots into the detective's chest. "Finally, we agree on something."

Getting shot in real life was not how the movies portrayed it. There was no flying backwards in spectacular fashion, propelled by the force of the impacting lead. Neither did a torrent of thick red mush explode from the entry wounds to spurt through the air in slow motion. Dyson simply stumbled a step and let out a violent cough. More shocked than gripped by agonising pain, he stared down at the two neat holes in his zipped-up jacket, perfectly grouped together above his heart, and brought his hand up to clamp over them. He felt his balance desert him, the building appearing to tilt to a steep angle that pitched him to one side. The room spun, fast like a fairground waltzer, his legs weakening and sinking him into an opposing twist that laid him out flat on his back. The office's colour palette shifted from magnolia to madness, bursts of insane, multicoloured light cast a billowing shadow that inched closer and closer. A warped image of Ratski slid into view, towering over him to speak words too distorted to hear. Then, with a final, gruesome breath, Dyson's vision blurred, everything wiped away by an invisible hand to leave a trailing smear that deepened and turned to the darkest of blacks.

TO BE CONTINUED…

COMING SOON

'Dyson had expected one adventure in 1888...but two?'

Want to know what happened in those missing seven days? Sign up to receive updates, exclusive offers, and giveaways on upcoming book releases, and download a copy of '*To Kill A Queen*' COMPLETELY FREE!

AUTHOR'S NOTE

If you're still digging Dyson's tale of woe, would you take a few moments to leave an honest rating on Amazon, and/or Goodreads.com? I can't stress how vitally important reviews are to independent authors. They're essential to help with a book's rankings—often deciding whether it lives or dies—and they assist other readers in determining if a book is a good fit for them. If you're feeling really generous, and are *really* enjoying the story, I'd doubly appreciate it if you could share the love and tell your friends and family about this book on your social media platforms too.

That's all, folks! See you in Part Four.

ACKNOWLEDGMENTS

Edited by Claire Rushbrook
Cover design by me

I'd like to say a special thank you to my little team of guinea pigs; especially Heather, Mark, and Monika, for all the help, feedback, and encouragement they provided.

Printed in Great Britain
by Amazon